DEVILS CRK.

ALSO BY TODD KEISLING

A Life Transparent
The Liminal Man
The Final Reconciliation
Ugly Little Things: Collected Horrors
The Smile Factory

DEVIL'S CREEK

A NOVEL

TODD KEISLING

This book is a work of fiction. Names, characters, places, and incidents either are the product of the author's imagination or are used fictitiously and any resemblance to actual persons, living or dead, business establishments, events, or locales is entirely coincidental.

Edited by Amelia Bennett, Kenneth W. Cain, & Renee Fountain
Proofread by Heather Cain
Cover artwork © 2019 by Greg Chapman
Cover & interior design by Dullington Design Co.
"Devil's Creek" photograph © 2019 by Erica Keisling
Interior illustrations © 2019 by Todd Keisling

Silver Shamrock Publishing, LLC.

CONTENTS

Dedicated to the memory of Frank Michaels Errington and Matt Molgaard.
We miss you.

DEVIL'S
CREEK

PART ONE

THAT OLD-TIME RELIGION

Outside Stauford, Kentucky
1983

CHAPTER ONE

The sun hung low along the western horizon, painting the forest with fractured orange flames, and Imogene Tremly knew in her heart the minister would be dead before it rose again. She'd prayed for this day, prayed the others would see the light of reason, and finally their time had come. In a past life, she would've said her lord had seen to it, but now she wasn't so sure.

These days she wasn't sure what was listening to those prayers she sent up into the dark, whispered in her most vulnerable moments. After the horrors she'd witnessed at the Lord's Church of Holy Voices, Imogene could no longer say with complete faith her god was benign.

Answered prayers? No. All she knew today was fortune had seen fit to smile upon her, and the others had finally gathered the courage to stand with her against Father Jacob. Her only fear was they'd waited too long to act, and the children of Jacob's infernal community were beyond saving.

The car shuddered and lurched as they drove over a pothole. Henry Prewitt took the winding curves of Devil's Creek Road at full speed, squealing tires and spitting up gravel in their wake.

Jerry Tate leaned forward from the back seat. His face was pale and his lips drawn thin in a grim frown. "Christ, Henry. We want to get there in one piece, y'know?"

Henry clenched his teeth, white-knuckling the steering wheel as they took another curve in the road. Jerry sat back in a huff, clutching the back of Henry's seat.

Headlights flashed in the rearview, piercing the evening gloom. Maggie Green followed several yards back in her rusted-out Ford pickup, and Roger Billings closed the rear in his old Dodge. Together, their motorcade snaked its way through the brush of Daniel Boone National Forest, tearing up the old access road with demonic fury as they sped toward their fate.

Imogene glanced over her shoulder at the back seat. Jerry looked like he might vomit; Gage Tiptree met her stare but said nothing.

Despite Jerry's protests, they both knew no matter how fast Henry drove, it wasn't fast enough.

"I still think we should've gone to the cops. At least then we wouldn't be going in alone."

Henry spoke flatly, his voice nothing more than air forced through corn husks. "We already tried, and it got us nowhere. They're just as afraid of him as we are. It's us or no one."

Silence fell over them as the Toyota rattled along the gravel road. Deep down, Imogene knew Jerry was right—they should've gone to the police one last time—but there was also truth in Henry's words as well. How many times had they tried calling attention to Father Jacob's nightly activities? How many anonymous reports of child abuse and rape would it take before the police would finally act?

Too long, Imogene thought. *Too long, and a handful of dead children.* Thoughts of her grandson Jackie propped up on Father Jacob's stone altar made her stomach twist in knots. She blinked away the grisly image and focused on the road ahead, as her mind wandered back to all the things she could have done to avoid this outcome. If only she'd opened her eyes sooner, maybe then she wouldn't have lost her daughter to Jacob's brainwashing.

Imogene closed her eyes and scolded herself. *What's done is done. You can't save Laura, but maybe you can save little Jackie.*

Henry slowed the car to a stop as they neared the turnabout. Two muddy ruts cut through a narrow clearing in the woods before disappearing around a bend several yards back. There, the gravel road was consumed by the overgrowth, turning back travelers for as long as any of them could remember. Those who belonged here, however, knew of another path.

Imogene opened her eyes. The trailhead beckoned to them like a gaping mouth, waiting to swallow them all. Half a mile down, the trail dipped into a gully where the creek trickled its way toward the Cumberland River. A wooden footbridge they'd built years before would carry them to the other side.

From there, any traveler would find a series of homes, nothing more than cardboard and sheet metal shacks. They'd all lived in those homes at one point or another, selling off their belongings for the sake of Jacob's vision, trading their lives of privilege and sin for those of piety and reverence. Beyond the village, the forest gave way to a clearing, and rising from its center was Calvary Hill. The heart of Jacob Masters's religious community sat atop Calvary: a one-room, white-washed church with a black steeple. And down in the pit below, deep in the heart of that blighted land, they would find the bastard.

Imogene's heart raced. She reached into her purse and pulled out her daddy's revolver, amazed by how such a small thing could bear such weight, hoping her daddy's lessons wouldn't fail her now.

Henry parked the car and shut off the engine. He popped the trunk and turned to the men in the backseat. "I won't blame either of you boys if you want to back out now."

Jerry and Gage remained silent, studying Henry's face. They nodded to one another, a tacit agreement between old friends that wasn't lost on Imogene. *See it through.*

"Genie," Henry said, "What about you?"

Imogene placed her daddy's revolver in her lap, absently tracing her finger along the loaded cylinders.

"Jacob took my Laura from me, and I didn't do nothin' because he told me it was God's will. I'm not going to make the same mistake with my grandson. He can't have him—he can't have any of those children. We're all they've got now. If I meet my maker tonight, I'll do it knowing I did what I could to make things right."

Her words clung to the air between them, resonating like church bells. They all knew Henry Prewitt's offer to turn back was an empty one; none of them could back out now even if they wanted to. Not after all they'd let happen. Tonight, they would atone for their sins, one way or another.

Imogene opened the door and broke the silence. The sound of low guttural chants sent her heart into her throat. Nestled between each lurching incantation were the shrill calls of children in song.

"It's begun," she whispered.

The men climbed out of the truck. Henry looked back at her, frowning. He understood this was their burden and theirs alone.

Henry retrieved his shotgun and chambered a round.

"Then let's end it."

CHAPTER TWO

1

Jacob Masters stood at the threshold of his church and gazed down the hill at his self-made paradise. His people chanted, calling out the many names of their new lord in preparation for their offering. Their children—*his* children—sang in harmony, speaking the forgotten words of God with their sweet cherubic voices. He leaned against the doorframe and closed his eyes, relishing the soft breeze rustling through the trees, whispering like the voice of a god in his ears. *Shhh*, that voice told him. *Breathe this in. Take it in. This is your will. Your will and the Old Ways are one.*

His will. Yes. Who else would have given everything to empower their flock? Not the false god of the heathens in Stauford. They had forgotten the Old Ways, turned away from their purified scripture by a deceiver and usurper. The heretics had traded the ways of blood and fire and tongues for a more hypocritical, self-righteous doctrine. Their sins were metaphorical, the devil a phantom of their own conjuring, nothing more than veiled attempts at filling the heads of their congregation with psychobabble and lies.

The path of the Chosen is gilded in fire, forged in blood, and patterned across the bones of the damned. The people of Stauford will remember the Old Ways, and soon.

His new lord told him as much, opened his eyes to the truth, and Jacob saw that truth before his eyes. The decadence and decay of modern society grew and festered around him like a cancer. How could he stand aside and let this filth overrun the earth?

Oh, how much time had he wasted leading his flock astray?

Jacob opened his eyes. *No longer,* he thought. *It is time we bring back the Old Ways.* A song from his youth crept from the corners of his memory, and the lyrics tickled the back of his throat until he could not help but give them voice.

"*Give me that old-time religion,*" he sang quietly, "*it's good enough for me.*"

Beyond the foot of the hill, where the clearing gave way to the forest, lights emerged from the shadows as the chanting grew louder. Jacob smiled when he saw the crimson figures emerge from the wood.

Six members of the congregation stood at the forest's edge, each draped in red robes dyed by their own hands in preparation for this day. Red to symbolize their sacrifice; red to pay tribute to their new lord. They each carried lanterns to light their way toward the church, and behind them, clad in robes of white, stood their sons and daughters.

My lambs, Jacob thought, relishing the sudden stiffness in his black trousers. He brushed a hand over his bulge and sucked in his breath at the sensation. His little lambs. Such a shame he must part with them so soon, at such a young age, but their lord had needs just as he, and in the end, he was a servant himself.

Sacrifice, after all, was at the core of the Old Ways. Sacrifice and so much suffering.

The chants intensified as the remaining members of Jacob's flock emerged from the forest, their faces aglow in lantern light. An intense sensation of joy rippled through him. His flock, his children, were here to see all their hard work come to fruition. Tonight, and every night after, would bring them one step closer to a new world. A new paradise on Earth, free from the heathens and heretics.

And here, where he'd first heard the whispered truths of their one true god, he would become his lord's apostle, his flock's savior.

Jacob knelt in the doorway and ran his fingers through the bald patch of soil at his feet. He dug his hand into the dirt, sensing the subtle vibrations of the earth and the god who slumbered within. When he extracted his fingers from the soil, a plump earthworm came with them, wrapped around his ring finger. He raised his hand before his face and smiled at the proposal.

"By your will, my lord, my love, my light." He plucked the worm from his finger, placed the writhing tip between his teeth, and bit off its lower half. The other half he dropped to his feet, where it squirmed in the open wound of dirt. He savored the bitter, metallic taste on his tongue and silently thanked his god for the gift. The worm curled in upon itself before seeking comfort in the loose soil. He watched until it was gone and swallowed the earthen mess in his mouth.

Only through blood will we regain dominion. Rend their flesh under the light of the moon and let their blood wash away the damned.

The lord spoke within him, and for the first time, Jacob truly felt like the right hand of God. He'd knelt at the pulpit of a false idol for far too long, watching hypocrites saunter into the pews every Sunday morning, praising their lord while harboring the very sins they despised in others. Their time would come. Oh yes, their time would come, in a tidal wave of blood so great it would rival the great flood of the Old Testament.

A sacrifice begets sacrifice. Changes are wrought with pain. Salvation comes not from sloth but from the cleansing fire of agony. The Old Ways mandated sacrifice and the spilling of blood. God willing, Jacob Masters would have both before the night was through.

2

"But Mommy, I'm scared."

Laura Tremly looked down at Jack and squeezed his hand. Her little lamb was always afraid, always questioning their faith and conviction. She smiled, quietly wishing their new god would silence him for good.

Soon, she wanted to tell him. *Tonight, Jacob will have you again, and then I will be free of you.*

Instead, Laura shushed him, and whispered, "Fear is a sin of the heart. Be strong for your lord, like we talked about."

Jack blinked back tears and wiped his face with the sleeve of his robe. He glanced at the other children, seeking comfort in their shared reactions, but they cast their eyes to their feet.

Laura watched her son and tried to read his face. She wondered if he would listen to Father Jacob. Would the boy do as instructed, even in the face of danger? And would their god accept him as a suitable offering?

Oh honey, your mind is wandering again.

Jacob's voice spoke in her head, whispering like a hushed breeze on a cool summer night. Laura closed her eyes and smiled as a delightful warmth washed over her. He always knew the right things to say to her, even without saying a word. Such was his power. He could see through her, into her, shining a light on the darkest corners of her heart. Not to expose or mock her, but to make her whole and cleanse her spirit.

My will and the Old Ways are one, he'd told her. And she'd given herself to him because he willed it. She'd given him her son like the others. Just as she would do again for one final time tonight.

We are yours, she thought, staring up the hill toward her savior. *I give you my life, and I give you our son. Take him as you took me.*

And peering down at her, Jacob spoke again in her head: *As you wish, my darling lamb.*

Laura closed her eyes and sucked the air through her teeth as a new wave of warmth flushed through her, down her belly and between her legs.

"Your will," she whispered, "and the Old Ways are one, my darling."

Jack squeezed her hand, yanking her back to this crude reality of flesh and sin. "Mommy?"

She looked down at her son and bit her lip so hard she pierced flesh. A trickle of coppery warmth filled her mouth.

"Be silent. Your time is at hand, child. Do you not see?"

Jack's eyes welled with tears. "Mommy—"

But she wasn't listening to him anymore. He was a part of her, yes, but a temporary part, a shred of flesh and blood picked clean from her body. There would be more children. She prayed they would be more grateful for the sacrifices that came before them.

Atop Calvary Hill, Jacob raised his arms to welcome his children home.

"Come to me, my lambs," he called, his voice carrying along the wind, through the leaves and branches, on the wings of every bird and chirp of every insect. By their new lord's will, Jacob Masters was everywhere, one with nature, one with the earth, one with their hearts.

Laura Tremly yanked her son's arm, dragging him forward up the hill to his fate. Jack cried out in both pain and terror, begging his mother to stop, but she did not hear him. She held her gaze with her master, her savior, her lover. *Your will be done.*

Jacob looked down at her, his eyes aglow in the fading light, and grinned.

3

Jack Tremly winced as his mother's fingers dug into his wrist. He turned to his sister Susan for comfort, her pale face half hidden beneath the white hood of her robe, cast aglow in the warmth of her mother's lantern.

Susan Prewitt sensed his desperation and met his terrified stare but didn't dare say anything. Instead, her eyes spoke for her: *Accept this. What else can we do?*

Jack searched her placid face for answers he knew weren't there, as his heart thudded in his chest. He looked to the other robed children. Chuck, Stephanie, Bobby, and Zeke appeared as calm as Susan was, but he saw the same terror in their eyes as he felt in his heart.

In the weeks before, as the weight of reality slowly pressed against them, Jack dared to question his mother on what she called "matters of the church." That he would question her at all was a sin in her eyes, a trespass which would be judged by their new lord, and his punishment was swift. He still bore the marks from the small tree branch she'd used to beat him, and he hadn't been able to sleep on his back for a week.

"That pain you're feelin' ain't nothin' but your sins, Jackie. You remember that when it's your turn at the altar."

Thinking about that day made the striped scars across his backside sting. He longed for the days when they lived in town, when he went to school, when church only happened on Sundays. That was before Pastor Jacob had his "awakening," when God spoke directly to him, ordering him to gather his flock.

Jack remembered the sermon and the way his mother flung herself upon the floor, writhing in agony, babbling words he didn't understand. That was the day Jack experienced an awakening of his own, but for the wrong reasons. *Mommy isn't Mommy anymore.* Those words raced through his mind as Laura Tremly pulled him forward with her up the side of Calvary Hill.

"No, Mommy, *no—*"

The world exploded before him as Laura's hand struck his cheek, knocking the words from his throat. His eyes watered and his face stung, but when he looked up at her through a glassy lens of sorrow, Jack told himself not to cry. Not this time.

"Our God hates a whiner, child. You are part of something so much greater. Why can't you see that?"

Jack fought the urge to scream and run. He turned and surveyed the hillside. To where could he run, anyway? The forest went on for miles, and without a lamp to light his way, he would surely be lost. Jacob would find him wandering in the woods, and then there truly would be a reckoning.

Laura yanked the hood back over Jack's head and wiped a tear from his cheek.

"Be the son I should've had," she whispered. "Go to God with dignity."

She took hold of his wrist and dragged him up the hill. Behind them, the chanting grew louder as the congregation followed.

4

The Lord's Church of Holy Voices was a one-room shrine to the ways of Jacob's heritage, when God was still up above in a heaven none of them would see. Pastor Thurmond Masters preached fire and damnation from the pulpit back in those days, working himself up to the brink of a stroke while one of the ladies of the congregation led a discordant rendition of "Old Rugged Cross" on the church's upright piano.

Ah, the old days, before Jacob heard the voice of their new lord coming not from above, but from within. After his father passed, Jacob took up the mantle to lead their flock toward salvation, steering the church toward the Promised Land, only to find their humble meeting place was planted above their lord all along. Their new lord's voice came from within, filling him with a vibrating hum that rattled his teeth and shook his bones.

God from within, he thought, watching the congregation fill the church to its brim, their lantern light illuminating the open wound in the earth before them. *Lies above, love below.*

He welcomed them into the room that would be their salvation. For it was here he'd first heard their lord, whispering to him from below, a hollow cavern deep down like the empty chambers in his heart.

Jacob raised his arms to his flock. "Welcome, brothers and sisters. Welcome all. Before we begin this joyous occasion, would Sister Tremly lead us in prayer?"

Shouts of "Amen" erupted from the throng of men and women in the room. Sister Laura Tremly bowed her head, and shadows slipped down her face from the hood of her robe. Jacob whispered the words which filled her throat, and together they spoke as one.

"Bless us, oh Lord, on this momentous occasion, when we pay tribute in blood, so we may cleanse our filthy spirits. Bless us as we commit our flesh to You below, so that You may free us from this earthly hell and plant the seeds of paradise. May the Old Ways guide our hands, let us see the lies above, and know our love below. Amen."

"Amen," Jacob continued. "Thank you, Sister Tremly, for that lovely benediction." He tiptoed forward from the lectern and circled the torn hole in the floor. The congregation followed his every step, swaying in unison like a slow-motion wave, ready to crash against the pews. A suffocating heat filled the church, hanging above their heads in a thick cloud that leeched the moisture from their pores. Beads of sweat slicked their foreheads and cheeks.

Jacob Masters waited at the precipice of the gaping wound in the floor. He sensed his flock's yearning for his words, could *feel* the ache in their souls, and the sensation made him smile. *My cup runneth over*, he mused, and raised his hand in the air.

"I've a confession to make, brothers and sisters." He placed his hand upon his heart and lowered his chin. "I have sinned. I am a sinner. My sins run through me like the precious blood of old, and with each beat of my heart, so goes another sin like the first. For years I was lost, teaching the ways of my father and his father before him—but then I heard the truth."

"Hallelujah!"

"Thank you, Brother Adams. Hallelujah. For years, I was taught there's a god above, using a proxy of flesh and bone to judge us. A god of silence. An absent god. A *lazy* god. And in my moment of need, when I questioned my faith in that god of liars, all I heard was the stillness of the air and the beating of sin in my heart. The god of my father wasn't listening, brothers and sisters. He never was, and he never will."

"Amen," hissed the congregation, swaying to the sound of his voice. Jacob smiled. *They're yours*, his lord told him. *They always were.*

"And I fell to my knees in this very house, a house built by my father, a house built in the name of their god! Every beam, every timber, was put here in His name. Did this false god speak to me, brothers and sisters? No, he did not. A child of His own flock, a messenger of His faith, wasn't worthy." Jacob pointed to the dark hole in the earth. "But it was then, my lambs, I heard the voice of another god. The one true god. And I discovered I'd been praying in the wrong direction. Our new lord was not silent, brothers and sisters. No, this god listens—"

He took a step into the hole, but he did not fall. Jacob walked across the air, hovering inches above the mouth of the pit, eliciting cries of praise and awe from his flock.

"This god listens, and this god rewards. Yes, brothers and sisters, the one true god spoke to me, as plain as I speak to you here and now, and told me I would build a new kingdom from this very hill, a kingdom from which a new world would spread. Our new lord told me of the Old Ways upon which our very beliefs are founded—and that, my brethren, is why we are gathered here tonight. We will fertilize the earth with the blood of the chosen, so a new kingdom may take root."

He pointed first to the ceiling and then to the hole beneath his hovering feet. "New lies above, and old love below. Can I get a hallelujah, brothers and sisters?"

The congregation erupted in jubilant cheers, a din of holy voices crying out in praise not to the heavens above, but the earth below. Jacob closed his eyes and drank in their praise. The taste of their sweat and subservience was divine. *This*, he realized, *is what Jesus must've felt like.*

Jacob smirked. The sweet knowledge of quiet domination, watching a throng of followers give themselves to him. Let this cup pass from his lips? Never. That proxy of flesh, birthed by his father's false god, was an absolute fool.

He held out his arms to mock the old cross hanging above the entrance, waiting a moment longer before looking down at the cheering faces before him.

"I share your glee, brothers and sisters. Tonight, we will birth a new world together. Tonight, we will pluck the fruit from the forbidden tree and watch it rot in the earth." He turned toward the row of red-robed women. "Sister Tremly, Sister Prewitt, Sister Tiptree, Sister Green, Sister Billings, and Sister Tate. My darlings. You six were chosen because of your faith and fertility. I've lain with you and planted the seeds of our reckoning, and today, we shall pluck the fruit of your wombs in offering of our new lord."

The six mothers spoke together: "Your will and the Old Ways are one, Father Jacob."

"Will you give your lambs to me?"

"Yes, Father Jacob."

"So be it," he said, twisting in the air to the men near the door. "Deacon Jones, Deacon Croner, would you be so kind as to lower the ladder for the lambs?"

A path parted through the congregation as the two doe-eyed men approached with an old rusted ladder. They nodded to Jacob in reverence before lowering the ladder into the pit.

"Thank you, my brothers."

Satisfied, Jacob willed the air to part beneath his feet. He sank into the pit like so many angels, held aloft by the wings of something far greater than himself. The boy at the edge of the pit—Laura's lamb, little Jackie—looked down and locked eyes with him, and for a moment, Jacob felt something stir within. A screaming voice echoing from the dark chambers of his heart, a shrill cry that gave him pause—

—except the scream was happening above him, somewhere beyond the confines of the church. The scream became several, and as the footsteps clamored above him, a gunshot erupted beyond his sight.

The heretics, his lord rasped. Jacob Masters wasted no time. He reached out, gripped the foot of Laura's son, and yanked the child down into the darkness with him.

CHAPTER THREE

1

Henry Prewitt's shotgun split the night, erupting in a hail of buckshot over the heads of their former friends. The sound startled Imogene and she almost dropped her revolver in the brush. They'd come upon Calvary Hill unannounced, their trek through the woods without incident. They had no need for their flashlights in the fading sunlight. The chants of their former brothers and sisters guided their way through the wilderness.

Standing at the tree line, where undergrowth met the weeds of the unkempt path leading up the knoll, Imogene watched their heads turn in shock. She raised her weapon and cocked the hammer but hesitated when she saw the gaunt face of someone at the edge of the congregation. He was young, barely eighteen by her estimation, and she didn't know him. There were so many converts now, the old white church could barely contain their numbers.

Her daddy spoke up in her head. *Remember, Genie, they ain't your brothers and sisters anymore. He's done things to 'em, and their souls are so filthy there ain't no comin' back from it.*

Henry racked another round in his shotgun as Maggie fired off a warning shot. Imogene watched as the others winced from the report, and she resisted the urge to dig her finger into her ear. The ringing of tinnitus would haunt her for the rest of her life.

"Y'all need to clear out right now," Maggie screamed. "You let our grandbabies go!"

"Fuck you and your blasphemous ways, whore."

Deacon Croner marched through the open doorway with a finger raised in accusation. Imogene shot a look at Gage, who caught her glance and frowned. Robby Croner used to be a heavy-set man, two meals away from a heart attack, with a gut so enormous the poor fellow could barely bend over. But in the weeks since their exile, he'd lost at least two hundred pounds. The scrawny thing marching down the hillside toward them was barely a man at all, reduced to a skeleton dipped in flesh and obscured in robes. A large fold of skin hung limp from his neck like moss from a dying maple.

"That's far enough, Robby." Gage raised his hunting rifle. "We don't want no trouble from you and your kin. We just want the kids."

Robby Croner spat at their feet. "Y'all ain't welcome here. Father Jacob cast you out for good reason. We ain't got time to be dealin' with no non-believers."

"You tell 'em, Deacon!"

Imogene glanced up the hill. One of the new parishioners, an obese woman she didn't recognize, heckled them from the safety of the church entrance. "That's right, sinner! We ain't scared a'you!"

Jerry Tate stepped out of the brush with a hand held out to their former friend. "Look, Robby, we want our grandkids. You send them out here to us, and we'll be on our way. No one has to get hurt here."

Deacon Croner grinned, his eyes filled with an ethereal shade of blue. Whatever that mad man unearthed in the knoll ate away at not just their bodies but their minds. This wasn't their old friend Robby; this was a husk of what he used to be, a puppet made to dance the dance of its master, and he was keeping perfect time.

Robby turned to face each of them, sizing them up. "That's where you're wrong, Jerry. You may have turned away from the good lord's teachings, but that don't mean they ain't true. Someone *does* have to get hurt. We can't have our new kingdom without the spilling of blood."

"Christ, Robby, listen to yourself." Roger Billings stepped from the woods and lowered his rifle. He pleaded to his old fishing buddy. "Jacob's filled your head with lies. He's dangerous, man. Can't you see that?" Roger lifted his gaze to the crowd outside the church. "Can't *any* of you see that?"

"We see what the good lord wants us to see, and what I see's nothin' but lies from blasphemers and whores. All I see's lies from a false god." Deacon Croner reached into the sleeve of his robe. "His will and the Old Ways are one."

The congregation chanted together in agreement. "*His will and the Old Ways are one.*"

Jerry was too distracted by the ominous chants to see the blade hidden in Croner's sleeve. Even Imogene looked away, her skin crawling from their discordant voices, her heart stumbling beneath the tension in the air. In later days, and for the rest of her life, Imogene Tremly would replay that night in her mind, questioning if any of them were prepared for what was about to happen.

Deacon Croner revealed the knife to them. Maggie cried out, and both Jerry and Roger raised their hands in protest. Henry and Gage lowered their weapons, stunned to silence by what they witnessed.

Deacon Robby Croner, once a prominent member of Stauford's Chamber of Commerce and a good God-fearing Christian, raised the serrated blade to his own throat. Carrion-black ichor seeped from his nose and ears, and thin trickles spilled from the corners of his eyes. He smiled at them all, and for a moment, Imogene thought she saw a glimmer of the man she once knew hidden behind the contorted mask he now wore for a face.

"By your will, my lord."

"Wait—" Gage began, but he was silenced by Maggie's screams.

Robby Croner buried the blade into his gullet, engulfing his hand in a torrent of blood. He cut as far as his Adam's apple before he collapsed. The world stopped around them, the air still and the sounds of crickets silenced as blackened gore oozed from their dead friend's open wound.

A scream worked its way into Imogene's mouth and would've found voice if not for what followed. One by one, the congregants of The Lord's Church of Holy Voices followed the path of Deacon Croner. One by one, they extracted blades from their robes, and within moments were sawing through their own throats.

The scream of a child carried over the collapsing bodies of the congregation and down the hillside. Imogene's heart lodged in her throat. *Jackie! Oh, dear God, please, not Jackie!*

She broke free of her fear and raced up the hill toward the church. Her friends cried out for her to stop, but she refused to listen. Jackie was in there—so were all their grandchildren—and she had to stop that madman from hurting them.

As she stepped over the bloodstained bodies of her former friends, Imogene prayed she was not too late.

2

Jack struggled to adjust to the gloom. A veil of light fell from the hole above them, but all around were shadows, and somewhere beyond them was Father Jacob. Motes of dust danced in the light, and he followed them down to the floor where he saw fragments of what looked like old pottery. Jack tried to move for a better look, but his left arm throbbed something fierce every time he tried to move it. So sharp was the pain that he cried out into the dark, but his voice seemed lessened in the void, dampened somehow by the suffocating emptiness.

"No one can hear you here, Jackie. You're here with us. With your new god."

A blue spark lit up the emptiness, revealing Father Jacob mere feet away from him. The boy watched the old pastor light a pair of candles with his finger. No matches, no lighters—just his finger. The realization made Jack's blood run cold.

Magic, he thought.

No magic, child. Only power. The power of blood and sacrifice. The power of our lord manifested in my flesh.

Father Jacob's words filled his head like black static. Jack winced, shaking his head to rid himself of the awful noise, but Jacob remained inside his mind, chipping away at his will, his spirit, his soul. More and more, Jack felt himself slipping away, a prisoner in his own body as something else took his place. Something shapeless, formless, something infinite. *A shadow*, he thought.

Jack turned away from the old man before him, struggling to tear his mind free of Jacob's influence. He glimpsed impossible things in the shifting candlelight. There were drawings on the walls, old inscriptions etched into stone, written with letters he'd never seen in school. Every surface was covered in dust and grime, untouched by man for what seemed like years. Maybe hundreds. Older than the dinosaurs, maybe. The sheer age of something like this eclipsed his scope of understanding, and the longer he focused on the markings, the more his head hurt.

The old pastor stood behind a stone slab, his face illuminated in a swirling mixture of light and dark, the shadows dripping down the contours of his face. When he spotted Jack staring at him, Jacob smiled. Shadows dripped from his mouth, too. The sight of the dark ooze made Jack's stomach churn.

"We are in the womb of the earth. Our new lord speaks to me here. He was beneath us all along. For centuries, maybe. I broke through the church's foundation until I met the earth, and then I pulled back the stones with my bare hands. And it's here that I found our lord."

Jacob raised his finger and touched the wick of a candle near the center of the slab. A spark lit up an adjacent figure which Jack hadn't seen before. The figure was carved from stone, its details crude but unmistakable. Deep lines ran up and down the sides of the idol, around its center into individual divots to mark out teeth, and into two deep holes for eyes. Even in the shifting light, Jack saw it was supposed to be a child of some sort. A deeply deformed, grinning child etched in stone.

Father Jacob lifted the idol to his face.

"My lord," he whispered, "I give this sacrifice to you. My father, my Omega, my guiding light, allow me to honor you with the blood of an innocent. Tonight, and forever onward. Let me spread this child's blood and water the fields with his life so your new kingdom may grow. Your will and the Old Ways are one."

The pastor's hand engulfed in flames, filling the room with a hazy azure glow, and Jack saw for the first time he was wrong about the floor. Those weren't fragments of old pottery beneath their feet. They were bones. Thousands of bones cracked and split apart. Broken skulls and ribs sat in piles around the altar.

Jack raised his face to the faint halo of light above and let loose a shriek that pierced the shifting shadows around them. Years before, he would've cried out to God, or even his mother. As his shrieks were lost to the chaos happening above, Jack's heart sank.

There was no one left to hear him.

3

"You're too late, Sister Tremly."

Imogene stood in the entrance of the church, gulping back her gag reflex as she witnessed the horrific tableau before her. Six figures clad in red stood over their fallen brethren, each with a blade in their hands. Hiding behind them were their sons and daughters in white, but Imogene's heart sank when she counted.

She cleared her throat. "Where's my grandson? Where's Jackie?" Imogene winced at the sound of her own voice. Dry, raspy, desperate. There was a time when she used to command the attention of her brothers and sisters within these walls. Those were better times. Now she felt weak, powerless, and uncertain of how this would play out. She had six rounds for a weapon she hadn't fired since she was a little girl. Deep down in her heart, she knew they wouldn't be enough.

"He's with our lord now."

One of the mothers stepped forward and lifted back her hood. Laura Tremly stared down her mother with a sickened grin. Splotches of sapphire dotted the whites of her eyes, and black veins splintered the flesh across her face. Imogene gasped in disgust.

"My God, what's he done to you, Laura?"

"He opened my eyes, Sister Tremly. Shown us the way to a kingdom on earth. He showed you the way, too, but you turned from him like Lot's wife. He'll do more than turn you to salt. He'll rape your soul."

The other mothers chittered at her words, forming a chorus of hateful mockery that made the hairs on Imogene's arms stand at attention. Laura raised her sacrificial blade. The pale light overhead illuminated the long scars down her naked arms, older wounds from Jacob's many bloodletting ceremonies.

Imogene took a step back and raised her weapon.

"Jackie's in the pit with his father, and his blood's gonna spill for the sake of the world. *So shall you all.*"

"So shall you all," chimed the other five. One by one, they turned and pushed their little ones into the pit below. Each child's shriek ripped through the stillness of the church, filling Imogene's belly with the leaden cold of dread. *No, dear God, no, no, no—*

"Tonight, we bleed for a new world, sisters." Laura flicked the tip of her blade toward Imogene, but her mother was too focused on the ladies at the wound in the floor. With their children down in the pit, there was no need for them to linger on this plane any longer. Imogene knew the blasphemous scripture by heart. She knew what came next, after their sacrificial offerings were presented to the godhead for final communion, and despite the knowledge she found she could not look away.

Remember this, her daddy whispered. *Hold on to this. For Jackie's sake.*

One by one, the five mothers of Jacob's seed raised their blades to their throats and spilled their own blood upon the floor. Gouts of viscous black oil spewed from their open wounds, writhing down the front of their robes. The wooden floor sizzled and steamed beneath them as their bodies collapsed.

Imogene swallowed air and grimaced at the sour taste. The heat of the room clouded her face, and her heart raced in her throat. She gripped the revolver and held her finger against the trigger. "Please don't make me do this, Laura. For your mother's sake, please—"

"My mother is dead to me," Laura spat. "You're nothin' more than a godless heretic, come to disrupt our communion with our one true god. But you may yet find salvation if you bleed. Bleed with us, heretic. Bleed for our lord's mercy."

The following moments happened quickly for Imogene Tremly. When she tried to recall them to the authorities later, she found her thoughts were out of focus and refracted, like staring at them through a pool of murky water.

Imogene's daughter lunged for her.

From behind, Henry Prewitt and Gage Tiptree called her name.

Laura Tremly's foot caught the edge of Brother Adams's corpse, and her knife swung wide in an arc as she stumbled forward.

Imogene screamed as the blade sliced up the left side of her face, cutting through her cornea, and forever blinding her left eye. She collapsed to her knees and clutched her face, panicking at the sudden warmth slickening her cheeks. Somewhere overhead, Roger yelled for Maggie and Jerry to hurry the fuck up, Genie's hurt.

"You'll all burn," Laura cried, but she was silenced by the butt of Henry's shotgun. A moment later, Henry was at Imogene's side. She winced as she looked up at him with her good eye. He'd gone pale, the color bled right out of him, and she'd later swear he'd aged ten years that night. All of them would.

A cry echoed from the hole in the floor, and Imogene shot to her feet, one hand covering the left side of her throbbing face. Blood oozed between her fingers. She tucked her daddy's gun into the waist of her dirty jeans.

"Genie, wait—"

"Never mind me, Henry Prewitt. Our babies are down there with that monster. We need to see this through."

And before they could stop her, Imogene Tremly staggered to the ladder and descended into the darkness of Calvary Hill.

4

Father Jacob placed the idol back on the altar and trained his eyes upon the children. They'd fallen into the chamber like angels from Heaven, if such a place existed. He used to think so, but those days, those lies, were behind him. When he moved, the children shivered in fear. They huddled together like rodents, packing themselves together like one writhing entity, attempting to scare off a predator.

But he was no predator. No. In his moments of Gethsemane, down here in the darkness of this earthen Golgotha, Jacob Masters had questioned his devotion and faith. He'd questioned the revelations bestowed upon him by the scripture writ upon these ancient walls, by the whispers of a god from within.

My lord, he'd asked, *why the blood of innocents? Why not the sacrifice of a lamb, a deer, a beast of the forest?*

And his lord spoke in myriad tongues, languages foreign and familiar all at once, a hissing tease of language rippling through his mind, his heart, into the core of his soul, and he knew it was true: *The innocents* are *beasts, my child. They are no different than the lambs in your book of lies. No seed will sprout without the sustenance of nature; so, too, must this earth be fed. It is my will as told in the Old Ways upon these walls.*

Jacob walked toward the ancient wall, tracing his dirty fingers over the etchings revealed to him in his time of need. These scriptures were his new Bible, comforting him when he needed it most. There was no other way. He knew it in his heart. Heaven could be a place here on Earth, and it would begin here, taking root from the throats of these six innocents.

There would be more, of course. Lifeblood from these children would only go so far. Stauford's children would feed the maw of his lord in time. There they would find redemption in the roiling belly of the nameless below.

Shouts from above rattled his mind, stealing his attention away from his meditations. The children whimpered in the gloom.

They come, my servant. The heretics come to stop our heaven on earth.

"I will stop them," he muttered, staring at the carvings on the wall. Thick rivulets of blackened sin leaked from the corners of his eyes, coating the contours of his face.

No, my child. You will not. But I can prepare your body. I can prepare your soul. Will you give yourself to me? Will you die for me?

Jacob Masters closed his eyes and smiled. He spoke without hesitation. "Yes. Take me, my lord."

A moment later, the idol's flame snuffed out, and the darkness moved in. Somewhere in that formless abyss, the children heard the muffled screams of their captor, a man devoured by the void.

CHAPTER FOUR

1

Imogene grit her teeth to hold back a tide of agony as she descended into the darkness. She heard voices, what sounded like Father Jacob crying to himself, and a dull hum reverberating from the rise and fall of his pitch. Beyond those sounds was the sobbing of children, tempering her resolve as she climbed into the murk.

"I'm coming, kids." Her voice echoed into the chamber, a pained and raspy sound reminding her just how tired and frail she really was. The last several years took a toll on her. How many of those years were wasted in servitude? She couldn't bear to think about it.

Only the children mattered now.

"Mamaw Genie?"

Her heart stopped. "Jackie? Is that you, baby?"

She looked down, following the curtain of light from above, illuminating centuries of earth and dust and bones. There were shapes beyond the circle. Small, fragile shapes, tiny arms and legs, little heads and terrified hearts. If she held her breath, she could almost hear the fear racing in their chests.

"I'm coming, darlin'. I'm almost there."

"Please come quick, Ms. Genie. Jackie's hurt, and somethin' happened to Father."

Little Stephanie Green. She'd recognize that sweet voice anywhere.

"I'm almost there, kids. Not much farther now."

Her descent was slow going with one hand pressed against her face, her other arm wrapped around each rung of the ladder. *One step at a time, lady.* Twinkling splotches of color swam before her face in the darkness, accompanied by a lightheadedness that could only be wrought by the blood seeping from her wound. She waited long enough to rest her face against the nearest rung.

"You okay, Genie?"

Imogene looked up and squinted against the light above. Jerry, Roger, and Henry peered down at her. "Yeah," she gasped. "Are Gage & Maggie taking care of my daughter?"

Jerry nodded. "Yes, ma'am."

Henry mounted the ladder. "I'm right behind ya, Genie."

Imogene peeled her forehead away from the rung. The thin metal bar was slick with her blood. Her head swam.

"Careful on the steps," she mumbled, fending off the droning bells in her head. *Keep going,* she told herself. *Almost there.*

Seconds later, Imogene's feet met the dirt floor of the earthen pillar rising from the dark. A series of chiseled steps led down to the floor of the temple, and she descended two at a time. Dusty bones of unsung sacrifices crunched beneath her as she steadied herself. The children crawled on aching limbs into the circle of light and crowded around, nearly toppling her in their desperate excitement. All except one.

She scanned the darkness with her good eye. Jack Tremly remained huddled in the dark, and she could barely make him out in the shadows.

"Mamaw Genie, I think my arm's broke. Is Mama okay?"

Imogene frowned. "Yes, darlin'. She's okay, and so are you. We can mend a broken arm, honey. One of your uncles can carry you up. Now, let's get all of you kids back up the ladder—"

A crackling noise erupted from the dark, disturbing the centuries of dust in the chamber. The children cried out and huddled behind her like chicks seeking shelter from a storm. She was their Mother Hen in this dark place, and whatever lurked in the shadows beyond the light would have to go through her to get to them. Imogene reached for the revolver in her jeans and shakily pointed it toward the noise. Jack gasped when she took her hand from her wound.

"It's okay, Jackie. I'll be okay. Your mamaw's had worse."

"Ah, Sister Tremly. Miss Imogene. *Genie.*"

Jacob's voice raised the hairs on her neck. More footsteps cracked across the bones from somewhere beyond the halo of light. She glanced up, saw Henry and Jerry were almost into the chamber, and felt some relief. At least she wouldn't have to face this bastard alone.

"You're done here, Jacob." Her voice was dry but commanding, betraying the weakness in her head, her bones. "You can't have these babies. I won't let you."

"You never were a true believer, darlin'. I could see it in you from the first day you brought your daughter to the church. That didn't stop you from leaving her with me, though. Did she tell you what I did to her?"

Imogene swallowed hard. Her throat clicked. *Don't let him get to you*, her daddy whispered. *He's trying to get in your head.*

"She didn't have to, Jacob. It's on her face. In her eyes."

Jacob's laughter sprang from the dark. The children clustered around her, held tighter, as if she might be plucked from their circle in an instant. Imogene shared their fear.

"You might say I came in the name of the lord, Sister. Your little bastard, Jackie, is proof. He was bred to be opened on our altar. His blood should be flowing right now. And it will. Perhaps not now, but soon. When you aren't here to protect him. When you aren't here to protect any of my little lambs."

Father Jacob Masters emerged from the shadows. His eyes glowed in the dark, filling the chamber with a sickly azure light that turned her stomach. Thick, black tears oozed down his cheeks, collected at the rim of his chin, and dripped in sporadic ropes. Black veins crisscrossed his pale flesh, shattering gaunt cheeks in a hundred pieces.

"I am steeped in my own sin, Genie. You know the only way to cleanse the soul is through bloodshed. The only way to temper the soul is through the fires of redemption." His fingertips sparked like matches, erupting in flames. He gestured to the etchings on the walls. "Our lord's scripture teaches these rites of the dead. Search your heart and you will know it is true. Tell me you didn't come here to shed my blood and burn my church to the ground."

Imogene didn't have to. Jacob knew her well—knew them all, in fact. He had that way about him, a way of seeing inside his flock, knowing what made them tick, which strings to pull. She didn't know if he'd always possessed that sight, or if the beast from the pit gave him such a gift. Either way, he'd worked his will upon her, whispering to her when she was at her most vulnerable, after her husband Steve died in a car accident.

Jacob took advantage of her weakness, suggesting she give her daughter to him, let him have his way with Laura so he would have a sacrifice, and like a good little lamb who'd felt betrayed by her god, she'd done as he wished. For the good of the church. For the promise of heaven on earth. For her new god.

The regret settled in her belly and burned there, eating a hole through her. She'd spend the rest of her life feeling that regret. She knew it, and worse, so did Jacob.

"Kids," she said, lowering her voice. "I need to you to close your eyes and cover your ears. You too, Jackie."

She didn't wait for them. Shaking, her heart full of hate and regret, Imogene raised her daddy's revolver and pulled the trigger. The flash from the muzzle lit up the room like lightning, painting Jacob's shadow across the wall for an instant before he fell backward against the altar. The stone effigy of their buried god sizzled in blue flames.

"Genie!" Henry shouted, dropping to the floor. He crumpled when he hit, hissing at the impact to his knees. "Christ, girl, what have you done?"

Imogene ignored her friend, his words muffled by the sudden ringing in her ears. She walked forward and stood over the bleeding body of the preacher. Jacob Masters looked up at her with pallid blue eyes and grinned.

"Blood and fire," he growled. "You'll have them tonight, but *I'll* have them in time." He raised a pale finger to the wound in his chest, covered the tip in blood, and lifted it to his forehead where he drew a crude symbol upon his flesh. A thick stench of burning meat sizzled upward from his touch. "The heretics will be my gateway. Death for life. So it is written." He leaned back and chuckled to himself. "As I am below, so shall I be above. My will and the Old Ways are one."

Imogene Tremly raised the revolver and clenched her teeth. She fired another round between Jacob's eyes and kept firing until the sickly light was gone from them for good. Even when the rounds were spent, she kept pulling the trigger, waiting for the bastard to stand back up.

She would for the rest of her life.

2

After they carried the children from the church, the men returned to the pit to bury the man who'd taken so much from them. They used the tools leftover from when Jacob dug his way into the forgotten chamber all those years ago. Even with his corpse lying there, Roger and Henry and Jerry and Gage swore they heard him whispering to them from the shadows, cursing them from beyond a veil they could neither see nor feel.

They dug a hole into the floor of the chamber, unearthing the bones of children less fortunate than their own. When they were done, they buried Jacob Masters face down in the earth so he could see Hell.

The sun was rising when they emerged from the church. Maggie and Imogene sat with the children in the shade of the poplars lining the clearing. The six babes were curled up among their guardians, fast asleep in the weeds. Laura Tremly sat against a nearby tree, her hands bound to the trunk. She drifted in and out of consciousness, babbling in tongues none of them could understand, nor did they want to.

Imogene sipped water from Maggie's canteen and held a bloody bandage to her face. She needed medical attention, but the pills Maggie gave her would keep the pain at bay for now. She leaned her head back against the trunk of a poplar and watched as the men set fire to the church.

They stayed for a while after and watched until the Lord's Church of Holy Voices was nothing more than a pile of ashes upon a cracked foundation. Only when the flames licked the heavens and the far-off sirens of the fire department wailed did she breathe a sigh of relief.

It's over, she thought. *Thank God, it's over.*

And for her, she was right.

But for the children, their nightmare wouldn't begin for another thirty years.

FROM THE JOURNAL OF IMOGENE TREMLY (1)

1

From the Stauford Tribune's Evening Edition, August 30th, 1983

STAUFORD DEATH CULT CLAIMS 57

STAUFORD, KY – The bodies of 57 men and women were found dead early Monday morning in an apparent suicide pact, local authorities said.

Officials confirmed they received a 911 call Monday morning around 6:30 a.m. reporting a fire at the church near Devil's Creek Road. Emergency responders arrived on the scene at about 7:05 a.m. and were met by thirteen survivors of the incident who led them to the burning church.

"There was nothing we could do," Fire Chief Doug Stewart said. "A place that isolated, all we could do was make sure the flames didn't spread to the trees."

According to Chief David Bell of the Stauford Police Department, members of the Lord's Church of Holy Voices took their own lives in what officials believe was a religious ceremony. "We're still trying to sort out the details. Obviously, there are lots of questions, and this is going to take time to make sense of it all," Chief Bell said. He later added, "This is one of the worst things I've ever seen in my twenty years on the force."

Authorities have withheld the names of the thirteen survivors and the deceased, pending further investigation. The Whately County coroner's office was not available for comment.

2

From the Landon Herald, September 1st, 1983

INVESTIGATION CONTINUES INTO STAUFORD SUICIDES

STAUFORD, KY – Local authorities continue to pick up the pieces following a mass suicide that occurred late Sunday evening outside Stauford's city limits. The Lord's Church of Holy Voices was a known religious community located in a section of Daniel Boone National Forest, locally known as Devil's Creek.

According to Stauford's City Commissioner, Wallace Getty, the investigation is currently focused on the background of Jacob Masters, the late reverend of the church. "Any Stauford local will tell you Masters had a way with words," Getty said. "I'm shocked by what's transpired but not at all surprised." Getty declined to comment further when asked for clarification.

The Lord's Church of Holy Voices was founded in 1919 by Thurmond Masters. Records indicate that Jacob Masters took ownership of the church in 1957 following his father's death. Herald readers may remember Jacob Masters was the subject of a state investigation into allegations of child abuse. At the time of this printing, the investigation was pending due to a lack of eye-witness testimony.

3

From the Breyersburg Bugle, March 27th, 1985

FAMILY CUSTODY GRANTED FOR STAUFORD SIX

STAUFORD, KY – Custody for the six minors orphaned following 1983's tragic mass suicide will be granted to their grandparents, Judge Thomas Mercer declared on Thursday. The court's decision follows months of deliberation which has drawn public criticism.

"The court has spoken," said one family's attorney, Glenn Wolfard, following the verdict. "These last several months have been trying for all involved. What's important now is that we move on from this horrible tragedy and allow these kids to live normal lives."

The 'Stauford Six,' a nickname given to the six minors who were rescued in late 1983 following a suicide pact at a local church, have been the subject of a heated public battle between state and local officials.

Reintegration of the Stauford Six into Stauford's public school system continues to divide the greater Stauford community.

"We don't want these tainted cult kids poisoning Stauford's youth," said Chief David Bell of Stauford's Police Department, as reported by the Stauford Tribune during a planned protest last December. Bell and others presented a petition containing over one thousand signatures to the court last week. Bell's office was not available for comment following the court's verdict.

4

From Usenet Newsgroup alt.urbanlegends.ky, June 13th, 1995

ANYONE EVER HEARD OF DEVIL'S CREEK?
[Note: First online mention of incident. —Genie]

User alien-head22 wrote: "Check this shit out, y'all. My mom just told me about this place out near Cumberland Falls. Place called Devil's Creek Road. Used to be an old church out there. Some rednecks were worshiping Satan and they burned down the place. Mom told me she and her friends used to go out there to party and they saw all kinds of weird shit. Any of yuns ever heard of it?"

User BullsFan23 wrote: "Oh yeah, I been there before. That where I fingered ur mom."

User cowjot47 wrote: "no shit I heard about this place. My dad told me they used to skin children out there and hang their body parts from the trees. Really f*cked up shit."

User meetwood-flack wrote: "Ain't that place near Dog Slaughter Creek? I heard they hung dog parts from the trees to warn people off the grounds."

User alien-head22 wrote: "I just asked my mom and she said it's near Dog Slaughter. She told me they saw shadows in the trees. Creepy figures without faces hiding in the woods and watching people there. She said they had blue eyes. Her and her friends heard spooky voices whisperin to em so they ran outta there real fast."

User BullsFan23 wrote: "How old are you alien_head22 you sound like ur 12."

User alien-head22 wrote: "Old enough to fuk ur mother."

User meetwood-flack wrote: "Oooh burn."

5

From the Lexington Quarterly, Fall Edition, October 1ˢᵗ, 2013

THE BOOGEYMAN OF STAUFORD, KENTUCKY

This time of year, the staff at *Lexington Quarterly* delight in sharing their favorite local haunts and legends. Some of these local Kentucky legends have become the subject of past editions (see our 2007 Fall Edition about the "Hillbilly Beast," or our 2011 piece on Bobby Mackey's haunted honkytonk bar), but this year, we decided to put out a call to you, our readers, for your favorite scary legend. One such reader submitted what we consider to be one of the more disturbing and unsettling tales, primarily due to the truth behind the legend. It was so unsettling, in fact, that our Editor-In-Chief refused to travel to the location for an on-site editorial.

As our reader suggested, we dug into the history of a little railroad town called Stauford. It's about eighty miles south of Lexington on I-75, a stone's throw from the Tennessee border. At a glance, one might assume this snapshot of Kentucky living is as idyllic as it is quaint, a quiet sort of place where a family can grow in relative peace and comfort. Obviously, since we're talking about it here, there's a darker side to this town which most folks in Stauford would rather forget.

The legend of the Devil's Creek Boogeyman began in the 1970s, although some might say it goes back further than that. An eccentric reverend by the name of Jacob Masters preached a different kind of sermon—

[PAGE IS TORN]

—the legend of Devil's Creek remains just that: a scary story told to spook the young, a story given occasional life by the whispers of a boogeyman named Jacob Masters who still haunts those woods. The few online discussions we found tell of dark shadows in the forest and hushed voices slipping from between the trees, usually accompanied by grainy photos too obscure to decipher. Perhaps more curious, however, is that despite our research, we found no recent mention of those who survived the fiery ordeal back in 1983.

There were six children who survived the inferno, dubbed the 'Stauford Six' by local media since the law forbade the release of their names. Records show they were eventually turned over to the guardianship of their grandparents, former members of the Masters cult who defected when things turned crazy. Aside from a *Stauford Tribune* article reflecting on the five-year anniversary of the incident, all mention of the survivors seems to have slipped between the cracks of history. At the time of this writing, the Stauford Six are just as much phantoms as the late Reverend Jacob Masters himself. Thirty years later, one mystery remains: *What happened to the Stauford Six?*

PART TWO

RITES OF PASSAGE

Stauford, Kentucky
Present Day

CHAPTER FIVE

1

A n uneasy calm fell over Jack Tremly when he passed the interstate sign announcing STAUFORD – 20 MILES. He was tired and strung-out, having spent the prior night in the uncomfortable bed of a no-name roadside motel across the river from Cincinnati. What was the name of the town? Newport? It didn't matter—Jack had lived in enough shitholes in his time and decided at first glance that Newport was one of them.

Part of him wanted to carry on in the night. Stauford, Kentucky was a few more hours down this stretch of I-75, and the sooner he arrived, the sooner he could get everything over with. The other part of him, the one that sometimes woke up screaming in the dark wanted to prolong the inevitable as much as possible. That part of him didn't want to go to Stauford at all, and for good reason.

His trepidation grew with each mile. The past stalked him like a cold shadow. Jack supposed the shadow had followed him his entire life, growing more chilling the older he got. Now, almost twenty years since he'd left Stauford, here he was again. Part of him wondered if the fires were still burning.

A steady buzz displaced the noise of morning talk radio. Smiling, Jack pressed the answer button on the steering wheel.

"Yes, my dear?"

"You sound too chipper for a weekday morning. Are you okay? Have the locals taken you hostage? Sniff twice if you're in distress."

His agent's voice was exactly what he needed first thing in the morning. Carly Dawes had a way of invigorating him, be it through her stern professionalism or her dry wit. Jack suspected it was a mixture of both.

"No worries, darlin'. If the locals couldn't assimilate me before, I doubt it'll work now."

Carly chuckled, filling the car with a surge of static. "But seriously, kiddo, are you okay? That's why I'm calling. You know, not because you're a top client or anything. Not because you have a gallery showing in four days."

"Is it because you care?"

"Of course. Because I care."

Jack smiled. She *did* care, in her own way. Many of his contemporaries spoke highly of Ms. Dawes but warned him she was all business. He didn't think that was a bad quality, and in truth, he was thankful for her no-nonsense approach. She'd managed to get his work through many doors he'd once thought impenetrable. Next week's gallery show was the latest in a long line of successes with his artwork, and he attributed that to her.

"So, what's on your agenda today, kiddo?"

"Meeting with the probate attorney, signing some paperwork, and then I'm going to go see the old homestead. I'm about twenty miles outside of town, and a few hours early. Couldn't sleep last night."

"Night terrors again?"

"Yeah, the usual."

"Good, keep 'em coming. There's a reason the critics call you the next Beksiński. I don't know what goes on in that fucked-up head of yours, but whatever it is, it sells. Anyway, are you sure you can't fly back? I don't understand why you couldn't fly down there and be on your way back to civilization before—"

"I told you, Carly, I don't like flying."

"Right, the claustrophobia thing. Sorry. Well, keep me in the loop, and if you can get back to the city ahead of time, try for that, too. Ciao!"

The line went dead, and the talk radio DJ resumed his banal commentary. Jack leaned back, braced his hands against the steering wheel, and yawned. Driving over twelve hours the day before caught up to him. The lack of sleep wasn't doing him any favors.

Perhaps Carly was right. He could've flown in half the time, been in and out of town in a day, and been done with his business; but that would've meant no time for preparation. A trip to Stauford meant more to him than throwing clothes into his overnight bag. He'd not been home in more than twenty years, a fact for which he refused to feel any sort of guilt, despite not being there for Mamaw Genie's funeral.

I told you to go, sweetie. So, go. Your place isn't here. We both know that.

Jack sighed. She was right. She'd always been right. College was his way out of town, and a string of sales and gallery showings got him the attention he needed to start a career. Twenty years later, he was on the way to one such gallery showing when he got the call from his grandmother's attorney.

Thinking on it now, replaying the message from Tiptree's secretary in his head, Jack's heart raced. He loved his grandmother dearly, but he couldn't bear the thought of putting her into the earth. She'd always been there, always guiding him in the right direction. Even when he was a thousand miles away, she was still there, checking in on him every weekend like clockwork. Their last conversation was as mundane as it was sweet. Like always, she asked if he'd met anyone, as she wasn't getting any younger and would like to have a great-grandchild. Like always, he rolled his eyes, laughed it off, and asked if she was remembering to take her medications.

And like always, they talked about the weather, because talking about his art scared them both. That topic was always off limits, because unlike his agent and contemporaries and his fanbase, they both knew where that darkness came from. They'd lived it, seen it with their own eyes, and it was enough for two lifetimes. Maybe more.

Now, Mamaw Genie was gone, another fatal victim of a heart attack.

The sign for Exit 29 loomed on the horizon. A numbness fell over him, easing the tension in his chest. His grandmother's voice spoke inside his head. *Relax*, she told him. *Everything is fine now. You're home, sweetie.*

That thought conjured a chill across his shoulders, raking its claws down his back, and he realized the shadow trailing him all his life hadn't really left at all. It was right here the whole time, waiting for him to come back.

He flipped on the Mazda's turn signal and merged onto the exit ramp. "I'm home, Mamaw."

2

He didn't go where he needed to right away. The appointment with the probate attorney wasn't until eleven. He'd not seen Chuck Tiptree since high school, long before that cocky little shit added "esquire" to his name, and Jack supposed a couple more hours wouldn't make much of a difference.

Off the highway, he drove east, noting businesses along the old Cumberland Gap Parkway had sprung up in his absence like fungus, the most notable being a giant Walmart Supercenter crawling with life even at 9 AM on a weekday. He surveyed the retail behemoth with idle curiosity before a nearby billboard stole his attention. A curly haired brunette stared down at traffic with a smirk on her face, one hand held up with her pinky and index fingers extended, defiantly throwing the devil horns to all newcomers from the highway.

Z105.1 – THE GOAT! KEEPING IT EVIL FOR ALL OF STAUFORD'S SINNERS!

A byline in smaller text read, "Featuring Stevie G. in the mornings!" The Goat? A rock station? Devil horns in this part of the Bible Belt?

Be still, my beating heart.

He punched in the radio station as the light turned green. A moment later, he was on his way, driven forward by the classic crunch of AC/DC's "Highway to Hell."

He followed the parkway east, more by memory than the guidance of his GPS, and the landscape was both foreign and familiar. The local economy had grown in the last twenty years, perhaps more so in the last five than the rest. His grandmother emailed some years back about the county finally legalizing the sale of alcohol, something which Stauford's older generations—and bootleggers—rallied against, but in the end, the promise of commerce and tourism dollars silenced the old guard. The empty fields and undeveloped plots of his youth were now home to chain restaurants, gas stations, and small shopping pavilions.

Off to his right, in the remains of the old Trademark Shopping Center, a bright blue sign proclaimed "Stauford's Only Drive-Thru Liquor Mart." And business was booming, even at this hour of the morning. After years of his friends paying a premium to get beer from Swafford's place over on Moore Hill, the thought of walking into a liquor store and buying a six-pack seemed hilarious and weird to him.

"Highway to Hell" faded into the opening riff of "Have a Drink on Me," and Jack laughed aloud at the irony. He made a promise to himself to get a drink later, if only to encourage the local hedonism, and drove another mile before turning off the parkway.

The remnants of the old Layne Camp High School stood off to the left at the top of a hill, empty and derelict for years, like the petrified body of a fallen giant. Across the street, the old football field remained dormant and overgrown. Newcomers wouldn't recognize it as anything more than a field now, with its metal stands and goalposts removed, but Jack remembered a time when those stands were packed every Friday night. The last time he was in town, he'd heard there were plans to build a new school elsewhere in the county, but he couldn't say when or where. He was off to college by then, and the goings on of Layne Camp might as well have been lightyears away.

Jack frowned when he reached the intersection at the bottom of the hill. Hurley's gas station sat empty, out of business by the look of things, its two pumps long dry. He sat for a moment, replaying happier days in his mind. Mr. Hurley—he never knew the old man's first name—always gave him a piece of bubble gum when Mamaw Genie stopped for gas.

"Five in the tank," she'd say, and hand the white-headed old man a crisp fiver. He'd pocket the bill and come back with a wrapped piece of gum in his hand.

"For the little one," he'd say, and offer Jack a sly wink. "Keep the change, young man."

The memory made him smile. He idly wondered what happened to good ol' Mr. Hurley. *Cancer, probably. A lifetime of pumping gas couldn't have done any favors for his health.* Jack sighed. *Mr. Positive strikes again*, he thought, and let off the brake.

He drove along Briar Cliff Avenue and through the neighborhood of his youth. Some of the yards were yellowing, others overgrown, and Mr. Miller's prized garden was nothing more than a patch of dead weeds.

"I used to help pull those weeds," he muttered, unaware he was speaking aloud, creeping along at a steady five miles an hour. Seeing the dead patch of earth in front of Mr. Miller's old place saddened him more than the state of the neighborhood. Time was not kind to his old stomping grounds, and he wondered how the rest of the town fared.

A quarter mile past Mr. Miller's former home, Briar Cliff split off into Standard Avenue, and Jack followed the road around the bend. From there, he could see Mamaw Genie's house atop the hill in the distance. Her home was hard to miss. The old Victorian style was once the talk of the town, even the featured article in one of the state's magazines.

(*"Jackie, a big-shot reporter came all the way down here from Frankfort! Can you believe it?"*)

He *could* believe it. The house stood out among its neighbors, a monument to his great-grandfather's classic taste. The story went, as Mamaw Genie told it, her daddy used to travel all over the country for work after the coal mine closed, and he loved New England so much he wanted to build one of their houses back home. "So he did just that," she'd said, pointing to the brick foundation. "Every brick was put there by my daddy—your great-grandpa Franklin, that is—and our family's lived here ever since."

Jack turned off Standard Avenue and guided the Mazda up the hill toward his grandmother's home. He parked the car in the drive and gave the house a once-over. A thin layer of dirt clung to the white vinyl siding of the old house, and small cracks splintered up through the brick foundation. The second-floor windows overlooking the driveway were covered in dust and bird shit, and the wraparound porch below them was covered in dead leaves and dried grass clippings. One of the white rocking chairs was tipped over on its side.

As Jack rounded the corner toward the porch steps, something caught his eye.

Thick streaks of red paint had drip-dried off the edge of the porch railing. A cool breeze picked up around him, swirling the leaves around his feet, their crackling sound driving a chill up his spine.

"What the hell?" He walked down the overgrown sidewalk toward the banister, wondering if Mamaw Genie hired someone to paint the house before she passed on. His heart sank when he saw the mess covering her front door. "Son of a bitch."

Both front windows were shattered, the curtains billowing lazily in the breeze, and thick red letters were scrawled across the front door. There was no effort in their construction, none of the stylistic grace found in true graffiti. Instead, they were swabbed in haste, forming seven words that made his stomach churn: *REJOICE! THE OLD WITCH BURNS IN HELL!*

Jack grit his teeth so hard his jaw ached. Mamaw Genie promised him the heckling and threats stopped years ago, but of course she'd lied to him so he'd stop worrying. He'd still made a call to the Stauford police department to ask that someone keep an eye on the place. Not that it did any good. *I guess not everything's changed around here,* he thought, pulling his phone from his pocket. He was so caught up in taking photos of the vandalism he didn't hear the old woman approach from behind.

"This is private property, young man."

He turned with a start. The old lady looked him over, her lips pursed and swollen hands balled together into gnarled fists. Jack hadn't seen her since he left town, but even after all these years, she still wore her hair in a tight bun, pulled back so far her forehead seemed stretched, and her eyes protruded with the slightest bulge. *Thyroid problems,* Mamaw Genie once told him. She'd not mentioned Mrs. McCormick in years, and his cheeks flushed with guilt as he stared. He'd assumed she'd passed away years ago.

"Ruth?"

The old woman's face softened at the sound of her name. She peered at him a moment longer before lifting a wrinkled hand to her cheek.

"Jackie Tremly? My lord, is that you, darlin'? Is it really you?"

He smiled. "Yeah, it's me. How've you been?"

But Ruth was crying, and she approached him with her arms out. They embraced, and she gave him the biggest hug he'd had in years. She smelled of lavender and mothballs. Some things hadn't changed after all.

3

"I think it was Ronny Cord's boy, 'cept I can't prove it. I called the chief, but he ain't done nothin' about it. More coffee?"

Ruth didn't wait for his reply. She tipped the coffee pot and refilled his mug. Jack drank deeply, enjoying the bitterness of the black brew. Ruth's kitchen hadn't changed since he was a kid, except everything seemed much bigger back then. Sitting at her table now, he felt two sizes too big for everything. The walls were still the same wooden paneling from the early 80s, and she still used the same knitted placemats. Time stopped for her when her husband Ed died some years back, and her home was just a place she waited out the days until she could join him.

"Who's the chief these days?"

Ruth returned to her seat. "That would be David Bell's boy, Ozzie. Did you go to school with him?"

Jack gulped his coffee and relished the burn in his throat. "Yeah," he sighed, "I did. We weren't friends." Ozzie Bell graduated a couple years ahead of him, and that was after being held back another two. Word around Stauford High was the administration let him graduate to be rid of him, but bad seeds like Ozzie always took root in the worst places. Jack had his own run-ins with Ozzie Bell and his friends back then. Being known around the school as the "pagan art fag" didn't help matters. Hearing Mr. Bell was Stauford's police chief crushed his hope of filing a formal report of the vandalism.

"Anyway," Ruth went on, "they told me they'd send someone out to look at the damage, but that was two days ago. I reckon Ozzie Bell would rather sit on his high horse a few more days with his thumb up his ass, but that's none of my business."

Jack smiled. He didn't remember Ruth having so much sass.

"I s'pose this ain't none of my business neither, but…" Ruth trailed off, stirring her coffee with her teaspoon. "Are you plannin' to visit your mother while you're here?"

He opened his mouth to reply, but the words weren't there. When he got the call from Chuck Tiptree's office to tell him his grandmother passed, he'd packed a bag, hopped in his car, and got on the road. Seeing his mother at the regional hospital hadn't crossed his mind once, and in truth, he'd not thought of her in years. Laura Tremly was a bad dream to him, a monster from the shadows of his past. That's where he preferred she remain.

"No," he said finally. "No, I hadn't planned on it."

Ruth nodded. "I s'pose that's just as well. Was an awful thing, what happened to you kids. Genie did right by you, though. I know she sure was proud of you and what you accomplished. Me, too, though…" She blushed. "Don't take this the wrong way, Jackie, but I don't have the stomach for the paintings you do."

He chuckled. "No offense taken, Ruth. I get that a lot."

"I'm glad you're able to do what you love, and that there's people out there who love it, too. It's so rare someone gets out of Stauford and succeeds. Then there's folks like that slut on the radio, pollutin' our air with her filth."

"Who's that?"

"Didn't you see those billboards everywhere, promotin' the devil's work on your way into town?"

"Oh," he said. "Stevie-something, right?"

"That's the one," Ruth spat. "Nothin' but filth comin' out of her mouth every morning. Me and the other ladies at First Baptist are tryin' to have that station shut down. Can't believe they let her on the air. This whole world's goin' down the toilet, if you ask me. First Genie's house is vandalized, the chief won't do nothin' about it, and we got this harlot playing devil music for the kids to hear…"

Jack smiled, choosing silence over commentary. Defending Stevie G's choice of music was not a hill he was willing to die on, especially at this time of morning. He checked his phone and saw he still had an hour to kill.

"Ruth, it's been great catching up with you, but I wanted to head out to the cemetery before my meeting with Chuck."

"That's fine, honey. You're welcome here any time. Thanks for sittin' and lettin' me ramble on."

She walked him across the street and up the hill to his car. Before he climbed in, he gave her a big hug and handed her his business card.

"I'll be in town for the next few days," he said. "If you need anything, call me."

Ruth took his card. "Genie raised a good man," she said. "Are you stayin' here in her house? Well, I guess it's your house now, too."

He looked up at the old Victorian. Until his arrival, Jack had planned on checking into a local hotel. Now that he was here, however, something about the place called to him. Part of him wanted to revisit the rooms of his youth, to understand the woman who'd raised him, nurtured him. The old Tremly homestead was his last, strongest connection to her. Not staying here seemed wrong somehow.

"Maybe," he said. "I'll be back this afternoon to take care of the windows. You're welcome to stop by if you want some company."

"I may do that, Jackie." She stood on her toes and kissed his cheek. "Tell Chuckie I said hello."

Minutes later, Jack was back on the road, headed toward the parkway. Stevie G. promised another hour of uninterrupted rock 'n roll, and when Marilyn Manson spewed from the Mazda's speakers, Jack cranked the volume until the windows rattled. *I dedicate this one to Ruth*, he thought, and laughed all the way to Layne Camp Cemetery.

4

A row of maples separated the cemetery grounds from the old church road, covering the pavement in a blanket of red leaves. Jack followed the path up the hillside before turning off into the nearby church parking lot. There were two other cars parked at the end of the lot, their drivers either inside the church or somewhere on the hillside, paying their respects to the dead.

He sat in the car for a time, watching the clouds roll overhead in the late summer sun. He hated this time of year in Kentucky. The days went on forever in a thick miasma of heat, humidity, and misery. The nights were not much better, albeit just cool enough to be bearable. Together, the air of the place heaved in and out like the hitching breaths of a season refusing to die.

Jack reached for his sunglasses and noticed his hands were shaking. He'd been in town for little more than an hour, and he was already a nervous wreck.

Foolish, he thought. *All that time on the road and you didn't let yourself grieve.* He was so absorbed with getting out of the city and getting on the road that he'd not considered being at his grandmother's grave.

Grandmother. Grave. Those two words didn't belong together. He leaned back in the seat and closed his eyes, listening to his heart, willing it to slow.

He'd talked to her a week ago. She'd seemed so vibrant on the phone, so full of life despite her age, and he remembered thinking afterward that she was going to live forever. Imogene Tremly was his whole world for a time, until she let him go to make the world his own. Everything he'd done in the years since, every pencil line, every brush stroke, was done to make her proud.

Jack opened his eyes and stared through the shaded view of the car's sunroof. A jet drifted miles above, leaving two fuzzy white trails in its wake.

"Get a grip on yourself," he whispered to no one. "The world goes on, and so do you." Years later, Mamaw Genie's words of wisdom still lived on.

He took a breath and climbed out of the car. The Tremly family plot was on the other side of the hill, beyond a white marble mausoleum. He never did like the old thing. On the occasions when he'd accompany Imogene to put flowers on her husband's grave, Jack always kept his distance. It reminded him too much of a horror film from his youth.

Farther down the hill, a thin blonde woman in a red T-shirt and jeans stood over one of the graves with her arms folded across her chest. He watched her for a few seconds before feeling like a creep, averting his gaze to the graves at his feet.

Two rows beyond the mausoleum, he spotted the fresh earth of his grandmother's grave. Bouquets of flowers lined the granite marker, offering color to an otherwise drab memorial, a detail which Mamaw Genie would've appreciated. Jack stood beside the rectangle of soil, collecting himself as he took in the scene.

MARTHA IMOGENE TREMLY
BELOVED WIFE AND GRANDMOTHER
"ET QUOD EST SUPERIUS EST SICUT QUOD EST INFERIUS"

A row of symbols was etched below the Latin phrase. Jack slept through most of his Classical Studies course in school and had no idea what the words said, nor had he seen those symbols before. Mamaw Genie was no strangers to symbols herself. She'd always worn a bracelet with a trio of silver charms—her "good luck" charms, she told him—and each charm was inscribed with curly runes in similar fashion, but he'd never summoned the courage to ask her what they meant.

Jack smiled as he knelt beside the demarcation of earth.

"I miss you," he said softly. "You always knew what was best." He traced his fingers through the soft earth. "I'm sorry I couldn't be there when they laid you to rest, Mamaw. I hope you'll forgive me. I hope you'll understand."

Jack pressed his hand into the dirt and left his imprint before climbing to his feet. He wiped the tears from his eyes and kissed the edge of the marble gravestone.

"I'll say goodbye before I leave town for good, Mamaw. I love you."

He was about to return to his car when he had an idea. *For later*, he thought, reaching into his pocket for his phone. He held up the device and snapped a photo of the grave marker. As he did so, the young woman he'd spotted earlier walked past, offering him a cursory nod before pausing long enough to glance at the gravestone.

"As above, so below."

Jack lowered his phone and turned. "Excuse me?"

The blonde woman stared at him blankly, her placid expression prompting his cheeks to flush with heat. It was the look of an elementary school teacher, strung out at the end of her day. *Why aren't you paying attention?* it asked. *How can you be so dense?*

The blonde woman raised one hand to the air, pointing up; with the other, she pointed to the earth.

"As above," she repeated, "so below." Then she pointed to the gravestone. "That's what it says."

Jack stared at her, agape with confusion. The coldness of her gaze stirred a memory, and he was struck with a sensation of déjà vu.

"Did you—"

The phone buzzed in his hand. *Know my grandmother,* Jack wanted to say, but the words failed him while he fumbled with the device, canceling the alarm he'd set for himself. He had fifteen minutes to get to Chuck Tiptree's office downtown.

"Sorry," he mumbled, but when he looked up from the phone, the blonde woman was already halfway up the hillside. "Huh."

Jack pocketed the phone and glanced back at his grandmother's gravestone. As above, so below. He wondered if the stranger was telling him the truth and not blowing smoke up his ass. Then again, he supposed the exchange was too odd not to have some truth to it. Mamaw Genie always told him knowledge often came in strange forms.

"Just like the apple from the tree," he whispered. "As above, so below. One mystery begets another."

Puzzled, Jack made his way back to the parking lot. One of the cars was gone. In its place was a white plastic bag full of trash. He shook his head, frowned, and climbed into the car.

As he drove away, a warm breeze swept over the cemetery lot, whispering through the trees and blowing the small bag across the asphalt. Its contents scattered. Fast food wrappers, a few candy bar wrappers, an empty fast food cup bled dry of its contents, and other detritus littered the parking lot—including an empty aerosol can of red spray paint.

CHAPTER SIX

1

J ack almost didn't make it to his appointment on time. At some point in the last twenty years, the confluence of East Mason Street and North Depot Street was overtaken by a behemoth of concrete and rebar. Dubbed the "Tom Thirston Memorial Overpass," this massive structure directed travelers over Layne Camp Creek and onto North Kentucky Street, which was now a one-way thoroughfare.

The car's GPS was as confused as he was, uttering stern directives demanding he perform a U-turn when possible—or else. He cursed quietly to himself as he shut off the device, certain he could find Chuck's office on his own. How much could Main Street change in twenty years?

A bit, he realized. He circled the block around what used to be First National, discovering a larger corporate bank had swallowed up his grandmother's bank of choice in his absence. Main Street itself wasn't the desolate strip he'd expected it would be. Cars and trucks lined the parking spaces, their owners bustling along the sidewalks, ignorant of this outsider in their midst. Stauford had grown up, or maybe it was always like this and he just didn't remember. In either case, Jack was taken aback by the signs of life, and was so absorbed in his memories he didn't see the light change. A car honked, and he turned left.

He circled the block again, this time following Kentucky Street to its conclusion, where it terminated at the south end of Main Street. He took the opportunity to turn back on to Main Street and see the town in all its modern glory.

Town Hall was remodeled in his years away, looking less like the old office building of his youth and more like something one would see at a state capitol, with white columns and a domed roof to match. He'd once witnessed the beginnings of a Klan rally on the building's front steps. Peering from the back seat of Mamaw Imogene's green Cadillac, he'd asked her why all those men were dressed up as ghosts. She'd looked back at him in the rearview and said, "They're bigots, honey."

"What's a bigot, Mamaw?"

She'd thought about it for a moment, but the answer came to her just as easily. "Bigots are cowards. They're dressed up so people can't see their faces."

"Are they scaredy cats?"

"*Dumb* scaredy cats."

Decades later, as he sat in traffic, he turned and saw the old municipal building across the street was now home to the Stauford Laundromat. A smaller sign in the window also claimed they bought gold for cash. The juxtaposition gave him a good laugh that lasted through most of the traffic.

Chuck Tiptree's office sat across the street from where Huffington's Drugstore used to be, except now the square, brick building was home to a small coffee shop. The next block over, what used to be Ron's Department Store was now a bar and restaurant called Devlin's On Main. Jack parked the car along the curb and sighed. The town had changed drastically in his time away. A new generation built over the bones of the old. The corpses were still there, but a new sort of creature inhabited them. Time finally moved in Stauford, something he'd once thought impossible.

Jack looked at himself in the rearview mirror. Had *he* changed all that much? He studied the lines on his face, the hints of silver in his hair, the darkening spots of age in his cheeks and forehead. The man in his reflection looked a lot different than the boy who'd wandered these streets on Halloween or watched the annual parade with an ice cream cone in his hand—but somewhere in the eyes, there was still a spark of youth. Somewhere, where his dreams still haunted him, and the darkness filled his lungs with the foul musty air of untold ages. That child was still in there somewhere, and he was screaming.

Hot air clouded his face, stealing his breath from him, and he escaped to fresh air and the smell of roasting coffee from across the street. The aroma lingered on his taste buds, and he wished he had time to get a cup before his meeting.

"Jack?"

He closed the door behind him and looked up. A paunchy man with cropped silver hair and a goatee to match stood in the office doorway. His bulbous cheeks were bright red and beaded with sweat. Jack would recognize that shitty grin anywhere.

"Chuckie?"

"Jackie, you lanky son of a bitch! Come 'ere."

Chuck Tiptree bounded across the sidewalk and gave Jack a bear hug. Jack tried to pat his old friend's back, grimacing slightly at the wetness of Chuck's sweaty shirt.

"Goddamn, man, how long's it been? Fifteen years? Twenty?"

"Twenty this month," Jack said, forcing a smile. "How've you been?"

Chuck nodded, gesturing to his office. "Not bad, man. Getting by, making ends meet. The usual." Silence fell between the two men as Chuck's words sank in. Jack was gone so long he didn't know what "the usual" entailed. Chuck Tiptree cleared his throat, his swollen cheeks suddenly pale. "Anyway, you've come a long way to meet with little ol' me. Step into my office, Mr. Tremly."

2

"Glass of ice water?"

Chuck's secretary, Diane, stuck her head through the open doorway of the conference room. Her withered cheeks were flushed, the buoyant poof of her bouffant hair nearly lost to heat and sweat. She stared down at him with wide yellowing eyes while fanning herself with the morning edition of the Stauford Tribune.

"Yes, please."

"Sorry, bud." Chuck wandered in after her and plunked down a box of paperwork on the table. "The A/C died a couple days ago and the repair guy can't get out here until this afternoon. So…"

He trailed off as he ducked out of the room. A moment later, Chuck returned with a portable desk fan. Warm, stale air blasted Jack's face.

"There," Chuck said, panting. He took a seat across from Jack as Diane brought in two tall glasses of ice water.

"Fresh from the dispenser," she said. "Here you go."

Chuck nodded. "Thanks, hon."

"No problem, Mr. Tiptree." She turned back for the door, but before she left, Diane placed her hand on Jack's shoulder. "I'm sorry for your loss, Mr. Tremly."

He offered her a thin smile. "Thank you." The pity on her wrinkled face told him his smile wasn't believable. She tightened her arthritic fingers on him, offering a firm gesture of condolence before leaving the room. Once she'd closed the door behind her, Jack reached for the glass and drank greedily.

"Bet you forgot about these hot Septembers, huh?"

Jack took one last gulp and wiped his mouth. "How's that?"

"I mean, with you livin' up in New England all these years, you must get, what, three days of summer?"

Jack laughed. "Hardly. You should come visit New York in the middle of a summer heatwave sometime."

Smiling, Chuck leaned back and looked at the file box between them. "So what were you saying earlier? Someone vandalized Genie's house?"

Jack nodded, pulled out his phone, and showed him the photos. Chuck's cheeks blossomed in fresh red splotches.

"Did you report it?"

"Didn't have to," Jack said, pocketing the phone. "Ruth McCormick told me she called the police station to report it a couple days ago. Thinks it might've been Ronny Cord's kid. She says hi, by the way."

Chuck sighed. "If it was Ronny's little shit stain, you can bet money Ozzie Bell won't do shit about it. Those Cro-Magnon window-lickers take care of their own. Anyway, I know a guy who does good window work. I can give him a call later if you want?"

"I'd like that," Jack said. "Thank you."

Chuck waved him off. "Forget about it," he said, unpacking several green legal folders wrapped in rubber bands. "I guess we should get down to business?"

"I guess so."

Chuck Tiptree went over the specifics of Imogene Tremly's last will and testament without much fanfare. Where he was all fun and games around his friends, he was nothing but professional when it came to his clients' legal affairs, a trait which Jack appreciated now more than ever. As she had no living spouse, and with her only child committed to the psychiatric ward of Baptist Regional, Imogene Tremly's affairs of estate would be handled by one Charles Tiptree, *Esquire*, whom she named sole executor.

"I had the opportunity to meet with your grandmother a handful of times before she passed. She considered you her only living heir, Jackie. The only one who matters, anyway. A small portion of her estate was set aside to be donated to the Stauford Fire Company for saving her daddy's barn back in the day. There are still some bills to collect and get paid. Less the government's cut and my fee—which is nominal—and provided no one comes out of the woodwork with a surprise claim, I'd say you've got yourself a nice nest egg to retire on. I think you'll find everything's in order." Chuck extracted a sheet from his file and slid it across the table. "Once you sign, we can get started, and you'll have a paycheck in six months or so. Easy-peasy."

Jack looked over the document, which was an itemization of estate assets, taxes, and Chuck's fees—which were, Jack discovered, quite nominal indeed. And the nest egg his friend mentioned was more than enough for Jack to retire on. All told, Mamaw Genie left him the better part of two million dollars. Jack did well for himself as an artist, far better than most in his profession, and he would not go down in history as one of the starving geniuses of the trade, but the net amount on that piece of paper made his heart stop. He didn't know Mamaw Genie had that kind of money.

"There's also the matter of her house to discuss."

He looked up as Chuck drained the last of his ice water from the glass. "I'm sorry?"

"Her house is part of the declared value. Not much in comparison to the rest of her liquidated assets, but…"

Chuck's words faded into the background hum of the oscillating fan. Jack closed his eyes and sighed, trying to hold back the tide of emotions churning inside him. He'd suspected she'd leave him the house—it was his birthright, after all. A family heirloom of the highest degree built with his grandfather's own hands. At the same time, however, he questioned how the hell he could take care of such a place. Jack spent most of his time either working on his art, talking about his art, presenting his art, or sleeping and dreaming nightmares which fed his art. Keeping up with the demands of a house were beyond his range of capabilities, much less one over a thousand miles away.

Chuck cleared his throat. "Jack? You still with me?"

"What?" Jack barked, stunned by the sound of his own voice. "Sorry, I'm…still processing all of this."

"S'all good, Jack. I understand. It can be a lot to take in, believe me. Is it the money or the house?"

"Both," Jack admitted. "I had no idea my grandmother had that kind of bread stashed away, and the house…" He held up his hands, flustered. "I can't come down here every time there's a problem, you know?"

Chuck nodded. "Understandable. The money's an easy one. Your grandmother invested well. Most of the money belonged to her daddy, which he passed on to her, and now she's leaving it to you. It's yours to do with as you wish. As for the house, that's not so simple. Legally, you're free to do what you want with it. There's no provision in the will that you can't sell the house…" He met Jack's gaze. "…but you and I both know Genie wouldn't care for that. The house and land have been in your family for generations."

"Now you sound like her," Jack mumbled.

"I know I do," Chuck said. "I'm the executor, remember? That's my job. Anyway, I'm sure a big shot like yourself can figure something out. Maybe fix it up, call it a summer home."

"Would *you* spend your summers here?"

Chuck gestured to his conference room, the oscillating fan, the stacks of file boxes lining the walls. "Baby, I'm living this every day. This shit's my life!"

They shared a laugh, but the mood died quickly, giving way to the low hum of the fan punctuating the silence between them. Chuck drummed his fingers on the table, mumbling to himself. Finally, he slapped his hand on the table, startling Jack from his thoughts.

"I almost forgot. There's one more thing."

Chuck dug into the file box and retrieved a small wooden case. He slid it across the table to his client.

Jack held the box in his hand. The wood was polished to a shine. Trembling, he opened the clamshell lid, and frowned when he saw its contents.

Laid out on a red velvet interior was an old metal key, its surface tarnished dark with age. He'd never seen it before, and he hadn't the faintest idea what it unlocked.

"Was there anything else with this?"

Chuck was in the middle of returning some of the folders to the box. He paused and shook his head. "That's all she gave me, man. I assumed you'd know what it's for."

Jack sighed. "No, I don't." He rolled the key in his hands, gauging its weight. The metal was thick, its teeth carved with an intricate design that would've taken its maker days to etch, and the rounded end was polished smooth. *They don't make 'em like this anymore*, he thought.

Chuck Tiptree closed the box and planted both plump hands on the table. "Say, you hungry? It's almost lunchtime and I'm starvin'. You can sign this paperwork later. Let's get a bite."

He'd not considered food since leaving Ruth's house, but now his stomach groaned in discontent at the thought of sustenance. "Yeah, now that you mention it. Is the old Burger Stand still in business?"

"My man," Chuck grinned. "Come on, my treat."

3

Chuck offered to drive, a gesture for which Jack was grateful. He'd happily admitted defeat to the changes wrought by time, and being a passenger afforded him an opportunity to sightsee for the first time that day.

Although Stauford's Main Street had undergone a facelift in recent years, Jack was delighted to discover some of its institutions hadn't changed at all. The powder blue water tower overlooking the town from atop Gordon Hill still stood, announcing "Stauford Welcomes You" in swirly red letters.

Banners stretched between buildings over Main Street, announcing the upcoming "Miss Stauford" beauty pageant, along with the dates of the town's fall street festival. Jack missed them until Chuck pointed them out.

"You wouldn't *believe* how much they wanna charge to advertise in the festival program."

They turned off Main Street and back on to Kentucky Avenue toward the south end of town. The Piggly Wiggly was no longer in business, replaced by a massive hardware store. The local pizza joint was still open, though, and seeing its subdued orange lettering on the windows brought back memories of his first date with a girl named Megan Briarson. They'd kissed awkwardly at the end of the night, their breath tainted with the stench of garlic, and the following week they'd acted like strangers to one another at school. Jack felt a pang of regret over that, and he idly wondered what she was up to these days. He hoped she was happy.

Half a mile up the road, Chuck turned right onto 18th Street. Jack craned his neck to take in the massive temple of asphalt and concrete at the corner, home to a Walgreens.

"There used to be a produce stand there," he said. "Mamaw Genie used to shop there every week."

"A lot's changed, brother. Tends to happen when you run off to be a big shot in the city." Chuck smiled when he said it, but Jack took the jab in the gut. He felt more than a little guilty, a feeling which he told himself was irrational, but the remorse sat like a hot lump of lead in his chest. He thought of the friends he knew, the promises to keep in touch, the bonds he thought would never be severed—and all of them were replaced by his drive to leave, to tackle the world, to transmute his pain into something he could sell.

Jack Tremly left Stauford to become something more than a dirty town secret. Maybe the others dealt with that legacy in their own ways, but not him. He had to get away, go someplace where no one knew him, and rebuild himself in any shape he wanted.

His task accomplished, he'd returned to find the world he once knew had changed and moved on without him, and how dare he feel entitled to anything different. *Time didn't stop with you leaving, honey. You can't expect it to. That's vanity.*

Mamaw Genie's words in his head again, guiding him through another silent crisis. Their comfort was always welcome, and he clung to them like a child to a soft blanket.

"And here it is, my man." Chucks words tore him from his reverie, and Jack looked up from the car's dashboard as they turned off the road into a crowded parking lot. A small, squat building sat in the center, with a large overhang extending half the length of the lot. Cars were parked underneath like calves suckling at their mother.

"One of the few reasons you'd ever want to leave I-75."

Jack smiled. "Is that your professional opinion?"

They found a spot at the far end of the lot and parked. Chuck turned off the engine and grinned. "As your attorney, I would strongly advise it."

The Stauford Burger Stand was a city icon. Opened in the summer of 1956, under a partnership between the brothers Willie and Donald Chastain, the Stauford Burger Stand earned itself a reputation of having the best burgers and chili in the region. He opened his window and took a deep breath. The scent of the grill and twangy country music swirled around him, taking him back to simpler times. His stomach growled in anticipation.

"God, I've missed this place."

"Tell me about it. I dream about this place, and I live here. Hasn't changed since you left and probably won't even after we're long gone. I'm having a Dixie burger. You?"

"I'll have the same," Jack said. "And fries. Root beer, too."

Chuck signaled to one of the waitresses in the kitchen, and a moment later, a thin blonde approached with a pen and notepad in her hand.

"Hey, Susan," Chuck said. "You'll never believe who's with me today."

Jack looked up and did a double take. She'd changed clothes since he'd seen her earlier in the cemetery, but there was no mistaking the dirty blonde hair spilling over her shoulders, the cold stare, and dimples betraying the promise of a smile.

Susan Prewitt leaned into the open window and smirked. "Jackie Tremly, as I live and breathe." She reached in, and he shook her hand, noting the circular tattoo on her wrist. "The years have been kind."

"Thanks. It's good to see you again," he said, stunned. "Since this morning, I mean."

She smiled, but her eyes told a different story, and for a moment he feared he might wither under her gaze. It was a stare of silent fury, the sort reserved for scolding mothers not wanting to make a scene. *Not another word*, that stare said. *Or else.*

"Just paying my respects, Jackie. Your grandma was a good lady." She clicked her pen. "Anyway, what can I get you boys?"

They placed their orders, and she left without a remark. When she was gone, Chuck shrugged. "What was that about?"

Jack watched her drop off the order at the kitchen window and walk out to a rusted Ford pickup. He'd never been close to Susan, not like they were when they were little kids. Not since what happened in the woods. Growing up, she was always the quiet one, commanding respect from their peers out of sheer will. Most kids of that sort always skittered through the halls like mice, afraid of being seen and singled out, but not Susan. She was a contradiction, a clique of one, who stood out by not standing out at all. Wherever she went, she went alone.

"I'm not sure," he said, finally. "Probably nothing."

Only he wasn't so sure, and he didn't understand why. Watching her take another order, Jack thought back to the morning. *One mystery begets another.*

4

Across the street, while Jack and Chuck waited for their food, another sort of mystery was unfolding in the spartan office of Stauford High School's assistant principal, Dave Myers.

"Mr. Tate." A bluish vein bulged from his forehead like a buried worm. "Are you ready to tell me what the hell you were thinking?"

Riley Tate sat in the hot seat across from Mr. Myers, picking at a crudely painted thumbnail he'd done himself. To be honest, Riley was trying to figure out the answer to that question himself. He frowned at the dirt on his ripped jeans.

"Mr. Tate?"

The fifteen-year-old looked up, dusting off the legs of his jeans. "Yes, Mr. Myers?"

"I asked you a question."

"And I heard you. I'm still thinking of the answer."

Assistant Principal Myers leaned back in his seat and scoffed. "Let me make sure I understand, Mr. Tate. You don't know why you attacked Jimmy Cord? You don't know why you blindsided him and broke his nose?"

Riley's eyes lit up. "I broke his nose?"

"Oh yes, Mr. Tate. You certainly broke his nose. He's at the hospital right now, having it reset."

Riley bit his cheeks and fought a smile. "Oh," he said. "Too bad."

"Oh yeah," Mr. Myers said, "it *is* too bad. It's too bad for him, because he'll probably have to miss tonight's game against Layne Camp. It's too bad for the Stauford Bulldogs because their quarterback was benched on account of a random attack by another student. It's too bad for all the folks in Stauford who bought tickets to tonight's game to see Jimmy Cord run sixty yards to the goal line."

Riley leaned back in his seat, fighting the smirk building in his face. The vein in Mr. Myers's forehead bulged with each subsequent word, and for a time, Riley secretly hoped an aneurysm would save him from another minute of this guy's bullshit.

"And it's too bad for you, Mr. Tate, because I have to make a decision here, today, in this office. Before I can do that, I need you to tell me what the hell you were thinking. So, please, Mr. Tate, enlighten me."

One of his father's axioms sprung from the cloudy tumult of Riley's mind: *Every man's got a choice, and every man is judged by the choices he makes.*

Riley couldn't remember from which one of the good Reverend Tate's sermons he'd heard that line. After a while, his father's Sunday morning monologues blended together into a buzzing mess of repentance, hellfire, and damnation. Still, Riley found his father's words particularly prescient at this moment, and he struggled with whether to tell the truth or not.

The easy way out would be to tell the lie burning on his tongue, the lie he'd made up before approaching Jimmy Cord. The lie was easy and convenient and didn't require a whole lot of explanation: Jimmy Cord was an asshole, and Riley didn't like him. Two statements which, on their own and out of context of his situation, weren't lies at all.

Jimmy Cord was, in fact, a complete and total asshole. Jimmy's reputation was established in the annals of Stauford lore, having slammed Mike Henly's head into a locker during Riley's freshman year. Mike Henly went to the hospital for a concussion and Jimmy went to varsity football practice. Even to a kid his age, Riley could see which direction the wind blew in Stauford, which made his lie so easy to tell.

But what about the hard way out? The truth of the matter? Riley struggled with the choice to tell Mr. Myers something he wouldn't believe.

Reputation was everything to a boy his age, especially in a town where one's roster of friends, vocation, and pedigree determined the pecking order. Riley had long ago established his own *modus operandi*, choosing to be the loner who sat alone at lunch, wore black T-shirts sporting logos of bands no one had ever heard of, and painted his nails with a color called "Satan's Heart." He'd done everything in his power to rebel against the status quo while terrifying his father and embracing the bitter irony of defying Stauford's many stereotypes by becoming one. Everyone around the high school knew Riley Tate cared for no one.

Except that wasn't true. He did care, in his own way, and when he saw Jimmy cornering Ben Taswell in the courtyard between second and third bell, something snapped.

Ben was the closest thing Riley had to a best friend. They'd grown up together in First Baptist's youth group. That is, their parents forced them to participate in it, and they hated having to do so. Otherwise, Riley and Ben had little else in common, but their tacit alliance over their shared hatred of the youth group was enough to warrant a bond of friendship which grew over the years.

The last thing Riley could abide was watching a kid twice Ben's size and half the intelligence beat his friend to a pulp. Jimmy had a fistful of Ben's collar, his other fist hovering above the poor kid's face like a hammer, and while other students crowded around to watch, Riley experienced a moment of clarity. He broke free of his social status, defied his reputation, and took hold of an empty lunch tray from a nearby table. No one saw him coming, especially Jimmy Cord.

"Hey, shithead."

Jimmy turned to look as Riley slammed the tray into his face. Blood gushed from the quarterback's nose. An instant later, Jimmy fell backward, landing on his ass with a dazed look on his face. Twin trails of dark red rolled out of his swollen nostrils like thick paint, staining the popped collar of his white polo. Riley stood over him, clenching his fists, ready for the bastard to climb to his feet, only Jimmy didn't. He sat on the ground, blinking.

"Thanks," Ben whispered.

"Don't mention it," Riley said, looking up as the lunch monitor, Mrs. Viars, pushed open the cafeteria doors and ran into the courtyard.

Half an hour later, Riley was in Mr. Myers's office, struggling to decide if he should betray his reputation by telling the truth. Would Mr. Myers believe him? Since when did Riley Tate have feelings? Or *friends*, for that matter? And what would the greater populace of Stauford High think of this recent revelation?

The possibilities turned his stomach.

"Well, Mr. Tate?"

Riley blinked and looked up at Mr. Myers. He smiled. "I felt like it."

"You *felt* like it?"

"Mmhmm," he said, nodding. "Can I go now?"

Exasperated, Assistant Principal Myers clenched his jaw and pinched the bridge of his nose. He shook his head. "You're suspended. One week. I'll call your father. Get the hell out of my office."

Riley Tate rose to his feet and opened the door. He tried not to smile as he walked out. After all, he had a reputation to keep.

5

Had Riley remained in Mr. Myers's office, he would've seen a rusted pickup truck pull into the parking lot of the Burger Stand across the street. The truck had seen better days, its surface once a bright banana yellow, but now all that remained was a shoddy husk of metal, duct tape, and Bondo. Its engine backfired as the truck drove over the curb and into the lot, coughing a plume of dark exhaust over the other customers.

The driver, a man by the name of Waylon Parks, brought the truck to a sputtering stop at the far end of the lot and shut off the engine. His passenger, Zeke Billings, rolled down the window. Another cloud of smoke just as odious rolled out of the open airway. He finished off his joint and ground the roach into the dashboard ashtray.

Waylon slammed his fist on the steering wheel and gave the horn three short honks. Zeke turned his head and winced at each shrill whine.

"Give that a rest, man. My fuckin' head hurts."

"I'm starving here. We got a schedule to keep." Waylon honked twice more. "Y'all hurry it up now."

Zeke leaned back and closed his eyes. He was awake until nearly dawn, poring over old chemistry books he'd checked out from the Stauford Library. Waylon was up just as late, searching for a cook site to prepare their first batch. Neither of them knew what the hell they were doing, but Zeke had enough sense to hit up the Stauford Library's computers for a little internet research first.

Saying no to their number one customer was out of the question. Zeke supposed having dirt on the town's chief of police was advantageous, assuming he ever had to do something with the information. Everyone had their vice of choice, and Ozzie Bell was no different, but their unique relationship allowed for more freedom than usual. Ozzie got his kicks, and Waylon and Zeke got to stay in business.

70

"Keep a low profile," Ozzie told him, "and we can keep this goin' until I retire. Hell, until *after* I retire, if you play your cards right. I get what I want, you get what you want, and everybody's happy."

Provided, of course, they could supply him with what he wanted, when he wanted it. Yesterday afternoon, when Chief Bell dropped by Waylon's trailer on the other side of Moore Hill, Zeke figured it was for the usual kinks.

"Y'all got any of that methamphetamine?"

Waylon spoke before Zeke could reply. "No, sir, but we can cook up a batch for ya right quick."

"How quick?"

"How's Sunday work for ya? Just in time for your Sunday schoolin'."

"That'll work," Ozzie agreed. "Anything to get through Tate's ramblin' sermons."

They all shook hands, even though Zeke didn't understand why. The deal was something Zeke's grandfather, Roger, used to call a "one-sided agreement." Truth was, Ozzie had them by the balls, and they all knew it. Ozzie Bell could've asked for the moon and Waylon would've promised it to him. That's why they were up so goddamn late, why they slept through Waylon's alarm, why they were late getting started, and why Zeke found himself wondering how in the hell they were going to get out of this deal.

"Hey, Ezekiel."

He opened his eyes and found Susan Prewitt leaning against the truck. "You know that ain't my name, Susie."

"Neither's Susie for me." She nudged his arm. "You'll never guess who's in town."

"Who's that? The President?"

"Even better. Our long-lost half-brother, the artist."

Zeke sat up, the stoner haze suddenly gone from his bloodshot eyes. "No shit?"

"No shit," Waylon said, drumming his fingers on the steering wheel. "Are you gonna take our order or not?"

"Give her a minute," Zeke snapped. "You're serious?" He studied Susan's face, trying to find the lie somewhere. *You don't trust a snake*, his grandpa Roger always told him, *they'll always bite when your back's turned.* She stared at him with the same blank mask she always wore. *Resting bitch face.*

She nodded, clicking her pen against the passenger door. "Talked to him ten minutes ago. He's down at the other end, if you can believe it. Saw him this morning at the cemetery, paying his respects."

"Kind of cold, not going to your own grandma's funeral."

"That's how all those big shots are. Then again, he probably didn't want nobody knowing he's related to a witch."

Zeke smirked. "Damn right about that, sis. She's lucky the town didn't burn her at the stake."

They shared a laugh, and for a moment Zeke felt at home with her again, like when they were kids. The shadows of their past hadn't seemed as terrifying when they could hold hands and face it together, but those days were long behind them.

Waylon cleared his throat. "Zeke, I hate to break up this here reunion, but we got a job to do."

"He's right," Zeke sighed.

Susan shrugged. "That's all right." She took out her notepad and glared at Waylon. "What'll it be?"

They gave their orders and watched her saunter back to the pickup window. Waylon let out a low whistle as she walked away, following the sway of her hips like a puppy on a leash.

"Damn shame she's your sister, man. I'd hit that faster 'n anything."

"Half-sister, but still blood. That makes her off limits." Zeke took a swing and punched Waylon's shoulder. "Goes for you too, you sick shit. I seen what you do to the girls you bring to the trailer."

Waylon slicked back his greasy hair and sniffed his fingers. "I got fond memories of Rhonda. You wouldn't believe the nasty shit she gets up to in the sack."

"Save it," Zeke said, grimacing. "And keep away from my sister."

"You ain't got nothin' to worry about there, brother. She ain't my type. Too stuck-up for my taste. I like 'em a little more plump, a little more broken on the inside."

Zeke rolled his eyes. Waylon's choice of partners was the emotionally scarred type, desperate enough to get with white trash like him, and willing enough not to say no. Susan Prewitt, on the other hand, was an entirely different breed of beast, more likely to gut a man for looking at her the wrong way than to submit. Waylon knew better than to catcall her, even in Zeke's absence.

"Besides," Waylon went on, "I don't know why you talk to that stuck-up bitch anyway."

"Because she's family," Zeke mumbled, leaning back in his seat. He closed his eyes and relaxed. He was closer to Susan Prewitt than he was the rest of his half-siblings, but that wasn't saying much. After his grandfather passed away from lung cancer, he went to live with Susan and her grandfather, Hank, until he turned eighteen. Even then, Susan was hard to read, his friend one minute and a stranger the next, and she always avoided him when they were at school. They had more in common now that he was into dealing—she liked to smoke from time to time, with the occasional blotter of acid on the side—but he still didn't trust her.

How could he, after that night in his bedroom.

Zeke opened his eyes and stared at the ceiling of the truck, charting a course between bald spots in the upholstery. *Put it out of your head*, he told himself. *It was a million years ago, and she still ain't worth the trouble.*

His heart, though, told him something different. He still got a fluttery feeling in his gut when she spoke to him, regardless of which mask she was wearing on a given day.

"Waylon," he said, sitting up. "Put on some music, would you?"

His friend obliged, pushing a mixtape into the console cassette deck. A moment later, the opening notes of Lynyrd Skynyrd's "Simple Man" filled his ears. He hummed along, taking the words to heart.

A few minutes passed, and Susan returned with their food. Zeke handed her a twenty and told her to keep the change.

"Thanks," she said, looking at the ruffled tarp stretched over the truck bed. "You going out to the woods?"

Waylon stopped unwrapping his burger and looked up, stunned. "How'd you know that?"

"Lucky guess," she said, smiling. "It's a full moon tonight, you know."

"So?"

"No reason. You boys enjoy yourselves." Susan tapped the roof of the truck and winked at Zeke. They watched her leave a second time. Waylon shook his head.

"Your sister's fuckin' weird, man."

"Yeah," Zeke said, watching her walk away. "Runs in the family."

"Ain't that the fuckin' truth!" Waylon laughed and nearly choked on a mouthful of food. He coughed up a chewed piece of burger and spat it out his window. He cleared his throat and wiped his mouth. "You ready to get to work?"

Zeke shoved a handful of fries into his mouth. "Let's do it."

"Right on." Waylon started the truck. A minute later, they squealed tires out of the parking lot and onto Cumberland Falls Highway. The sun hung above them at its zenith, the sky was clear except for a few clouds, and traffic was light. With Skynyrd blaring through the speakers and a full tank of gas, life couldn't get any better.

And it wouldn't. Waylon would be dead before the sun rose again.

≈

6

Jack returned to his grandmother's house two hours later with a full belly. He stopped at a hardware store along the way and bought some plastic sheeting to cover the broken windows, along with a bucket, sponges, and enough liquid soap to clear up the graffiti. Chuck had handed over the house keys when they got back to his office, but Jack kept them in his pocket. Staring up at the old house, he realized he wasn't ready to return to its halls and the memories awaiting him inside. Not yet.

Instead, he busied himself with cleaning up the mess left by the vandals. He found an old broom hanging inside the door of the garden shed and used it to sweep the porch. Ruth called up to him from the foot of the driveway, asking if he wanted any help, but he waved her off and thanked her anyway.

"Maybe tomorrow," he told her, and went back to work. Normally he wouldn't mind the company or the help, but right now he needed time to clear his head. Mamaw Genie used to call him a nervous worker. Working with his hands busied his mind with something other than the problem. He couldn't work on his art while preoccupied with such matters. The trivialities of real life poisoned his creative well. Besides, he preferred to leave his art to the realm of his nightmares, something which had served him well so far.

Once the porch was cleared, he set about scrubbing off the paint, filling the bucket from the outside spigot, and made a mental note to thank Chuck for keeping the utilities paid up. A few passes with the sponge yielded some results, staining the water a murky crimson color that took his thoughts back to darker places. He paused, searching the dusty corners of his mind for the memory irritating him most, a persistent itch inside his skull.

Fire, he thought. He was barely ten, not even out of elementary school yet. The night terrors were at their worst then, when he'd wake up screaming, kicking the blankets from his bed, punching the air at unseen creatures clawing at him from the dark. He'd woken up in a fury, chased into consciousness by faceless things, and heard men outside. They were loud and vulgar, and there was a faint orange glow coming from his window. The orange light danced erratically, casting horrible shadows across his cartoon posters, forcing their faces to change, to blink, to speak.

They're burning your house down, they whispered to him, and in his half-sleeping delirium he believed them. He lay there, terrified of the men outside who were preparing to burn down Mamaw Genie's home. He found he couldn't move, beads of sweat rolling down his forehead, into his eyes, the salt stinging so much and yet he was so scared he couldn't blink. The orange glow grew brighter through his closed curtains, and the men laughed with horrible, raw voices like starved, rabid dogs.

His memories shifted, scratched reels of a mental film he couldn't stop. He'd climbed out of bed at some point, broken free of the paralyzing fear holding him there, and he'd padded down the hallway in his bare feet. Mamaw Genie wasn't in her room. A nest of blankets lay in a crumpled heap on her bed, and the curtains were pulled back from the window.

Downstairs, then. He found the front door standing wide open, his grandmother waiting on the porch in her nightgown, bathed in a shifting orange light. A cool breeze made the white cotton fabric billow behind her like a cape, and in his half-dreaming state, Jack remembered thinking she looked like a superhero from his comic books.

The gunshot startled him. Mamaw Genie pointed her revolver to the sky and fired a second round. Jackie tip-toed toward the doorway, toward the light burning from the front yard. Because something *was* burning, he remembered. The smell of smoke was palpable, carried into the house by the breeze, and the musty plume blowing toward him made his eyes burn. He squinted, blinking away tears.

There were ghosts in the front yard. Loud, raucous ghosts in white sheets, their heads covered in pale masks with holes for eyes. And the grass was on fire, two roiling lines bisecting each other, rising into the night, tasting the air like serpent tongues.

"Get off my property," Imogene said. She lowered her weapon and trained it on the nearest ghost. "You ain't welcome here."

"Neither's you, witch. We don't take kindly to your pagan ways."

"I won't ask again," she growled. Jack remembered her tone. They were all in trouble, oh yes, and they'd be lucky if they didn't get a switch across their backsides.

And then something happened he couldn't explain. The memory, once buried in the recesses of his mind, was hazy enough to be confused for a half-forgotten dream. Mamaw Genie raised her free hand to the sky, commanding a force none of them could see, and the flames licking the night slithered toward the ghosts in a twisting coil. One of the ghost's white robes caught fire, and two of his friends rushed to his aid to pull him back from the inferno, stamping out the flickering orange climbing up his body.

Jack remembered the man screaming in panic. He remembered all of them screaming, urging each other to retreat.

"This ain't over, witch!"

And for a while, it wasn't. Jack held the sponge in his hand, gripping so tightly all the water seeped out. Suds bubbled and popped along the siding. He blinked, wiped the sweat from his brow, and looked at the remaining letters bleeding red trails down the white panel.

Old witch burns in hell.

He stared at the words, then turned his gaze back to the front door. The key was heavy in his pocket, a cosmic weight imbued with its own sort of gravity, and it was pulling at him.

"One step at a time, Mamaw."

When he was finished, Jack tossed the sponge into the bucket of murky water and dried his hands on his pant leg. He pulled out his phone and dialed Chuck's number. Three rings later, his old friend answered.

"Chuck, it's Jack. You want to go get a drink?"

CHAPTER SEVEN

1

The red "ON AIR" light went out, and Stephanie "Stevie" Green pushed the microphone away from her face. Her producer's voice filled the studio.

"Steph, you can't say shit like that on the air."

She threaded her curly hair free of the headphones and tied it back behind her head. When she was finished, Stephanie leaned toward the microphone and shot a side-eye glance toward Ryan on the other side of the window.

"It's my station," she said, "and I'll say whatever the fuck I want."

"Within reason, Steph. The FCC's one thing, but pissing off your listeners is a whole other ballgame, and—"

Stephanie pulled off the headphones. When she looked up, Ryan Corliss was still talking. She waved at him, pantomimed "I can't hear you" while pointing to her head, and laughed when he gave her the finger. Their argument wasn't a new one. Ever since the station opened a year ago, she'd met resistance every step of the way. She could accept complaints from the locals, but she wasn't going to take shit from her producer as well. Not when it came to matters of content.

She collected her purse, drained the coffee from her mug, and exited the studio. Ryan met her in the hallway.

"I'm serious, Steph. Some of these people want your head on a spike. They say you're preaching Satan's gospel. When you tell them to drink one for the Goat Lord tonight, you're reinforcing their mode of thinking."

She shook her head and brushed past him into the mixing room, pausing long enough to give the broadcast schedule a once-over. A block of old Metallica, a block of Swedish death metal, grunge, The Yellow Kings memoriam block, the 80s hair metal power hour leading up to a block of pre-recorded listener requests… Something was missing. Stephanie plucked a dry-erase marker from the tray and scribbled "More Industrial" across the top of the board. She turned back to Ryan and pointed to the board. "Tell Cindy to swap out the grunge every other day. We need to be playing Ministry and Nine Inch Nails as much as Nirvana and Alice in Chains."

Ryan shook his head. "Ministry? In southeastern Kentucky? Are you fucking serious?"

"As a heart attack, darlin'." She playfully patted his cheek. "We don't follow the rules, remember? We play what we want, and what we want is all forms of metal."

"Yeah? Tell that to this guy." Ryan handed her a folded sheet of paper. "More fan mail?"

"Uh huh. This time it's a doozy."

Stephanie took a seat on the leather sofa and unfolded the letter. The words weren't printed so much as scribbled, but the message was loud and clear:

ATTN SATAN WORSHIPING WHORE
CLOSE UR STATION
YOU ARNT WELCOME
GET OUT OR ELSE!!!

She crumpled the paper and tossed it across the room. The paper ball bounced off the edge of a trash can and fell into a pile of other complaints.

"So close," she said. "One of these days I'll get two points."

Ryan rolled his chair toward her and sat. He frowned at her with sad puppy eyes, a trait she adored about him. The look reminded her of the way her second boyfriend used to playfully pout when he wanted a kiss. Staring at Ryan, who was happily committed to a wonderful man named Victor, Stephanie reminded herself to keep her instincts at bay.

"I'm serious," Ryan said softly. "You're getting threats, for God's sake."

"Which is how I know we're on to something, Ryan. Did Elvis stop shaking his hips because of pissed-off parents?"

Ryan pursed his lips. "I wish you'd take this more seriously."

"I'm sorry." She put both hands on his cheeks and kissed his forehead. "I appreciate your concern, I really do, but I know what I'm doing. You forget I grew up here. I remember what it's like growing up in this shithole, not having an outlet of rock. Did you see the latest numbers on our audience? Those numbers don't lie."

He sat back in his seat and crossed his arms in a huff. *Gotcha*, she thought. Ryan couldn't argue with the numbers. They *were* reaching their intended audience. The work was grueling, and she'd spent more hours in the studio since opening a year ago than she had in her apartment, but the demand was there. After years of toiling in obscurity at the region's larger country stations, she'd had her fill of pop country music and would rather endure waterboarding than listen to it again.

So, she did what every other American entrepreneur did: saved her pennies, did her homework, wrote a business plan, and got a loan. A few months later, she broke ground on a small plot of land on the north side of Gordon Hill, and Z105.1 was born.

The numbers didn't lie, either. Stauford needed something other than country and gospel in its diet. They needed something with an edge, something to tap into the angst simmering among the town's youth, and Stephanie had the answer. She remembered all too well what it was like growing up in the asshole of the south, searching for something you could relate to, and only finding the art of your parents, just out of reach and years out of touch.

Stauford's youth heard their message: it's okay to be different. The town's older generations didn't agree, and they didn't appreciate the way the station went about getting attention. Stephanie glanced at the growing mountain of wadded complaint letters next to the wastebasket. Doubt dripped slowly into the cracks of her stony resolve, seeping into the dark places, inching deeper toward her heart. Maybe Ryan was right? Maybe she should take things seriously?

Her grandma Maggie spoke up in her head. *Remember what happened to Genie? Remember all the crosses they burned in her yard? She couldn't go shopping in town anymore, had to go all the way to Landon to do it so she wouldn't get dirty looks.*

A slow chill crept along Stephanie's shoulders. Poor Genie, gone two weeks already. Stephanie hoped Genie finally found peace, wherever she was. Her thoughts turned to Genie's grandson, Jack. They'd lost touch after college when he'd moved away to New England. She still followed him online, though. A print of his most famous work, *Midnight Baptism*, hung over the toilet in her bathroom. Ryan once asked her why she put it there, and she told him it was a good conversation piece.

The painting featured a faceless man baptizing a group of blindfolded children in a lake of blood while a congregation of masturbating parishioners watched from the shore. A jaundiced moon hung overhead with craters like unblinking eyes. Most guests at her apartment were repulsed by it, some found it fascinating, and all wanted to know why the hell she had it hanging in her home.

Because my brother painted it, she'd tell them. Only that's as far as she'd take the conversation. Any further would require more alcohol than she could handle at any given moment, and besides, these days she'd rather not relive the past.

"Steph?"

"Huh?"

Ryan shook his head, smiling. "You didn't hear a word I said, did you?"

"No," she said. "I was a million miles away."

"Uh huh," he said. "I said I'd finish up here if you want to head out."

"Are you sure?"

"Yeah," Ryan said. "You've worked ten days straight without a break. We've got enough pre-recorded to last us a month if necessary. Take a night off."

Smiling, Stephanie peeled herself off the leather sofa and grabbed her purse. Her phone buzzed from within, and when she checked the lock screen, she saw a text message from her old friend Chuck.

"Speak of the devil," she muttered.

Ryan looked away from the mixing board. "What's that? Still here?"

"No," she said absently. "I'm going."

Five minutes later, she was gone.

2

The rusted yellow pickup squealed tires and kicked up rocks as Waylon turned onto Devil's Creek Road. He snuck a glance at his partner after they passed the road sign. Zeke was fast asleep, a slim string of drool hanging limply from his lower lip.

Good, Waylon thought. *Last thing I need is you shitting your pants when you see where we're goin'.*

Like everyone else in Stauford, he'd heard the stories about his friend. Who hadn't? Anyone who'd grown up in the town heard all about the mysterious goings-on out at Devil's Creek, heard about the Stauford Six who'd been rescued from the death cult living out there. He grew up hearing those kids came back marked somehow. Bad luck, some folks said. Cursed, his grandpappy said.

Waylon didn't give two shits. All he cared about was delivering what he'd promised to Chief Bell, and Devil's Creek was the place to do it. He'd driven out here once when he was a teen, on a dare from his older brother, Wayne. The place was isolated, quiet, a void of civilization where something bad happened back in the 80s. Shit, didn't everything bad happen in the 80s?

The area was a ghost story the parents of Stauford told their children, forbidding them from venturing into the woods. Waylon knew about as much as anyone else: the old church, black magic, mutilated dog parts hanging from the trees. That last part he'd heard was how the neighboring Dog Slaughter Creek got its name, but he wasn't sure how true it was. Regardless of how much was truth or rumor, Waylon counted on the legend to give them the privacy they needed to get their work done.

He'd once tried getting Zeke drunk enough to talk about it, but his friend clammed up when he mentioned the place. Zeke cried himself into a stupor and wouldn't talk to Waylon for a week. When he finally came to his senses, all Zeke would tell him was he never wanted to go back there. "It's like a nightmare I can't wake up from," Zeke said. "A big goddamn cloud hangin' over my head for my whole shitty life."

Sorry, bro. You'll thank me when Ozzie puts a wad of twenties in your hand.

The road snaked its way into the forest. The twelve propane tanks in the back of the truck clanked against one another when he took a turn too sharply, and Zeke stirred. Waylon looked over, willing his friend back to sleep. Zeke's eyes cracked open for an instant before closing once more.

Waylon felt a pang of regret, a slight hint of guilt for steering Zeke toward a place that terrified him, but such trivial emotions were washed away when he rounded the curve and spotted the gravel turn-off. A few more miles into the forest, and they'd come upon an overgrown trailhead. Another mile beyond, they'd find a small village of abandoned shacks left behind by the cult, suffocated with weeds and left to rot with the passage of time.

Overhead, the sun slipped behind a thick bank of clouds, draping them in shadow. A chill crept along Waylon's arms and up the back of his neck.

Zeke awoke as the pickup skidded to a stop, kicking up gravel in the wheel wells and conjuring a cloud of dust. Waylon put the truck in park, shut off the engine, and turned to his friend.

"Ready to work, sleeping beauty?"

"Yeah," Zeke said, wiping sleep from his eyes. "Where are we?"

"That place I told you about. Come on, let's get movin'. I want to get set up before we lose the daylight."

Waylon climbed out of the truck before Zeke could protest, pulled off the tarp, and went to work taking inventory. Twelve propane tanks, a roll of rubber tubing, a milk crate full of starter fluid and nasal decongestants, bottles of ammonia, cans of acetone, boxes of matches, empty pots and pans, rubber gloves, coffee filters, five gallons of distilled water, a chemistry textbook Zeke stole from the library, and a small camping stove filled the truck bed.

He looked over everything, ticking off a mental check list. The last thing he wanted was to get started and realize halfway through the cook they needed more starter fluid or filters.

Zeke got out of the truck and surveyed the goods.

"Did you remember masks?"

"What do you mean?" Waylon grunted, heaving one of the propane tanks out of the back. "Masks for what?"

Zeke shook his head. "For our lungs, dipshit. Didn't you read any of the shit I gave you this morning? Don't you have any idea what sort of fumes we're gonna be breathing in?"

"It'll be fine," Waylon said. "Are you going to fuckin' help me or not?"

Waylon led the way with one of the propane tanks in tow while Zeke followed behind, carrying the crate of chemicals and medicine. They'd need at least four trips to the truck, maybe a fifth or sixth, and Waylon tried to move as fast as he could without tripping over his own feet. Time was money out here in the woods, and they were already behind schedule.

The sun disappeared overhead as they traveled beneath the forest canopy, offering only glimpses of its brilliance in narrow sheets filtering through the leaves. Gnats swarmed around their heads, humming in their ears a warning neither man would understand. Zeke hesitated when they reached the small wooden footbridge stretching over the babbling creek. A bullfrog barked and leapt into the water when they approached, stirring up a cloud of silt from the creek bed.

Zeke cleared his throat. "Wait a minute, Waylon. This ain't right."

Waylon was already on the other side of the bridge. He shifted his weight, hefting the bulk of the propane tank from one arm to the other. Sweat dripped off his forehead and down the curve of his nose. *Aw fuck*, he thought. *Here we go.*

"What's up?"

Zeke stared at the creek, squinting as sweat rolled into his eyes. "Do you know where we are?"

The question took Waylon by surprise, if only because he'd expected something far less innocent to fly out of Zeke's mouth. He'd expected a fight, to beg and plead Zeke to stay and help him cook, but this was something else altogether. Here, then, was a moral dilemma: tell his friend the truth or play dumb?

Waylon weighed his options and decided to err on the side of ignorance. He'd made it this far in life by letting people think him dumb. No sense in stopping now. "Nuh uh. I found this spot yesterday. It's quiet and no one'll bother us out here. Why?"

Zeke stared at him for a moment, reading his face, looking for a con. And there *was* a con, but Waylon wasn't about to let him see it. Instead, Waylon screwed up his face and grunted, shifting the weight of the propane tank once again. "Come on," he said, "let's keep moving. This fucker's heavy."

Finally, Zeke took a breath and closed his eyes. A soft breeze picked up around them, easing the burden of heat pressing upon their faces.

"It's…yeah, it's nothing. Never mind." Zeke took a step toward the footbridge, and then another. "Let's keep going."

Waylon Parks watched his friend move on by, following the faint outline of an overgrown trail sloping upward into the brush. Birds chirped overhead, calling out another warning both men couldn't understand.

3

Suspended. My son, suspended. For hitting another kid.

Reverend Bobby Tate took a breath as he waited in the hallway outside his son's room. He stood before a small decorative hutch, above which hung photos of his late wife and Riley when he was younger. Between the photos hung a cross, representing a trinity of everything Bobby Tate held dear in this world. *Please, Lord, grant me patience and understanding. Please give me the strength to resist killing my son. Amen.*

He didn't mean that last part but including it in his prayer did make him feel better. Riley had tested his patience before, seemingly every day since the boy turned thirteen, slipping into the devilish throes of adolescence. Bobby suspected his son's rebellion was the lord's way of making him pay penance for his own misdeeds as a teenager. God knew Bobby had his share of arguments with his grandfather, Jerry, many of which ended with Bobby's backside meeting the business end of a paddle.

Those punishments helped shape him into the man he was today. A respected figure among the community, a devout Christian, a leader of a congregation of good-hearted souls who did what they could for the church, and for each other. Years from now, when people looked back on Bobby Tate's tenure as reverend of First Baptist, they'd say good things about him.

They'd say Jerry Tate did a great job raising his grandson. They'd say Bobby Tate was a good man, with a good heart, a man who did the best he could raising his son after his wife, Janet, passed away from cancer.

They'd say he had a smart-ass weirdo for a son.

They *did* say he had a smart-ass weirdo for a son. At least, that's what Ronny Cord told him over the phone five minutes after he got the call from the school. Cord said some other things, too, but Bobby tuned him out. He was in the middle of planning his Sunday sermon when the calls happened; afterward, he had to think about hiring an attorney. All because of Riley. Always because of Riley.

How could he possibly approach this as a parent? They barely spoke to one another as it was, and when they did, it was usually in one- or two-sentence affirmations and platitudes. And just when he thought he had his son figured out, the boy went and did something to surprise him, shaking up the status quo. First, it was the awful, evil music, and then the black clothing, the nail polish, the backtalk and isolation. He spent most of his free time on his phone or on his computer. His grades were still good, thank God, but Bobby questioned how much longer they would last.

Despite his new turn in identity, Riley remained involved with his Youth Group at First Baptist, something which Bobby was eternally grateful for. He didn't fully understand why, given his son's new penchant for rebelling against everything Bobby wanted for him, but who was he to question divine providence? The lord worked in mysterious ways.

Bobby wanted to believe there was a good reason for his son's actions this afternoon, but he was hard-pressed to find one. Regardless, some sort of punishment was in order. Grounding the boy was an option, but Bobby was torn on keeping his son from the camping trip the Youth Group planned for the weekend. He feared keeping his son from the one thing he still wanted to do would make him resent Bobby even more.

He sighed and stared at the cross hanging on the wall. *My lord, help me find a middle ground with my son. I fear I've lost my little boy. If only Janet were still with me—*

Riley uttered a loud belch as he left his room. Bobby pursed his lips in disgust, wanted to curse at the boy, but practiced restraint in front of his savior. Instead, Bobby turned from the cross, mumbled "Amen" under his breath, and took a step toward his son. Riley was dressed in those awful ripped jeans Bobby hated so much ("They make you look like you're too poor to afford decent clothes."), a black T-shirt by that band of Stauford boys who all burned to death out west ("God rest their souls, amen."), and nails freshly painted black.

They called them goths back in Bobby's day. God knew what they called them now, and despite his best efforts, his son became one seemingly overnight.

"Son?"

Riley turned to him, instantly put out by the sound of his father's voice. Bobby's blood pressure rose a few points, but he held back the tide of anger, reminding himself he was an acolyte of the lord. Janet's sweet voice chimed in his head. *You'll catch more flies with honey than vinegar, hon.*

He cleared his throat. "Listen, I know you don't want to talk to me right now, but I need to understand why you did what you did."

Riley stepped back, leaning against his room's doorframe. Bobby knew this maneuver. One wrong word and his son would shut the door, shut him out, shut out the whole world if necessary. *God, grant me patience and understanding...*

"Violence is never the answer," Bobby went on, "no matter how much it might seem like a solution at the time. I'm sure you think Jimmy Cord deserved it." He snorted, fighting back a chuckle. "Heck, knowing what I know of his daddy, I wouldn't doubt it one bit if Ronny's son did something to deserve it. But my point is, it ain't your place to pass judgment. It's the—"

Riley rolled his eyes. "It's the lord's place, yeah, I got that, Dad. Can I go now? Ben's supposed to be here soon. I don't want to be late."

"Wait a minute, Riley." He put his hand on his son's shoulder and gave him a firm squeeze. "You can't do what you did without facing consequences. That's not how the world works." Riley bristled at the suggestion. "Relax, I'm not going to keep you from the camping trip. But we are going to have to work out a suitable punishment."

"Fine," Riley said. "I can live with that."

"Good," Bobby said, smiling. "I want you to know you can talk to me, son. I know we don't see eye to eye on everything, and I know I don't always give you the answers you want, but I will still listen to you."

"Dad," Riley said, returning the gesture, putting his hand on his father's shoulder. The boy smirked, a look Bobby knew too well these last few years, and in hindsight, he should've seen what was coming. "I know. And I mean this when I tell you, the bastard deserved it."

Bobby slapped his son across the mouth, hard enough to bloody the boy's lip. The pop of flesh smacking flesh startled them both. Bobby recoiled, stunned by his reaction. Riley, however, wiped his mouth and examined the bead of crimson on his fingertip. He blinked away tears and curled back his lip like Janet used to do when she was angry.

"I thought violence was never the answer?"

Bobby Tate slunk back into the hallway, his limbs filled with jelly, his heart broken. He wanted to say he was sorry, to plead for his son's forgiveness, but a deeper fire raging within told him not to. *You deserved it, you disrespectful little shit.*

He ignored the fire, reaching out to console his son. "Riley, I didn't—look, I'm sorry, I shouldn't have done that."

But Riley wasn't listening. He shouldered his backpack, shut off the light to his bedroom, and retreated down the hall toward the stairs without saying a word. Bobby watched him go. When his son was out of sight, he gasped as tears trickled down his cheeks.

He looked up at the cross on the wall, to his savior for comfort, but Jesus had more pressing matters of His own.

4

Riley unslung the backpack from his shoulder and dropped it on the porch steps. He nursed the wound on his lip, hoping like hell it didn't swell or bruise. The last thing he needed was to be made fun of all weekend by the other kids, especially since Rachel Matthews was going to be there. Then again, that old saying about chicks digging scars had to have some truth. He took a seat on the porch steps and busied himself with checking messages on his phone.

Ben texted ten minutes ago—"On our way!"—while Riley was busy avoiding his father and packing for the trip. Their confrontation was inevitable, although it hadn't gone quite like Riley expected it to. Riley didn't think his father would ever strike him, but with his lip throbbing, he wasn't surprised, either.

All that preaching on Sundays was hot air. His father's actions proved what Riley always knew in his heart.

Still, the pain he felt ran deeper than his swollen lip. It hurt his pride, his heart, and when he looked up from his phone, he discovered the world was glassy, clouded. He blinked away tears, wiped them on his sleeve, and snorted back a quiet agony growing inside him. Janet Tate would be gone three years this October, and every day she was absent, Riley felt a little more alone in the world, a little more like a stranger in his own home.

"Dammit," he mumbled, wiping his eyes again. No matter how hard he tried to keep them back, the tears kept coming, flooding over his cheeks.

Miss you, Mom. Wish you were still here.

Janet was loved among the community, and her loss was felt by everyone, but perhaps none more so than her son. When his father was too busy with the church, Janet took the time to attend to Riley's needs in school, helping him with homework, talking to him about his reading assignments, and though she didn't understand his taste in music, she at least tried to.

His father, on the other hand, dismissed his son's choices as acts of rebellion, pushing him toward a life of devotion to the church. Any time his father tried to connect with him on some superficial level, it was with the pretense of teaching some biblical lesson. Bobby Tate counted his son as part of his flock, a fact which troubled Riley more than anything else.

"You care about that fuckin' church more than me," he whispered, picking at the excess nail polish along the ridge of his thumb. "Mom would've listened. All you do is talk."

A loud honk startled him from his thoughts. Riley looked up to see the baby blue church bus turn slowly into his driveway. Ben's older brother, Daniel, sat behind the wheel and gave the horn a series of taps as Riley climbed to his feet. The loud bursts lifted the cloud from his head, offering some much-needed levity to his mind. He even managed a smile as he walked toward the bus.

"Riley?"

The boy's blood went cold at the sound of his father's voice. He looked back at Bobby.

"Yeah?"

"Be careful, son. I…" Bobby trailed off, frowning as he considered his words. He waited a beat and then waved. "Have a good time. I love you."

Riley sighed, swallowing back a mouthful of sarcastic retorts. "Love you, too."

The words left a bitter taste of copper on his tongue. He shouldered his backpack and marched for the bus. Onboard, he surveyed the seating arrangement. Boys in the front, girls in the back. He caught Rachel's eye as he took a seat next to Ben. She smiled at him, and he felt a familiar flutter in his gut. *See you later*, he thought, secretly hoping she could hear him.

"What happened to your lip?"

"Nothing," Riley said. The word tasted of copper as well.

5

Twenty minutes later, as the First Baptist church bus made its way to the south end of town toward the Cumberland Falls Highway, Jack Tremly parked his Mazda across the street from a place called Devlin's On Main.

He didn't see Chuck's car, so he waited a few minutes, checking messages on his phone. His agent asked, "Everything going okay?"

Jack typed a brief reply—"Kidnapped by locals. Forced into sideshow act. Send help"—and sent the message with a smile on his face.

A long shadow fell over his car as the sun dipped toward the horizon. Minutes later, the restaurant sign lit up in bright red neon, promising fine dining and spirits. Jack looked up, stunned by the sudden reddish glow. He tried to remember what Main Street looked like after hours. Dead, for the most part. Most businesses closed at a decent hour back in those days. Now, however, many of the storefronts along Stauford's main thoroughfare kept their lights on and their doors open.

Two couples and a group of young women went inside Devlin's On Main. A young man in a black apron passed them on his way out; a moment later, he stood beneath the corner streetlight and lit a cigarette.

Jack watched the busboy for a few minutes, taking interest in the contrast of red glow and phosphorous light, the way the cigarette smoke looked like a lazy tendril reaching down from the sky. He wished he'd brought his sketchbook, so he took a photo with his phone for later reference.

Chuck Tiptree parked his BMW in an open space behind Jack's Mazda. A minute later, they made their way into the restaurant. While they waited to be seated, Jack took in the décor. The place was fancier than it had any right to be, especially in a tiny town like Stauford, with recessed lights offering dim halos around a series of tables adorned with candles and red tablecloths. A live band played a slow folk cover of Roy Orbison's "In Dreams" at the far end of the room, and Jack was surprised to see a few couples were even slow dancing in front of the small stage. The bar sat in the center of the room, every stool occupied with patrons nursing drinks, sulking over their phones, commiserating over another dime earned, another week gone.

What caught Jack's eye, however, was the framed image hanging over one section of the bar, between the drink menu and a series of framed photographs of various celebrities. The framed print featured a pale woman looking back over her shoulder, with half her face obscured by locks of reddish-brown hair. A black robe draped over one side of her body, dipping low enough to reveal the tentacle tattoo on the curve of her thigh. A bright red apple sat in her hand, held up in offering to a falling star while the world burned to cinders around her.

Jack knew the image well, having labored for weeks over capturing the model's proportions. The model's name was Audra Gray, and he'd slept with her after each painting session, enough times he thought they meant something to each other. He had entire sketchbooks of her sleeping figure, captured in the early hours when his nightmares sent him screaming from slumber. She'd left him for the west coast and its promise of fame, citing his lack of success as a reason for ending their relationship.

Morning Star was his first professional sale. Six months after the sale, he'd had his first gallery showing, he'd signed with Carly, and he was in talks to produce concept art for an upcoming horror film. The last he'd heard, Audra was waiting tables at a club called The Hyades on the Sunset Strip, but that was a couple of years ago, long before the place burned to the ground. Seeing the painting and her lithe figure once again, he felt a somber tinge of nostalgia, the ghost of heartache rattling its chains. He hoped she was okay.

Chuck leaned close and said, "Table or bar?"

"Table," Jack said instantly. He hadn't eaten since lunch, and the smell of food from the grill made his stomach grumble.

After they were seated, Jack turned to Chuck and pointed out the painting. "Looks like I've got at least one fan here in town."

Chuck turned around, looking back at the bar. "Yes, indeed. One of the owners is a fan of yours. She'll be joining us soon."

"She?" Jack arched his brow. "Anyone I know?"

"Easy there, tiger. It ain't like that. And yeah, in a matter of speaking, you do know her."

"That so?"

"Yeah."

Jack smiled. "Fair enough. I'll wait in suspense in the meantime. What about the other owner?"

Chuck beamed. "You're lookin' at him."

A young bubbly waitress approached their table. "Hi, Mr. Tiptree. Will you be having the usual today?"

"Sure will, Darla."

After they ordered drinks, Jack shifted back in his seat and laughed. "Never took you for an entrepreneur."

Chuck shrugged. "One does what one can. Food and drink are on the house, by the way."

"Much obliged," Jack said. "How long have you owned this place?"

"Few years now. Bought it when Big Ron Taswell retired and sold the place."

Although the restaurant seemed to be a welcome addition to the town, Jack felt a tinge of sadness knowing Ron's Department Store was no longer in business. Mamaw Genie used to take him there to buy school clothes every August and January. He remembered Big Ron always had a handful of pretzels, and when he spoke, crumbs flew from his mouth in all directions. Nostalgia aside, Jack wasn't sure what surprised him more: that "Big" Ron Taswell didn't pass on the family business to his sons, or that Chuck Tiptree owned a restaurant.

"About a year after I bought it, I took on a partner to help manage the renovations. We opened a year and a half ago and have been going strong ever since. Especially since the community voted to allow the sale of liquor."

After Darla brought their drinks—a dirty martini for Chuck, a beer for Jack—Chuck slid a piece of paper across the table. "Here's the number for the contractor I told you about earlier. Tell 'em I sent you. Should give you a good rate on the windows."

Jack took the note and put it in his pocket. "Thanks, man. I managed to get the paint off the siding and covered the windows in plastic, but not much else."

"Yeah, I wondered about that." Chuck took a sip of his martini. "To be honest, I was kind of surprised when you called. You seemed upset. Everything okay?"

Jack ran the tip of his thumb along the mouth of the bottle, thinking back to the memories of his grandmother and the men in sheets on their property. Were they memories? Or were they half-remembered dreams distorted by the passage of time, twisted into a shadow resembling reality? He couldn't say. So many years had passed between that night and the present, years in which he'd forgotten the scene altogether, he found the demarcation between dream and waking life faded from view.

He *wanted* to believe it was the dream of a child with an overactive imagination, but deep down he suspected that wasn't the case. The details were too vivid, the memory a little too real.

"Jack?" Chuck drummed his fingers on the table. "You with me, bud?"

"Yeah," he said, emerging from his thoughts. "Sorry. I was elsewhere."

"I noticed. I'll ask again: Is everything okay?"

Jack took another gulp of his beer. "Yeah, I'm fine. It's been a long day. You know how it is. Long drive, emotionally draining probate experience, the usual."

"I'll drink to that," Chuck said, raising his glass. They toasted each other and shared a laugh, but the levity did little to extinguish a burning dread in Jack's gut. A dread he would have to return to his grandmother's house sooner or later and sift through her belongings. The mere thought of it made him feel like a ghoul, digging up graves to pillage the dead.

"Hang on," Chuck said, climbing to his feet. "Hey, Steph. Over here."

Jack looked up from his drink as a familiar, curly-haired brunette sauntered over to their table. She had tattoos down both arms, piercings in her eyebrows and nose, and wore a plum shade of lipstick. He recognized her from the billboard he'd spotted on his way into town. They locked eyes and stared at one another for a moment before realization struck. He *knew* that smirk.

"Holy shit," he muttered. "Stephanie? Is that really you?"

"Hey, stranger. Give me a hug."

Together, the three siblings reminisced over food and drinks, recounting the last twenty years. Chuck regaled them with tales of his law school bacchanalia, passing the state bar exam on his second try because he was too hungover for the first. He'd had plenty of girlfriends but no wives, a statistic he seemed proud of.

Stephanie recounted her years since college, studying broadcast journalism, pursuing a dream of opening her own station. Both, it seemed, were doing well for themselves, a fact which Jack pointed out. She downed her second whiskey sour and shrugged. "It's all relative, Jackie. Advertisers love us now, but that could turn on a dime, you know? If the Jesus Brigade has their way, The Goat is done for."

"What do you mean?" Jack asked.

"They've been getting threats," Chuck cut in.

Stephanie clenched her jaw and raised a finger to the air. "We're preachin' the devil's gospel, corruptin' all the innocent chil'ren with the music of Lucifer!"

Chuck laughed. "What was they called it in the Tribune? 'Satan's Pornography' or something?"

"The ladies of First Baptist bought a full-page ad in the paper, trying to drum up support for a vote to shut us down. Didn't work, though. The kids love us!"

Jack smiled, thinking of Ruth's rant earlier that morning. He thought of telling Stephanie about Ruth's comments, but decided against it. Instead, he changed the subject.

"What about Bobby? Or Zeke?"

"Bobby's doing well, for the most part." Chuck offered. "He's the reverend of First Baptist these days. Got his hands full with Riley, though. Ever since Janet died."

Jack blinked, the air sucked out of him like he'd been punched. "Janet passed away?"

"Cancer," Stephanie sighed. "Poor guy took it in stride, but he's been a shell without her. I help out with Riley here and there, but Bobby won't talk to me much because he thinks I'm a bad influence. And Chuck keeps in touch, too."

"I try to," Chuck said, "but sometimes he's hard to reach. The guy buries himself in the church. You know how that goes."

They all nodded solemnly, giving the table some air while they collected their thoughts. Jack thought of Bobby's late wife, Janet, and tipped back his beer in her honor. He'd never met her, but he'd heard about her, and heard about the happiness she'd brought Bobby. Knowing she was gone was still a blow.

His thoughts returned to Zeke, and he asked again. Stephanie and Chuck exchanged glances, as if to say, *"Do you want to take this, or should I?"*

Finally, Stephanie spoke up, lifting a cherry stem from her empty glass. "Zeke's in a bad way. Drugs. Meth, I think. Ever since he fell in with Waylon Parks—"

"Waylon Parks?" Jack scoffed. "Jesus, that guy's still alive?"

"Uh huh," Chuck said. "Hard to believe, ain't it? That guy was snorting coke when he was in elementary school. And Zeke, well, you know he was never the brightest bulb in the pack..."

Jack nodded. "Yeah, the guy was always in summer school to keep from getting held back. Didn't he live with Susan for a while?"

"He did, Jack." Susan Prewitt approached their table, emerging from a crowd of restaurant patrons. She was dressed for a night on the town, in a slender black dress and knee-high leather boots. Jack looked up at her, stunned by her sudden appearance. Chuck lifted his glass.

"Evenin', Susan."

"I didn't know this was going to be a party," Susan said, smiling. Her cool stare fell over each of them, testing their resolve, waiting to see who would wither first. "I guess I missed the invitation."

"It's not like that," Jack said, sliding over in his seat. "Join us."

"Oh, that's okay, Jackie. I'm here with someone, anyway."

Before he could ask, a tall fellow in a dark blue police officer's uniform sidled up to her and slipped his hand around her waist. The badge on his chest caught the light from above, illuminating the word "BELL" in capital letters. Jack stared at the badge for a moment, allowing the word to sink in before his eyes climbed up the tree trunk of a man he'd once thought inhuman.

Age hadn't changed Ozzie Bell much, except he now had a sizeable gut protruding over the rim of his belt. The cocky sneer seemingly cemented on his face by a rigid jawline, the pointed nose, and the icy eyes hadn't changed at all, were still as terrifying as the last time Jack saw him. That someone saw fit to elect this man as head of the Stauford police department was equally terrifying to him, and Jack imagined Ozzie would look just as at home in a black uniform adorned with an iron eagle crest and a swastika. *Sieg Heil, Herr Bell.*

The uniform only gave authority to a jackass who'd bullied and maimed more of Jack's classmates than he could count. Staring up from his seat, Jack suddenly felt fifteen and helpless again, and he wished he could slink away without being seen.

"Evening," Ozzie said, nodding to Chuck and Stephanie. He paused when his eyes fell upon Jack. "Well I'll be damned. Jack Tremly. I ain't seen you since high school. You still an art fag?"

Silence fell over their table, the air sucked out of them with Ozzie's insult. Jack exhaled slowly through his nose and nodded, smiling. He heard his agent pipe up in his head. *Don't, Jack. Let it go.*

Only he couldn't. Twenty years gone, and this guy was still trying to assert dominance over him like the old days? No. Not anymore.

"Yeah, Oz," he said. "I'm still an art fag. I see you're still a mouth breather. Glad that worked out for you. Fascism suits you, by the way."

Ozzie's face flushed, his cheeks filling with red splotches like bruises. He smiled, opening his mouth to retort, but Susan put her hand on his shoulder. "Come on," she said. "Let's leave them to their reunion. I had too much to drink, anyway. Drive me home, would ya?" She stood on her toes and kissed the tip of his chin, and his cheeks lightened in hue.

Chuck raised his glass again. "See you later, Chief."

Jack turned to watch them leave, biting his lip to keep from saying anything else. Stephanie leaned forward and grinned sheepishly.

"You're still a troublemaker, Jack Tremly. I love it. Welcome home."

6

Zeke regretted not stopping his friend at the footbridge. He doubted Waylon's ignorance, of course, but Zeke was a grown man, and the monster haunting his dreams was long dead. The last thing he wanted was to look like a pussy in front of his friend. Besides, what harm would there be in them camping at the old compound? So what if they spent a couple days in the woods near the site of a grisly mass suicide? All the shit that happened when he was a kid was probably a spate of nightmares anyway. There might've been some truth at the heart of them, but a child's imagination is a wild and feral thing, capable of dragging an innocent truth off into the dark to be devoured.

These lies failed to abate the constant chill crawling over his skin as they hiked into the abandoned village. Even while they were setting up the cook site in one of the shacks, even while sweat rolled down his neck, his back, into the crack of his ass, the chill ran deep into his marrow. Twice he stopped because of an uncontrollable shiver. If it were any other day, in any other place, he would've thought himself ill.

You're terrified, boy. Just like when you used to wake up in the night, soaked through to the bone with sweat, screaming the pastor was comin' to get you, to feed you to his god. His god was hungry, always seeking you out in the dark, crawling toward you, trying to taste you with its many tongues, trying to tear into you with its many teeth…

Zeke shook off the voice of his grandfather, gathered his wits, and focused on the work at hand. He and Waylon followed the instructions he'd found online, working by way of flashlight when they lost the sun, and even with his mind elsewhere, the persistent shivers wouldn't cease.

Once everything was set up, Waylon suggested they take a break before switching on the burner.

"Give me the flashlight," he said, "I need to go take a leak."

Zeke hesitated before handing over the light. A cold spike bisected his gut, filling him with the sort of dread that made his bowels clench, his testicles shrivel.

"Don't go far," he said, and instantly felt foolish. Waylon raised the light to his face and stuck out his tongue.

"Thanks, Dad. I'll try to watch out for the boogeyman."

Zeke gave a lighthearted chuckle, but the dread grew colder when Waylon left the shack, leaving him to sit alone in the dark on an old folding chair. A minute later, he heard Waylon cursing about flies as he wandered deeper into the village.

And then he was alone except for the drone of nocturnal insects in the distance, the hushed sigh of leaves rustling in a low breeze. He waited for his eyes to adjust to the darkness, following the outline of the crude, rotting door hanging limp from one wall of the shack. The floor was dirt and leaves, and when the breeze blew harder, he smelled the musty odor of an animal's droppings somewhere nearby. An old mattress sat in the far corner of the shack, covered in dark stains and reeking of mildew.

Zeke wondered how the hell anyone could've lived out here in the woods, without running water or electricity. Sure, people had done it for thousands of years, but only because they didn't have a choice. The moment man had light on command and fresh water to wash his ass whenever he wanted was a true turning point in civilization, yes sir.

"And yet we lived out here for years. Momma, you were out of your goddamn mind."

What little Zeke remembered of his mother was encompassed in shadowy vignettes, burned to a crisp at the edges, the pictures faded with time. She beat him so much he thought she hated him, despite being told the contrary. "You're special," she always told him. "You're one of the lord's chosen."

He didn't feel chosen for anything. His life was a gag reel of colossal fuck-ups, one quiet tragedy after another. The other kids who'd survived, the rest of the Stauford Six, they'd all moved on to make something of themselves. But not Zeke. Instead of being out on the town with a girl, or sitting at home with a family, here he was, squatting in a rundown shack in the middle of nowhere, waiting to cook a batch of impure methamphetamine. If he was supposed to do important things, he'd missed the bus by a few hours at least.

One of the lord's chosen, he thought. *Fuck off.*

How ignorant could all those people have been? He barely remembered their faces, but he did remember their utter devotion, their happiness and bliss whenever his father spoke before the crowd. He wondered how so many could give up so much based on the word of a mortal man.

Ah, but Ezekiel, he wasn't just any man. He was your daddy. He was your savior. He was the word, the voice, the hand of our lord. He was. He is. There'll come a reckoning one day soon, oh yes, because your daddy ain't done with his business. He's diggin' his way up from hell right now, and like the savior of the heretics, he's comin' home to set his people free.

His mind wandered into the dark, and his imagination had its way with him again. Being alone in this ghost town unsettled him, put him on edge like he'd never felt before. He felt like a trespasser in a graveyard. The folks who'd pulled up stakes, sold all their belongings, and given it to his father's church for the sake of building a utopia in the forest all died here. Their spirits would roam here for the rest of eternity, walking hand in hand, replaying the final moments of their lives.

"Stop it," he said, ignoring the chattering of his teeth. "You're scaring yourself."

Maybe it was the dark. Maybe it was the empty village of the dead. Maybe it was the fact his friend hadn't come back.

Oh shit.

Zeke stood and crept to the edge of the doorway. He peered out. Moonlight filtered through the trees, illuminating a path through the remains of the holy compound.

"Waylon?" The forest rustled and breathed around him. He cleared his throat and spoke louder. "Waylon, stop fuckin' around, man."

The forest said nothing, and neither did his friend. Another chill swept over him, racking his body with shivers for a full minute until he got a grip on himself.

This is stupid, he thought. *You're freaking yourself out for nothing. That dipshit is out there laughing his ass off at you. He knew all along what this place meant to you, and he brought you here just to fuck with you.*

"And it's working," he mumbled. The forest absorbed his voice, masking it with the primitive sounds of nature, of crickets and rodents in the brush and brambles, of rustling leaves in a wind far too cold for this time of year. He called out to Waylon again and waited, listening to his heart thud heavily in his chest.

One-one-thousand.

Two-one-thousand.

Three-one-thousand.

Four-one—

A guttural scream tore through the night, shredding any hope of this being a joke. Heart racing, his legs like jelly, Zeke scrambled out of the shack and into the fractured moonlight. He called to Waylon once more, but his friend was silent. The forest swallowed his cries as easily as it swallowed his mind, projecting phantoms through the undergrowth, shadow puppets in the dim glow of the moon. Everything moved around him, driven by the wind, and the constant hiss of rustling leaves filled his head with serpents.

Confused, his heart in the grip of an icy terror he'd not felt since he was a child, Zeke Billings pumped his legs and forced himself forward into the dark. He followed the dim outline of a trail through the center of the village, past a dozen overgrown structures, their slipshod windows filled with the faces of the dead. He saw them from the corner of his eye as he ran, and he told himself they weren't there, they were tricks of moonlight, broken by the limbs and leaves and reassembled by his feral imagination.

His drive to find Waylon was fueled by a desire to leave this place, to leave its silent memory of servitude and damnation behind forever, cast back into the darkened halls of his nightmares.

So he ran. He ran until a phantom fist clenched at his ribs, tugging with each step he took. He ran until his heart pumped steam and his lungs burst with fire. Tears streamed down his face as he shot forward to the clearing ahead, each step more laborious than the last, and when his feet caught the rotted husk of a fallen log, he welcomed the sweet collapse. The hard, musty earth and soft grass of an open field met his face.

Zeke pushed himself from the ground and rose to his knees. He wiped his eyes, and when his vision finally cleared, his heart sank deep into his gut.

"No, no, no, not here, anywhere but here…"

Calvary Hill rose in the center of the clearing, the old stony pathway up its face overgrown with weeds. The church was long gone, of course, burned to cinders and ash decades before, but its ghost remained in the window of his imagination.

A full moon hung overhead, aligned perfectly over the hill like the unblinking eye of God. Susan's words filled his head, a memory from earlier when the world still made some semblance of sense to him. *It's a full moon tonight.*

Zeke stood on his knees, staring up at the silent monument of his childhood, watching incredulously as the earth breathed in the moonlit glow. He was so enraptured by the sight, he didn't register movement from the corner of his eye.

There were sucking sounds coming from behind him. Slurping, cracking, crunching sounds. A spike of fear wedged itself into his belly, filling him with a numbing cold leeching his last ounce of resolve. Slowly, Zeke turned his head toward the sounds, his heart shooting back into high gear when he saw the hulking shadow leaning over the dead log.

The shadow moved, allowing the moonlight to wash over the log, and Zeke froze in horror.

Waylon lay sprawled on the grass, one leg twisted back at an impossible angle, his glassy eyes locked on the indifferent sky above, and a grotesque sneer of agony frozen to his face. His shirt was ripped open, his chest nothing more than a cavity of exposed meat and gore. A light tendril of steam rose from the warmth of his entrails.

The shadow reached into the hole of Waylon's chest, snapped off one of his ribs, and began sucking on the marrow.

"Oh God," Zeke mumbled, the words barely more than a rasp, and the shadow heard him. It raised its head and turned toward him, revealing a face coated in mud and blood. Worms writhed through the thing's greasy hair, feeling their way along the curve of its forehead and around the dried "o" of an old gunshot wound. The shadow crunched down on Waylon's broken rib and cast its gaze upon him. Its eyes glowed, two sapphire orbs floating in the dark.

Zeke Billings met the living face of his nightmare and began to scream.

Jacob Masters flashed a grim smile. "My little lamb," he rasped.

CHAPTER EIGHT

1

A thin sheet of moonlight slipped through the open bedroom window, and Susan Prewitt stood in its brilliance, allowing the pale sheen to coat her naked body. Ozzie groaned in his sleep and tried to roll over, but his one hand was still cuffed to the bedpost, and he came to rest at an odd contorted angle, his head forward against his chest. A rolling snore erupted from his nose.

She looked over at him, frowning. How long, she wondered, would it take to choke the life from him? Or to simply suffocate him with a pillow? She played out the ensuing conversation in her mind: *Why, officer, he was fine when we went to sleep, although he did snore quite a bit. Why, no, he never did go for that sleep study, but I kept telling him to do it. They say sleep apnea is a silent killer, but…*

Another snore filled the room. The floor vibrated beneath her feet.

Maybe not so silent, she mused, feeling a sudden rush of warmth between her legs. She thought about rousing him from sleep and taking him for another ride, but the shots he'd downed at the bar already worked their magic. He'd spend half an hour trying to get an erection, and by then, she'd be asleep, the heat of her desire extinguished in cold, damp boredom. Ozzie Bell had that effect on her, and she idly wondered how such a big man who talked such a big game could be so goddamn dull.

With such a little cock, she thought, smirking. *But even small things have their purpose.*

The people of Stauford loved their talk, and she and Ozzie's many nights out on the town were the subject of such chatter as of late.

The chief's found himself a nice girl to settle down with—

Oh, but wasn't she one of those poor kids from that church—

One of the Stauford Six, that's right—

Maybe Chief Bell could do better, find himself a girl with less of a history—

Working at the Burger Stand, Susan was privy to all sorts of gossip, one of the reasons she'd held the job for the last six years. She was fascinated by how much a person could learn by simply pretending not to listen. The righteous Baptists of Stauford loved to talk. She figured their shallow hearts couldn't contain all those secrets.

"Let them talk," she whispered to no one, returning her gaze to the moon. Her confidante, a brilliant portal and guide. How many conversations had she held with the moon? Countless, surely, but she dared not speak her heart's desires to anyone else in town, not even Ozzie. Stauford couldn't keep its mouth shut, and the last thing she needed was to be branded a witch like Imogene Tremly. The moon would listen, though, and it wouldn't judge. It watched over her, guiding her hand to do the deeds that must only be done in the twilit hours. Her father spoke to her through the moon's unblinking eye. He told her secrets. He told her his plans. And she waited.

From the moon, her father told her to lay with the town's chief of police. *He will become your eyes and ears. He will be your shield.* And like a good daughter, she had done so for months now, drinking Ozzie's seed, opening herself up to him in places he should not go, just to appease her suitor.

From the moon, her father told her to desecrate the home of the heretic witch. *Defile her birthplace. Defile where she rots in the earth.* And like a good daughter, she drove to the hardware store and purchased cans of spray paint. She marked the old Victorian house outside of town, and later, Imogene's gravestone. Except she'd heard the cemetery's keeper found her graffiti and cleaned the paint from the chiseled granite. Susan drove out to the cemetery a few days later to finish her work, only to find Jack Tremly there, a sight which stunned her. He was the last person she expected would return. But no matter. She would continue to do what her father bade her.

From the moon, her father told her to wait. *When all heretics rot and the moon is full once more, I will return to you, my daughter. We will build paradise upon this world's ashes.*

And like a good daughter, she waited, marking her calendar for the rise of the first full moon after Imogene Tremly was in the ground.

She waited, staring up at the white eye silvering her body, mind, and soul. A soft breeze rustled the trees outside and filled the room with cool air. Her skin bristled with gooseflesh, and her nipples hardened. She traced the moon's place in the sky with her finger, forming the sacred half-circle in her mind.

A drop of blood plopped on the nail of her big toe. She looked down, wondering if she was asleep and dreaming this, but then another tear of blood fell.

Susan looked up at the moon, at her outstretched hand and finger, and noticed the half-circle of blood on her wrist. Blackened tears seeped out of her skin, following the inked marks of the tattoo she'd commissioned years ago. The symbol her father burned upon his face before the witch took his life. She stared in awe at the seeping wound on her wrist. Tears flooded her eyes.

I come again, my little lamb. I was and I am.

"You always will be," she whimpered, freeing the tears as she sank to her knees. Blood trickled from her wound, dotting her thighs and hips, staining the floor in a Pollock painting of sacrifice and devotion.

Susan raised her bloody hand to the window in supplication. She smiled and said, "Your will and the Old Ways are one."

The moon said nothing in return.

2

Nor did the moon say anything to Zeke, despite his pleas and screams. The shape of his father moved before him, blocking out the moonlight, and ran a dirt-caked hand through Zeke's hair. He trembled at the touch, his skin crawling from the coarse texture of his father's crumbling fingertips. His stomach churned from the musty smell of the grave, the stench of rot covered in decades of soil and ash, and twice choked back the bile threatening to spew from his gut.

Zeke's mind ran circles around itself, questioning the reality of what was happening. His father was dead. He'd watched Imogene Tremly put a bullet in his chest, another in his head, watched her empty all her rounds into his father's bleeding corpse. The grotesque scene had haunted him all his life, forcing him into an existence of sleep deprivation and depression.

And yet here his father stood, caked in mud and gore from Waylon's steaming corpse. Zeke's eyes filled with tears.

"Do not weep, my lamb." Jacob's voice was dry, raspy, a sound of weeds whispering in the wind and soil blowing in fallow fields. "Your friend gave his life willingly to the lord, a sacrament of flesh and blood." He wiped his chin and smiled. "We have much rejoicing to do."

Jacob gripped Zeke's chin and lifted his head. Zeke forced himself to gaze into the glowing blue eyes of the thing that was once his father. Blackened worms clung to the revenant's face, seeking the air in trembling gyrations as if sensing Zeke's tears, his sorrow. Tasting his fear.

"But I must know, little lamb, what has become of our lord's idol?"

Zeke didn't have an answer, didn't even know what the hell Jacob was talking about. His voice failed him, amounting to nothing more than a few choked expectorations. Jacob gripped his son's cheeks and squeezed.

"Where is the idol, child?"

But Zeke couldn't reply. Instead, he screamed until his throat was raw, crying for help that wouldn't come.

Jacob Masters held his hand over Zeke's face to muffle the sounds of his wailing, panicked child. Black worms writhed across Jacob's flesh and into Zeke's mouth, his nose, his eyes. The world went dark, snuffed out like a match, but he could still feel the thick, pulsing things inching their way into his mind.

"You will help me find it," Jacob said, running a blackened, bloated tongue across his charred teeth. "And we will build paradise together."

Zeke said nothing, his mouth full of dirt and worms and a viscous gore tasting of oil and rot. But in his head, in the darkness behind his eyes itching with the sensation of clumps of crawling things, he said, *Yes, Father. Let's build paradise together.*

His father smiled up into the moonlight, and the circular glyph in his forehead began to bleed.

3

"So, do you kids want to hear a scary story?"

Ben Taswell's brother tossed another log on the campfire and grinned like a devil as embers sputtered into the night. The wavering dance of flames projected a shifting display of shadows upon his face. Ben thought Daniel looked like a madman in the firelight and found he couldn't help but match his older brother's grin. His smile faltered a little when he glanced at Riley and saw his friend wasn't paying attention to the flames but was instead whispering something into the ear of Rachel Matthews. They were holding hands. Ben looked away.

The other kids in the youth group cheered, confirming a unanimous vote for scary stories around the fire. Dan Taswell motioned toward the flames. "Gather 'round, then. I've got a really scary one for ya." Daniel shot a wink to the other chaperone, Glenda Martin, another college kid home for the weekend. She took Daniel's cue and shrank back into the shadows for a moment. When she returned, she held a small black bag in her hand. She gave it to Daniel before joining the group around the fire.

Ben leaned forward, trying to get his brother's attention, silently projecting his curiosity. What was in the bag? Soon, he thought, they would all know—but being the storyteller's younger brother often afforded him exception, and he wanted to be in on the gag before the rest of the kids.

If Daniel noticed the curious look on his brother's face, he made no indication. Instead, he stuck his hand in the bag. The orange light reflected in his glasses, painting his eyes the color of Jack-O-Lanterns and Halloween.

"You ready?"

Their bellies full of s'mores and warm cocoa, the youth group of First Baptist huddled together around the fire and gave Daniel their full attention. All except for Rachel and Riley. They were sharing a quiet laugh with one another. Ben tried to get his brother's attention, tried to avert Daniel's gaze toward the young couple, but his brother was too caught up in his monologue to notice.

For an instant, Ben thought about ratting out Riley when they returned on Sunday. He was sure Reverend Tate would be none too pleased to hear his son spent the weekend making out with Rachel Matthews, but then his cheeks flushed with the warmth of shame. *Not a way to treat a friend*, a voice said. *Not after he saved your life from Jimmy Cord this afternoon.*

Ben sighed. He did owe Riley. The whole scene happened so fast— first Jimmy had him cornered, for reasons he couldn't even remember, and then there was Riley with his lunch tray, and then Jimmy was bleeding and Riley was smiling and—

"Ben?"

He looked up, snapped from his reverie. "Yeah, Dan?"

"Pay attention, will ya? They're paying me by the hour here."

Glenda Martin chuckled at the line, but the other kids in the group remained silent. Ben nodded for his brother to go on.

"So, you know, there was a church out here once. Many years ago, before they built the dam down at Holly Bay. Did any of you know that?"

The children said nothing, but Ben found he could barely contain his excitement. He inched forward, willing his brother to continue. From the corner of his eye, he saw Riley was finally paying attention, but the grim look on his face spoke volumes.

"I expect you wouldn't. Not many folks talk about it these days. Not many of them are left." Daniel let those ominous words hang in the air for a moment as he pulled his hand from the bag. White powder slipped through his fingers and gave life to the flames, filling their circle with a whoosh of orange light. The children exchanged glances with shared awe.

Ben's friend Toby Gilpin nudged his arm. He leaned over and whispered, "Dude, I didn't know your brother was a magician."

"Me neither," Ben whispered, more to himself than his friend.

"The old church was a few miles from here," Daniel went on. "Way out here in these woods, just off Devil's Creek Road. A small group of Stauford folks used to congregate out there, and an old minister by the name of Jacob Masters presided over his flock with sermons of hellfire and brimstone—what my papaw used to call 'old-time religion.' Brother Masters built a whole community out here in these woods for his people to live, so they could worship how they wanted to without fear of people interfering."

Daniel Taswell paused, more to catch his breath than for effect, and an owl hooted from somewhere off in the distance, giving some of the children a start. He cleared his throat and continued.

"Anyhow, word spread there was devil worship going on back here in the woods. People heard all sorts of stories about animal sacrifices, strange sounds and lights after sundown, chanting, people in robes. I was a young man when I first heard these stories, no older than you, Ben."

All the kids looked at him, even Riley. Ben's cheeks burned.

"Everyone knew not to go out to Devil's Creek. Jacob Masters had a reputation in town for being a little off his rocker. So did the rest of his followers. His gospel wasn't like what we teach on Sundays at First Baptist. Over time, the rumors kept building and building until, one day, some kids went missing."

First Baptist's youth looked amongst themselves with wide-eyed concern. Glenda Martin shifted in her seat and put a hand over her mouth to hide her smile. Daniel had them in the palm of his hand.

"One thing led to another, and before too long, the people of Stauford formed a mob. They drove out to Jacob's church here in the woods, and do you know what they found?"

Ben leaned forward, waiting on the edge of his brother's words. Toby did the same, as did the other children. The only one who didn't was Riley, who now sat with his arms crossed, his eyes ablaze with an anger Ben had only seen once before, earlier that afternoon.

"They found the missing children—parts of them, I mean, hanging from the trees like wind chimes. The rumors were true, and the good people of Stauford had waited too long to act. They rounded up Jacob's flock to take them back to town and try them for murder, but before they left, they set fire to Jacob's church."

"That isn't how it happened," Riley mumbled, but only Rachel and Ben heard him.

Daniel reached into the bag and pulled out another handful of white powder. In that moment, before his brother tossed the powder on the flames, Ben realized what it was: coffee creamer. He'd seen the canister packed in his brother's bag earlier that day and wondered why because Daniel never drank coffee. A thin smile spread across Ben's face as he watched his brother conjure another burst of flames from the pit. Daniel Taswell waited for the flames to settle. He licked his lips, measuring their faces before going on.

"The old man was locked inside when they set fire to the building. My papaw used to say the screams coming from inside the church weren't from a man, but something else. Something inhuman. When there was nothing left but ashes, those who stayed combed through the cinders in search of Jacob's remains—but they didn't find them. Old man Masters vanished that day, but if you listen closely on cool autumn nights like this one, they say you can hear him screaming... *What's that over there?*"

Ben's brother shot to his feet with a jolt and cackled as the whole group of kids shrieked in horror. A moment of panic overcame them as they searched the shadows with fire-blind eyes, trying to find the shape of the evil Jacob Masters, killer of children. He wasn't there, of course. Ben saw his brother's ruse coming a mile away, but he played along, feigning surprise before joining in the laughter.

"Very funny, Dan." Toby looked back at Ben. "Your brother's lame."

"Whatever," Ben grinned. "I saw you jump a mile out of your shoes."

Glenda Martin clapped her hands. "All right, kids. We've got a long hike ahead of us in the morning, so you should all get some sleep. Come on, back to your tents. Let's get some shut-eye."

Riley remained while the children dispersed. Ben watched him say goodbye to Rachel, sneaking a quick wink before she trotted off with the other girls to their tents.

Daniel called out to him. "Hey Ben, help me put out the fire."

He did as his brother asked, kicking dirt into the fire pit. The flames were almost out when Riley approached from the shadows.

"Daniel," he said, "that's not how the story goes."

Daniel chuckled, shrugging off the criticism. "Come on, it's just a story, Riley. Let's get some sleep, huh?"

"Yeah," Riley said, frowning. He caught Ben's stare before leaving the circle. Ben thought he heard Riley say something else as he walked off into the darkness. *It's not just a story.*

Ben's pulse quickened from the implication, and he made short work of the fire pit, kicking up plumes of dust and dirt to mask the flames. With the last embers glowing in the dark of the forest, Ben doubled his pace to catch up to his friend so he wouldn't have to walk alone.

4

Riley climbed inside their tent. He activated a small handheld LED lantern, filling the dome tent with a pale white light and waited for Ben to return. Daniel's comment nagged him, taking small bites at his brain, filling his mind with an itch he couldn't scratch.

It wasn't just a story. At least, not how Riley understood it. He'd heard the spooky legends growing up. What child in Stauford hadn't? Someone's older sibling or cousin always spilled the truth, usually in hushed whispers with a feral sort of glee in their eye. Scary stories were primal things, passed on as warnings, but mostly—and Riley figured this was more truth than speculation—for the sadistic pleasure of scaring someone else with mere words. And like most scary stories, there was always a grain of truth to them.

In Riley's case, a kid named Chad Simmons shared the town's dark legend one sunny day on the playground of Stauford Elementary. Chad heard the story from his older brother, Dirk, who in turn heard it from an unidentified brother of someone who was *actually there*, man. Never mind the discrepancy of years. Such details were trivial to a young boy when there was a scary story to be heard.

Chad Simmons's version of the story was closer to the truth but left out one integral piece Riley would not discover until years later when he was in high school. That version was announced by Jimmy Cord to the entire freshman class during a school assembly: "Ain't your daddy one of those cursed Devil's Creek kids?"

The question was enough to spark the curiosity of every young teenager in the school auditorium, and by the end of the day, Riley Tate's reputation was fully metastasized.

His father looked like he'd been struck when Riley asked him about it. *"Are you one of the cursed Devil's Creek kids?"*

And for an hour afterward, Bobby Tate was behind the closed door of his bedroom, on the phone having a rather loud argument with someone whom Riley could only imagine was Jimmy Cord's father.

When his father emerged, he looked like he'd aged ten years, his eyes sunken, his cheeks drawn, his posture slouched and defeated. Bobby Tate wasn't a drinking man, but Riley suspected if they'd had bourbon in the house, his father would've imbibed.

That night Riley learned the truth of his lineage, and if his mother were still alive, he would've held her hand or sought her embrace for comfort. Her absence hit him harder than ever before. All the kids at school were right: he was a freak from a fucked-up family.

"But try to make the most of this," his father told him. *"If I worried about what people thought of me, I wouldn't have become a preacher."*

Riley's decision to embrace the image everyone projected on him seemed like the easiest course of action. After going to school with most of his classmates since Kindergarten, he knew what would happen if he tried to escape the bubble in which they'd placed him. Anyone who tried to rise above their social status in Stauford was swiftly rejected and dealt with. Being the monster they thought he was made sense, and after a few days of painting his nails and wearing black clothing, Riley realized he kind of liked being that monster. It allowed him to feel comfortable in his own skin for once.

There were others who liked that monster, too. Others, like Rachel Matthews, who were drawn into the mystique he'd built around himself. Being the monster did have its benefits. And unlike his father, Riley intended to have good stories to tell his children someday.

Ben climbed into the tent. He looked down at Riley and frowned.

"Something wrong? You're not still pissed about what my brother said, are you?"

"No," Riley lied. "I do need to talk to you, though."

Ben went about unrolling his sleeping bag. "About this afternoon?"

Riley paused. In the hours after school with his father, he'd almost forgotten about the incident at school. Yes, he supposed he did need to talk to Ben about it. About keeping his distance from Jimmy Cord as much as possible.

"Look," Ben went on, "you didn't have to do what you did. I owe you one. Thanks."

"I didn't, but if not me, then who?"

The boys went quiet as those words hung between them. Ben finished making his bed and climbed inside the sleeping bag. He rolled over and looked at Riley, propping his head up with one hand.

"Cord's going to beat the shit out of you, you know."

"Let him try."

Ben laughed. "He'll do more than try, jackass. I'm not the one who has to worry about him now. Hey, ain't you going to bed?"

"No," Riley said. "I'm not. Not yet. I told Rachel I'd meet her in the woods after lights out."

Ben sat up. "You're kidding."

Riley shook his head. "I'm not."

"To do what?"

"To talk."

Ben's cheeks flushed red even in the pale LED glow. "You know how much trouble you'll be in if you get caught? I mean, your dad probably won't let you come to any more of these trips. Shit, they'll probably stop the girls from coming along with us, and—"

"Ben, I'm not going to get caught. We're just going to talk."

"Uh huh," Ben smirked. "And hold hands like you were doing tonight. And suck face. Maybe she'll let you touch her boobs, too."

Riley's cheeks filled with heat, more out of embarrassment than lust. He liked Rachel Matthews a lot, and he thought she liked him, too, but he hadn't told her as much. Not yet. Their interactions were passing notes in class, texting one another at night, chatting on Skype. Whenever there was a project due for class, they always gravitated toward the same group. They always laughed at one another's jokes and looked away when the other caught them staring. She *liked* him, wasn't put off by the monster he claimed to be, and—

"Are you going to let her touch your knob?"

"Shut up," Riley sneered, smacking his friend playfully on the head. "You're not funny."

"Oh, come on. Don't tell me you haven't thought about it."

He smirked but said nothing. His silence was enough of an answer, and Ben didn't need words to confirm what Riley was thinking. He *had* thought about it, many times, and usually after they'd said goodnight to one another. But not tonight. Tonight, he wanted to talk to her more, free of open ears and prying eyes, when they could speak honestly.

And, maybe, a kiss or two.

Riley's phone buzzed. He checked the screen. His heart leapt into this throat, and his stomach fluttered. Rachel's message read, "Leaving in thirty min. See you soon <3".

Ben puckered his face and made kissing sounds as Riley stretched out on his sleeping bag.

"You're so immature," Riley whispered, and switched off the lamp.

5

Zeke Billings wandered in the dark, blazing a trail through the forest. The hushed whisper of his father's words seeped into his mind, while his father's shadow trailed a few paces behind, a lithe phantom slipping over the weeds and brambles like oil through water.

Do you know what the darkness told me, child?

"What, Father?"

Jacob, it said, you will spill your seed in my name, and from your seed you will spill your blood, and from your blood you will set alight the world from which paradise will grow. Paradise, son. Heaven on earth. A true heaven, born of ash and cinder, cities built upon the charred bones of the damned. Their sins will flow, and they will drown beneath waters of their own making. Do you understand?

Mosquitoes hummed about his ears and cheeks as he stumbled forward, pushing away fragile limbs that swung and scratched his face. He thought he heard himself say yes, he did understand, but the sound of his voice was miles away, his vision clouded in a darkened fog. There were worms in his mind, inching their way to his heart. He felt them there, darkened tendrils seeking for more of what made him himself, sipping at his life force, tasting it.

Zeke felt less in control with each step, his functions usurped by the slender fingers working in his brain and the dark shadow following close behind. He felt his father's fingertips on his shoulder more than once, steering him forward into the unknown. Zeke welcomed the touch, welcomed the comfort it brought him. All his life he'd longed for a real father to show him the way, and now, after decades of mistakes and tribulations, he finally got his wish.

Only Jacob was so much more.

Blood of my blood, my seed, my little lamb. I've so many secrets to share with you. Secrets of the earth, of the grave, of our new lord. The heretics pulled a veil down over your virgin eyes and hid the true world away from you. I promise you, child, there is so much more. This body you wear, this pain you feel, all this flesh is nothing more than a shroud. Our new lord will show you. Our new lord will show all your brothers and sisters.

"When, Father?"

Soon, my son. We must acquire our lord's idol. And there is something else we must do. We must build paradise on earth one stone at a time, and we will need help.

"Help, Father?"

Twigs snapped beneath Zeke's heavy boots. The murk in his eyes cleared enough for him to see the dying embers of a campfire ahead. Lazy tendrils of smoke sought the air above, and the pungent aroma made his nostrils tingle. He heard the muffled laughter of children. Boys and girls.

Yes, my son. The babes of the earth, for their innocence will sway the hearts of the damned. From these seeds of Babylon, a new paradise will grow.

The shadow urged him forward. Zeke obeyed.

6

Jack Tremly awoke from fevered dreams of faceless things in the dark, kicking the blanket from his legs and sitting up with a short cry. The creatures of his night terrors faded away into the dimly lit living room of his grandmother's house, a place both familiar and foreign to him beyond the threshold of sleep. Sweat beaded on his forehead and bare chest. Once he had his bearings, Jack wiped his face with the blanket, an old afghan Imogene knitted when he was a teenager. He stared at it for a few minutes, trying to remember when he covered himself but coming up short.

What he did remember was drinking way too much at the restaurant. Stephanie gave him a ride home, and after waving goodbye to her, he'd wandered into his grandmother's house for the first time in decades, the alcohol in his system robbing him of any nostalgic fanfare. After a piss that lasted for years, he'd fallen face-first into the old sofa and promptly passed out. He didn't remember taking off his shirt or wrapping himself in a blanket.

The lights were still on, the squeaky ceiling fan spinning above, and everything was just how he'd remembered it. Mamaw Genie's brown armchair sat in the opposite corner of the room, with a stack of magazines and newspapers propped up on one side of the ottoman. Her cabinet stereo and turntable, end tables, lamps, coffee table, and even her old wooden console television were in the same places they'd always been.

Everything used to be bigger, he thought, smiling at his foolishness. Of course it did. He'd spent most of his young life here, and he was sure if he checked the kitchen doorframe, the check marks indicating his growth spurts would still be there. Even the cabinet and loveseat with her princess-style rotary phone were still there next to the living room entrance, and he recalled the phone number as easily as his social security number or ATM pin.

He whispered the number to himself. Saying the words aloud made his heart hurt.

Jack climbed to his feet, swaying slightly as his head spun, and he resolved to get a drink of water before the worst of his inevitable hangover set in.

Once his thirst was sated and the world stopped tumbling over itself, Jack returned to the living room and opened one of the windows. A cool breeze blew back the curtains, covering his bare skin in gooseflesh, and he welcomed the sensation.

Something caught his eye when he switched off the lights. A dim glow emanated from beyond the living room.

"What the hell?"

A thin slug of anxiety crawled across his mind, covering him in a film of unease. The glow felt familiar, and for as much as he wanted to go back to sleep, his mind wouldn't leave it alone. There was a memory there, half-buried in the shadowy folds of his brain, one tip exposed and yearning to be unearthed. Jack knew himself well enough to know sleep wouldn't come until he discovered the source.

Exhausted, his head still fuzzy from the booze, Jack wandered down the hall. The light, he discovered, wasn't coming from the first floor at all. Nothing out of the ordinary was plugged into the walls of the dining room or kitchen. Light seeped down the far wall of the foyer like slow-moving water, capturing motes of floating dust. He followed it up the side of the wall to the stairwell. From where he stood, the upstairs hall was bathed in sapphire.

Maybe it's a nightlight, he thought, but his curiosity held him there. He looked up, dazed and half-dreaming, wondering if he could add somnambulism to his list of sleep-related ailments. He flipped on the upstairs light and ascended the steps. Imogene's bedroom door was slightly ajar, offering a slim crack into the room beyond. The glow pulsed slowly, rhythmically, like something taking deep breaths.

Jack stood in the hallway, watching the ebb and flow of the light spill from the room. His head hurt the longer he stared at the light, and he forced himself to look away. The nagging feeling he'd seen this light before prodded his curiosity despite the uneasiness he felt. Each passing second was another he wanted to turn in retreat, but he couldn't get the light out of his head. He was drawn to it, each slow pulse a beacon calling out to him.

"The hell with it," he mumbled, forcing himself forward. He pushed open the door and flipped on the bedroom light.

Mamaw Genie's room was as he remembered it, save a few exceptions. Her wardrobe still stood in the far corner adjacent to her four-post canopy bed, her boudoir was still cluttered with boxes of jewelry, perfumes, and cans of hairspray, and the cedar chest full of extra blankets and linens still sat at the foot of the bed.

New to the room, however, were two additions. The first was a signed and numbered print of his painting *Midnight Baptism* he'd sent her, which now hung on the wall next to the window. She'd given it a home in a nice wooden frame that probably set her back a few hundred dollars, given the size.

The second addition was her old roll-top desk. Light pulsed from between the slats of the lid.

He crossed the room and pushed against the lid, but the wooden slats wouldn't move. With his fingertips pressed against it, Jack felt a soft vibration coursing through the lid. The whole desk hummed in time with the pulsing light, and after giving the lid another shove, he noticed a keyhole in the center. Light seeped out of the metal opening. He ran his finger over it, remembering the wooden box he'd received in Chuck's office.

"Okay, Mamaw. What've you got hidden in there?"

Five minutes later, after rummaging through the pockets of his discarded jeans, Jack returned with the key in hand. He didn't wait to collect his wits. He was tired, the hour was late, and he had shit to do tomorrow. Jack pushed the key into the desk and turned until the lock gave way. A moment later, the lid rolled upward, and the air left Jack's lungs in a series of hitched exhalations.

No, he thought, his mouth suddenly dry. *This isn't real. It was all a nightmare. It can't be.*

Sitting on the desk surface, beside a wrinkled notebook, was a stone idol carved to look like an obscene grinning child. He knew that grin all too well. It had haunted his sleep since he was a kid. The sickly blue light pulsed from its grimy surface.

Jack fell to his knees and stared at the ancient thing, his tired mind racing with questions. What was it doing here? Why did Mamaw Genie keep this awful thing? What little Jack remembered of it was the stuff of nightmares—memories of sermons in the old church, memories of being down in the pit with his father, molested and raped in the light of this malignant rock.

A moment passed before Jack realized he was crying. Tears flooded his eyes, occulting the items on the desk. He wiped his face, plucked the notebook from the desk, and closed the lid.

Why did you leave this for me to find, Mamaw?

He leaned against the side of the bed and held the notebook to his chest like a protective sigil. A series of low sobs rocked him, filling him with tremors of emotion he'd not felt in years, and for the first time since he was a child, Jack Tremly truly felt afraid.

Ben lay alone in the dark of the tent, listening to the chatter of crickets while trying to sleep. His idle thoughts wandered into places they weren't supposed to go. Places like the locker room of Stauford High where the girls track team changed and showered. He thought of the day he saw Rachel Matthews doing stretches in the gym, thought of her legs, firm and smooth and covered in a glistening sheen of sweat.

He thought of her now, somewhere in the woods with Riley, sucking face, touching each other, and his whole body shuddered, suddenly flush with a heat and stiffness in his boxers. He thought about touching himself there, maybe working himself up in his hand like he did at home but stopped short of doing the deed.

No, he thought. *That ain't right. Not here.*

But he wanted to. God, he wanted to. It's not that he liked Rachel Matthews, not really. She had an obnoxious laugh, wore too much perfume, and didn't have an ass to speak of, but those legs killed him every time she walked by in biology class—

Crack.

The sound stole his attention, and he jerked his hands out of his sleeping bag. His heart thudded heavily in his chest, his throat, his skull. Was Riley back so soon? The last thing he wanted was for Riley to catch him jerking off in their tent. He sucked in his breath and waited, listening for his friend's footsteps, the eventual unzipping of the tent.

Minutes passed, and the forest remained still around him.

Must've been an animal, he thought, slipping his hand back into the warmth of his boxers. But the sudden noise and fear of being caught drove away his lust, and the urge was no longer there. Disappointed, Ben rolled onto his side and closed his eyes, listening to the lull of crickets.

His thoughts drifted away from Rachel Matthews's toned legs and into darker spaces, twirling in circles until his mind wound itself down. He thought back to the story his brother Daniel told over the campfire an hour before. A slow, creeping fear emerged from somewhere in the darkness of his eyelids, driven on the back of a charging possibility some parts of Daniel's story might be true.

Don't be stupid, he scolded himself. *You're too old to believe in the boogeyman.*

To which a nagging, curious voice in the back of his head squeaked, *What about the Devil?*

Ah yes, the Devil. The original boogeyman. He'd heard plenty of stories about Lucifer in the basement of First Baptist Church, from the fall of Adam and Eve to the temptation of Christ in the desert. Stauford's local evangelists did their best to put the fear of ultimate evil in Ben from infancy, but as he grew older, the same threats of damnation were tired and worn. When he got down to the heart of the matter, the Devil didn't scare Ben all that much anymore.

The threat of Jacob Masters, on the other hand…

He thought he heard Toby's laughter carry across the campsite. Ben sighed, reaching blindly in the dark for his backpack.

Another sharp crack startled him with a jolt. He sat up, his heart running first in a thudding marathon. The side of the tent fluttered as a breeze blew past, rustling the leaves above. He thought about rolling over, but this time another sound caught his attention. Shifting, dragging, the rattling sound of trenches dug through pits of tiny pebbles—just like when he'd kicked his feet through the campsite on numerous occasions the day before.

He held his breath and listened. An owl hooted from somewhere above. After another beat, all he heard was his slowing heart and the rustling of dead leaves in the wind. The crickets ceased their chatter.

One of the other kids must've gone to the bathroom.

That made enough sense to set his tired mind at ease, and he was about to stretch out once more before another noise made his blood run cold.

Pained, muffled cries carried along the breeze, followed by more dragging noises across the gravel of the campsite. A cold spike of fear stabbed his gut. Why couldn't Riley be back? Why did he have to sneak out? He'd know what to do. Ben, on the other hand, cowered in the dark like a terrified animal, and he considered rolling over, closing his eyes, and hoping it was all a bad dream wrought from his brother's stupid ghost story.

But maybe someone's hurt, he thought. Maybe one of the other kids tripped on their way to the campground facilities. Probably Kenny Simpson. He was such a klutz at school.

Just take a look, he thought. *Open the tent, wave your flashlight around, see what's out there, and be done with it. It's probably nothing anyway. Maybe a raccoon. You'll see. Just take the light—*

He did, holding his hand over the lens as he clicked it on.

—unzip the tent—

He pulled the zipper, cringing as each metallic tooth separated with clicks amplified in the silence. When he'd unzipped the door enough to open a flap, Ben sucked in his breath.

—count to three—

"One," he whispered, his words nothing more than hisses of air through clenched teeth. "Two, three—"

—and take a look. Nothing to it.

Ben exhaled, his chest shuddering violently from his pounding heart, and opened the tent flap. The flashlight's beam darted between two nearby tents as his hand shook. He steadied himself, angling the light at the other tents, going from one to the next until he fell upon Toby's tent. His breath caught in his throat as his heart froze.

The flap was open, swaying lazily in a soft breeze sweeping through the forest. Two deep trenches were dug into the gravel, leading away from the tent and into the shadows of the night.

Ben remembered to breathe, and his heart resumed its frantic pace. Trembling, he reached over and unzipped the opening the rest of the way. The flap folded outward with a slippery noise, and he cringed.

You got this, he told himself. *Put your shoes on and run like hell to Daniel's tent. Wake him up. Call the cops. Get help.*

But when he'd slipped on his sneakers and surveyed the pair of ruts on the ground, he realized they led off in the same direction as his brother's tent. His heart sank. He'd have to follow the same path, risk facing whatever it was that took his friend.

His cheeks flushed. How did he know something took his friend? Was he jumping to conclusions? Ben stared hard at the deep grooves. He considered the righteous hell he would catch from Daniel if he woke his brother for something stupid, and then considered the possibility he was right, that Toby was dragged off into the forest by a ghost, a mad man, a wild animal, or all of the above. His imagination ran wild with possibilities, and all the while he sat in the opening of his tent, trembling like a frightened child and wasting time.

"Stop it," he said aloud, ignoring the trepidation in his voice. "Go get Daniel."

Ben climbed out of the tent and into the cool night air. His bare arms erupted in gooseflesh, and he was struck by the sheer silence of the forest. There was only the wind, the rattle and hiss of leaves in the trees, and the unblinking gaze of the moon from above.

And choked, muffled noises coming from somewhere in the dark.

Shaking, Ben trained the flashlight's beam on the ground and followed the ruts down the path toward his brother's tent.

This is stupid, he told himself. *There's nothing wrong. You're an idiot wandering in the dark, and you're about to piss off your brother in a big way by waking him up. There's nothing out here—*

The beam fell upon two shapes in the clearing next to the fire pit. One knelt over the other. Ben remembered to breathe, and he was about to scream for Daniel when the power of his voice drained from him. A puff of warm air rasped out of his throat instead.

The sleeve of Toby's neon green hoodie glowed in the beam of Ben's flashlight. His friend's left foot was bare and twitched uncontrollably as the second, bigger figure held him down. Even in the light, the ghoulish shape was drenched in shadow, his clothes tattered and charred and impossibly carrion black, the very essence of a void.

The ghoul turned toward him, toward the light, and snarled.

Ben's mind gave way to fear, freezing him in his place, and he struggled to keep his bladder from letting loose. The boogeyman, a figure he was too old to believe in, stared back at him with pale blue eyes glowing in the dark. Black worms wriggled out of holes in his face, and in the dark clump of slimy earth he shoved into Toby's mouth.

He met the dark figure's stare and tried to scream. There was no boogeyman, and there was no Devil. There was only the burned minister from his brother's stupid ghost story. Jacob Masters, the mad cult leader in the woods, knelt over his friend's body. Thick, maggoty tendrils squirmed out of his forehead and cheeks. His brittle teeth clenched in a skeletal smile that withered Ben's mind.

"Sinner," the ghoul rasped.

Ben Taswell closed his eyes and tried to scream, but a shadow fell upon him and clamped a cold, clammy hand over his mouth.

CHAPTER NINE

1

In a small two-story house on the central side of Gordon Hill, Ozzie Bell's phone rang. Susan stirred behind him, jabbing the back of her foot into Ozzie's thigh and rousing him from sleep. He opened his eyes and winced. His wrist was still cuffed to the bedpost and his hand was numb.

"Get the phone," he mumbled, but Susan grunted and buried her face into her pillow. He waited, hoping the caller would give up.

Ozzie opened his eyes. What time *was* it? He was asleep long enough to leave behind the cloud of booze and stupor of rough sex. The thought of Susan straddling him brought a twinge to his crotch, but the sensation was short lived. His bladder was full and screaming. The phone rang once more and fell silent.

He twiddled his numb fingers while he reached for the key on the nightstand with his free hand. His palm felt disconnected and full of cotton, like a scarecrow's mitt affixed to a dead arm. Blood rushed to his extremities after he unlocked the cuff, prompting him to grimace and suck in his breath as the prickling pain surged in his fingertips. He waited a minute for it to subside before climbing out of bed and trotting to the bathroom.

Susan hadn't moved in his absence. Her bare ass stuck out from the tangle of sheets, revealing the black serpent tattoo just above her right cheek, and he contemplated giving her one good smack for leaving him cuffed to the bedpost.

The sharp trill of the phone stole his attention, and he frowned when he saw the caller notification light up the screen.

"Goddammit." Ozzie sat on the edge of the bed and answered the call. "This had better be fucking good, Marcus. I'm tryin' to have a little personal time, if you get my drift."

He doubted it. Officer Marcus Gray was barely out of high school and greener than a garter snake, as his daddy used to say. The kid was an officer by act of favor alone, a repayment for a debt Ozzie owed the kid's father, Harlan Gray. That was the first and only time Ozzie wrote a check his ass couldn't cash, and he'd learned his lesson the hard way. Harlan Gray's boy was dumb as a brick.

"Sorry, Chief, but we just got a 911 call from Danny Taswell, and I used to go to school with him a few years ago, but anyways, he called and said someone attacked his little brother and—"

"Slow down," Ozzie sighed. He wished he had a joint. "Start over."

"Uh, sorry, Chief. Danny Taswell and Glenda Martin—I went to school with her too—have got a busload of kids out near Holly Bay for some kind of weekend church group thing. We got a 911 call from Danny ten minutes ago, sayin' someone came out of the woods and attacked Johnny Gilpin's son and Danny's little brother, Ben."

Ozzie squinted at his watch. A quarter past two in the morning. "We got a patrol out that way?"

"Yes, sir. Fugate and Cox are on their way now."

"Get your boots on. We're goin' out to the woods tonight."

He canceled the call and tossed the phone onto the bed.

Someone came out of the woods, he thought. *Probably some tweaker who couldn't handle his shit.*

Ozzie's thoughts turned to those two idiots from the far side of Moore Hill. Waylon promised him a batch of meth to sell by Sunday. He doubted the inbred prick could boil water, much less cook meth, but Zeke might be able to pull it off. The product might not be entirely pure, but the discerning masses of Stauford's greater addict population didn't care about purity if the high was right. He ought to know. He'd put most of them away himself.

Smiling, Ozzie made a mental note to check in with Waylon and Zeke later on. After he dressed, Ozzie sat next to Susan and ran his hand along the length of her back.

"Hey."

She stirred, rolling over to look up at him. Her eyes fluttered open. "What's wrong?"

"Gotta go to work. Some kids were attacked out near the lake."

"Be careful, then."

"You got it, darlin'." He leaned down and kissed her, fishing his hand underneath the sheet. He pinched her nipple. Susan bit her lower lip.

"Don't start what you can't finish, Chief."

"I intend to," he said. "Just keep that bed warm for me. I'll be back in a few hours."

2

A few miles north along old US 25, just off the Tom Thirston Memorial Overpass, the fluorescent lights of Garvey's Gas 'n Go hummed and buzzed over an empty lot. A red neon sign blinked off and on in the front window, announcing to all who could see lottery tickets were for sale, while a pair of beer lights for Budweiser and Coors flickered in tandem. Three pay phone kiosks stood at the far end of the storefront sidewalk, remnants of a bygone era when collect calls and dial-up Internet were still a thing. Promotional posters for various cigarette brands, propane tanks, and prepaid cell phone minutes littered the store-wide picture window.

And inside this lonely self-service island of commerce, the son of the store's owner stood behind the counter, bored out of his mind.

David Garvey looked away from his comic book, first to the clock—2:30 a.m.—and then to the parking lot, which sat empty since a few high school kids rolled through a couple hours earlier, celebrating Stauford's win at tonight's football game. There were three and a half hours left on his shift before Crystal relieved him at six.

He flipped the last page of his comic book and turned it over in his hands to look at the cover. He'd picked up the comic book from the magazine rack because the cover caught his eye. There was a dark painting in place of the usual hand-drawn gothic superheroes, vivid in its detail and grotesquerie. "Guest Artist Jack Tremly," the cover read. David thought he recognized the name but couldn't place where. He was about to pull out his phone and google the name when movement caught his eye.

A short figure in a dirty gray hoodie and black sweatpants trundled across the parking lot. A bright neon yellow baseball cap sat on his head, and thick silver curls spilled from it. David rolled his eyes when he saw the slouching man walking toward the store.

"Not again," he whispered, and moved around the counter to the front door.

This was the fifth night in a week Gary "Skippy" Dawson visited David at the Gas 'n Go. David's generation often referred to Skippy as the town mascot, a waving idiot who'd greet anyone and everyone in town as he walked its streets. Rumors about Skippy circulated for as long as David could remember, ranging from conspiracy ("I heard he was a reject from some CIA experiment, man. MK-something.") to medical ("Didn't you know? The guy had a lobotomy, man. They cut out, like, three-quarters of his brain."), but the truth behind Stauford's favorite simpleton was far more tragic. Once the star quarterback of Stauford's football team, Skippy was in a horrible motorcycle crash one night after a game. He wasn't wearing a helmet, and the brain damage he suffered was both permanent and far-reaching.

David pushed open the door and greeted Skippy with a smile. "Skip, what're you doing out this late? Didn't we talk about this last night?"

And the night before, he thought. *And the night before that.*

Skippy pulled off his hat and scratched his head. He grinned, revealing the gap in his front teeth. "I knows, Mr. Gravy, but I's just needed to check the phones again. I hear 'em sometimes, callin' me when I tries to sleep."

David smirked. He'd been "Mr. Gravy" for a few nights now, although every once in a while, old Skippy would get his name right. A light breeze brushed past them, blowing back the matted curls from Skippy's shoulders.

"I know, Skip, but I keep telling you those phones ain't gonna ring any time soon. Hell, I don't think they've rang since I was in grade school."

"But they *will* ring, Mr. Gravy. Sooner or later. You'll see."

David glanced at the bank of payphones and shook his head. His father mentioned more than once he needed to remove them, but so far, the task sat at the bottom of his to-do list. David caught Skippy standing at the phones around 4 a.m. earlier that week, going back and forth from one handset to the next, asking if anyone was there. No amount of reasoning would deter him from checking those phones, and David idly wondered if there was something Skippy could hear that he couldn't. *Like a phone ringing in his head,* he thought. *Poor guy, going through life like that.*

The folks at Stauford Assisted Living were probably wondering where Skippy was at this hour.

"Skip, I'm gonna call your caretaker, okay? You sit tight. In fact, why don't you come inside with me—"

One of the payphones rang, filling the night with a shrill and ancient noise David had not heard since he was a child. Both men looked at one another in surprise, although Skippy Dawson was far more elated than his counterpart. The old man hopped up and down in his sneakers, the worn soles squeaking against the pavement and punctuating his hoarse, choked laughter. A chill of fear crept down David's spine, leaving him frozen in place, one foot on the parking lot and another on the sidewalk. The lines were disconnected a decade ago.

"Ain't you gonna answer it, Mr. Gravy? I bet it's for you."

David glared at Skippy. *Don't you put this on me, you ignorant shit. There's no goddamn reason that call would be for me. You're the curious one.*

The truth was, David was at least a *little* curious, if not entirely eager to silence the shrill noise filling the night.

"Maybe you should answer it, Skip." David looked at him and forced a smile. "I mean, you've been coming out here every night for this."

"But I already knows what it's gonna say, Mr. Gravy."

David's face fell, a familiar chill climbing back up the length of his spine. "And what's that, Skip? Care to tell me?"

Skippy grinned and shook his head. "Nuh uh, Mr. Gravy. You has to answer the phone."

The phone rang once more, driving home Skippy Dawson's cryptic edict. Frowning, David Garvey padded along the sidewalk in front of the store and approached the ringing payphone. The blaring noise made his head swim, painting the world around him with a frantic uneasiness.

He hesitated, sucked in his breath, and picked up the receiver. The ringing ceased. He lifted the phone to his ear and met Skippy's gaze.

"Hello?"

Silence answered him. Silence, and a coarse grit of static scraping through his ear. And from that hissing noise spoke a hollow voice with subdued glee, filling David's mind with terror.

"He lives," whispered the voice, backed by grating static and the shrill, ululating sounds of laughing children. "He lives."

The line went dead, but the sounds continued in David's mind, caught in a permanent loop. *He lives, he lives, he lives.* He returned the receiver to its cradle and leaned against the wall of the store, rubbing absently at his forehead. A thrumming pressure settled behind his eyes, pulsing in time with his heart.

"Now you know, Mr. Gravy," Skippy said, laughing as he hopped up and down across the parking lot. "Soon, everybody'll know! He lives! *He lives!*"

Skippy Dawson's prophecy faded into the night as he trotted across the parking lot, into the shadows, and away toward town. David watched him go, thankful he was alone, terrified he was alone. He stared at the bank of payphones with reservation before returning to the store.

Five minutes later, he locked the doors and shut off the lights. He'd think of an excuse to tell his father in the morning.

3

Bobby Tate switched on the bedside lamp and fumbled for his glasses. He'd had the worst nightmare, a tapestry of hellish horrors and agony, but with his eyes open and the light on, those dark phantoms were banished from memory. Only the dread remained. There was something else, though, something his waking mind took a few moments to understand.

The phone. His phone was ringing.

He looked at the nightstand, and his heart lodged in his throat. The screen lit up, announcing an incoming call from Riley. Bobby checked his watch as he reached for the phone. 2:37 a.m.

Oh God, he thought, his belly filling with a sickening dread like concrete. *Please let him be okay. Please, Lord, let my son be okay.*

Bobby held his breath and accepted the call.

"Dad?"

Riley's shaky voice was like angels singing in his ear. *Oh, thank you, Jesus, thank you.*

"I'm here, Riley. What's wrong? Is everything okay?"

"No," Riley said, his voice rising an octave, trembling. "No, it's Ben. And Toby. They're… Dad, they're gone."

Bobby sat up, kicking back the blankets and planting his feet on the cold wooden floor. "What do you mean, 'they're gone?'"

"I mean, they're gone."

His son's raw voice made Bobby's heart palpitate. The bold, rebellious fifteen-year-old with whom he'd fought earlier was now reduced to the frightened six-year-old he loved and missed so much. Riley's fear forced Bobby's paternal instincts to surge. He needed to get dressed and go get his son. His son needed him, needed his father right now, and—

"Someone came to the camp and took them."

"*Took* them?" Bobby rolled the word over in his head. "Riley, weren't you in the same tent? Tell me exactly what happened."

Silence filled the line. Bobby heard his son breathing, thinking how to reply, and a pit opened in his gut as he slowly put the pieces together. He closed his eyes and made a silent prayer to God, hoping beyond measure he was wrong.

"It's my fault, Dad."

Bobby's heart, the whole world, fell through his stomach. He opened his eyes and clenched his jaw.

"I'm listening, son."

"I wasn't in the tent. I was…out. In the woods. With Rachel Matthews."

"Riley James," Bobby hissed, too late to catch his anger before giving it voice. He waited a moment to collect himself, for the heat to bleed from his cheeks. "Look, we can talk about all that when you get home. I'm coming to get you."

"I can't leave yet. The cops are on their way. I have to give a statement."

Bobby sighed. *Of course*, he thought. *Ozzie Bell is going to have a field day with this. And when Don and Harriet find out what their daughter was doing with my son…oh Jesus, please grant me grace and patience.*

"If I'd been there, Dad, I could've done something. I could've…"

"Son, right now I need you to be strong, okay? You need to focus on what you remember, anything you saw, and tell the police when they get there. We can talk about…what you were doing when you get home. I'll be on my way to get you in a few minutes. Which campsite are you camping at tonight?"

Riley told him, and after a brief exchange of endearment, Bobby canceled the call with his son. His mind raced with questions and concerns, but underscoring the swelling maelstrom of anger, fear, and disappointment was a growing alarm for how close they were to the old church site near Devil's Creek.

The mounting realization brought long-buried memories to the surface of his mind, and as he rose to his feet to dress, fragments of his nightmare slowly faded into focus. There were hands in the murk, reaching to pull back a shroud of dust and ash, revealing blue torch fires burning in the pit below the old foundation. Ethereal echoes of children's laughter filled the cavern, rising and falling in waves as they sang an old church hymn.

"Give me that old-time religion, it's good enough for me."

A slow chill crept across Bobby Tate's back with the faint itch of spider legs. He shivered and shrugged off the sensation, dismissing the memory of song as nothing more than a nightmare. Minutes later, Bobby was on his way toward the west end of town and the twilit wilderness beyond. The uneasiness followed like a lost dog, always trotting a few steps behind, faithful in its resolve. No matter where Bobby Tate went, that old unease was always sure to follow.

❧

4

At the summit of Gordon Hill, the radio tower of Z105.1 hummed with transmissions of the damned. Power chords, double bass drum kicks, and growls seeped from the tower, infecting the airwaves with all manner of metal. The radio signal wasn't the only thing teeming with life; inside the small station sat the third-shift DJ, Cindy Farris, doing her best to enlighten the masses of Stauford with music from the witching hour.

The song faded to dead air, and Cindy licked her lips as she leaned into the microphone.

"Evenin', Stauford. That was a little Faith No More to get your blood pumping. I don't know about you ladies out there, but Mike Patton's voice makes me melt, if you get my drift. I see the boards are lit up with requests, so what do you say we get to them?" Cindy punched the blinking red light on her telephone console. "Next caller, you're on the air. Welcome to the Witching Hour. What can I play for you tonight?"

A gruff voice filled her headphones. "Oh hey, Cindy, how you doin' tonight, babe?"

She rolled her eyes, picked up her pen, and drew another tick mark next to "drunken admirers" on her notepad.

"I'm doin' just fine, handsome. What can I play for you tonight?"

"You can play me like a fiddle—"

Cindy canceled the call and pulled the microphone closer. "And thank you, generous caller, for that lovely rendition of 'Are You Lonesome Tonight.' Next caller, you're on the air."

To her relief, a woman's voice filled her headphones. "Hi, Cindy. Any chance you could play 'Holes in the Fabric' by the Yellow Kings?"

"Absolutely," Cindy said, smiling. "I will always play one from Stauford's fallen soldiers. What's your name, sweetheart?"

"Mandy. Could you dedicate it to my brother, Tommy?"

"You got it, Mandy." Cindy canceled the call and queued up the request. "Here's one from Stauford's own Yellow Kings, gods rest their souls. From Mandy to Tommy, two kids braving the southern wastes. This one's for you."

The red "ON AIR" light blinked off as the song began to play. On her way out of the studio, Cindy stopped to admire the corkboard in the hallway. Dozens of letters were pinned to the board, beneath a sign reading "Wall of Shame." Hate mail, some of them addressed with names, most of them from anonymous senders, all filled with the same fire-and-brimstone rhetoric: *Stop doing the Devil's work!*

"Busybodies," Cindy mumbled, and walked to the restroom. She'd grown up in the northern part of the state, and while the self-righteousness of Christian denominations was prevalent there, her hometown of Newport had nothing on Stauford. The town was a hive of religious goings-on, with a minimum of three churches in every quadrant. She'd never seen so many Baptist and Pentecostal centers in her entire life. The station heard from them all, but none so much as First Baptist. Bobby Tate's congregation.

In her first couple weeks working for the station, Cindy heard a rumor Stephanie was related to Bobby in some way, but she hadn't worked up the nerve to inquire. Cindy knew enough about small towns to know she wasn't a resident long enough to involve herself in rumors. Besides, she admired Stephanie, respected her, and was also partially afraid of her. Anyone who had the salt to set up a rock-focused radio station in the shiny buckle of the Bible Belt was someone who deserved admiration; anyone who had the balls to stand up and defy the religious masses demanding the station's closure, well, that was someone to be feared, too.

Stephanie stoked the flames a few weeks ago when she was interviewed by Michael Lot, a reporter for the Stauford Tribune, about the station's apparent success despite its vocal detractors. "It's time Stauford faced its reflection," she'd said. "The Goat is here to hold up the mirror."

Ryan had framed the news article and hung it outside the studio. A pink Post-It note with Stephanie's scrawl clung the glass: "OUR MISSION STATEMENT!!!"

Goddamn right, Cindy thought. She felt empowered every time she walked by the article. The empowerment is what kept her here in this shitty town. It was the knowledge she was taking part in something greater, something that might help the youth of this closeted town break free of religious expectations and find the courage to be themselves.

Cindy Farris sat back in her rolling chair and adjusted the microphone. The final notes of "Holes in the Fabric" faded out to dead air as she put on her headphones and went live.

"I love that song so much," she said. "For those of you out there in Stauford who are just tuning in, I'm Cindy Lou and this is the Witching Hour. That was Stauford's own Yellow Kings, a special request from Mandy to Tommy, two siblings fighting the good fight in this war we call rock 'n roll. I'll be your guide through the fog as we walk hand-in-hand toward the dawn. Next caller, you're on the air."

Silence filled the line. Cindy's finger hovered over the board, ready to move on to the next call. "Caller, you're live on the Witching Hour. What's your request?"

A shrill chuckle rose from the silence like a serpent from water, slick and agile and coated in a slime of anxiety. The sound forced a hitch in Cindy's breath, the air forming a hard bubble in her throat. She turned away from the microphone to gasp. Voices folded over one another as the laughter rose in waves, and she felt the sharp sting of panic rising in her when she realized they were children on the line.

"*We* request," one said.

"We *request*," said another.

"*We request,*" the voices said as one, "*your young. Your seeds to grow paradise from bones and ash. We demand blood and fire. Blood of the damned, fire for the purge, for he lives. Rejoice, for he lives. He lives. HE LIVES!*"

A chorus of chattering youth surged through her headphones, overpowering the speakers and devolving into static noise. Cindy jabbed her finger on the board, canceling the call, and gave herself a moment to breathe before realizing there was dead silence on the air. She collected herself and cleared her throat.

"And thank you for that lovely message, creepy children. We don't shy away from the dark side here on the Witching Hour. Next caller, what's your request?"

She punched the blinking light on the console and held her breath.

"Hey there, Cindy Lou. Anyone ever tell you ya got a purdy mouth?"

Thank God, she thought. "Mmm, I sure do, darlin'. You got a request for me?"

"Yeah, I got a request. How 'bout you stuff my—"

Cindy canceled the call and exhaled. She picked up her pen and marked the notepad with another tick mark. Her hand trembled.

5

"...next caller, you're live on the Witching Hour. What's your request?"

Ruth McCormick set aside her notebook and sipped her tea, rocking idly in her late husband's recliner. The Devil's station was coming in clear tonight. Some nights all she could get was a few words and static, but not tonight. Tonight, she had audience with the followers of Satan, and like a good acolyte of the lord, she would transcribe their infractions for presentation to the ladies' church group on Sunday morning. *Soon*, she thought, *everyone will know what crude, awful things those people are promotin' on their station. Allegiance to the Great Adversary, witching hours, pagan defiance, instruction to embrace nonconformity, and that horrid music...*

A barrage of crunching guitars and machine gun drumming rattled forth from her tiny radio's speakers. An instant later, a man began shrieking in tongues, a language she couldn't fathom, nor did she wish to. Ruth set down her teacup and saucer, her gnarled arthritic hands shaking as she made her way across the living room. She switched off the radio.

"I'm sorry, Lord, but my soul can't take no more of that tonight. Forgive me."

Ruth stared at the radio, almost expecting her god to respond from within, but He never did. And why should He? His work was in her hands, and what good hands they were. The lord trusted Ruth McCormick. She was a God-fearing sinner, a lady soldier carrying the Christian banner into the battlefield of Armageddon. She believed this with conviction in her heart and had done so ever since she'd rededicated her life following Ed's departure.

"I know you're up there," she said, picking up the empty dishes and wandering toward the kitchen. "Ed, I know you're watching over me. You tell our Heavenly Father I'm doin' the best I can, but even His soldiers have to sleep sometime."

Sleep. Yes, she needed her sleep, and she'd done what she could to squeeze in a few hours earlier that night, but the dreams kept her from rest. She tried to remember what they were as she rinsed her teacup in the sink. No, they weren't dreams, they were nightmares. Awful things, really. There were children and the smell of smoke, deep down in a bottomless darkness, a darkness so thick it was fluid like oil, and the voice, dear God, the voice speaking from inside the murk was something that made her heart grow cold.

Ruth's hands shook as she thought about it, the teacup and saucer rattling in her fingers. She shut off the faucet, put the dishes in the strainer, and dried her hands.

What was it the darkness said to her? Something about "old ways?" About rising again? Jesus rose again, rose right out of the pits of a fiery hell for He held all the keys, letting loose the condemned into His father's kingdom of heaven. But the darkness of her dreams was different. Jesus wasn't there in her dreams, He wasn't there in the shadows. There was only strange writing on the walls of a cavern, the stench of incense and smoke, and somewhere in the dark, children linked hands and danced around a small stone carving. She tried to remember what the carving looked like, but her memory failed her. All she could recall was the color blue, and a pair of words repeated like a mantra looping in her head over and over again: *He lives, he lives, he lives...*

"He lives," she whispered. The sound of her voice startled her, and the kitchen darkened at the utterance of those words, the pale nightlight above the kitchen counter dimming somehow. A chill fell over her, and she rubbed her arms for warmth. *He lives*, she thought again. *But of course He lives. He died on that cross and emerged three days later, hallelujah.*

Hallelujah, spoke a voice, a mere whisper coming from inside the living room. Ruth tilted her head and listened. *Hallelujah, my love. He lives. He is risen.*

"Ed?"

Her husband's name fell flat in the empty kitchen, and she felt foolish for even entertaining the idea. Ed McCormick was by the lord's side in Heaven, hallelujah, and would remain there for all eternity until she, Lord willing, would join him in paradise. And yet that soft and caring voice sounded like her husband, didn't it? Ruth took a step toward the living room and listened, her frail heart humming in her chest, her paper-thin fingers trembling with the slightest unease.

She waited a moment longer before sighing, holding back tears. "You silly old thing," she told herself. "You're goin' senile faster than anything else, I declare."

Come to me, my darling.

Ruth held her breath, her whole body shaking now, the beating in her chest like the rumble and roar of a freight train. She swallowed hard and winced at the raw click of her dry throat.

"Eddie?"

It's me, my love. Come to me. I'm in here.

Hesitant, Ruth tip-toed to the demarcation between kitchen and living room. There, she reached out with one shaking hand and peered around the corner, but with her eyes closed. *He's not there*, she thought, *he's in Heaven, Ed's in Heaven, and the only ghost is the Holy Ghost, hallelujah.*

She opened her eyes. A rush of relief swept through her. Her late husband's recliner was empty.

"Thank you, Jesus."

Over here, my love.

Her heart ascended to her throat as panic set in. Ruth scanned the room, trying to hold her terror at bay, fearing someone had broken into her home and the awful intruder was imitating her dead husband. Her gaze fell upon the radio sitting atop her television cabinet. The frequency dial was illuminated with a pale blue light, the backlit screen reading a jumble of numbers circulating across all bands, AM and FM.

Ruth stared incredulously at the device, certain she'd turned it off.

Hadn't she? Her memory was fuzzy, like the remnants of that awful dream, and the room felt closer, the walls a few inches further inward, the air acrid, smoky. The light on the radio pulsed, picking up words from each rambling station, forming sentences, intoning the voice her husband.

I want you to listen to me, my love. My darling. My angel from Heaven.

"Ed?" she spoke again. "Am I dreaming, honey?"

The greatest dream of all, my dear. I want you to listen, now. Get your pen and your notebook. The lord has a plan for you.

"He has a plan for us all," she whispered.

That's right, my dear, He truly does. Rejoice for He is risen. He lives. He lives. Not the god of false prophets and liars, but the one true apostle. Old lies above, and true love below. Rejoice, for His will and the Old Ways are one.

"The one true apostle..." she whispered, retrieving her notebook as her husband asked. "...His will and the Old Ways are one..."

That's right, my darling. Now listen and bear witness—

Ruth listened to what the darkness had to say, and she wrote it down.

6

Near dawn, as the sleeping babe of Stauford stirred in its cosmic crib beneath the deadened glow of the moon, one more phone rang at the psychiatric ward of Baptist Regional.

Head nurse Madeline Ross lifted her gaze from the paperback she was reading and answered the nurse station's phone.

"Maddy Ross," she said, licking her index finger to turn the page. Nurse Nichols filled her ear with panic and fright.

"Maddy, we've got a situation in B Wing. I've—well, it's best you come down here yourself."

"Uh huh," Maddy said, half-listening, half-reading the pulp novel in her hand. "What's the trouble now? Mr. Frederick eating out of his bedpan again?"

An exasperated laugh swelled from the phone receiver. "No, uh, it's Ms. Tremly."

Maddy Ross dropped her book. She gripped the receiver and focused on the panicking nurse on the other end.

"What is she doing, Darlene?"

"She's...well, she's, uh, floating."

Maddy blinked. "Floating?"

"That's right. Floating. Now would you *please* get over here?"

Maddy didn't wait. She hung up the phone, grabbed her badge and keys, and jogged down the hall toward B Wing. She was no stranger to that side of the ward, having done her time monitoring the special cases and administering their meds as needed. Out of all the patients currently interned in B Wing, Laura Tremly was the only one who'd been there when Maddy started. The poor woman was little more than a vegetable at this point, having suffered spells of hysteria, delusions, and night terrors. Especially the night terrors.

As her white sneakers clapped down the tile hallway, Maddy remembered many occasions on which she'd had to restrain Ms. Tremly, for both her safety and the nurses who attended to her needs. The restraints remained a necessity in the ensuing years, for she usually experienced bizarre convulsions and seizures in the night, often attributed to her manic dream state.

Only in the last few years had she finally calmed down, and the sudden swing in her manner caught the attention of various medical professionals. Laura Tremly was a classic subject for study, exhibiting symptoms and traits that refused diagnosis, earning her no less than four observations in the last year alone from doctors around the globe. And now she'd finally decided to wake up from her catatonia. Maddy Ross could almost believe it, more so than Nurse Nichols's claims of levitation.

Maddy swiped her keycard and waited for the automatic lock to disengage. She heard the laughter echoing down the hall as the doors swung open. Nurses Nichols and Dwyer stood outside Ms. Tremly's room, gawking in stupefied horror at what they saw. She pushed them aside and peered through the glass, working up a tongue lashing for the ages.

"Ladies, I should remind you, this hospital expects you to maintain your professionalism no matter—"

What, she wanted to say, but the word stopped short of her tongue. A dark ruby streak filled one side of the observation window. Through the other half of the safety glass, Maddy saw the restraints sitting in lifeless coils on the unkempt hospital bed, the bands frayed where they'd been chewed apart, the sheets stained blackish-red in thick spurts.

Maddy joined her subordinates, gaping at the gruesome impossibility before her.

Laura Tremly hovered before the grated window of her room, her arms held out to reveal the tears in her wrists. Thick shoestrings of blood dripped from her open wounds, but gravity held no sway in this room. The dollops of precious lifeblood fell upward, pooling on the ceiling in a viscous puddle boiling with an impossible heat.

The moon hung over Laura's shoulder, and she laughed with unsettling glee like a child, her chest heaving in deep convulsions. Her figure bobbed in the air, held afloat by unseen hands, and treading invisible waters.

"He lives," she cried, cackling madly at the light of the moon.

The trio stared in awe as Laura ripped at her gown, pulling it from her body in long shreds of linen. Bleeding, hovering, she clawed one hand down her naked thigh and between her legs.

"Oh my God," Nurse Nichols gasped. "Christ, shouldn't we—"

"My father, my lover, my apostle, accept this blood from me now. I rejoice with you for now you live! *You live!*" Laura Tremly spun in place, exposing herself in bloody display to the gaping nurses outside. Blood lined the contours of her ribs, forming a semi-circle design across her stomach. The blackish lines sizzled with heat, burning into her flesh, but if she felt pain, she gave no sign. No, she laughed and writhed in ecstasy, rubbing one hand between her legs while offering her blood with the other.

Nurse Dwyer turned her head and vomited, and Maddy covered her mouth for fear she might join the poor woman.

"He lives," Laura cried, rubbing herself so hard blood leaked down the side of her thigh. "Rejoice, sinners, for *He lives!*"

7

The full moon crept slowly above the small town of Stauford like the watchful eye of a silent sentinel, casting a pale glow over all who slept and dreamed. For some, the moon's presence was a welcome comfort, an open eye of God watching over them, a symbol of His loving brilliance and protection. For those fortunate few, their god was in His heaven, shining a light over all His wonderful sinners even when the sun was gone. The light of the moon was their security blanket, and they lay tucked in their beds, sleeping peacefully knowing their lord was watching from above.

What angry, jealous being would grant them light even in the dark? A light by which man would find his way in the wilderness. A light to comfort him even in a valley of shadows. The moon would never betray them. The moon, like their lord, always was and would always be.

But as the moon rose to its zenith and began a slow arcing descent toward the horizon in the twilit hours, the people of Stauford were haunted by troubling visions and restless dreams. They tossed and turned in their beds, chased through impossible hallways by pale-faced phantoms and creatures of the dark. Beasts with blue eyes and black worms protruding from their skin. Faceless men and women with shrouds over their eyes, their bloated lips ruby red, and their cheeks marked in black spider veins.

That night, the people of Stauford slept with the primal fear the moon had betrayed them. The moon, once their silent guardian, withheld a secret none of them could possibly know. Its light dimmed, its pull on the earth now maligned by old words not spoken by a mortal tongue in a millennium.

And somewhere above, their god was no longer watching from His golden throne.

Their god looked away, and the moon ushered in the very shadows which now plagued their weary minds.

The people of Stauford rolled in their beds, for they knew in their dreams their god had never been, His glorious kingdom above nothing more than fiction. That god of fantasy was one they didn't deserve.

No, the god they deserved was far below, sleeping beneath their feet, nestled among the crawling worms and roots of the earth, cradled by bedrock and shale, and blanketed by centuries of lies and legends.

They trembled, for one of his apostles now walked the earth.

FROM THE JOURNAL OF IMOGENE TREMLY (2)

1

From the Landon Herald's Morning Edition, May 19ᵗʰ, 1996

LOCAL PROFESSOR'S NATIVE RESEARCH HIGHLIGHTED

LANDON, KY – The recent work of Dr. Tyler Booth, professor of anthropology at Sue Bennett College, will appear in the quarterly edition of the *Journal of Southern Anthropology* this summer.

The feature highlights his studies of Native American burial mounds in the eastern and southeastern Appalachian regions during the 1993 school year. Dr. Booth's expedition was funded by a grant from the Thomas R. Trosper Foundation, awarded for efforts of furthering research and understanding of regional tribes.

"It's an honor," Dr. Booth said. "I'm grateful for the support from the college, the foundation, and the staff at the journal."

Dr. Booth's full thesis will be published by Sue Bennett's Keystone Press later this fall. The *Journal of Southern Anthropology's* summer edition will be available next month.

2

Excerpted from the Journal of Southern Anthropology, Summer Ed., 1996

[…] most well-known among local anthropological and archaeological circles for his continued efforts of preserving known Adena burial sites, Dr. Tyler M. Booth of Sue Bennett College confesses he is also something of a romantic.

"I love the mystery," Dr. Booth said. "Consider this: even the name 'Adena' is a Hebrew title thrust upon this group of hunter-gatherers, based on nothing more than a former Ohio governor's whim. The name has been adapted by modern scientists out of pure convenience, perhaps to occult the fact that we know very little about them."

(The Ohio governor mentioned above is one Thomas Worthington, whose estate contains the first documented burial mound attributed to the Adena culture. – Ed.)

Fellow anthropologists may be scratching their heads at the professor's remarks. Modern records indicate a great deal of information gleaned from more than 200 known burial mounds, ranging from hunting habits to agricultural progress and artistic tendency. We raised these points with Dr. Booth, and he had the following commentary to add.

"I'm not discounting prior discoveries. Please don't misunderstand me. I'm saying that while we have recorded evidence of what these people left behind, we know very little about who they were. The name given to them is something the anthropological community did for their own benefit. I'm driven by the mystery of who they were, and in my opinion, I believe that mystery can be solved by more in-depth research of their ceremonial rites."

We asked the professor to expound on that statement, and he was admittedly coy with his answer.

"I can't give everything away here," he said. "All I can say is that my team uncovered evidence during my last expedition that suggests there's more to the 'Adena' puzzle, especially regarding their burial rites. A full rundown of my findings will be published in a few months from Keystone […]"

Maybe he's my guy. Get copy of thesis. –Genie.

3

Highlighted passages from "A Puzzle of Rites: Discerning the True Nature of the Adena" by Dr. Tyler M. Booth

[...] began with the discovery of a former ceremonial site on the property of Jasper Goins, a tobacco farmer from East Bernstadt, Kentucky. Mr. Goins happened upon a sinkhole at the far end of his field while tilling in preparation for the planting season. The sinkhole, he discovered, was roughly the size of an inground swimming pool and no deeper than six feet. He would've filled in the pit himself except for one detail: the collapse had exposed skeletal remains along the north-facing wall [...]

[...] nine such bodies were pieced together, four male and five female, estimated to have been between the ages of six and ten when they met their demise. The remains exhibited signs of various trauma, ranging from notches in the bone (suggesting blunt force from cutting tools) to scratch and gnaw marks from either human or animal origin. Carbon dating on the remains placed their lifetime well within the period of known Adena habitation in the area. The mystery, then, revolves around the nature of the site itself. To date, no prior Adena burial sites have suggested human sacrifice or cannibalism. [...]

[...] However, the most compelling find within the Goins site concerns carvings etched in a stone marker found within the center of the pit itself. The stone stands approximately one foot tall and is roughly the size of a tree stump. Its surface is riddled with various notches and cavities, suggesting the stone was used as a rudimentary cutting board or sacrificial altar. Marking its rounded edges are etched symbols of unknown meaning, and on the western-facing side is a crude painting of a figure with blue eyes [...]

Definitely my guy. Will visit college next week. —Genie.

4

Notebook entry following Dr. Booth's essay—Date unknown

Met with Dr. Booth this morning. He was skeptical but didn't say no. With any luck, the idol is still there, and I can continue my research. I should hear from the professor within the month.

I hope so. He's handsome.

PART THREE

SEEDS OF BABYLON

Stauford – Landon, Kentucky
Present Day

CHAPTER TEN

1

J ack Tremly read until dawn, wading through the many notes and newspaper clippings stuffed inside the notebook's pages, until his eyelids hung heavy in the gray morning light. He felt drunk with knowledge, his mind tilted askew by the burden of weight his late grandmother set upon his shoulders, the room shifting in the haze of a hangover tinged with understanding and terror. The confusing puzzle in his grandmother's notebook set his spirit alight.

But despite the thoughts racing through his head, sleep found him.

Sleep always found him, and so did the things waiting in the dark.

2

The nightmare is always the same. He is well-acquainted with its twists and turns, the vividness of its depiction, the sensory effects hyperreal in the dream space.

Sunlight beaming through the passenger window of his grandmother's green Cadillac heats his arm to an uncomfortable degree, so much the skin reddens in the morning light. Summers in Stauford are always sweltering, a haven for flies and mosquitos, the trees drooping in depression. Outside, a forest passes them by in a swirling green haze, and the floor beneath his tiny feet rattle from gravel kicking and spitting up in the wheel well.

He can't remember his age but guesses he's somewhere between four and six years old. He's dressed in dark leather sandals, neatly pressed khakis, and a green checkered button-down. Without looking, he knows his hair is slicked back and parted to the side.

Mamaw Genie drives in silence, leading them along a forest path in the morning sun. Her hair is pristine, a silvery dome coiffed and immaculately sculpted into a perfect bouffant by the finest artists at Arlene's Beauty Shop. She wears her favorite earrings: a pair of dangling butterflies adorned with emerald jewels. A gift from her late husband, Jack remembers, although he can't recall his grandfather's face. He died in a car accident when Jack was a baby.

The nightmare shifts here, a rapid jump-cut to a different scene, one projector switched out for another. Mamaw Genie holds his hand and leads him into the forest. The path is overgrown with weeds and wildflowers. Stones older than time lay embedded in the earth, covered in patches of moss and etched with crude symbols.

Deeper into the forest, the world is a kaleidoscope of light and shadow, the sun filtering through the trees in a shadowbox display. Mamaw Genie leads him down a small slope into a gully overgrown with ferns and dandelions. A creek slices through the gully in an erratic line, its waters babbling over stones and under deadfalls. Birds chirp overhead, and the trees whisper about this pair of visitors wandering beneath their branches.

Jack stops at the wooden footbridge and tugs on his grandmother's hand. "Why do they call it Devil's Creek, Mamaw?"

This is the only detail of his nightmare that changes. Imogene Tremly turns to him, and sometimes she's smiling, sometimes she's laughing, sometimes she's crying. Sometimes, like this time, she doesn't have an expression, her lips a single thin line across her face.

"The waters split up ahead," she says, pointing out toward the forest, which now seems so dense it's like a thick green curtain draped over the world. "They split off like the Devil's pitchfork, so old timers called it Devil's Creek. But we both know there ain't no Devil. Ain't that right, honey?"

"No, ma'am."

They continue deeper into the forest, where a village of shacks is being constructed. Tools and supplies strewn about the foliage, hammers and saws and nails and beams of lumber and sheet metal, a town grown from the old stones of the earth beneath them. The village smells of rotted meat, and Jack understands why as they near the clearing. Animal carcasses hang from the limbs of trees at the foot of the clearing, odd sacrifices lifted to the sky in offering to gods Jack can't pronounce with his elementary tongue. Flies swarm around the rotting limbs in thick black clouds, and Jack's stomach churns as the stench hits him. He vomits a breakfast of milk and cereal all over his shoes, and Mamaw Genie scolds him for getting his clothes dirty on their way to church.

Another shift in scene, another projector reel swapped out, and they're at the summit of Calvary Hill. The Lord's Church of Holy Voices stands before them, and the lilting sound of the choir seeps through the old white beams. Mamaw Genie runs her fingers through Jack's hair until she is satisfied with how it looks. She takes his hand once more.

"Now," she says, "be quiet. We're late for the invocation."

She opens the door and leads him into the single room of the old church. The pews are shoved back against the perimeter walls, and motes of dust dance in the beams of morning light piercing through the windows. Straight ahead, the lectern lies on its side, and the upright piano sits against the wall, forever out of tune. The room is vacant except for the sounds of the humming choir rising from a hole in the floor.

Mamaw Genie leads Jack to the edge of the hole where they peer into the depths. There's a light down there, flickering orange flames fill the cavern with shadows, and Jack resists his grandmother's pull.

"We're late," she whispers, and releases his hand to descend the ladder before them. He watches her, helpless as she sinks into the shadows, and in a moment of terror, Jack considers fleeing for the door.

"Jackie," his grandmother whispers, "are you coming?"

His cheeks flush with shame. He doesn't want to let her down, doesn't want to earn her scorn, and descends into the dark.

The reel changes again, and they're in an open cavern far below the foundation of the church. Dome-like, insulated in the depths of Calvary Hill, the cavern walls are lined with cracked stone plates upon which are carved symbols that hurt Jack's eyes when he looks at them. A pillar of earth rises from one end, circled with steps carved from stone. The center of the cavern is lit with torches positioned around the perimeter, illuminating mounds of dust and bones. In the infinite wisdom of dream logic, Jack knows there are countless bones buried beneath their feet if they would only dig a little further, and he scrapes the heel of his foot in the dirt. A gray jawbone protrudes from the dirt, its baby teeth caked in dark soil and worms. *Hello*, it says, *won't you join me?*

Jack turns away, frightened by the sight, but he finds no respite here in the cavern. The members of his grandmother's church sit in the center, their bodies pressed closely to one another, swaying in time with their singing. White shrouds are draped over their faces, obscuring their eyes and noses, so Jack can only see their mouths. The song they sing is one he has never heard before, a hymn of the Old Ways written upon the walls, and their voices form a vacuous hum that drones on and on in his ears until he fears his head might pop. Mamaw Genie joins the circle, joins their mechanical swaying, and leaves him in the flickering shadows near the edge of the room.

His father stands outside the circle, beyond a stone altar etched with the same bizarre symbols. A low droning hum erupts from the figure as he lifts his hands to the dark, offering praise to something Jack cannot see but can feel. This unseen thing, this impossible something, it feels gigantic in his dream, a shapeless form that defies logic and wields its own gravity. A giant of dark matter, a self-contained void hanging above them all, lording over its congregation like the vastness of space. Jack can't bring himself to follow the direction of his father's praising hands.

Shaking, Jack taps his grandmother's shoulder. "Please," he whispers, "I'm scared. Can we please go?"

Imogene Tremly is annoyed, but her face softens when she sees the terror on his face. "Okay," she says.

The congregation sings and sways while their pastor reaches for the unseen, a sentient cosmos deep within the earth. Before they ascend the ladder, Jack looks back at his father, a faceless man he will never understand and never love, a figure of fear and mystery that will haunt him into adulthood. Jacob Masters turns away from the void and casts a darkening gaze upon them.

"Sister Tremly," he rasps, "where are you taking my son?"

The reels swap one final time, the scene shifting from the dark of the cavern below to the golden sun-filled church above. Jack stands at the threshold, peering down the path along the side of Calvary Hill. Behind him, Mamaw Genie waits at the edge of the hole. She is panicked and afraid, and she beckons to her grandson.

"Go," she tells him. "Run, Jackie. For God's sake, *run!*"

And Jackie does as she commands, sprinting from the doorway and into the failing sunlight. Time has ceased to have meaning, the rules broken in this terrible dreamscape, and in the moments they spent underground an entire day has passed them by. The sun is setting, clouds rolling by overhead, obscuring the light and bleeding the world of warmth.

Behind him, something is approaching. Something dark. Something wearing the face of his father and the skin of a man, with terrible blue eyes.

Something hidden. Something horribly old.

Jack runs as fast as his little legs will take him, but no matter how many times he dreams, no matter how far he pushes himself, he never outruns the thing lurking behind him. He never sees it, never gazes upon its vastness, only senses its size, a terrible dark wave seeping from the earth beneath the foundation of the old church. This impossibly formless thing, this unescapable void, it crashes over the threshold, spilling over everything in its wake, swallowing the world as it swallows minds and souls.

The void licks at his heels, and he cries out in horror. It sweeps over him. Jack screams—

3

"Mamaw!"

He woke himself with a jolt, kicking a blanket from the sofa and knocking over a lamp from the adjacent end table. Jack sat up, covered in sweat, his heart racing. Fragments of the dream reached for him from the far shadows of the room like disembodied hands, threatening to pull him back into the depths, but then his eyes focused on the sheet of sunlight filtering through the curtains.

Jack wiped sweat from his face and looked to the floor. His grandmother's diary lay open to the page with all the strange symbols. Most of them he'd never seen before, save for a few at the bottom of the page. Mamaw Genie had remarked near the bottom in her delicate scrawl: "Cleansing Runes." There were four of them, scribbled in red ink:

He studied them for a moment longer while the horrid dream seeped away from reality. For years he was haunted by the same dark vision, and no matter how often he was subjected to the phantasmagoric film, the effect was always the same: He awoke, terrified, grasping for safety from the unseen thing behind him. The terrors cost him sleep, cost him money with ongoing therapy bills, and cost him more relationships than he cared to admit. He'd told himself it was all a nightmare, the curse of an overactive imagination subjected to early childhood trauma and abuse.

Except it wasn't. His mind wandered to the stone idol, which he'd left inside the old roll-top desk upstairs. A chill crawled over him, stretching from his neck all the way to his feet. Jack glanced at the diary. Mamaw Genie could only speculate on its nature, even after dedicating years to researching its existence, but death found her before she could discern its secrets. The only truth she'd gleaned from her research was it should be kept as far away from its infernal altar as possible.

A dull thump reverberated in his skull, and he closed his eyes to stem the tide of discomfort crashing at the base of his forehead. His evening exploits had caught up to him, and he considered going back to sleep when he remembered he'd left his car downtown.

He reached for his phone and called Stephanie for a ride. She answered after the second ring.

"Yeah?"

He smirked. "That's how you answer the phone?"

"It is when I've had too much to drink," she croaked. "What's up?"

"Need a ride into town to pick up my car."

"The things I do for my favorite brother. Give me an hour."

"Thanks," he said, and was about to say goodbye when she hung up. An hour afforded him time to clean himself up, but before he stood, he reached down to collect his grandmother's notebook. He flipped back to the first page and Mamaw Genie's note. He read her words again for comfort, despite their grim warning:

My darling Jackie,

If you're reading this, I am gone, and Chuck has delivered the key to you per my wishes. I can't imagine how confused you must be, finding this among my things, but I hope to set things straight with you by the end of these pages. I began keeping this book many years ago, but I didn't do it for nostalgia like most grandmas might. I guess I didn't do a lot of things like most grandmas, but I tried to raise you right, and give you the best life I could considering all that happened.

Everything I've done here was to keep you safe, honey. Those people in Stauford are going to say nasty things about me when I'm gone, that I was a witch and a pagan, a devil worshiper from the old church, that I practiced black magic.

You and I both know which parts are true, but I never told you why. Let me do that now while I'm still breathing. I can only hope you won't put this down in anger, that you'll read through to the end and weigh my words in your heart.

Because this concerns you, Jackie. This concerns all your brothers and sisters. It's about what happened at Devil's Creek.

He frowned, flipping back to the end of the book. The last few pages were blank, the notes incomplete. One of the pages had been torn out.

"You did the best you could," he whispered, his eyes flooding with tears as he set the black notebook aside. A small beige business card fell from between the blank pages and landed on his lap. He squinted at the print: "Tyler M. Booth, Ph.D. – Department of Anthropology, Sue Bennett College."

He flipped the card over. His grandmother's notable scrawl filled the back side with an address and phone number.

"Huh," he mumbled, tucking the card back into the notebook. He remembered when Sue Bennett College shut down back in the 90s due to low attendance. Jack couldn't remember his grandmother ever having ties to the school or its faculty. Then again, he supposed, his childhood memories weren't what they used to be. He left the notebook on the end table, but as he went about showering and getting dressed, his idle thoughts returned to the blank pages and the business card tucked away between them.

4

Stephanie Green canceled her brother's call and buried her face in her pillow. The phone had disturbed her beauty rest, although there was nothing beautiful about it. Nightmares plagued her all night, but now their remains lay fractured and burned in the waking light. Each time she attempted to piece together what they once were, their ashes slipped through her fingers.

She was no stranger to nightmares, of course. Her therapist told her they were normal for victims of traumatic experiences, a category into which she fit neatly, comfortably, perhaps even happily. Jack probably fit as neatly into their shared niche, but while he'd embraced the trauma in his art, she doubted he did so with as much enthusiasm as she did. Still, it was great to see him last night, and while she fought the urge to mute her phone and return to the disturbing wasteland of her dreams, she considered inviting him to the studio for an interview.

The prospect was enticing enough to drag her from her near-comatose state. Stephanie opened her eyes and glared at the sunlight streaming through her bedroom window.

"Be gone," she mumbled, plodding down the hallway to the bathroom. "You're not wanted here, sunlight. Your presence offends me."

After relieving herself, Stephanie stared at her brother's painting hanging above the toilet. She found she couldn't stare at it for long. The grotesque image of faceless men and women surrounding the children in the water recalled too many dark memories, shadowy things tiptoeing on the line between dream and reality, tinged with just enough detail that made her question their nature.

Instead, Stephanie considered the source of the macabre piece. Seeing Jack last night was a welcome surprise, something she'd not thought would happen again. They'd not spoken since college, and even then, their conversations were in passing, the two of them too busy with their own lives to acknowledge the other. Years later, Stephanie grew to accept their limited interaction had more to do with the pain of their shared past. Chuck kept in touch, primarily through Imogene, and later discussions with Stephanie revealed a sort of survivor's guilt rooted in the heart of Jack's decision to leave town. Jack's mother was the only one of their mothers to survive, although without her sanity intact, and while he'd never said as much, Stephanie long suspected he blamed himself for their mutual predicament.

Staring at the grim painting before her, Stephanie decided she'd ask him for an interview. Not only would it be good for the station, it would be good for her to better understand him. Knowing how far apart they'd drifted over the years made her heart hurt. She'd bridge that chasm between them somehow, and if she knew anything about artists, the best way to get them to talk was by bringing up their art.

There were two voicemails waiting for her when she got out of the shower. The first was a morning update from Cindy, wrapping up her shift at the station. The second was from Chuck: "Stephanie, I'm headed over to Bobby's. Something happened last night. Call me when you wake up."

Stephanie hesitated, her thumb hovering over the "call back" option on the screen. The last time Bobby Tate had a crisis, it was because he'd found "Satanic paraphernalia" in Riley's bedroom. Said paraphernalia turned out to be a Slayer album, loaned to him by a friend at school, and a collection of stories by H.P. Lovecraft he'd checked out from the school library.

She returned to that day in Bobby's house, when she'd witnessed him losing his mind over such insignificant things, and she questioned if today's crisis was something similar. Maybe he'd found porn on Riley's computer, or worse, a collection of albums by Ghost or Marilyn Manson. Maybe—and she hoped this was the case—his son had finally renounced the faith of his father, having grown tired of the oppressive Christian regime which Bobby lorded over with an iron fist.

Oh, if only. She wanted to be present for the fallout if that's what happened—but she doubted it. The truth was Stephanie would be there for her brother regardless of the nature of his crisis, because she still cared about him despite their differences, despite the fact his congregation was out to murder her business, and despite that he was subconsciously pushing his son away.

Something her grandmother Maggie once told her flitted through her mind with the lithe wings of a butterfly. *Family's family. You can't change that, Steph. When everything's breakin' down, who else can you turn to but family?*

Stephanie dressed and texted Jack. She'd already made up her mind to go check on Bobby by the time she reached the front door.

5

Saturday was a cloudy one for Stauford, the sky painted in wide swathes of graying clouds stretching over the town, sealing in a late summer humidity that would not relent. Stephanie drove with her AC cranked as high as it would go, but even with the cool air blasting her face, sweat still dotted her forehead.

She escaped the early Saturday traffic by turning at the corner of Main Street and Kidd Avenue, passing under the railroad tracks. She knew these byways well, having learned to drive in the neighborhood beyond Stauford's football field and recreational center, and when she crossed the bridge over Layne Camp Creek, a memory of grandma Maggie playing backseat driver crept into her mind. *"Brake, for God's sake, Stephanie! You're going to kill us both!"*

Stephanie had braked, but not before hitting the gas pedal at the wrong time, shooting her grandmother's old Ford over the curb and toward the hill overlooking the creek. The look on Maggie Green's face when they finally came to a halt was something she'd never forgotten: the utter terror, the surprise, the humor of it all. Those were better days, and when she crossed the bridge, Stephanie felt a hint of sadness wash over her, complemented by the dull sky above.

Kidd Avenue forked at Granger and Harmon Streets, and Stephanie took a right onto Granger, driving through their old neighborhood. Maggie Green's house was fourth on the left, an old brick two-story in which Stephanie spent most of her youth after the incident at Devil's Creek. She slowed as she drove by, pleased to see the current owners were taking care of the place. Even the tire swing was still there, suspended from the great arm of the old oak standing in the front yard beside the driveway.

Seeing the old place took her back to lazy summers when Jack and Chuck biked to her house to plan a day of misadventures. Her house was the midway point between them, with Chuck all the way on the other side of the creek. Susan, Bobby, and Zeke were scattered across opposite parts of town, beyond Moore Hill and Gordon Hill, respectively. Bobby joined them a few times, even Zeke for that matter, but never Susan. She'd always kept to herself, but even more so as they grew older. Zeke's visits stopped when he moved in with Susan and her grandfather, and Bobby's stopped when he found Jesus.

Their differences and absences aside, Stephanie had fond memories of traveling the roads of Stauford with her brothers, splashing across the shallows of Layne Camp Creek on warmer days, fishing in the deeper parts, and catching the wind to cool off as they rode their bikes down the inclines of Gordon Hill. Those days lasted forever in her memory, like warm impressionist paintings where the sun is always setting, the sky on the cusp of fading from orange to purple, and the fireflies indistinguishable from the stars. They'd made an unspoken pact to stick together in those forgotten afternoons, taking care of each other even when the rest of the world was against them.

Somehow, in the wisdom of their youth, they'd decided to make the most of what life dealt them. Somehow, in the years since, they'd lost sight of that decision, and some more than others.

She sighed. Those were better days, indeed.

When she reached the end of the block, Stephanie took a left onto Brennen Road and continued up the hill toward Standard Avenue; there, when she looked to turn right, she saw the weathervane atop the Tremly house. When she was a kid, she'd pretend the old Victorian was like a castle, filled with secret corridors and books of magic. Jack's grandmother Imogene was like a sorceress to her, the black eyepatch a strange badge of honor. She didn't learn about all the rumors until she was a teenager, and by then she and Jack had drifted apart, their adventures more infrequent, given away in favor of newer friends with lighter pasts.

All those rumors, she thought. *Old lady Tremly's a witch, she eats children and bathes in the blood of virgins, and she worships the devil beneath the light of a full moon.* She rolled her eyes. Such stories were ridiculous, and yet…she wondered if there wasn't some truth to them. The rumors had to start somewhere, and she hoped to reconcile those stories with Jack this evening, if he'd let her. She and Chuck had a tacit agreement not to discuss what happened all those years ago, but Jack was a different story.

She turned off Standard Avenue and up the driveway toward the Tremly place. Jack sat on the edge of the porch, a sketchbook in his lap. He was sketching one of the trees in the front yard.

Stephanie slowed to a stop and lowered her window. "How much for the drawing?"

Jack Tremly closed the sketchbook and tucked it into his messenger bag. "Twelve grand." He smiled. "For thirteen, I'll even sign it."

"Deal," she said, unlocking the door. He climbed in beside her and buckled up. "I guess you do that often?"

"What, sketch?"

She nodded, turning the car around in the driveway. "Yeah, I mean, isn't it like riding a bike? Once you know how to do it…"

"Nah, it's not like that," Jack said. "You always have to practice, like playing a piano. You have to warm up, keep your fingers limber, and remind them how to draw the right shapes."

"Is that how you did *Midnight Baptism*?"

He crossed his arms and blushed. "Is this an interview?"

"It could be," she grinned.

Stephanie made her pitch as they turned out of the driveway and drove back to town.

Across the street, Ruth McCormick sat in her window, watching them leave. Reddish-purple bags clung to her eyes, tears slipping down her cheeks. She fervently scribbled across the ruled lines of her notebook, taking dictation from a voice only she could hear, filling the pages with the truth of the world before the coming of man and the gods he made.

6

Jack closed the passenger door and leaned down into the open window. "See you tonight," he said. "Do I need to bring anything?"

Stephanie shook her head. "It's radio. Just bring your voice."

"You got it. Thanks for the ride."

He watched her speed away before unlocking his car. Inside, he retrieved his grandmother's notebook from his messenger bag. He'd considered telling Stephanie about last night's discovery but thought better of it. For all he knew, there wasn't anything to his grandmother's research, but he had to know for sure before telling her.

Jack started the car and entered Mr. Booth's address into the dashboard GPS. The GPS plotted a route along old Highway 25 on the way north to Landon. He wasn't as familiar with the town of Landon, even though his mother was born there. Today, he realized, would be a day of knowledge in more ways than he thought.

He hoped Mr. Booth would be a willing teacher.

Seconds later, Jack put on his turn signal, waited for a break in the Saturday morning traffic, and went on his way toward US 25.

7

Across town, while Jack sat in traffic at the junction of Main Street and Highway 25, Chuck Tiptree checked his phone for messages. This wasn't how he wanted to spend his Saturday morning, listening to Bobby Tate tiptoe between rage and whining, but here he was. It's not that he didn't want to be there for his brother, but so far Bobby had spent more time losing his mind over Riley sneaking out with a girl than the concern of legal action for Riley's assault on Ronny Cord's son yesterday.

Chuck supposed this was the real reason he took Bobby's call so early in the morning, knowing the good reverend would focus on the wrong concerns and worry himself into an early grave. As he sat in the den of Bobby Tate's home, sunken into the cushy folds of his brother's armchair, Bobby ranted on about the hellfire and brimstone that had befallen his family since his wife's untimely demise. Chuck decided he knew his brother better than he cared to admit.

"Where did I go wrong?" Bobby wondered aloud, a rhetorical question which Chuck restrained himself from answering. *You had kids*, Chuck thought. In all his years and many, many relationships throughout, Charles Tiptree had one rule: No kids. There was cursed blood in his veins. The last thing he wanted to do was pass it on, siring another generation of their father's lineage. No, Chuck Tiptree decided years ago his particular branch of the Masters family tree would wither, snap, and fall into the forgotten void of history.

That's not to say he disliked Riley. He adored the kid, especially when he defied his father—"It's good for both of them," he'd once told Stephanie, before erupting in a fit of laughter—but Riley fell into a slim, acceptable category of "Someone Else's Problem." Chuck loved his nephew, loved spoiling him, but at the end of the day, Riley went home. He didn't stick around Chuck's place, didn't raid his refrigerator, and didn't whine about his teenage problems. No, Chuck didn't need that kind of complication in his life. Watching his brother go through the motions over Riley's recent trespasses clinched that for him, and he quietly wondered if the boy's issues had something to do with their bloodline.

Put the idea out of your head, he told himself. *All Riley's done wrong is be a teenager in a broken home.*

"Talking to him is like talking to a brick wall," Bobby said, standing at the fireplace mantle and staring at a picture of Janet in happier times. "I feel like the lord is testing me, Chuck. It's one thing after another with this kid."

"Bobby," Chuck offered, "I think you need to take a minute and breathe, okay? Sit down and take a time-out. Let's talk about this carefully, rationally."

Bobby Tate turned away from the photo and wandered reluctantly across the room. Chuck thought he looked like a lost child, still seven years old and taking panicked breaths down in the suffocating darkness. In some ways, Chuck thought it made sense Bobby had rediscovered religion in his teenage years. The poor guy needed some kind of coping mechanism to help him get through the drudgery of everyday life. He was wound up so tight a mouse fart might give him a heart attack.

Bobby sat on the sofa and slouched in defeat. "Okay, Chuck. Okay." He took a breath and exhaled. Chuck noticed Bobby's hands were shaking.

"Are you still on your meds?"

"No," Bobby said absently, clasping his hands on his knees. He averted his gaze from Chuck, suddenly preoccupied with the patterns on the sofa. "Not for a few months now. They gave me nightmares, and…well, you know."

Chuck nodded. He *did* know. All six of them suffered from nightmares and terrors after the incident at the church, and by his count, they'd all undergone some form of therapy in their tween years to help them cope. Their grandparents pooled their resources to hire the therapist, Dr. Benjamin Mosier, a frumpy sort of fellow with thick glasses. Dr. Mosier's therapy involved urging them to find a vocation, something through which they could channel their fear and anxiety, and for most of them, the therapy worked.

Had religion truly helped Bobby find peace? Chuck liked to think so, although ever since Janet died, the church seemed more like a burden than anything else. The man who sat before him didn't look rested or at peace; in fact, he looked manically depressed, a slipshod effigy of a man held together by prayers, anger, and minimal sleep.

Chuck cleared his throat. "Are you, uh, sure kicking the meds is wise, Bobby? I mean, after Janet passed on…"

Bobby waved him off. "They helped for a time, but they dulled my focus. I felt distanced from reality, if that makes sense. Like the world was covered in cotton, soft at the edges. Like I was a ghost."

"All I'm saying is maybe they would help clear your head."

"Yeah, I got it." Bobby shrugged. "But that's not why you're here. I need a lawyer, Chuck, not a doctor."

Chuck nodded. "So you do." He leaned back in the chair and rubbed his hand against the grit of stubble on his cheek. "You know this isn't the sort of law I practice, Bob, but I can refer you to a friend who does.

You know Craig Paige? Just opened his practice over on Kentucky Street. Me and Craig go way back. I can give him a call this afternoon, even. He'll be happy to help you with Ronny Cord."

"What about Don Matthews?" Bobby seemed incredulous, stunned Chuck would skip over such an urgent matter. "Shouldn't we be more concerned with what Riley and Don's daughter were up to in the woods last night? While those two boys were kidnapped?"

Chuck sighed and shook his head. "Bobby," he said, measuring his words, trying to keep his heart rate at a reasonable pace. "We'll get there. Do you know for certain what Riley and Rachel did? Did Riley tell you?"

His brother fell silent, wringing his hands the way Chuck's grandma used to when she was worrying over something. Bobby suddenly looked very old to him, worn down and aged like a fallen log in the forest, its bark brittle and flaking at the edges. "No," Bobby said finally. "No, I didn't ask him. Not that he would tell me, anyway."

"Uh huh." Chuck nodded. "So, you're working from the basis of assumption, is that right?"

Bobby nodded again, his gaze turned down like a scolded puppy.

"In that case it's an equal assumption to say Riley and Rachel Matthews didn't do anything wrong." Bobby opened his mouth to speak, but Chuck held up his hand to silence him. "The truth is, Bob, we don't know, do we? So, it's like I said—we'll get there. In the meantime, let's deal with what we *do* know, okay?"

"Okay," Bobby whispered, and Chuck almost smiled at the sound of defeat in his brother's voice. Good ol' Bobby, always so quick to jump to conclusions. They were the land mines in the hopscotch game to Hell, as his grandfather Gage used to say.

"Great," Chuck went on. "Now we've got that settled, let's talk about what Ronny Cord said."

8

"So I said to that holy-rollin' fuckstick, I says, 'I'm gonna sue the shit out of your righteous ass.' And you know what he said to me, Tony? 'There ain't no cause for that language, sir.' Can you believe that shit?"

Ronny Cord barked into his phone between sips of a lukewarm Miller High Life while his son, Jimmy, listened from his bedroom. Jimmy's old man laughed like a hyena when he was drunk, and this morning was no exception. Every wet, phlegmy chuckle rose an octave higher than Jimmy could stand, lifting the dull ache pulsing in his skull to new heights.

His old man's morning call with Tony Burgess was something of a ritual in the Cord household, or at least it was for as long as Jimmy could remember. Ronny Cord worked third shift for the railroad, sweeping the floors of the offices down at the train depot on the south side of town. Tony worked across town for A&Z construction. He and Ronny were old high school buddies, way back when Stauford football mattered in the local scheme, and they'd kept in touch in the years after graduation.

Jimmy once joked his old man and Tony were secretly gay for each other, a quip that earned him a smack across the mouth. Ronny hadn't said anything to his son about it, letting the sting of his backhand speak for him, and Jimmy never said a word about it again.

When he'd heard enough of his father's raucous retelling—"And then I said, 'I'll shove that Bible so far up your ass, preacher, you'll be shittin' proverbs for a week.' I'll tell ya Tony, he didn't care for that none, no sir."—Jimmy crawled out of bed, wincing as he moved, and went to close his bedroom door. Before he did so, however, he heard his father mention something about a couple of kids going missing last night.

"Yeah, I heard somethin' about that on the morning news. Nah, just a couple losers, no one my boy would pal 'round with. Don't surprise me none. You ask me, I'd say the preacher's kid did it. I mean, shit, look what he did to Jimmy yesterday!"

Jimmy closed his door. He couldn't listen anymore. Brilliantly sharp sheets of blinding pain sliced through his skull as he crossed the room and sweat beaded on his forehead by the time he returned to his bed. A prescription bottle of codeine-laced Tylenol sat on his nightstand, and he indulged himself, tapping three tablets into the palm of his hand. He washed them down with a glass of water, wiped his mouth, and slowly, carefully, Jimmy leaned the back of his head against the wall.

This fucking sucks, he thought. He'd played football all through middle school and into his high school years, graduating to the varsity team when he was still in eighth grade, and he'd never broken a bone before. Even with that extra year he gained when he failed his freshman year of high school, Jimmy Cord never so much as sprained a toe on the field.

Everything changed yesterday when that little shit, that emo-goth fag Riley Tate, introduced Jimmy's face to the back side of a lunch tray. Thinking about it sent a spike of pain shooting through the bridge of his nose. Jimmy hadn't done anything to provoke him—hell, they didn't even have cause to cross paths with one another. Riley was one of those creepy psycho kids who looked like one bad day might make him snap and go all Columbine on the school.

Jimmy wasn't afraid of that five-foot-nothin' queer, but he'd no reason to bully the punk. Riley stayed out of his way, stayed out of everyone's way, so when Jimmy set his sights on Ben Taswell over something he'd heard in homeroom that morning, he didn't think he'd face any sort of opposition.

Jimmy Cord's head swam, his mouth filled with a metallic taste, and he closed his eyes as dull colors erupted across a wide expanse of encroaching darkness.

What was it Ben Taswell said about him? Or, rather, what was it Carla Reed said Ben said about him? He couldn't remember now, the last 24 hours a pained blur of suffering and medication. All he remembered now was Riley Tate caused him to miss the game last night, a game which he'd been looking forward to for weeks—not for the macho glory he'd bask in afterward, but for the promise his girlfriend, Amber Rogers, made to him the prior week.

He thought of her now, of the tight round bubble of her ass stretching out a pair of gray yoga pants she knew drove him crazy. She'd met him after practice last week, her hair pulled back in a dirty blonde ponytail, her skin salty with sweat from her dance team try-outs.

"Are we going out after the game?" he'd asked her, and she'd smiled wryly, her baby blue eyes shimmering in the failing afternoon sunlight.

"Oh, maybe we can," she'd said, tracing a finger along the ridge of his jawline. "Maybe just the two us?"

He'd nodded, stuffing his equipment into his gym bag. Most of the other guys had left the locker room. They were alone, and he wondered now why he hadn't made a move then.

"Maybe," she whispered, leaning in close to his ear, "maybe I'll even suck your dick."

He stiffened at the thought of her now. Why, oh why, hadn't he made a move then? She'd never blown him before—in truth, he'd never experienced that delightful act, but God, he'd heard stories from the other guys on the team, the juniors and seniors who'd regaled their younger teammates on the bus rides home from away games with stories of their many sexual conquests.

The thought of her on her knees, her blonde head bobbing up and down on his dick, took his mind off the pain in his face. But the sensation didn't last.

A surge of anger rushed through him, reddening his vision, and he ground his teeth to hold back the tide, clenching his fists so tight they shook. Riley Tate, that Goth fuck, if only he'd left him alone, Jimmy would've won the game for them last night. He would've driven off with Amber to some shady spot outside of town, and there he would've received a celebratory blowjob. Christ, his balls ached just thinking about it.

"You fucking bastard," Jimmy mumbled, the codeine painkillers beginning to take hold. He closed his eyes once more, imagining what he'd do to Riley Tate once he got his hands on him. Break his arm, maybe. No, break his nose, and then his arm. Maybe he'd pull off those shiny black fingernails first.

Ah, the possibilities. Jimmy Cord had plenty of time to plan his revenge. As he drifted off into a drug-induced sleep, Jimmy's erection returned, and for entirely different reasons.

9

Riley sat on the edge of his bed, listening to the muffled voices of his father and his uncle Chuck. He knew they were talking about him. The ebb and flow of pitch in his father's voice pretty much confirmed his suspicions.

Instead, Riley occupied himself with his phone, scrolling through the list of text messages on the screen. The last message he'd received from Ben was from yesterday, telling Riley he and Daniel were on their way. Riley stared at the message for a full minute, debating on whether to send a reply or not, before setting the phone aside and burying his face in his hands. The sobs came quickly, filling his soul with a kind of sadness he'd not experienced since his mother died.

If only you'd been there, a voice whispered. He knew that voice well, a soft and confident voice speaking over his shoulder, right into his ear. *If you'd been there, you might've kept him from going out into the night. Maybe you could've even stopped whoever took him. Maybe if you weren't so concerned about yourself for once, Ben would still be here. You'd still be in the forest, on a hike toward Laurel Lake, happily skipping along a beaten trail through the brush, stealing glances at Rachel Matthews.*

His gut lurched, and he sucked in his breath to hold back the sobs. Memories of the night played back in slow motion: Leaving the tent, wandering through the dark, finding Rachel waiting for him on a fallen log, her face aglow in the moonlight. They'd held hands and talked, mostly about nothing, but sometimes about the spark of "something" between them which neither wanted to name. A feeling inside, like having the ground pulled out from beneath them and gravity working its magic on their guts. Maybe it was a crush, maybe it was nothing at all. Riley wasn't sure, and neither was Rachel, but they both agreed something was there, even if it was nothing. A friendship, maybe, or possibly more. The inconsistent nature of it terrified them and excited them, and in the twilit hours, as the moon charted its lazy path overhead, Riley leaned forward to kiss her.

Thinking about it now, Riley felt foolish—no, he felt utterly stupid for doing it. He wasn't even sure why he did it. Hadn't they agreed they weren't sure what "it" was between them? Well, sure, but there was that instinctual tickle in his belly, a flush of heat in his cheeks, and the racing gallop of his heart telling him to go for it, kiss her, the time is right.

Only it wasn't right. He'd kissed her on the lips, she'd pulled back in shock, and the look on her face wasn't quite one of revulsion, but of betrayal. Her expression made him feel disgusting and ashamed, and he'd tried to stammer an apology when a soft cry erupted from the darkness.

The rest of the night played out in shattered fragments: Rachel and Riley racing back to camp, finding Ben's tent empty, spotting two figures silhouetted in the moonlight. One carried a body slung over its shoulder, the other dragging something behind it. And the eyes. God, the eyes. A shiver ripped through Riley's body, and his arms erupted in gooseflesh.

The second figure, dragging what he could only imagine was either Ben or Toby, looked at him with blue eyes. Terribly blue shimmering eyes piercing the night like two cold headlights. Riley froze, his mind struggling to make sense of what he witnessed. He'd later asked Rachel if she'd seen them, but she'd shaken her head. Had the sight not terrified Riley so much, he might've withheld that detail when he was questioned by the cops, but when asked what he remembered, those eyes were the first thing that came to mind.

Riley's cheeks flushed with embarrassment. One night in the woods had reduced him to a terrified child, his imagination gone wild with impossible fantasies of teenage love and boogeymen in the woods.

And now, his best friend Ben was missing. His only friend, really. He didn't know Toby all that well, but the boy's absence stung just as much. Yet another boy lost on account of Riley's recklessness.

As for Rachel, well, he'd probably crossed the line. He could say goodbye to whatever "it" was between them. Even if she'd reacted differently, even if she'd kissed him back, Riley's father would've put a stop to any sort of relationship. It was bad enough Bobby Tate thought his son snuck out to have pre-marital sex, but the look of disappointment on the man's face, the pure disdain he projected toward his son when he picked him up at the campground earlier that morning, made the bile churn in Riley's gut.

"I thought I raised you better," Bobby said, and Riley sat in silence during the long car ride home. Riley leaned back on his bed, plugged his ears with earbuds, and shut his eyes, replaying all the things he wanted to say to his father but didn't have the energy to do so.

Nirvana's plucky acoustic cover of "Lake of Fire" filled his head as exhaustion finally found him. He slept dreamlessly, restfully, until a knock on his door roused him from the dark. Riley opened his bleary eyes and found his aunt Stephanie standing in the doorway. She smiled and crossed the room, taking a seat beside him. Riley pulled the earbuds from his ears. Stephanie took one and put it in her ear.

"This is a great album," she said. "I prefer the Alice in Chains acoustic set, though. Have you heard that one?"

Riley shook his head.

"We'll have to fix that," Stephanie said, removing the earbud. She lifted his phone and paused the music. A long sigh escaped her lips, and Riley saw she was working her way toward something. "Your dad told me what happened." She smirked. "Well, *his* side of what happened. I'd like to hear more about it from you, though. How're you holding up, kiddo?"

He turned away from her, rolling to face his pillows and a framed photo of his mother on the nightstand. "I really don't want to talk about it right now."

"Fair enough," she said. "I hope you know I'll be here when you do. If you want me to be."

Riley looked back and nodded. "I know, Steph. Thank you. I think, right now, I just want to sleep. Can I call you later?"

"Of course you can," she said, and leaned over to plant a kiss on his forehead. "I'll be at the station this evening, but you're welcome to join me if you want."

He smiled. "That would be awesome."

"Cool," she said, rising to her feet. She walked to the corner of his room where his desk stood. An assortment of posters clung to the wall—mostly bands like Ghost, Opeth, Tool, even one for Black Sabbath—but what caught her eye was one of Riley's prized possessions: a print of his uncle Jack's *Midnight Baptism*.

"Did you know Jack is in town?"

Riley perked up. "He is? Seriously?"

Aunt Stephanie nodded. "Got in yesterday. I'm interviewing him at the station tonight."

"No shit," he whispered.

"No shit." Stephanie grinned. "So, what do you say I swing by here later, we go grab a bite to eat, and then you can meet your famous uncle?"

"I'd love that, but…" Riley's face fell, remembering the deep shit he was in with his father. "I'm not sure Dad will go for it. He's kind of pissed."

Stephanie ruffled his hair. "Let me take care of that. He may seem scary to you, but I grew up with the guy. Trust me, he's a pushover."

"Thanks, Steph."

"Any time, kiddo. I'll see you tonight."

Stephanie left the room. Riley grinned, and for the first time in weeks, the weight on his heart lifted. Stephanie always treated him kindly, recognizing he wasn't like his dad and nurturing his darker interests. Most of the music he listened to was because of her, and even his interest in his uncle Jack's art—a man he'd never met, and probably wouldn't have known existed had it not been for his aunt—sprang from listening to Stephanie talk about it in passing.

Riley wasn't sure what it was about Jack's art he found appealing, whether it was the dark subject matter or the vivid portrayal of such horrible twilit creatures, but despite its macabre nature, he found himself drawn to it. The first time he saw *Midnight Baptism*, he knew he had to have a print of it, his father's protests be damned. His mom was still alive then, and she'd ordered the print for him without his father's knowledge. The dark scene hung on his wall for months before Bobby Tate noticed, but by then, Janet Tate had fallen ill and there were more pressing things to stress about.

He closed his eyes and pushed those troubling memories out of his mind. After a few moments, sleep found him again, but this time there were other things waiting for him in the dark. Their sharp teeth glowed in the impossible light of an unseen moon above, and somewhere in the shadows, his best friend Ben was screaming.

10

Ben Taswell *was* screaming, but no one heard him—no one who cared, anyway. He was in a musty cave of some kind, with a thin curtain of morning light piercing the center of the dark. A rickety ladder descended from the ceiling to a pillar near the edge of the shadows. The ground beneath him was dirt and something fine, like sand, but when he ran his fingers through it, he discovered there were bits of stone in the mix.

And the smell—God, the smell was awful. A wet and moldy stench of rot, like the time he'd forgotten to empty the grass clippings from his dad's lawnmower. The smell was pungent enough to make him retch on the spot, and now, as he lay sprawled on the dusty floor of this cavern, he felt his stomach churning once again.

Don't, he told himself, but the cramps in his stomach were terrible pinching things, like fists clenching his insides. Colors swam before him, and a low droning bell sounded in his ears as the churning intensified, working its way up from his guts and into his throat. Ben was struck with terror as he realized the moldy stench of the cavern was inside him. He tasted it, the fetid offal of time and the earth, decaying in his mouth, his throat, his guts.

Ben cried out into the dark, but his voice was silenced by his gag reflex, and he tried to choke back the awful sludge seeping up from his throat. Panic seized him when he realized the phlegm was creeping out his nose as well. He wiped his nose on the back of his hand and saw a thick streak of black sludge smeared across his skin. It was moving, writhing with startled life like worms driven to the surface by the pattering of rain.

"Oh God," he cried, wiping his hand in the dirt, trying to clean himself of this awful thing.

"God," a raspy voice said, "is not here, child. But I am, and I can take your pain away."

Panicking, Ben clamored to his feet, but a ripping agony tore through his insides. He doubled over and fell hard to his knees. Thick ropes of the black sludge dribbled from his lips and pooled on the ground beneath him. Shaking, his eyes alight with bursts of shimmering color, Ben looked up toward the halo of light above. There was a man peering down, his face draped in shadow, his blue piercing the dark.

"H-Help me," Ben pleaded, but the figure turned away.

"I can help you, child."

The raspy voice was closer, and Ben turned toward the shadows surrounding him. At first, he saw only the dark, his eyes blinded by the sunlight from above. Shapes swirled before him, phantoms conjured from the fear gripping his mind. He tried to move, but his muscles cried out in agony, the pinch in his stomach closing a little more.

Footsteps now. Steady footfalls, crunching over the shards of stone in the sediment.

"My god is a living god, child, and through me, he speaks. The way to salvation is through suffering. Anything else is a lie. Your little head has been filled with these lies since birth, child. These walls around us show a simpler way, a way of truth. These Old Ways were written long before the God of lies took root in this world."

Jacob Masters emerged from the shadows and took Ben's face in his hands. The colors swimming before the boy's eyes cleared, and for a single moment, he saw with total clarity the monstrous face before him.

Shimmering eyes illuminated the cracked visage of a dead man, his flesh a moistened mess of rot and age. Tendrils of the black sludge sought the air from holes in his face, and just before Ben's mind finally cracked from the weight of this impossible horror before him, the boy glimpsed his friend Toby approach from beyond.

"It's his will," Toby said. "His will and the Old Ways are one."

A wrenching pain tore through Ben's chest, forcing a wheezing cry from his throat. *It's got me*, he thought. *The boogeyman's got me. I'm sorry, Daniel. I'm sorry, Mom and Dad. I'm s—*

Jacob Masters placed his palm over Ben's face and squeezed. "Suffering is the way to salvation, my child. You are not quite there yet."

CHAPTER ELEVEN

1

Jack slowed alongside a large wooden mailbox with "BOOTH" printed on its side in dingy white letters. He parked behind a beat-up red minivan in the driveway. The van's back bumper was blemished with rust and dented at both ends. A slender crack stretched across the left corner of the back windshield, accented by a religious decal along the lower edge of the glass. "He is Risen!" it read.

Jack sighed, and for the first time since leaving Stauford, he questioned what he was doing here. His grandmother must've had this person's business card for a reason, but why? Did Mamaw Genie have a secret passion for anthropology?

The only person left who could answer that question was Dr. Booth himself, but Jack's doubts almost got the best of him then when he spotted the sticker in the van's window. He knew the sort of people who sported slogans like this one. He'd been haunted by them his whole life. His grandmother lost her eye trying to save him from people like that, an act which earned her the derision of an entire town, harassment in the form of men wearing white sheets, men who came in the middle of the night to set fire to her yard. They were the sort of men who hid behind their religious convictions, spouting scripture that suited their views. They were men who believed they were doing their lord's work.

Those cowards had sons and daughters who ridiculed Jack and his siblings, and in some ways, the wounds from their jabs and insults never healed. Not for Jack, anyway. He looked at his reflection in the rearview mirror, replaying all those nasty things they'd called him in school. Even the teachers regarded them with caution and contempt. They were living reminders of Stauford's dirty secret.

He realized he was white-knuckling the steering wheel. *They called us the Stauford Six. The cursed Devil's Creek kids.*

Wasn't the constant ridicule and stigma the reason Mamaw Genie told him to leave and not look back? *"This place ain't for you,"* she'd said. *"When you finish school, don't come back to Stauford, honey. You and me, we both know there ain't nothin' left for you here, Jackie. Your whole life you've been hurt by this place. It's time you go heal now."*

"But what about you, Mamaw?"

"I'll be fine, darlin'. My work here isn't done yet, Jackie."

He remembered trying to ask her what she meant, but she'd changed the subject, asking him to go get her a glass of iced tea.

He'd grown up hearing his grandmother was a witch, a devil worshiper, an enemy of God. Their ridicule never made sense to him— Mamaw Genie was one of the kindest people he ever knew—but looking back, he wondered if there was a shred of truth to those awful remarks. He thought of the cryptic symbols in his grandmother's notes, the glowing idol in her desk. *Hell*, he thought, *maybe they were right.*

"Only one way to find out," he sighed. He gathered his things, climbed out of the car, and walked toward the front door. Along the way, he noticed small figurines positioned in the adjacent flowerbeds. They weren't lawn gnomes, as was typical in most suburban neighborhoods. These were wooden, crudely carved animal figures with rudimentary features. Jack was about to kneel and get a closer look when someone said, "They're protective totems. Made them myself."

Jack looked up with a start. A stocky old man with thick-rimmed spectacles stood in the doorway, his thinning white hair slicked back over a patch of bald skin. He crossed his arms.

"Help you with somethin', son?"

"As a matter of fact, yes. At least, I hope so. Are you Dr. Booth?"

"Who's askin'? You a salesman?"

Jack extended his hand. "No, not a salesman. I'm Jack Tremly. I think you knew my grandmother. Or maybe she knew you, at least." He gave the old business card to the professor.

Dr. Booth took the card and examined it. "I haven't seen one of these in a long time. My teachin' days closed up with the college, and…" He locked eyes with Jack. "Yes, son, I knew your grandmother. Briefly, anyway. I'm guessin' by the look in your eye that you're taking up her quest."

"Her quest?"

The old professor pursed his lips and frowned. "Right, then. Come on in, son. I'll put on some coffee, and then we'll talk."

2

Ozzie Bell sat behind the wheel of his cruiser, watching Officer Gray speak with a pair of park rangers while another squadron of officers combed the campsite. They'd let the kids go a few hours beforehand, but not before he'd taken his turn grilling the Tate boy over the disappearance of his tent mate. Ozzie knew all about the kid, knew he was already in hot water with Ronny Cord's son, and he'd taken pleasure in watching the young punk squirm. What was it the kid said? One of the suspects had glowing eyes?

Sure, he could buy Riley's story about sneaking out with the Matthews girl, but he couldn't buy the glowing eyes bit. Maybe one of the suspects had glasses. Maybe the light was reflecting off the lenses.

"Bullshit," Ozzie muttered, drumming his fingers along the steering wheel. A few droplets of rain pattered against the windshield, and he craned his neck to look up at the gray blanket of clouds rolling overhead. His men had ground to cover today, and the last thing he wanted to hear was bitching and moaning about having to walk in the rain. Never mind the matter of tracks being swept away in a downpour.

And there *were* tracks. He watched Officer Danton photograph what they'd found in the grass leading toward the tree line: two sets of footprints, one deeper than the other, with a trailing pair of trenches scraped into the ground. Chief Bell recalled the boy's statement. One man carried someone over his shoulder. The other looked like he was dragging something. Logic dictated those trenches probably belonged to a pair of heels. Whether it was the Taswell boy or the Gilpin boy didn't matter; what mattered to Ozzie Bell was where those tracks were headed.

There were miles of forest in that direction. Hundreds of thousands of acres, as a matter of fact, if what he'd heard from one of the rangers was correct. A whole lot of nothing but mosquitos, deer flies, and undergrowth between here and the Cumberland River.

His phone buzzed with a text message alert. He glanced at it, saw the message was from Susan, and put the phone back on the console. He was on to something then. Something sharp, sticking out of his brain, exposed enough to stumble over, and—

Susan sent another message. Ozzie paused, clicking his tongue. Devil's Creek Road wasn't too far from here. Maybe a few miles in the same direction as those tracks, but a half-hour drive to get there thanks to the winding rural access roads, little more than gravel-strewn paths snaking through the wilderness.

Chief Bell honked the horn and gestured to Officer Gray. A moment later, Marcus trotted over to the car.

"Yeah, Chief?"

"Going for a drive, Marcus. Don't fuck anything up while I'm gone."

"You got it, sir. You can count on—"

Ozzie closed the window and started the car. He checked his messages. Susan wanted to know how the investigation was going. He typed a quick reply—"In progress"—and threw the cruiser into gear. Gravel and dust spewed from the tires as he turned the car around in the cul-de-sac.

Minutes later, he was back on Rural Route 1193, heading south toward the Cumberland Falls Highway.

3

Fifteen miles east, Jack Tremly sat in Professor Booth's kitchen, stirring sugar into his coffee. Professor Tyler Booth took a seat across from him at the small kitchenette table. The furniture was far too small for the large room, which was decorated with various masks and carvings of native origin. From what he'd seen, the whole house was decorated in similar fashion. A pair of long tribal spears were mounted on the wall above Booth's television, accompanied by a series of framed photographs from various sojourns across the world. The man in those photographs looked younger, more vibrant, and more importantly, he looked happy.

The fellow before him now had not aged gracefully. Large bags clung beneath his bulging eyes, dark spidery veins burst across the bridge of his nose, and the left corner of his lower lip was cursed with a nervous twitch.

"I'm sorry, by the way." Dr. Booth folded his hands together and placed them on the table. Jack looked up, confused.

"Pardon?"

"Your grandmother," Booth said. "I'm sorry for your loss. I didn't find out about her passing until several days later, so I couldn't make it to the funeral. I've been meaning to pay my respects, but I don't get down to Stauford much these days."

"Thank you," Jack said. He sipped his coffee and swallowed hard. "I appreciate you saying that. I...wasn't able to make it to the funeral myself." He met the professor's gaze and frowned. "Listen, I don't want to take up too much of your time. I'm honestly not even sure what I'm doing here."

"It's quite all right," Booth said. "I'd be confused, too." He gestured to the worn notebook, its cover tattered and frayed, stuffed with a variety of notes and newspaper clippings. "I didn't know Imogene well, but I still thought of her as a friend. She had a kind soul. So, if I can help you solve a mystery, then I'm happy to do it."

Jack nodded, smiling. "Thank you, Dr. Booth."

"Oh, please." Booth waved away Jack's words with a smile. "No one's called me that since my Sue Bennett days. Please, just call me Tyler."

"Okay," Jack said, "Tyler it is."

He ran his fingers across the cover of the notebook, tracing the contours of its coarse texture while he sought the right words, the right place to begin. There was no rhyme or reason to the notebook's contents. Its pages were filled with various memoranda, some written in a scrawl so quick and narrow their words were difficult to decipher. From those passages, he gleaned his grandmother had developed her own form of shorthand, filling some pages with abbreviated words in patterns that looked like code. If he'd found the notebook in a kitchen cupboard, he would've mistaken them for recipes of a sort.

Complementing her passages were articles from local newspapers, Op-Ed columns about the dark side of religious freedom, assorted update pieces about the status of the minors the media dubbed the "Stauford Six," the formal inquiries from state officials about the goings-on at the church, and more recently, articles revisiting the horrid event five years gone, ten years gone, and even one about the twentieth anniversary. The final article in the book ended with a note in his grandmother's script, four words scrawled in red pencil: "No mention of temple."

From there, Jack lost the narrative his grandmother was trying to convey, the articles set aside in favor of her odd shorthand, esoteric symbols, possible meanings, and something involving the cycles of the moon. Affixed to one of the pages was an old Polaroid of a dimly lit carving in stone. The carving depicted more symbols, much like the ones etched into her tombstone, but with one difference: a semi-circular design with a smaller circle in its center. Looking at it made his head hurt, and from the shadows of his mind crept a whispered phrase in a voice that was not his own. *Old lies above, new love below.*

Together, her notes and collected articles served not as a sort of dark scrapbook compiled for the sake of nostalgia, but as a record of what happened, a bible of instruction for…what, exactly? A ceremony of some kind? Cycles of the moon? The spirit of religion dwelled in the pages of this notebook, more than he ever expected his grandmother to behold after all that happened at their church. She'd sworn off all manner of faith after the incident, a fact which the many townsfolk of Stauford refused to let her forget. How many times had they ventured down to the IGA for their weekly grocery trip and felt the hateful stares burning into their backs? Or what about all the times someone spat at her feet and called her a godless witch?

Too many, Jack thought. He opened the notebook and flipped through its pages, searching for the place to begin. *My work isn't done yet, Jackie.*

This wasn't like the Imogene Tremly he remembered. This wasn't a bible. No, it was more like a grimoire.

"Jack?"

Tyler Booth stared at him with a twitching smile betraying the concern he tried to hide.

"Sorry," Jack said. "I was a million miles away for a minute there."

"That's quite all right," Tyler said. "Perhaps I should tell you how I knew your grandma?"

Jack nodded. He sipped his weak coffee and listened. The old professor folded his arms across his chest and looked off into the distance, thinking.

"Your grandma paid me a visit when I was still teaching. This was…1996, I believe. Near the end of the fall semester. Sue Bennett College was on its last legs then. Financial trouble. They lost their accreditation a year later and that was that." Tyler shrugged. "Anyway, she'd sat in on one of my lectures and approached me afterward while I was packing up my notes. She said, 'Are you the man who digs up old things?'"

Jack smiled. "Yeah, that was Mamaw Genie, all right."

"It's not every day a lady with an eyepatch pays me a visit, you know. We talked for a few minutes before she got down to business. She wasn't one to mince words, your grandma."

"No, she really wasn't. Why was she there to see you?"

"She wanted to hire me. She'd read an essay I'd written on the discovery of strange Adena ceremony sites in the southeastern region, and said she knew of one I hadn't mentioned."

"Calvary Hill?"

Tyler nodded. "Yes, sir. Calvary Hill, off Devil's Creek Road. I suppose you're…well, I guess you'd rather not think about that."

"It's okay," Jack said. "I've come to terms with it."

Tyler eyed him carefully, the twitch in his lip more prominent now. Jack suspected if Tyler knew anything of his artwork, then the professor would know Jack was lying to him. Anyone who knew Jack's past could see his pain on the canvas.

"Yes," Tyler said, and cleared his throat. "As I was saying, Calvary Hill wasn't a part of my article, because I'd never heard of it. I mean, I'd heard of what happened at the church back in the 80s, but I don't think anyone in the anthropological community ever considered the hill to be a Native American tumulus."

"So, she hired you to…what, exactly? Go explore Calvary Hill?"

Tyler nodded. "Mostly correct. She asked me to go down there and find something for her." He lifted his coffee mug and saucer. The porcelain rattled together as his hands shook. "And I did. I went down there once. I won't go down there again."

"I'm not asking—"

The old professor raised his hand. "I know, son. I just…well, a man my age has to put his foot down, make his boundaries known. Twenty years ago, I wasn't so keen to say no. If I'd known then what I know now, you and me wouldn't be sittin' here having this conversation."

"Fair enough," Jack said. He sighed. "Will you at least tell me what you found down there?"

Dr. Booth rose from the table, opened a cabinet over the stove, and plucked a bottle of dark rum from the shelf. He poured a good amount into the mug.

"Care for some liquid bravery?"

The offer was tempting, but Jack remembered the previous evening and thought better of it. He smiled and shook his head. Tyler shrugged. "Suit yourself."

When he was seated, the old professor sipped his spiked coffee and smacked his lips. "That'll do." He waited a few seconds, collecting himself. "I've never been much of a religious man. Not really. At least, I wasn't until I went where your grandma paid me to go. Even then, I'm still not sure of a higher power. Not in the sense my mama and papa believed. What I do believe is there are things in this world we aren't meant to understand."

Jack nodded. "But what about the sticker on your van? That seems to be rather…*focused*, in a religious sort of way, don't you think?"

"That?" Tyler chuckled, but there was no humor in his voice. "It's another totem, son. I'm sure you've noticed they're all over my house. You saw the ones in my front yard."

"I'm not sure I follow."

"After what happened at Devil's Creek, I've tried to surround myself with protective energy. Positive reinforcement. Something to keep…" The old professor scratched the white stubble on his chin, searching for the right words. "…something to keep the wolf from the door."

Jack pushed his coffee aside and leaned forward. He stared hard into the old man's eyes.

"Please tell me what happened to you. Why did my grandmother pay you to go there?"

Dr. Tyler Booth lifted his mug and drained its contents in three loud gulps. He wiped his mouth with the back of his hand and met Jack's stare. There was a cold intensity in his eyes, the thousand-yard gaze of a man who'd seen something he wasn't meant to see.

"Have it your way, Mr. Tremly. Here's what I can tell you…"

4

"I left here early one Saturday morning in mid-October. The college was in the practice of instituting a 'fall break' after midterms, and to be honest, I'd been looking forward to it as much as my students. Drafting exams and grading essays is about as exciting as it sounds. Truth is, I'd been looking forward to checking out the place your grandmother told me about for weeks. I just didn't have an opportunity to get away until that weekend…"

Dr. Tyler M. Booth closed the door to his white 1990 sedan and slung the strap of his backpack over his shoulder. He looked up at the sky, noting the late morning sun overhead. Sweat dotted his forehead, and an uncomfortable dampness seeped into his armpits.

He'd forgotten what it meant to dress appropriately for such adventures. Although he'd overseen an excavation two years earlier, Tyler had not been on a proper expedition since the 70s, when he'd done graduate work excavating several burial sites on the islands off the coast of the Carolinas. That was back before popular films made archaeology sexy and intriguing to the general public, when telling someone "I'm an anthropology major" resulted in a quick change of subject. These days, everyone wanted to go into anthropology and its understudies because of Indiana Jones and some video game about raiding tombs.

These days, most of his prospective students dropped the class after the first week when they learned how much research and study was involved. "This is a science," he'd reminded his most recent class. "We're studying native cultures with what little they've left behind. We're not looting tombs and digging up buried treasure."

Except here he was, on his way to explore an uncharted burial mound and retrieve an artifact for a nice old lady who'd paid him a thousand dollars in advance for his trouble. The irony wasn't lost on him, and he smiled as he stepped off the gravel road and found the old trail into the woods.

A blanket of fallen foliage covered the path, painted orange and yellow and brown from the deciduous canopy overhead. Imogene gave him detailed instructions from memory, but he still had to stop several times to get his bearings due to the overgrowth. The babble of water from a nearby creek led him toward the footbridge. Once there, he stripped off his flannel shirt and tied it around his waist.

Birds chattered at one another in the distance as he surveyed the path ahead. The fiery blanket of leaves spread out for as far as he could see, coating the forest floor with vibrant patchwork foliage. Something small—perhaps a chipmunk—skittered through the leaves on the other side of the creek. Overhead, two squirrels argued over a cache of walnuts in their nest. Gnats hummed in his ear.

Tyler closed his eyes, listening to the language of nature, wondering what stories it might have to tell him. Something horrible happened here years ago, something senseless and terrifying, but he was more interested in the other untold secrets this area had to whisper in his ear. He'd done as much research as time allowed in the weeks leading up to this moment, poring over what articles he could find in the college's limited library catalog, searching for any mention of a Cherokee or Adena burial mound in this part of the state. All searches yielded nothing. How had no one heard of this burial mound? Furthermore, how had a little old lady from Stauford known about this anthropological anomaly?

These were the questions he hoped to answer today. Imogene Tremly wanted him to collect an artifact from the wreckage of her old church, but Tyler Booth hoped to unravel this local mystery which, to his knowledge, had not come up once in regional lore. That was his reward for this little trip—and the thousand bucks sitting in his bank account.

He fished his canteen from his backpack, took a drink, and continued on his way.

"When I was a kid, my daddy took me and my mama on a family vacation across the country. We stopped at all those funny roadside attractions. You know the ones I'm talking about? 'Come See the Largest Paperclip in the World,' things like that. Well, we stopped at one of these roadside places out west—New Mexico, I think, or maybe it was Arizona. The attraction was a literal ghost town—one of those single-street towns you see in all those Western movies with Clint Eastwood or John Wayne. This place—Dry Gulch or Gulch Junction or some sort of 'gulchy' town—had been abandoned for decades after a gang of raiders drove through and murdered the folks who lived there.

"The tour guide was really big on playing up the 'ghost' angle of the place. You know what I mean. He'd say things like, 'And sometimes we can still hear them screaming,' and other such nonsense. He was trying to scare me, of course, me being a kid and all, except I don't remember being scared. I felt sad. That old town sat dormant since the 1800s, its last living residents slaughtered in cold blood.

"I mention all of this, Jack, because that's what it was like when I walked through the old shantytown you used to call home. It was eerie, sure, but I also felt a profound sadness there. Those houses were still standing, no one bothered to tear 'em down, and it was like walking through a graveyard. Every house was a grave marker. The names weren't etched on their doors, but that didn't matter. I knew what had happened—doesn't everyone, even if they don't want to talk about it?

"But I'll tell you one thing, son. One thing different about that shantytown I didn't feel at the old ghost town out west."

"What's that?" Jack asked.

Dr. Booth wiped his lips and shook his head. "It felt haunted."

As Tyler wandered slowly between the two rows of shacks, he was struck with the nagging sensation of eyes upon him. The shacks themselves sat abandoned for thirteen years, but the knowledge did not set his mind at ease. He remembered the ghost town of his youth, the way the buildings sagged with age like rotten fruit, their windows and doorways slightly askew, the angles a few degrees wrong somehow, all staring at him, all watching—

Stop it. There's no one here but you, and you're just scaring yourself.

Tyler wasn't the only one to visit. There were signs of others. Graffiti, mostly, on sides of some of the shacks in faded neon pink paint. "Ricky + Julia 4-EVAR," "SKYNYRD!," and in one hilarious case, "Worship Stan!" On the other side of the hut were the leftover cans of spray paint, smudged with pink trails down their sides, the metal marred with spots of rust. A few feet down the path, Tyler spotted a cluster of crushed beer cans and what appeared to be a makeshift fire pit.

He'd heard of kids driving out here to have parties. Part of him thought this was a shame, that society had slipped a few inches further down the slope into debauchery when even the dead couldn't be honored. Another part of him, however, understood the appeal. The place was isolated, miles from anywhere, there were no neighbors to complain about the noise, and to get there, you had to hike over a mile into the woods. It was the perfect place to have a party.

Or to start a cult.

Tyler lingered near the edge of the empty village and looked back at the two rows of rundown shacks. *People lived here,* he thought. *People actually* lived *here. They bathed in the creek. No running water. No electricity. They chose to live like this.* He shook his head. The conviction it would take for someone to forego the amenities of modern life for the sake of their faith was something he admired and also something that terrified him.

He tried to contemplate the sort of power a person would have to possess to influence and manipulate people. Such power was beyond him, but he admired it. Respected it. Feared it, and for good reason. Humanity had its limits for a reason. We were flawed creatures, truly unworthy of our own success. The power to convince people to give up their lives in servitude to a god they couldn't see was the sort of power man wasn't meant to have.

Of course, to hear Imogene's daughter speak of Jacob Masters, one might think he was the second coming of Christ. Tyler felt a pang of sadness in his heart, knowing a nice lady like Imogene Tremly had such an insane child, but that spike of emotional pain was short lived. A woman like Imogene wasn't innocent. Wasn't she just as complicit in what happened here? Hadn't she helped build this half-assed Jonestown in the forest outside Stauford?

Years later, as he recounted this story to Imogene's grandson, he'd keep this detail to himself, but his gut instinct remained constant over the years: Imogene was partially to blame for what happened here. He felt that in his bones.

And later, after he went down in the depths of the barrow, he'd try to hold her accountable for what would eventually happen to him, but his heart would have other plans.

"When I left the canopy of the forest and stepped into the clearing for the first time, I felt something I'd never felt before. There's an energy to the place, like standing near a power station. A low-grade hum you can't hear but feel in your fingers and toes, down to your bones. A slow vibration, almost hypnotic, buzzing through my head like a swarm of bees. Pulsing, breathing in rhythm, and it was whispering to me, Jack. I could hear a voice in the drone."

Jack watched the old man get up and make himself another drink. When Tyler sat back down, Jack asked, "What did the voice say?"

The professor sipped from his mug—now more rum than coffee—and shook his head. "It didn't say anything. At least, nothing I could understand. And maybe I misspoke before. It wasn't just a voice, but voices. They were singing in chorus, and for a moment I thought I could make out what they were singing…"

Tyler stood at the foot of the hill and cocked his head, listening. The voices were louder here, and they said something he understood, but what was it? Rejoice? He took another step up the overgrown path winding its way up the hill.

The chirping birds ceased, and the insects weren't singing anymore. There were only the voices, an absurd chorus filling his thoughts like church hymns.

You're letting yourself get scared by ghosts, he told himself. He continued along the path up the slope.

Calvary Hill was surprisingly larger than he expected it to be, at least twice the size of a typical burial mound in width and height. When he looked up at the summit, he imagined what this place must've looked like when the church still stood. All around him were charred remnants of its presence, piece of rotted timbers and rusted hinges, fragments of scratched glass embedded in the earth, the half-buried steeple overtaken with weeds.

A thick blanket of ash awaited him at the summit. He surveyed the pit, a barren scar on which the church once stood, and from which nothing would ever grow again. Sweat beaded on his forehead and dripped from the tip of his nose. When he turned back to look at his progress, he noted how bald the area was in comparison to the forest. Aside from the grass which blanketed the clearing, no other plants grew there. No weeds or wildflowers.

Rejoice.

Startled, Tyler spun on his heels and looked across the ashen patch. The low sing-song chorus hummed in his ear, the voices positioned next to his head. He'd heard them clear as day, but when he turned, there was no one. He was alone here, alone for miles, and an icy nail scraped slowly down his back as a heart-dropping realization occurred to him: No one knew he was here.

So stupid, he scolded himself. Sweat trickled down the back of his neck. A feeling in his gut urged him to turn around, leave, go now while you can because something is wrong here, Tyler, something is *incredibly wrong*, and if you don't go now, something *incredibly wrong* is going to happen to you—

"*Rejoice.*"

He heard the chorus this time, not in his head, but here in the physical world. A chorus of voices singing from within the earth. The voices were sweet, lurid, and they wanted him to follow. *"Rejoice, for the words are yours. Our ways are yours. Rejoice, our child. Come and see…"*

Tyler Booth took two steps toward the center of the ashen pit and felt the ground give way. He had no time to react. The earth collapsed beneath him, and he fell into the dark.

"You're probably wondering why I was so careless. Truth is, your grandma did warn me about the drop. Hell, I'd even packed rope for the descent, not that it would've mattered. There was nothing to anchor myself to anyway. Even all these years later, I can't tell you why I wandered to the far edge of the ash pit. I knew there was an opening there, but the voices had...an effect on me. They told me to come and see, and I wanted to. I really wanted to. How could something so sweet be so malign? And like sailors to a siren, I went toward them, dumbstruck by what they told me. I stepped on some old charred, rotted timbers and shingling covering the rift and that's when the world fell away from me."

Jack shivered. The old professor's words coaxed a memory to the forefront of his mind, one of descent and cold, of darkness and voices and dim candles spread out along the cavern floor.

"I don't know how long I was unconscious. Hours, probably. Far longer than I'd planned to be there. When I came to, my whole body ached from the impact, and my head was pounding. Somehow, I'd managed to fall more than twenty feet in a dead drop without breaking anything. I remember thinking, 'So this is how I die. Alone, in a dark hole, in the middle of nowhere.' But I was wrong. There was light down in the barrow. And I certainly wasn't alone."

Tyler sneezed, his sinuses agitated by the dust and ash in the musty air of the cavern. The pressure in his skull was exquisite, pulsing in time with his heart, hammering against the interior of his forehead and eye sockets. He sat up and cried out in agony. Pain crashed over him in churning waves, and for a time, he remained still, counting the rhythm of his heart and taking slow breaths to calm himself.

He surveyed his surroundings. A halo of light fell from the ceiling in a bright curtain, banishing the darkness to the outer recesses of the room. The depth of the barrow and its hollow nature confused him. This wasn't a burial mound at all, he realized. This was something else, something that didn't make sense with his understanding of the local native culture. When the old woman told him there was a burial mound in southeastern Kentucky, he expected something of Adena origin, or maybe even Cherokee, but this wasn't anything like the mounds left behind by those tribes.

No, this was something he'd never seen before at all. Tyler searched his surroundings for his backpack, wincing at the sharp nails of pain driving into his skull, and felt one of the fabric straps. He pulled the backpack toward him, fumbled in the dark for his flashlight, and clicked on the beam.

Crude stonework supported the outer layers of earth, their asymmetrical shapes held together by a primitive mortar he'd never seen before. The grout between stones was porous, pockmarked with tiny holes and clefts like coral. A viscous black liquid seeped from the openings, covering the stones in a grimy wet sheen. Tyler's heart climbed into his gullet.

Get a grip on yourself, he thought. He turned away from the nearby wall and slowly, painfully, rose to his feet. A spell of vertigo struck him when he stood, but he found his bearings a few seconds later. The room ceased its spinning, but the air—no, the fabric of reality—continued to breathe, swelling in and out before him, and he thought he heard the thrum and drop of a heartbeat reverberating from somewhere in the dark.

Tyler dismissed the sound, certain he was hearing his own terrified heart and steadied the flashlight as he set off to explore. A narrow pillar of earth stood near the center of the room, with stone stairs leading to its summit. To the side of the steps sat a stone altar covered in soot. The whole floor was covered in dirt and ash, mounds of it some places, and nearly bare in others, revealing more of the primitive stonework inches beneath his feet. He spotted the buried legs of an old aluminum extension ladder and felt a rush of relief wash over him. At least he'd have a way out of this place—but not yet. He wasn't done here yet.

Along the far wall, the stones were covered in strange glyphs, but he couldn't make them out in the dim light.

He took a step. Something crunched beneath his sneaker.

Confused, Tyler shifted the beam to his feet and stepped back. There were bits of stone in the mound of earth beneath him. He traced the tip of his shoe into the mound, seeking the hardened thing he'd cracked with his weight. There it was, something pale and brittle, something—

Oh God.

The femur was small, belonging to a child of no more than five or six years. Tyler stared at it for a long time, fixated on the contours of those brittle remains and the implications they posed. What the hell was this place? A primitive abattoir, built for the purpose of human sacrifice?

His mind raced with questions, seeking answers where there were none. This place defied known record. The cultures that had inhabited this area thousands of years ago all buried their dead in mounds, sure, but they weren't known to sacrifice their own. And if they hadn't built this place, then who?

A soft voice whispered from the shadows beyond the altar.

Our prophet is sleeping, child. Would you baptize yourself in the blood of midnight and become an infant in his cosmic womb? Would you seek rebirth in his court of bones and serve on your knees in a palace of fire?

Fear seized him. He pivoted on his heels, searching the room for a person, a shape, anything to explain the voice whispering in his ear. Those weren't his words, the voice in his head was not his conscience.

A sickening glow pulsed from beyond the altar, bathing the room in sapphire. The grip of fear slackened, and he found the will to move his feet, stepping carefully through the mounds of ash surrounding the stone altar. There was something buried on the other side of the structure, something emanating a blue light, illuminating the carvings and drawings along the stone walls.

Illuminating an opening in the wall itself.

"I don't remember if the doorway was there before. It was all so dark, my mind was waging a war between terror and curiosity, and the throbbing in my head made it hard to focus on any one thing for long. All I can tell you is it might've been there before, or maybe it wasn't. I don't know."

Jack nodded, flipping through the pages of his grandmother's notebook. He found the old Polaroid photo, pushed it across the table, and averted his eyes. Looking at it for too long made his forehead throb.

Dr. Booth glanced at the photo, nodded, and closed the book. He pinched the bridge of his nose and winced. "I took that, just before I dug out the glowing thing in the dirt. The idol your grandmother wanted. I should've charged her more than a thousand dollars. I should've said no in the first place."

The Polaroid flash lit up the cavern, and for a split-second, he glimpsed the room in totality, a dome framed in old stones covered in writing carved a millennium before. Maybe even longer.

He didn't wait for the photo to develop. Instead, he shoved the camera and photo print into his backpack and moved to the other side of the altar. A driving desire to leave this place clung to him, eroding any resolve he had to document everything, and—

All thought ceased when he spotted the open passageway in the wall.

In his younger days, even just five years before, he might've ventured through the dark doorway, but not now. Staring at the opening, at the way light retreated from its corridor, he was filled with a terror he'd never experienced before. The sort of terror that makes one's gut drop to their feet, their blood run cold, their mind seize like a corroded engine. It was the kind of terror born from facing the impossible, the unnatural, and knowing what one is seeing *simply cannot be.*

And the opening, whether it was there before or not, filled him with a horrific leaden sensation in his belly. However deep he was inside the bowels of Calvary Hill wasn't deep enough to accommodate such a passage, for its ceiling would break the surface of the earth beyond the hillside. What he saw mere feet away was impossible—and yet there it stood, taunting him, beckoning to him.

Would you explore us, child?

Would you baptize yourself in the blood of midnight?

Would you kneel before a throne of fire?

Tyler's head swam as he stuck his hand into the earth and retrieved the glowing object. It was as Imogene described: a rough stone carving in the shape of a grinning figure. The figure was cold and stung his flesh. He shoved it into his backpack, teetering on the heels of his feet as the world swirled around him. A moment later, he steadied himself, and gave one final glance toward the impossible doorway.

There were stars in the darkness. Bright blue stars lining the stone walls of a hallway, stretching into the vast darkness of the cosmos. Because it *was* the cosmos—a shimmering tapestry of stars and galaxies, the cold uncaring vacuum of space framed here in this place that should not be. The universe illuminated a grotto at the end of the corridor, with large porous walls climbing into the twilit abyss above. Black ichor seeped from the wounds in the stone, trickling down the sheer rock walls into a lake below. He heard the lazy slapping of waves against an impossible shoreline, pulled forward by an unnatural gravity down here in the earth.

And in the brief instance when he glimpsed the twilit grotto, Tyler was filled with a maddening epiphany that would haunt him in the years to come: *Those aren't stars. Oh God, they're eyes.*

As if they'd heard his panicked thought, the stars blinked and twitched erratically, all turning to focus upon this stranger at their threshold. A low groan erupted from beyond the lapping waves.

We see you, child. Do not take what does not belong to you.

Tears streamed from Tyler's cheeks. He scrambled to the ladder, dragging it up the steps of the earthen pillar, crying out as he banged his shin against one of the metal legs. His heart hammered in his chest as he set the ladder against the opening in the ceiling. He was halfway up before he looked back, and immediately wished he hadn't. The passage was gone, replaced by a darkening void spilling over the floor like a rich oil seeping up from the earth. A moment later, the room was coated in darkness. Even the failing sunlight from above cast no glare on the surface. What light fell upon the dark was consumed in a liquid nothingness.

Tyler Booth scrambled out of the opening and onto the ashen summit of Calvary Hill. He stumbled as he raced down the slope, rolling to a painful stop at the tree line. Pain shot up through his ankle, but the dull throbbing in his head finally began to abate. Exhausted, the fear draining from him in beads of acrid sweat, Tyler leaned against a nearby tree and sobbed.

5

Jack watched as the old man wiped his eyes with shivering, gnarled hands. Dr. Booth had finished off the bottle of rum, but even the alcohol wasn't enough to quiet the tremors. The men sat in silence for a few minutes, the professor collecting himself after reliving such a horrible experience, and Jack wrestling with the sudden guilt of asking Tyler to do so.

"I'm sorry," Jack whispered. "I had no idea…"

Except he *did* have an idea. Those voices down in the dark, the carvings on the wall, the grotto beneath a sky full of eyes—weren't these the very things of his nightmares? Had he not built a career from mining the horrible images embedded from years of childhood trauma? What the professor described was the very setting of *Midnight Baptism*.

"It's no matter," Tyler mumbled. "She paid me to do it. I didn't have to, but I—well, money is money. That says it all right there. I delivered as promised. When the college went belly up the following year, I took the opportunity to retire. But…" The old man's voice hung in his throat with a dry croak as he considered his words. "…but that place still haunted me. In my dreams. Even now, Mr. Tremly, I can't sleep a wink without visiting that awful place. That's why…"

He gestured to the window, and then at the various masks and effigies hanging along the walls of the house.

"Did my grandmother ever say why she wanted the idol?"

Tyler thought for a moment and then nodded. "She did say one thing. The day I returned with the idol, she mentioned something about 'breaking a curse,' but when I asked her to repeat herself, she told me it was nothing. After the hell I'd gone through, I'd already decided then and there not to press further. I didn't want to know." The professor met Jack's gaze with heavy eyes. "I still don't want to."

Jack caught his drift and nodded slowly. He checked his watch and smiled. "Well, Dr. Booth, I appreciate you taking the time to speak with me. Before I go, I do have one more question."

"Shoot."

"Does the phrase 'As above, so below' mean anything to you?"

"As a matter of fact, it does. It's an old Hermetic saying. It implies balance. As things are in the heavens, so shall they be here on earth. Or some horseshit like that."

"Hermetic?"

"Well, yes. I'm far from a scholar on the occult, but after what happened, I did a fair bit of research to…well, protect myself. From whatever it was down there. You understand."

Jack nodded. He did, in a weird sort of way. Instead of speaking, he opened his grandmother's notebook and flipped to the page with the symbols he'd seen on her gravestone.

"What about these? Do these mean anything?"

Dr. Booth studied them, his eyes dancing excitedly from one glyph to the next, and Jack saw the spark was still there. The desire for knowledge, for understanding another fragment of the greater human puzzle. And then the spark was gone again, the light fading from the old man's eyes.

"No," Tyler whispered. "I've never seen them before."

"You're sure?"

"Yes," Tyler said, smiling. He looked over his shoulder at the kitchen clock. "Listen, I hate to be rude, but I have some errands I have to run."

Jack smiled, held up his hand. "No, it's okay. I need to be going."

The old professor saw him to the door and watched as Jack walked to his car. Before Jack climbed inside, he turned back and said, "Hey, Doc?"

"Yes?"

"If you were to ever get the itch to figure out what those symbols mean, it would be a great deal of help to me. I'd pay you, even."

Tyler smiled but waved him away. "I appreciate that, son, but like I said before, I'd rather not know."

Jack nodded. "I get it," he said, "but…well, they're etched into my mamaw's gravestone. I'd just like to know what they mean."

"Maybe you aren't meant to," Tyler said. "Have a good afternoon, son."

The old man closed the door. Jack walked back to his car, puzzled by the afternoon's revelations. *What were you up to, Mamaw?* He climbed into the car and started the engine. *What curse were you trying to break?*

6

Dr. Tyler Booth watched from behind the curtains as the car backed out of his driveway and sped off. He remained there even after the young man was out of sight.

"Why'd you lie to Genie's grandson," he muttered to no one. The empty house said nothing in reply, offering only the subdued gesture of a ticking clock from the kitchen. His many totems looked on from their resting places along the walls, their faces slack, lifeless, and free of judgment.

Because, he thought, *she was trying to save him from that mess. Save us all, for that matter.*

Tyler stepped away from the window, wincing at the stiffness in his knees. There was moisture in the air, maybe even rain on the way, and the ache in his joints sang a chorus in its honor. He left the living room and walked down the hall to his bedroom. There, he closed the door and reclined on his bed. He leaned over and took hold of a framed photograph on the nightstand.

The photo had aged, but the two smiling faces had not. They were forever preserved behind glass. He looked at his younger self, just ten years ago now, with his arm around the lady he loved. There was a moment, earlier in his life, when he thought he'd missed his chance at finding someone with whom he could spend the rest of his days. Maybe he was too dull, too unattractive, and too odd in his ways.

Imogene Tremly proved him wrong. He'd delighted in aiding her in her grim quest, if for no other reason than it brought them together. But now she was gone, her quest unfulfilled, and if what she believed proved to be true, then there would be hell to pay. By everyone.

You should've helped him, he scolded himself. *For Genie's sake.*

Maybe, maybe not. Maybe what Genie told him and what she believed was nothing but a farce.

And maybe...well, that would be something, wouldn't it? Wasn't the moon currently in its full phase for the next few days? Maybe he could ask her himself.

"As above, so below." He wiped a tear from his eye, tracing a wet finger along her face, leaving a smudge on the glass. "My God, Genie, I hope you were wrong."

7

Chief Bell missed the turn-off for Devil's Creek Road, going nearly as far as the old road to Cumberland Falls before realizing his error. He was deep in thought as he drove, reliving the days of his youth, all the times he'd taken girls out to Devil's Creek to get high and screw.

The Cumberland Falls Highway made such reveries easy, of course. The road was mostly a straightaway running east to west, carrying travelers beyond the city limits and into the wilderness of Whately County. There was a whole lot of nothing between the town and the turnoff for the state park, fields and farmhouses and the Stauford Speedway, where rednecks from three counties away were already parking to get a good seat for the night's race. In the great cultural desert of Kentucky, Stauford itself was an oasis, if a somewhat dubious one. Beyond its borders, there was plenty of nothing for travelers to get lost in their thoughts, hypnotized by the doldrums of the road, and Ozzie Bell was no different.

When he doubled back to the turnoff for Devil's Creek Road, Ozzie was struck with a memory from his high school days. He'd driven out here one night—was it after a football game? He couldn't remember—with one of the cheerleaders, Peggy Darling. They'd dated briefly during his junior year, what couldn't have been more than a couple of months but might have been years to their young love-struck hearts, and they'd driven out here for some quality "alone" time.

Ozzie couldn't keep himself from smiling as he passed the old barn on the right with the sign reading "Devil's Creek." He'd fucked the hell out of Peggy on the other side of the barn, amidst the sour smell of mildewed haybales and the faint aroma of cow shit wafting in the air around them. She'd gotten pregnant, and he'd taken up selling weed to pay for her abortion. They didn't talk much afterward, and Peggy dropped out of school a few months later amid rumors she'd miscarried Ozzie's child. His reputation as a star athlete for the football team protected him from such scrutiny, but the cheerleaders were fair game in the eyes of the Stauford elite. They didn't bring in the money like those Stauford boys did. Last he'd heard, she was living in a trailer park somewhere in Landon, collecting welfare.

What a shit-show, he thought. What was it he'd said to his pal Ronny Cord after the deed was done? When Ronny said he couldn't believe it?

A wicked laugh erupted from his throat, causing him to swerve into the other lane.

"I kid you not," he cackled, laughing so hard tears spilled down his cheeks. He jerked the wheel, guiding the cruiser back into its correct lane. A mile past the old barn, the pavement gave way to gravel as the road snaked its way into the forest. Not too far now.

Another thought crept into his balding skull, on the heels of the wreckage he'd made of Peggy Darling's life. Hadn't he dreamed of Devil's Creek last night? The phone call from Officer Gray pulled him out of it, and in his grogginess, he'd nearly forgotten about the horrible picture show going on behind his eyes. In the dream, he was tied to Susan's bed (which wasn't out of the ordinary—she liked to be on top), but there was something wrong with her. Her skin was wrinkled, her entire body pruning like a finger held underwater for too long, and she looked as though she'd aged fifty years. The bed rocked and creaked with their motion, but somehow, with the impossible logic of dreams, he knew they weren't in her bedroom. No, they were in a large cavern of some sort, filled with a radiant blue light. And Susan—who wasn't really Susan anymore, at least not by appearance, but instead an old crone having her way with him—chattered and gnashed her blackened teeth as she ground her hips against him. Maggots and flies fell from her mouth and nostrils. *He lives,* she'd cried. *He lives!*

Officer Gray's phone call saved him from the rest, but now, as he approached the end of Devil's Creek Road and the trail leading toward the old church site, Ozzie realized he and Susan were *here* in his dream. Somehow, even though they were in a cave of some kind, he was gripped with this impossible knowledge they were at Devil's Creek, deep down in its womb.

"He lives," Ozzie whispered, slowing the cruiser to a stop. "And what do we have here?"

The fragments of his dream fell away in favor of the present. There was a truck here, parked alongside the road. He recognized that rusty yellow pickup truck. Most of Stauford's sleazier residents would, too.

Ozzie parked the cruiser and climbed out. He unbuckled his holster but did not draw his weapon. Not yet. Had he made a mistake in driving out here? A pair of crows cawed overhead, answering the unsettling question he'd asked himself. The last thing he wanted to do was interrupt Waylon and Zeke's little operation, especially since he'd been the one to hire them in the first place, but there was the matter of the missing boys to consider as well. He stared at the truck for a few minutes, contemplating what to do.

The crows cawed and cackled again from somewhere nearby, startling him from his thoughts. Ozzie approached the pickup, walked toward the front, and placed his hand on the hood. The surface was cold.

Did you boys cook here all night?

A soft breeze swept by him, forcing a whisper from the tree line. He looked toward the old trail, wondering if the forest had any secrets it wanted to share. The scattering of branches waved to him in the wind like gnarled bones. *Come and see,* they said. *Come and see.*

The last thing he wanted to do was wander across a cook site, especially while on official business. Sure, he was the chief of police, and he could come and go as he pleased, but he preferred to keep a layer of separation between himself and the "side hustle," as kids today were fond of saying. Politicians might've called it plausible deniability, but Ozzie preferred to think of it as being smart. The less he knew about how and where his drugs were made, the better.

He wiped sweat from his balding pate, wishing he'd brought a joint with him. Branches snapped beyond the tree line, punctuated by a rustling of dry leaves in the breezes. That same pair of crows cawed once more in the distance, mocking him.

What's all this, his inner voice chided. *Stauford's greatest chief and good ol' boy, Ozzie Bell, afraid of a stroll through the woods? Say it ain't so.*

It *was* so, and he knew it. The dream had set him on edge. He didn't understand why and honestly didn't care to. All he knew was the dream left a sour twist in his guts, and finding Waylon's truck here was like…what, a bad omen? Devil's Creek wasn't far from the campsite, after all. And for as much as Ozzie wanted to backhand the little shit, Riley Tate's testimony was all they had to go on. Two men carried off those two boys from the camp. Two men.

Two. Men.

The crows cawed again, now overhead. One of them shit on the hood of the truck. The loud splat startled him, and he took a step back in disgust.

"Ah, fuck this," he growled, starting toward the path in the forest. He pushed his way through the underbrush, swatting away errant weeds and limbs, barreling through a trail of flattened leaves with the grace of a bulldozer.

He'd gone as far as the footbridge when he spotted the lone figure standing in the bushes on the other side of the creek. Ozzie froze, dropped his hand to his hip, and drew his firearm.

"Police," Ozzie said, his voice nearly crowded by the babbling waters. "Come out of there. Slowly. Keep your hands up."

His voice sounded mechanical in his ears, a flat vibration filling his skull in the pattern of words. Ozzie blinked sweat from his eyes. A cloud of gnats hummed around his ears.

The figure in the weeds did as he'd instructed, pivoting in place with an almost leisurely gait. Zeke Billings met Ozzie's stare with deadened eyes and a pallid face, but he wore a big smile that seemed wrong somehow.

"Zeke," Ozzie said, ignoring the tremor in his voice. He resisted the urge to holster his weapon. "What the hell are you doing out here?"

"Afternoon, Chief." Zeke's dead stare betrayed the jovial nature of his smile. It was too wide. Too happy, too *euphoric* for Ozzie's taste. *Fuck*, he wondered, *has this dipshit been sampling the goods?*

Ozzie swallowed back the lump in his throat. He repeated himself. "What are you doing here, Zeke?"

"Waylon sent me up here to keep watch. In case anyone tried to crash our party." Zeke giggled, his dead eyes staring straight ahead, into Ozzie's skull, through him. "But you're invited, of course."

"You're cooking down there?"

Zeke nodded. "Uh huh. We're cooking real good, Chief. It'll be the best stuff you've ever had. It'll give you a religious experience. You might even see God."

"Is that a fact?"

"Oh yes," Zeke said, drawing his gaze down toward the creek. "It's like my father used to say. Old lies above, new love below."

"Right," Ozzie said flatly, squinting to get a better look at the husk of a man standing before him. Dark veins splintered outward from the corners of Zeke's eyes, fracturing the flesh of his face into pale shards like a dried riverbed. "You look like shit, Zeke."

"But I feel wonderful, Chief."

"Uh huh," Ozzie said, tightening his hands around the pistol grip. The weapon felt heavier now, a fifty-pound weight in his hands. He sucked in his breath and exhaled slowly, telling himself to keep cool, keep it together, don't let this doper see you rattled.

"So, what brings you out this way, Chief Bell?"

"A couple boys were kidnapped last night. From a campsite a few miles from here. You and Waylon wouldn't have anything to do with that, would ya?"

The smile on Zeke's face, an impossibly happy thing, widened even more. Thin black lines drew across the man's cracked cheeks. "Not at all, Chief. Waylon and I have been here since yesterday, doing as you asked us to. Cooking up magic for you. For everyone."

Christ, he really is stoned out of his mind.

"Where is Waylon?" Ozzie asked. He shifted his weight from one foot to the other, wincing at the sudden pop in his knee. "I think I'd like to see him. Talk to him, I mean."

"Waylon is busy, Chief. He is cooking his magic for you. But you will see him tomorrow. I promise."

The official part of Ozzie Bell, the part commanding the authority of the Stauford Police Department, wanted to insist on seeing Waylon right now. The rational part, however, saw something entirely wrong in Zeke's eyes and face, and demanded Ozzie leave immediately, haul ass back to the cruiser, and forget he ever drove out here. Something wasn't right. The smile, those eyes, the cracks in his face—Jesus, had they poisoned themselves making the meth? Had they mixed the chemicals wrong?

Ozzie's head swam from the sudden heat clouding his face. The hum of gnats in his ears and the babbling of the creek collided in a swirling vortex of auditory overload, and the burning sickness in his guts roiled upward.

"Something wrong, Chief Bell?"

"N-Nothing," Ozzie said, finally holstering his weapon. "Go get back to work."

"I will," Zeke said, grinning. He stood in place, his skin waxen and cracked like a discarded storefront mannequin. "We'll be seeing you tomorrow, then."

But Ozzie was already walking back up the trail, away from the creek, away from the unnatural visage of Zeke Billings.

Just before wandering back up the slope into the thicket of trees, he looked over his shoulder toward the creek. Zeke wasn't there.

Ozzie muttered "fuck" under his breath and ran back to the road, his cruiser, and away from Devil's Creek.

CHAPTER TWELVE

1

By midday, the sky over Stauford was a delicate shade of gray, the clouds forming a thick blanket that showered in some areas and merely sprinkled in others. The late summer heat did not relent, the air pregnant with a kind of humidity that clung to one's face like a wet pillow. Those mid-September days in southeastern Kentucky were oppressive, the nights a teaser for what fall might bring.

And like the weather, the greater tri-county area bore some semblance of predictability. The gears of late Saturday machinery spun as they always had, cogs greased by the hopes and dreams of a populace saturated in their own self-importance. This wasn't to say Stauford was like any other small Kentucky town. Quite the contrary, in fact.

Founded in 1885 and later incorporated in 1905 at the height of its economic affluence, the city sat upon the nexus of county borders, earning itself an early nickname of "Kentucky's Tri-County Oasis." A pair of railways bisected the city and ran parallel along US 25, diverting through Stauford's train depot which served as a popular stop for many visitors on their way to and from Chattanooga and would do so for a period of fifty years before the decline in railway travel.

In its day, Stauford was a bustling epicenter of southern life, its main thoroughfares lined with storefronts, several of which were still around when Jack and his siblings were children. Even after the passenger trains ceased operations and tourism dried up, Stauford continued to thrive thanks to the old highway slicing through the town from north to south.

Sadly, the construction of I-75 to the west of town in the mid-60s and early 1970s leeched vital business traffic from the town, and old US 25 became just another road for local travel. The new highway drove home a harsh reality for many: despite being the center of the region—and the known universe for its small settlement of residents—Stauford was still a long way from anything of significance, and for a long time, the local economy suffered because of it.

If asked, some of the old-timers like the Corbins and the Hudsons and even the Taswells, families who'd lived in Stauford for generations going all the way back to its founding, would've said the downswing in jobs and prosperity had more to do with the "Masters Curse" than the economy. No oil embargo in the early 70s, or even a shift in preferred travel in the 60s, had much to do with the rise of unemployment, they'd say.

They'd say it had more to do with Jacob Masters and the curse his people placed on the town. They'd say his father, Thurmond, couldn't hack it in the city limits as an honest preacher, so he'd guided his flock out to the wilderness like Moses. They'd say he blamed the people of Stauford for his failures, for not being pure, for their fine little town being a bed of sin.

And they'd say Thurmond's son, Jacob, turned away from the god of his father. They'd say he'd turned toward something older, something far more dangerous, something malignant sleeping beneath the earth.

These days, Stauford's old-timers knew better than to whisper about such things. They'd dismiss such claims, change the subject, or flat-out refuse to answer. Those tales were ghost stories for another generation. The youth today were better off not knowing. There were bigger boogeymen in the world than the ghost of a crazy dead preacher. May the ashes of his madness remain buried in the dirt.

Besides, they were just stories. And like all good stories, seeds of truth were buried in the fiction. They'd taken root there, fed with the blood of the innocent, and after decades of gestation they were soon ready to sprout.

2

Skippy Dawson remembered the stories. He'd seen a change befall the town once before, and there were hints of it in the air now, a bitter taste on the tip of his tongue like those sour candies he used to buy for pocket change. *Just like last time,* he thought, wandering along the empty sidewalk of Main Street. There was a bad man—there was *always* a bad man—but he couldn't remember the how or the why.

What happened before? Skippy searched his memories, struggling to put his finger on the one thing nagging at him. An itch inside his head, a thought screaming to be heard, but he'd be damned if he could remember its name.

Skippy wandered as far as the park across the street from where First National Bank used to be. There, he took a seat on a bench beneath a poplar tree and focused his efforts.

Something happened with a bad man. He hurt children and people died. But why did everyone seem upset?

The children were safe.

The children…

"Ah ha!" Skippy snapped his fingers, startling a pair of squirrels frolicking in the grass beside him. "I found it!"

Indeed, Skippy reflected on a simpler time, right after his accident. This was back in the mid-80s, during the height of the so-called "Satanic Panic," when Main Street USA was under threat not just from the Soviets, but from the Satanists as well. In a small town like Stauford, the threat was even greater than most realized, what with the children of a devil church being allowed to roam free, to *integrate* with the town's own Christian sons and daughters. Those were trying times, friends. And no one in town knew it more than Skippy.

Most days, Skippy wandered around town, smiling and waving at passersby, welcoming them to his favorite town on earth. He'd taken to that routine ever since his accident. He was lucky to be alive, a fact which filled him with an unmeasurable happiness too good not to be shared.

In the years following his recovery, Skippy Dawson took to the streets to spread his joy with as many people as possible. He was ignored at first, dismissed as the town retard despite his prior reputation as the best quarterback Stauford's football team had ever known. So quick were the townsfolk to forget their heroes, but Skippy wasn't dismayed. He'd win them over, one smile, one wave at a time.

But something was wrong in Stauford. There was a poisonous cloud hanging over the town setting everyone on edge. He couldn't see it, but it was up there somewhere, making everyone frown. Making everyone angry. Even James Isaacs, the short chubby man who watered the flowers on Main Street in the summertime, didn't return his smile or even wave, and Jim *always* waved at Skippy when he could.

The same went for Arlene Watson, proprietor of Arlene's Beauty Shop. She always laughed and smiled whenever she saw Skippy waving on the corner, but during that time—the Bad Time, he'd decided to call it—Arlene didn't laugh, and she certainly didn't smile.

He remembered overhearing a couple of old men passing the time on the bench outside Mr. Fugate's Barber Shop. Skippy couldn't remember their names, but he remembered what they'd said because their words frightened him:

"Can't believe they're letting those kids go to our school."

"Hell of a thing, ain't it? Those six freaks going to Stauford?"

"It's horseshit, is what it is. You know what I heard? One of them kid's grandma's a witch."

"A witch? Bull. You're pullin' my leg."

"Hand to Jesus, I ain't. She lives in that big ol' house out near Layne Camp. Heard all sorts of stories from folks, sayin' they heard chanting and seen weird lights in the windows and shit."

"You think it's a coincidence there's six of them kids?"

"Nah sir, I don't. Six is the number of the devil. Who knows what Masters was up to out in the woods. Summonin' the devil into our little town, that's what I think. And those 'Stauford Six' they call 'em in the papers, they're just here to do the devil's work."

"You know what I think? I think they ought to get the Klan together and run 'em out of town, just like they did them negroes back in the day. Load 'em all up on a cattle car and ship 'em off to Chattienooga."

Skippy sat up in his seat when he remembered that phrase. The Stauford Six. Those were the kids. He'd never met them—he was too old to talk to kids, his mama told him—but he'd heard of them. Everyone in Stauford had, and they were angry about it.

They didn't want the Stauford Six anywhere near their kids. Those kids were cursed, reminders of something from Stauford's past everyone wanted to forget. Skippy thought this was a bit like when he had chicken pox and he kept scratching at the scabs until they bled. The kids had picked off the scab somehow, upsetting everyone.

He'd asked his grandpa once. Edmund Dawson said it had something to do with the bad man in the woods. And the kids, the Stauford Six, they reminded everyone of the bad man, but…

"Things got better," he whispered, "so why's it all seem bad now?"

Maybe it had to do with the dream? He'd heard one of the nurses at Stauford Assisted Living complaining of strange dreams last night, and even he'd experienced them himself.

"He lives," Skippy muttered, unsure of who he was talking about and assuming "he" was Jesus, like the ladies at First Baptist taught him in Sunday School. But would Jesus know how to use a phone? And even if He did, why would He call the Gas 'n Go so late at night?

A large tanker truck rumbled past and Skippy waved to the driver. The driver did not return the gesture.

Maybe it is *the dreams,* he thought, shrugging to himself. But as the day wore on, Skippy feared the Bad Time was coming again. Worse, he feared the blue-eyed bad man from his dreams was coming, too.

3

"Want some of my fries?"

Riley looked away from the window and across the table at his aunt Stephanie. She held up a greasy container of French fries smothered in ketchup. He wasn't hungry, hadn't been all day, but she insisted they stop for food because she was starving.

She'd said it with the hope of pulling a smile across his face, but Riley wasn't in the mood. Still, he was grateful she'd managed to get him out of the house despite his father's protests and humored her with a forced grin.

He plucked a soggy French fry from the basket and stuffed it into his mouth. Stephanie watched him with a tired smile.

"That's more like it," she said, taking a sip from her drink. Riley turned back to the window, watching rain spit and spot the glass, snaking down in erratic globules and distorting the outside world. He wanted to leave the brightly lit safety of the diner and wander into the storm. His skin itched with a prickling electricity, had done so ever since he got back from the campsite, and he felt guilty for not being out there, helping to look for his friends. He felt guilty because he was sure Rachel was in trouble with her folks. Part of him wondered if he'd see her at church tomorrow; that same part thought going to church tomorrow was a bad idea.

More than anything, Riley didn't want to be around people right now. His aunt Stephanie was a rare exception—she was one of the few people he thought understood him, one of the few who hadn't forgotten what being an outsider felt like. But being around people was sometimes a necessity, something she told him when they parked along the curb outside of Marleen's Diner at the far end of Main Street.

"I get it," Stephanie said. "You don't want to be here, and you don't want to talk." She waited for him to reply, but Riley kept his gaze on the falling rain outside. His friends were out there, somewhere, being…what, exactly? What would the man with blue eyes want with them? *Maybe he's a pedo,* he thought. A child molester. What some of the kids at school jokingly called a Chester.

"But here's the thing, kiddo. You don't get somethin' for nothin', understand? I got you out of your dad's house for the day because stewing there is the last thing you wanna do. But if you want to hang out with me at the studio tonight and meet your uncle Jack, I need some conversation. So, talk to me, Riley. What's been going on?"

He caught her stare, and this time he smiled for real. She always called him by his name. She never looked down at him for being younger. He was a regular person in her eyes, not a burden, not a weirdo. A human being, and not a lesser one because he was a nephew.

"Which part?"

She nodded. "Whichever part you feel like talking about. We'll go from there."

Riley took a breath, weighed his options, and told her about attacking Jimmy Cord the day before. Stephanie sat back, listening, even cracking a smile when he said Jimmy was a dick, but she didn't interject, and she didn't judge. She let him talk.

"But the truth is, Steph, I couldn't stand to see him pick on Ben. Someone half his size, y'know? As far as I'm concerned, the bastard got what was coming to him. He walks through the school like he's a celebrity, like nothing can touch him. Like he's God or something. It's sickening. I hate it. So, when I saw him bullying Ben, something snapped."

"I get that," Stephanie said. "I do. Good on you for standing up to him, Riley. I respect that about you."

He measured her gaze, looking for a sign she was joking, but he didn't find one. Stephanie smiled and sipped her drink. "What?"

"Nothin'," Riley said. "I expected you to give me shit for it, like Dad did. He's scared he's going to get sued by Jimmy's dad."

Stephanie laughed and counted off with her fingers. "Number one, I ain't like your dad. You ought to know by now. He always had a stick up his ass about things. Number two, yeah, he might be scared, but Ronny Cord ain't got a leg to stand on. Chuck knows the judge, knows lots of people in this town, and furthermore, he knows Ronny's got a bench warrant for missing traffic court. If he weren't up Ozzie Bell's ass, Ronny wouldn't have his license right now. Trust me, your dad's not getting sued." She leaned forward and lowered her voice. "And three, Jimmy's dad wasn't any better when he was in school. If the little prick needed his ass kicked, I say good on you for being the one to do it."

Riley laughed. "Like father, like son?"

"Oh yeah," Stephanie said, crossing her arms. Her eyes drifted upward as she recalled her high school days. "He and Ozzie used to pick on all of us, but no one got it worse than your uncle Jack. Jack was the artsy kid, the one who wasn't afraid of wearing different clothes, listening to different music…" She trailed off, settling her eyes upon him. She stared at him, long enough to make Riley blush. "Come to think of it, you remind me a lot of him. You two have a lot in common. I can't wait for you two to meet."

She plucked a couple of fries from their basket and shoved them into her mouth. Riley gave some air to the conversation, wondering about his famous uncle. His father never said much about Uncle Jack, presumably because of the dark—and at times blasphemous—content of Jack's artwork. The few times when Riley asked, his father was always dismissive, deflecting the question to some other issue or errand. He'd assumed it all had something to do with what happened when they were kids, a topic which Riley wasn't entirely comfortable bringing up. He knew how much stress it caused his father; he didn't want his dear aunt to feel the same.

"What's on your mind?"

"Nothing."

"Bullshit," she said, pushing her basket of fries across the table again. "Help me eat these. Tell me your problems."

Riley sighed, the words on his tongue, unsure if he should. Stephanie nudged him under the table with her foot. "Spit it out. I'm all ears."

"Look, I know you and Dad had a hard time as kids, but…well, I hear things. At school. Rumors, mostly, but y'know, they're the same thing over and over."

"And you're wondering if there's truth to those rumors?"

"Well, yeah," he shrugged. "I've grown up hearing Jack's mom was a witch, you're the spawn of the devil…" He looked up, hesitant to go on, expecting Stephanie would be upset, but to his surprise, she wasn't. She was smiling. Riley went on: "…like I've heard everyone in my family was born out of some Satanic pact, you guys were part of a cult. And…"

He thought of the man with glowing eyes. His blood ran cold, his breath thinning in his lungs.

"And?"

"And… your father was a bad man. An evil man."

"Bobby never talked to you about this?"

He shook his head. "Dad always finds some excuse not to. I mean, if it's true what I've heard, then I guess I get it, but I'd like to…I dunno, I'd like to know who my family is, y'know?"

"Okay, honey. Let's get some things straight." Stephanie pushed the basket of soggy, cooling fries aside and met his gaze. She swiped one of her curls from her face. "People in this town are gonna talk and gossip all day long. That's fine, that's Stauford's way. That's how it's been and how it'll always be until the end of time, I guess. But here's something else that isn't going to change." She reached out and placed her hand on his. "Your dad is your family, and so am I. So's your uncle Chuck. Jack, too. Even…" She faltered, thinking of Susan and Zeke. Saying their names left a bitter taste on her tongue. "Even your aunt Susan and uncle Zeke. You have no reason to doubt that."

"That's not…never mind."

"No, tell me, Riley. Talk to me. That's why we're here. If no one else, you can talk to me. Always."

She squeezed his hand. Riley hadn't cried since his mom's funeral, made it a point to fight the urge to do so ever since but seeing the heartfelt honesty in his aunt's eyes made his own well up with tears.

"It's okay," she whispered.

When Riley spoke, his words came in a flood. "It's just…I feel like my dad has kept a lot from me. Like, I don't even know him, y'know? I don't know anything about him except he loved Mom, and he loves Jesus, and sometimes I think he puts himself into the church so he won't have to look at me. He only notices when I do something wrong or do something that puts him in a bad light.

"So, last night, when he came to get me at the campsite, all I heard was about how my fuck-up would make him look bad. What would people think, with the pastor's son being caught with a girl after dark? He kept saying, 'Why weren't you in your tent, Riley? Why didn't you stay in your tent?' And he didn't say it, but I knew he wanted to. I knew he wanted to say, 'If you'd only been there, Riley, your friend Ben would be okay.' And he's right, Steph. If I had been there…"

The tears spilled down his cheeks. Stephanie handed him a napkin.

"Look, Riley, you can't blame yourself for that. So, what if you'd stayed? Who's to say you wouldn't have been one of the kids taken last night?" She let her words sink in and then said, "Your dad's a worrier. He always has been. I don't think he's afraid to face you, I think he's afraid of raising you alone."

Riley wiped his eyes and blew his nose. She had a point, on both counts. There was a good chance he could've been slung over the shoulder of Mr. Blue Eyes last night. And Dad hadn't been the same since Mom died. He recalled something Bobby told him one night about a week after her funeral. *I see your mother when I look at you,* he'd said. *You always did look just like her.*

He'd never considered he might be a reminder of a love lost. No wonder his dad avoided him sometimes. Riley couldn't blame him.

"Thanks," he mumbled, blowing his nose again into another napkin. "You're the best."

"I know," she said, grinning. "I hope you feel better. But let's get something straight, okay? The waterworks won't make me spill my guts about what happened at Devil's Creek. I could tell you, but your dad would probably kill me. I'll leave that up to him to tell you when he thinks the time is right."

Riley cracked a smile and blushed. "I wasn't trying—"

"I know," Stephanie said, "but I'm making it clear now. I know how you Tate boys are with words. If your dad can get hundreds of folks to drop their dimes into the collection plate, there ain't no telling what his son can do."

He laughed, and for an instant, all his troubles were forgotten. There was just the two of them in the diner, enjoying each other's company. It could've been any other Saturday in Stauford, when circumstances were better, less stressed.

"Now, what do you say we grab a couple of milkshakes before we head over to the station?"

"I'd like that," he said.

"Do you still like malt?"

"Of course."

"Good," Stephanie said, climbing out of their booth. "When we're on our way, you can tell me all about this Rachel chick while you're at it…"

4

Across town, Jimmy Cord's phone buzzed, pulling him out of a late afternoon doze. His head hummed with a dull ache as he reached under his pillow, felt the vibrating device, and lifted it to his ear.

"Yeah?" Eyes still closed, not bothering to check the screen. Somewhere else in the darkness, his father was singing an old Hank Williams tune out of key while he got ready for work.

"Hey, sexy."

Amber's smoky voice filled his ear, and the blood drained from his face into his groin. Even through the pain pulsing in his face, Jimmy still found his libido intact. He reached under his sheet and touched himself.

"Hey, babe."

"How're you feeling?"

"Like ass," he grunted. "The pain pills are wearing off, but I can't take any more of 'em for at least an hour."

"Poor baby," she cooed. Jimmy smirked, feeling a twinge down below. He loved when she talked to him like that. "I bet I could make you feel better."

"Huh, I bet you could."

"So, did you hear the latest?"

"About the goth freak and the other guys in the woods? Yeah, I heard my old man talking about it on the phone this morning."

"But did ya hear about what the goth freak was up to?"

"Nah, I didn't. What was he doin'?"

"I heard from Samantha Jones that Rachel Matthews was givin' Riley a handy."

Jimmy sat up in surprise and immediately wished he hadn't. The thudding in his skull intensified, a phantom hammer pounding away at the front of his face. He winced and sank back into bed. "Get the fuck out. Seriously?"

"Uh huh. I heard she was close to finishin' him off when Ben and Toby were attacked."

"Wait, how'd Samantha find out? Was she camping too?"

"No, she heard from Joanne Wallace. Mrs. Wallace goes to First Baptist with Rachel's mom, and…well, you know how uptight Mr. and Mrs. Matthews are. They had to give Rachel 'the talk' as soon as she got home."

"Ugh, God." He remembered when his old man gave him "the talk." They'd sat in their backyard in a pair of lawn chairs, Ronny Cord halfway through his second case of beer. Their two German Shepherds were going at it. Jimmy sat in utter horror while his old man slurred on about the birds and the bees. *And all I's tryin' to say is, Jimmy, don't go fuckin' anythin' without a condom. Tha'sh how I ended up with you.*

The fact Rachel's parents hadn't yet given her the talk didn't surprise him, though. Her folks were old-fashioned, always dressing up even to go shop at Walmart, never letting Rachel have a social life to speak of unless it was church related. Jimmy found out the hard way when he'd asked her to a Friday night dance back in middle school. She'd turned him down but invited him to church that Sunday. His hormones almost convinced him to do it, too.

His cheeks flushed with embarrassment, and he was thankful Amber couldn't see him now.

"So gross," Amber said, "her and Riley. I can't wait until Monday, though. It's gonna be hilarious."

"Yeah," Jimmy sighed, closing his eyes. He struggled to focus on her words. "Listen, babe, I'm really hurting. Can I call you later tonight?"

"Aww, but don't you want to see me tonight?"

"Of course I do. It ain't like that at all, Amber. My face, it's just…"

"I made you a promise, didn't I?"

Jimmy's eyes snapped open. His erection throbbed. "Well, yeah, but that was before that faggot broke my nose."

"How 'bout I come pick you up tonight? Your old man's working third shift tonight at the railroad, ain't he?"

"Well, yeah, but—"

"Don't you want me to suck your cock?"

"Well…yeah."

"Good," she giggled. "I'll pick you up 'round nine. See you then."

The line was dead before he had a chance to reply. Jimmy winced as a jolt of pain ripped through his nose. *Fuck this,* he thought, reaching for the prescription bottle on his nightstand. He popped two pills and swallowed them down with a gulp of water.

5

A bank of storm clouds rolled in from the west, blanketing the forest in a downpour that ended the day's search for the two boys with a depressing flourish. The officers were covered in ponchos, having prepared for the possibility of poor weather, but the civilians who'd joined the search—including the Gilpins and Taswells—had done so quickly, and now marched their way back to the campsite parking lot in drenched clothing. No one spoke a word, their voices raw from calling out the names of Ben and Toby, and the mood among the party was sour long before the rains came.

Officer Gray tried to keep his spirits high despite the lack of any solid leads. The heavy footprints leading them beyond the tree line vanished in the undergrowth. Whoever took Ben Taswell and Toby Gilpin could be anywhere, traveling miles from here in the hours they'd spent searching the woods. A nagging thought intruded upon his otherwise positive demeanor: *They're dead, man. You know as well as everyone else does. You saw the look on Grant Taswell's face. He knows it, too.*

Indeed, the look on Grant's face alarmed Marcus. It was the look of utter defeat, a father's instinct that his son wasn't coming back.

John Gilpin wasn't much better. He passed Marcus on the way back to their cars, and Marcus said, "Don't worry, sir. We'll find your boy." Mr. Gilpin looked back, his eyes swollen red, his cheeks pallid. He began to say something but stopped short and offered the officer a weak nod.

Marcus watched the defeated man walk down the gravel path toward his parked sedan. *Poor guy.* He stripped off his poncho and climbed into the car. He'd hated to call off the search, but the inclement weather would only worsen their slow trek into the brush of Daniel Boone National Forest. Though they'd walked a search line for the better part of a day, he estimated they'd covered less than two miles, and found nothing more than the occasional deadfall, animal spoor, or patch of poison ivy. The woods had swallowed every trace of the boys, a thought which drove a chill right down the young officer's spine.

Of course he'd heard the stories. Some bad voodoo went down out here back in the day, long before he was even a twinkle in his daddy's eye, and though the chief hadn't said anything, Marcus figured that's where he was headed when he left earlier. Devil's Creek Road wasn't too far from here, a straight walk through the woods for a few miles, and he wondered if that was the dark cloud hanging over the search party all day. Were they all thinking the boogeyman from Devil's Creek took those boys?

Surely not. Those were ghost stories told by the old folks to scare kids from going out there to party. God knew Marcus had attended his share of drinking parties out near the old church site, amid the skeletal remains of the tiny cultist village, but he'd never seen anything out there. Sure, there were rumors of people hearing children laughing from beyond the tree line, somewhere near the hilltop where the church used to stand, but he'd never heard such things himself.

The creepiest thing he ever saw was a carving in one of the trees out there. A strange symbol, like something out of those tabletop fantasy games his older brother used to play in the basement with his friends on Friday nights. Something foreign and bizarre, a symbol of erratic lines carved together to form a sigil of some kind. A rune. A warning.

His phone vibrated in his pocket, startling him out of his reverie. Marcus pulled out his phone and checked the screen. A text from Chief Bell: Went to Devil's Creek. Nothing there. How is search?

He replied: Pouring rain here. Called off search until tomorrow morning.

A moment later, Bell responded: Headed to station and then home. See you in morning.

Marcus frowned. Sometimes he questioned the chief's sense of duty, but on the other hand, he wouldn't have this job if it weren't for Ozzie Bell. Besides, who was he to doubt Bell's authority? *Nobody,* he thought, starting the car. *That's who.*

As Officer Gray shifted into gear and drove away from the campsite, he found his thoughts returning to the old stories he heard growing up.

The shadows, he thought. *They used to say there were shadows stalking through the trees.*

"Shadows with blue eyes…" he whispered. Another chill crawled down the back of his neck, prompting him to press down on the gas pedal.

6

Agnes Belview stifled a yawn as she parked her Cadillac in Ruth McCormick's driveway. She'd not slept well at all last night. "A bad case of the night haunts," she'd told her husband, Jerry, before packing up her tote bag full of church paperwork. Only they weren't really haunts at all but full-fledged nightmares. Horrible things, with pale children guided by a dark man like a demonic pied piper, his glowing eyes lighting up the darkness of her dreams.

She shivered, pausing to listen to the radio a moment longer before turning off the ignition. The radio DJ spoke of an ongoing search in the woods near Holly Bay Marina following the apparent abduction of two boys. The DJ didn't say the names, nor did he have to—Agnes already knew who they were, courtesy of a phone call from Maddie Gray. Her son, Marcus, called her earlier that morning—the poor boy couldn't do his business without checking in with his dear mother—and let slip the names of the two children who'd been taken. By lunch time, the whole town knew Toby Gilpin and Ben Taswell were missing, and volunteers had departed to offer whatever aid they could in the search.

Agnes gave a silent prayer for the wellbeing of those poor boys, collected her things, and climbed out of the car. She was already twenty minutes late for her church meeting with Ruth. She'd made a habit of meeting every Saturday after Ed McCormick passed away years back, primarily out of comfort for her grieving friend, but also out of their shared duty to lead the ladies of First Baptist to a higher understanding of their lord. Lately their meetings had more to do with the evil sermons from that awful radio station and how the bold Christian women of this town would unite to combat the devil in all his vile incarnations.

But Agnes found she was distracted today. What was this world coming to, when a couple of good Christian kids couldn't go camping in the woods anymore? She shook her head as she walked up the sidewalk toward Ruth's home.

Agnes pulled herself together and rang the doorbell. When a full minute passed, she opened the screen door and knocked.

"Ruth? It's Aggie. Did you forget about our meeting?"

There was movement somewhere in the house—the subtle *pop* of the foundation settling, the weight of someone walking across the room in slow stride.

Agnes knocked again. "Ruth, dear? I can come back if you aren't feeling well. I can—"

The latch clicked and the doorknob turned. Agnes stepped back, the sound stealing breath from her throat. The door opened slowly, and Ruth appeared in the entrance.

Oh my God.

Ruth's eyes were swollen and red, her cheeks pale and her forehead beaded with sweat.

"Good afternoon, Aggie. I'm sorry, I forgot all about our meeting."

"That's...that's all right, Ruthie. I can see you aren't feeling well. I can come back another time, maybe next Saturday." Agnes backed away, turning toward her car, already planning to call Maddie Gray and tell her all about what horrible illness Ruth had come down with.

"Oh, stop that, Aggie. I'm right as rain. Come in." Ruth opened the door wider.

"Are you sure, Ruth? It's no trouble at all to postpone, we're just going over the daily lesson plan, and..."

Ruth smiled. A weak, almost pathetic sort of expression, the smile of someone feeling their age, and worse, someone starved for company. Ruth had been so alone since Ed passed away, and then her neighbor, Imogene, went just a couple of weeks ago. Who else did Ruth have if not her dear friend Agnes?

She turned, and with the slightest hesitation, walked over the threshold into Ruth's home. The dim living room was lit by a single reading lamp next to Ruth's recliner. Musty air filled her nostrils, punctuated with the hint of something sweet and ripe, the pungent odor of fruit nearly gone bad. Static hissed from a small portable radio next to the window, the white noise broken erratically by a voice she didn't recognize. She listened and thought the noise sounded like a sermon of some kind.

A stack of notebooks sat beside the recliner in a haphazard tower, their pages ruffled at the ends. Agnes stared at them for a minute while her eyes adjusted to the gloom. She knew Ruth was staying up late to record the infractions of the late-night devil's broadcasts, but this was too much. Had she literally written down everything?

"Been writing, I see." Agnes cleared her throat, inviting in the stuffy air of this domestic tomb. "Is that all from last night?"

"Not quite," Ruth said, wandering across the living room toward the recliner. She took her seat, plucked a notebook from the top of the pile, and opened it to a marked page. Ruth cocked her head toward the radio like a curious puppy.

Agnes watched her friend for several minutes as she scribbled across the page, her eyes transfixed on the radio. A tear beaded from the rim of her eye and slowly dripped down her cheek into the pursed crevasse of her lips. Ruth wiped it away absently and kept writing.

"W-what are you writing, Ruth? May I see?"

"I'm writing the gospel of our lord, Aggie. Can't you hear Him?" Ruth gestured to the radio. Intermittent static burst from the tiny speaker.

She must be running a fever, Agnes thought.

Agnes tried to steer the conversation back to something tangible, something to engage her friend and bring her back to earth. "Did you hear about those two boys who went missing out in the woods last night? Awful, awful news."

Ruth kept writing, her arthritic hands scribbling across the page at an erratic rate, faster than Agnes could keep up with her eyes. She tilted her head to see what Ruth was writing. Jagged symbols lined the page, a primitive tableau depicting a story she couldn't read. Staring at the odd geometric glyphs made her eyes and head hurt, and she looked away to the door.

"Ruth, maybe you should see a doctor." Agnes reached out, placing her hand on the old woman's forehead. Ruth's skin was ice cold. "I can drive you. Really, I don't mind. I think—"

"Aggie," Ruth said quietly. She put down her pen, set aside her notebook, and stared up at her friend. "I promise you, I've never felt better. Honest."

She took Agnes's hand. Agnes squeaked at the sensation of her friend's touch. Ruth's hands were cold, clammy, the thinning skin pulled tight over her bones.

Like a corpse, oh God, she's dead, she's dead, she's DEAD—

"Now, if you don't mind, I've got more writing to do."

Ruth let go of her friend's hand and took up her pen. Stunned, Agnes slowly backed away toward the door. The radio static grew louder with swollen bursts, mocking her.

"Will I see you at church tomorrow?" The meek rasp of her voice startled her, forcing the air in her throat to hitch.

Ruth didn't look up from her notebook, kept scribbling those weird symbols down the page. "Uh huh. I'll be there, honey. Wouldn't miss it for the world."

Agnes nodded, nearly jumping out of her skin as she backed into the door. A moment later, she was outside and racing to her car, her heart pounding with a fear she didn't fully understand.

The front door stood open, the static laughter seeping out like an aural infection, a chorus bleeding through from beyond.

CHAPTER THIRTEEN

1

Susan wandered across the street from the Burger Stand, toward a pair of red picnic tables in front of the high school. She planted herself on the nearest table and lit a cigarette. A soft breeze brushed her hair back from her forehead, cooling the sweat beading there, offering a slight respite from the day's humidity.

She checked her phone. No texts and no missed calls. She'd not heard from Ozzie since that morning. The latest news she'd heard came via radio chatter from a customer's open window. A search party was underway in the woods, but that was hours ago. Susan looked toward the horizon again and frowned. Dark clouds rolled eastward. Thick gray sheets of rain fell in a distant haze.

A twinge of concern for her boyfriend poked the back of her brain, but the sensation passed as quickly as the breeze. In its place was a growing apathy toward their relationship, a sense that whatever it was between them had run its course and he was only good for the sex—which, let's be honest, wasn't even good to begin with. He was a lumbering ox of a man, intelligent enough to tie his shoes and do his job, but vapid when it came to conversation about things that mattered.

They had nothing in common, and for good reason. In their younger days, Susan was well aware of Ozzie's notoriety. Everyone in Stauford's school system knew who he was. He ran with Ronny Cord and Tony Burgess, a trio of bullies who ruled over the halls of Stauford High like the football gods they were. Ronny was a violent drunk who scraped through life by cleaning the floors of the train depot. Tony worked construction like his old man and would probably die of a heart attack on the job like his old man.

Only Ozzie had amounted to anything, rising to the rank of chief like his daddy before him. His religion was football and hunting, money and drugs. She'd known this going into their relationship, when she'd pursued him at the insistence of her father's godly voice in her head. Before then, however, they were non-entities in each other's lives, two fish on opposite sides of the Stauford pond.

Ozzie had friends, a crowd, he was known in the popular circles. Susan was an outcast like her brothers and sister from the church, one of the cursed Stauford Six. Her siblings were her crowd, and even to them she was an outcast. They might have been kin, bound by their father's blood, but they weren't siblings in the true sense. Susan never felt tied to them. They were inconsequential beings in the great scheme, flesh and blood birthed for offering to their buried lord.

Like her mother, Susan Prewitt was ready to give her life for the sake of their church. This was her purpose in life, an act she was literally born to perform, and the opportunity was stolen from her. Her memories of childhood were marred by a profound sadness, a low-hanging cloud of sorrow hovering over her life for years and evading her understanding—until she bled for the first time. That's when her father finally spoke to her, an errant voice from the grotto of her youth, a place in the earth but filled with the stars of another place. A place where their lord sat upon His throne.

She'd dreamed of the grotto for years, but after the mortifying conversation she'd had with her grandfather about what her bleeding meant, she was haunted with visions before her eyes. Phantoms of the church congregants, standing at her bedside, tracing the symbols of the temple into the walls of her room with their blood. They filled every surface with the lord's scripture, tracing the Old Ways in those odd symbols she couldn't read but could *feel*, each glyph resonating with an electricity in her bones.

Her father stood before her, a spirit cast in impossible moonlight. He looked almost real, almost plausible, and for the first time in her young life, Susan felt something like true happiness.

My little lamb, do you love your father?

"I do," she'd whispered, lying in the darkness of her room, crying with happiness that she wasn't alone and shivering with fear that she might be losing her mind.

Will you be my hand, my eyes and ears? My disciple?

"I will."

She'd made a vow that day and had done so every day since. The sound of her spoken vow softened the world around her, the air suddenly thick and fluttering, a curtain draped over reality itself. There was a paradise behind this world, and soon her father would pull back the curtain to allow her passage. She felt the promise in her bones, her fingertips electric, her nipples hardening, a swell of warmth between her legs. Her mind wandered back to her early memories, to those nights in the grotto with her father, when he'd touched her in the ways society wouldn't understand.

Unlike the others, she welcomed his touch, a desire following her into adulthood. Susan embraced her lineage, running toward her fate. She was alone in her pursuit for so long, until now.

She smiled, her cheeks flushed with warmth when she thought of her brother Zeke. She'd tried to help him years ago, through the ways of flesh and lust, but he wasn't ready to understand. But Zeke understood now. He was with their father. She saw him in her dreams last night, held tightly in their father's embrace. Finally, they would be a family once more—

A sharp jolt ran through her fingertips, and she dropped the smoldering cigarette. She stuck her finger in her mouth to quell the burn. The phone in her apron buzzed. Ozzie's face lit up the screen.

She answered. "Been trying to reach you all day."

"Yeah, I know. I was busy." He spoke with a lazy, stoned drawl. *He's been smoking up.* Susan rolled her eyes. *No wonder he never answered.* "When's your shift over?"

"Hour and a half from now. Why?"

"Need to talk to you."

"About?"

"Your brother."

Susan opened her mouth to ask which one, but she already knew. He was going to ask about the only brother who mattered to her.

"What about Zeke? Is something wrong?"

And then he told her, and Susan decided her relationship with Ozzie Bell might come to an end sooner than she'd planned.

2

Chuck sat in the far corner booth at Devlin's, sipping scotch and looking over the prior day's ledger, wondering if he'd spent all those years in law school to become an overpaid accountant. *Entrepreneur,* he reminded himself as he scrolled down the list of transactions making up Friday night's orders, alcoholic and otherwise. After nearly an hour of reconciling figures, he leaned back and yawned. *I want a vacation,* he thought. *I need a vacation.*

He'd promised himself a trip to the beach—South Carolina, maybe, or even along the gulf somewhere—but then Imogene had passed and managing her estate occupied him more than he cared to admit. Imogene was one of his first clients after he started his practice. She'd hired him years ago to draft her Last Will and Testament, and she'd paid him handsomely to do it. More than he was charging, more than he felt was necessary, but she'd insisted he take it for services rendered. Every year since, she'd paid him a visit to review the document, but only once had she ever made a significant change.

Chuck took another sip of his drink, reflecting on their last meeting. Imogene Tremly was always a chipper old thing, with a smile that could light up a cave and one good eye shimmering with life. The day she walked into his office, however, she'd been anything but those qualities. Her hair was stringy and unwashed, her clothes wrinkled, her good eye puffy and bloodshot from a lack of sleep. She looked as though she'd aged ten years in the month since he'd last seen her at the Kroger in town. He'd passed her in the frozen foods section, smiled, said hello. She'd done the same, and everything was right in the world.

Something was rotten and wrong, but he'd been too afraid to pry, too afraid to ask.

And why's that, Chuck?

He sipped his scotch, savoring the taste of burning smoke as it coated his throat.

Because I was afraid of her.

Which was a foolish notion. If it weren't for Genie Tremly and the other grandparents, he'd be another statistic, another name in the newspapers whenever the infamous "Stauford Death Cult" rose again into public consciousness. His body would still be down there with the rest of them, buried in the ashes.

There were the rumors she was a witch, carrying on the practices of the church even after saving the children from Jacob Masters. Rumors she'd defied Father Jacob and sought to lead the church on her own. Those were just rumors, of course. The people of Stauford were full of shit when it came to their rumors, one of the few universal constants left in that part of the world. But what about the things she'd told him in confidence?

Ah, yes, Chuck, what about those privileged things?

He took another sip and grimaced back the liquid fire.

The burden of his attorney-client privilege weighed heavily on him at first, but the weight grew easier to bear with each substantial payment from Ms. Tremly. Most of what Imogene had to confide in him had happened when he was a child, still in therapy after the fire and suicides.

There were several unresolved questions in the fallout of the Devil's Church scandal. Jacob Masters convinced most of his congregation to sell off their property and belongings and donate the proceeds to The Lord's Church of Holy Voices. The assumption, then, was Masters had hoarded the money for his personal gain, but when authorities froze the remaining assets in Masters's name, they found his bank accounts empty.

The man who was Jacob Masters severed most of his ties with the modern world prior to building his community in the woods, and what little he'd left behind wasn't worth much more than a few thousand dollars. No deed to the property in the forest was ever found, nor was there ever any record such a deed existed. The small house Masters inherited from his father was sparsely decorated and lacked any sign of renovation or luxury and was eventually sold at auction to a property developer who leveled the structure as soon as the ink was dry.

And the money? Some speculated it was buried out in the woods somewhere, or that Masters burned it. What happened to the missing "Masters fund" remained a mystery for the better part of twenty years until Imogene walked into Chuck's office one afternoon and asked about getting her affairs in order.

Let's be honest, Chuck. Did you really think your grandpa could afford to pay for law school out of his own pocket?

No, he didn't, but whenever he'd brought it up to his grandfather, Gage Tiptree waved him off. *It's taken care of*, he said. *Just worry about your studies.*

Chuck wondered if Jack had questioned Imogene, or if he'd ever wondered where she found the money to pay for art school. Had Stephanie questioned how her grandmother managed to put so much money away, money which Maggie Green bequeathed to Stephanie in her will? Money which Stephanie used to help start her radio station? Or what about Bobby and Susan? Had they batted an eye during the estate settlements when they learned they were entitled to substantial sums? Money which they'd used to buy their homes? Hell, even Zeke received a stipend from his grandpa Roger's estate, but he'd blown most of it on drugs and forfeited a chunk of it to the state after he was arrested for possession all those years ago.

The day Imogene dropped a bomb on him, he'd made a down payment on a new car out of his own pocket, money he'd earned through his own hard work in a profession he'd studied to practice. And his education? Paid for with blood money.

No, he thought, *you weren't afraid to ask. You've never been too afraid to ask. You just didn't want to know. You didn't want her to tell you what she'd been up to over the years while Jack was out of town. You didn't want to know if there was truth to what the townsfolk said about her, about the chanting and strange lights out at her house, about what those men in the Klan said happened one night with the fire. Just like you didn't want to know about the money, about the six-way split among the grandparents.*

There was only one question he'd asked her about the whole thing, aside from how she wanted her estate to be handled. One question he simply needed to know, lest his image of her be completely shattered forever.

"Is the money the real reason you left the church? Is that what started all of this?"

She'd sat staring at him for several minutes, not blinking, her smile failing her as the air between them grew warm, suffocating. Finally, Imogene had said, *"It wasn't about the money. We didn't even think about the money, not until after it was all said and done. And we all agreed it would be better served takin' care of you kids than lettin' it get swallered up by the state."*

He'd played their meeting over and over in his mind for years, wondering if she'd told him the truth, feeling ungrateful for speculating on her intentions. He wouldn't be alive if not for Imogene and the others. None of them would.

He leaned back in the seat, watching the restaurant fill up, and thought about breaching a client's confidentiality for the first time in his life. Maybe he'd tell Jack and Stephanie and even Bobby, if the poor guy could handle it.

Chuck raised his glass and downed the rest of the scotch in a single gulp, setting his throat and gut on fire. Elsewhere in the restaurant, the house band began the opening notes of their cover of "Goodbye, Horses." *Then again,* he thought, *maybe telling them is not such a great idea.*

He closed his laptop. In his profession, telling the truth often caused as much harm as good.

3

Jack parked outside the small modular building and looked up at the adjacent radio tower. Z105.1 flashed above, bathing the surrounding hillside in red neon. Over the hill, beyond a line of trees, traffic sped across the overpass and down Main Street. Two other cars were parked in the parking lot, and though he was already a few minutes late, Jack remained seated, collecting himself before going inside.

He'd driven home after the meeting with the professor, but the things the old man said remained with Jack in the hours since. They lingered in the forefront of his mind as he returned to his grandmother's house and wandered its rooms like a ghost, struggling to make sense of everything. He busied himself with cleaning up the broken glass in the foyer, reinforcing the seal of plastic over the shattered windows, and leaving a message for the repair guy Chuck recommended, but the mystery left behind by his late grandmother persisted.

Her final years were devoted entirely to research on the nature of Devil's Creek, and he couldn't shake the feeling her breadcrumb trail was missing a vital piece, something that would tie everything up and let him move on. Maybe she was simply obsessed with that part of her life—and why not? What happened out there in the woods all those years ago defined her.

Only that didn't make sense to him. Mamaw Genie told him everything, promising she'd never keep a secret. The revelation of what she'd been up to didn't bother him nearly as much as the fact she'd kept it from him. Even the money she'd left him in her will was a shock, especially when he remembered some weeks she'd pinched pennies to fulfill a grocery order, when her checks from the state came a day or two later than usual and her brow furrowed with worry like a looming storm.

There was a whole other part of Imogene Tremly's life he'd missed, another side that left him feeling cold and confused, worsened by the fact he couldn't face her and ask why. Why was she digging up the past? Why was she researching Hermetic symbols? And why did she need that creepy idol?

Part of him wished he'd stayed in New York. The other part wished he'd left town yesterday after his meeting with Chuck, before his nagging curiosity got the better of him.

His phone vibrated, and he checked the screen. A new text from his agent: "Checking in. Everything okay?" Jack stared at the message, his fingers hovering over the digital keyboard, but his mind was frozen. What could he say? *No, everything's not okay, I just learned my grandma was up to some weird shit that had to do with the cult we were a part of when I was a kid. My father was a fucked-up preacher who molested me and my brothers as part of some twisted ritual underneath our church.*

Instead, he replied: "All is well. Doing interview with local radio DJ. Will call later."

He sent the text without second-guessing himself and stepped out into the low evening light. The afternoon storms broke the day's humidity, and the world breathed a collective sigh of relief with a soft breeze that felt good against his hot skin. Jack closed the car door and relished the scent of autumn lingering in the air: dead leaves and cut grass. For so much that changed in Stauford, the look and feel of southern Kentucky's dusky light on his face felt familiar, a kiss from an old friend he'd not seen in years. The sensation felt like his childhood. The good parts, anyway.

Refreshed, the troubling thoughts shoved safely away to the back part of his mind, Jack put on his game face and walked toward the building. A couple minutes later, he stood in the front office of the radio station. A lanky fellow with black hair and glasses sat behind the receptionist's desk with a phone perched between his shoulder and ear. He offered Jack a smile and mouthed *one minute* before gesturing to the row of empty seats.

Jack took a seat, half-listening to the phone conversation while taking in the décor. Several framed newspaper articles hung on the walls, sporting headlines such as "New Station Riles Listeners" and "Christian Groups Protest Rock Radio." One such headline was printed in large blocky text from the Tribune's Op-Ed section: "THE GOAT GETS OUR GOAT." Above them all hung a larger decal of the station's mascot with the station's call sign.

The thin fellow behind the desk hung up his phone. He stuck out his hand as Jack rose to meet him.

"Sorry. I'm Ryan Corliss, the station's producer."

"Jack Tremly. Stephanie's brother."

Ryan smiled. "The famous artist. I've heard a lot about you."

Jack shrugged, his cheeks warming at the recognition.

"Good things, I hope?"

"Nothing but," Ryan said. "Stephanie and Riley are in the studio. I'll walk you."

Riley? Jack wondered, searching his memory, and then remembered: Bobby's son. He'd not expected to meet his nephew tonight and had only seen the occasional photos of the boy over the years courtesy of his grandmother's emails. The sudden prospect excited and terrified him.

His trepidation slipped away as Ryan led him down a short hallway and into the control room. Stephanie sat at the mixing board, checking emails on her phone while Chris Cornell sang "Black Hole Sun" through the surround sound speakers. A plush leather sofa lined the wall on the opposite side of the room, and there sat a slim teenager dressed in ripped jeans, black combat boots, and a snug T-shirt sporting the skeletal logo of The Misfits. He held a smartphone in his hands. The kid's nails were painted glossy black.

Jack smiled. *I can definitely see who his favorite aunt is.*

Stephanie stood to meet them. She reached out and gave Jack a hug. "Thanks for coming," she said, turning to Ryan. "Thanks for showing him in."

Ryan shrugged. "Hey, no problem, boss. Now, if you don't mind, I have a date to be getting to."

"Meeting Victor tonight?"

Ryan winked at her. "You know it."

"Have fun, tiger."

After Ryan saw himself out of the control room, Stephanie turned her attention to Riley. "Jack, I'd like you to meet our nephew. Riley, meet Jack."

The boy stood—except he wasn't a boy at all, not anymore, not the serious child Jack recognized from his grandmother's photos. He'd grown into a young man, the tell-tale hints of stubble shadowing his chin and upper lip. Jack saw a glimpse of Riley's father in his portrait, a living flashback to the boy Jack remembered racing down Main Street, fishing in the shallows of Layne Camp Creek, or trembling in fear in the dark recesses beneath the old church.

"I love your work," he said. "Steph's told me all about you. I've got one of your prints hanging in my room, and I've even got that art book you wrote a few years ago. Is it true you get your ideas from dreams? I heard you only sleep, like, two hours a night—"

Jack shot Stephanie a glance, smiling. "Big fan?"

"Huge," she said, placing her hand on Riley's shoulder. "You guys have plenty of time to talk, but right now, he's my interview. Got it?"

Riley blushed. "Sorry, Jack."

"No worries, man. We'll chat in a few." Jack turned to his sister, who held open the door to the studio. "You promise this will be painless?"

Stephanie thought for a moment and grinned. "No, but it's like we used to say when we were kids: sometimes good things hurt."

He snorted back a laugh. He'd forgotten all about the old saying, really nothing more than a joke between them, lifted out of a newspaper clipping talking about the Stauford Six. Some state senator had chimed in about their debacle, suggesting they be divided from their families and given a fresh start.

Sometimes good things hurt, he thought, walking into the studio. *I guess there's some truth in that statement.*

4

Ozzie Bell kicked off his boots and reclined on Susan's sofa, awash in the radiant glow of the TV screen. Condensation dripped down the neck of his beer onto his hand, where he let it collect for a few minutes before rubbing the cool water along his forehead. He closed his eyes, listening to the thrum of his heart and the babble of the news station out of Hazard, Kentucky. A pretty young blonde talked about the latest tragedy unfolding out of Stauford, two young boys who were abducted by two unknown assailants while on a camping trip. Officer Gray appeared on screen for a brief statement recorded earlier that day.

Should've been you, Oz. I didn't raise you to be no loser. The late David Bell's voice rose from the crowded halls of Ozzie's mind. He knew the voice well, the deep sound of a giant walking through a forest, certain in its purpose and determined to destroy everything in its way. The voice of Ozzie's doubt always took on the voice of the former police chief. After all, hadn't David Bell always been the monster in Ozzie's closet?

I ain't no pussy. He took a sip of his beer.

Could'a fooled me, boy. What are you drinkin'? Coors? That's pussy beer. A real man would be drinkin' Pabst. Hell, a real *man would be drinkin' something even stronger. Ain't you got nothin' better to drink, you pussy?*

Ozzie finished off his beer in another gulp, grimacing at the swill's shallow taste. He remembered the liquor Susan kept in the cabinet above her refrigerator. Good old Kentucky bourbon bled right from the mountains. Something stronger, something more refined. Something his father would drink.

"I ain't no pussy," he muttered. He certainly felt like a pussy. Oh, sure, he'd left the crime scene to pursue a possible lead, full of good intentions, ready to play the hero and deliver those two boys safe from harm, but Zeke's appearance at Devil's Creek spooked him. Zeke's face was all wrong—he was too happy, too conscious, his eyes filled with a dangerous sort of intelligence which Ozzie had never seen in the man before. Zeke Billings was the fuck-up, the drug-dealing dope fiend Ozzie kept in his pocket for a side-hustle whenever he needed the extra cash, or better yet, some good shit for himself.

Like the meth Zeke and Waylon were supposedly cooking for him right now. Ozzie would sell some of it, sure, but he had every intention of sampling the wares. God, he could use something right now to take the edge off, but he'd smoked the last of his weed earlier. All she had in the house was booze, and the cheap shit at that.

When he opened the cabinet, there was a half-gallon bottle of bourbon. He uncapped the bottle and tipped it back. Liquid fire poured down his throat, and he coughed twice before taking another quick shot.

"Fuckin' hell," he croaked, carrying the bottle back to the comfort of the sofa. With his belly and throat burning, Ozzie sank into the cushions. Saturday night's sports scores flashed on the screen, but his mind drifted to darker matters, driven by the booming voice of his dead father.

You say you ain't a pussy, but I ain't so convinced, boy. A real man wouldn't think about arrestin' his girlfriend's brother for kidnappin' those two kids in the woods. A real man would do the work, find the real perps, and save the day.

But the circumstances were too convenient. The kidnappers were in the same area as Devil's Creek, headed off in that direction by the Tate boy's eyewitness account. There were two kidnappers, and Ozzie happened to hire two idiots to cook a batch of meth the day before. Two idiots who'd need a quiet, secluded place to do the job.

What about a motive, boy? Ain't you even got that? What would those two druggie dumbfucks want with those boys? Why would they travel a couple miles through the woods and take two kids? Yer whole story's fulla holes, boy. It's lazy police work.

All he could think about was the look in Zeke's eyes. Hadn't his father also told him there's no such thing as a coincidence when it comes to being a cop? Finding Zeke Billings in the same area as those missing boys was one hell of a coincidence. Two kidnappers. Two meth cooks. Too easy.

Something was wrong, you pussy. You knew he was actin' funny, but ya turned tail and ran. You got spooked by a scary campfire story. You was raised better'n that.

Ozzie grunted in reply to the voice in his head. David Bell was fond of telling the story about Devil's Creek, especially after he'd downed a few beers himself. Ozzie heard all those stories when he was a kid, courtesy of his braggart father. His mother, Eileen Bell, disapproved of such stories, but Daddy Bell wasn't one to quiet himself because of a woman. He'd sat Ozzie on his knee and regaled him with tales of blood-soaked bodies decorating the landscape. Ozzie heard all about the weird Satanic shit Jacob Masters got up to out in the woods, the voices people heard coming from within the earth, the shadows lurking among the trees. He'd had nightmares for weeks.

Ozzie's mind drifted, the room slowly spinning in a thick, warm haze. He closed his eyes and let his thoughts wander.

Sure, he'd gotten spooked by a scary campfire story, but who could blame him? Certainly not his father. David Bell passed away five years ago from a heart attack, God rest his soul. Ozzie was sure his father would disapprove of him dating one of the kids from the church, too. David Bell was one of the folks in town who'd spoken out against the reintegration of the Stauford Six into the school system, even from his position as an elected official. After all, wasn't David Bell the protector of the town, the voice of local law? *Those kids will poison the well,* David Bell said to a Tribune reporter. He'd framed the article, and it hung in his office until his death.

Speaking out publicly wasn't the only thing David Bell did. As the Grand Dragon of Stauford's Brotherhood of White Purity, Chief David Bell led his fellow white-sheeted brothers in an organized "protest" in front of Imogene Tremly's home. Their efforts hadn't gone well—"The witch still has some magic left in her," his father said—and the Brotherhood went quiet in the following weeks, but the rumors of Genie Tremly's witchcraft and her association with the church were just beginning to bubble to the surface. Ozzie didn't know for sure, but he suspected his old man had something to do with that as well.

A small town like Stauford thrived on rumors, manufacturing drama almost daily, and it loved nothing more than to bask in the shadow of a boogeyman. The old Tremly woman fit the bill even with Jacob Masters out of the picture, and in the years since the church's destruction, everyone had a Tremly story. They'd either seen strange lights pulsing from the upstairs windows of her house, heard ominous chanting leaking through the walls, or knew someone who had. The gossip train had left the station, charging full steam ahead with the old woman tied firmly to its tracks. Ozzie felt a stab of empathy for the old woman, but the sensation was muted by the alcohol in his bloodstream.

All those folks at Devil's Creek got a raw deal, but none more so than the ones who survived. What happened to those kids wasn't right. Maybe they'd outgrown the stigma, maybe what happened to them slipped into the shadows of Stauford's history, but that didn't change the fact they'd all been treated poorly. God knows, he'd done his share of treating them that way when they were kids, and he supposed he'd have to answer for that. *Someday,* he thought.

His mind drifted back to Susan, and he wondered where she was. Didn't she say she'd be home soon? Wasn't she bringing him a late dinner?

He couldn't remember. His memory was fuzzy. They'd spoken on the phone, he'd talked to her about his suspicions of Zeke, and something had happened. Her voice grew cold, mechanical. *She didn't sound like herself,* he thought. *She was different.*

A flash of Zeke's wide eyes, his vein-streaked face pulled back into an impossible smile, one so wide it split his cheeks in half and could swallow the world.

"She sounded like him," he muttered to the dark. A chill crawled across his arms. He fumbled for the blanket draped over the back of the sofa and pulled it around his shoulders for comfort, but the cold would not abate. Sleep offered no solace, and when he dreamed, he found Zeke's horrifying face smiling in the dark.

5

Jack shifted uncomfortably in his seat. A muffled boom microphone hung before his face, and he eyed it warily as Stephanie situated herself at her desk. He spied Riley through the soundproof glass. The young man looked away when he saw Jack watching, shifting his gaze to the phone in his hands.

"Okay," Stephanie said, swiveling in her seat to face him. "We are ready to roll. All set?"

Jack forced himself to smile. The pre-interview jitters were something he'd never shaken, not even since fame found him in the world of art and film, and although he told himself he was only talking to Stephanie, the fact made his jitters even worse. Maybe it was because she'd know where he was coming from with his inspirations. They'd shared the horror in their childhood, and if anyone could relate, she would.

"Hey, are you all right?"

"Huh?" Jack blinked, startled from his thoughts. "Yeah, sorry. I get...tense when I do this sort of thing."

Stephanie smiled. "Don't worry. We aren't live. This is being recorded, and you can give your blessing before we take it to air. Deal?"

"Deal."

"Right then," Stephanie said, pressing a button on her console. A red light blinked on. "We're recording now. I'll do an introduction after the fact. For now, let's talk a little bit about your history. You're a Stauford native. Why'd you leave this fine town of ours?" When he wrinkled his nose at the question, Stephanie smirked. "Be honest, Mr. Tremly."

Jack blurted out the first thing that came to mind. "Because there's nothing for me here. I mean, let's face it. Stauford, Kentucky isn't exactly the art capitol of the world, you know?"

Stephanie grinned. "Felt good to get that out, didn't it?"

"It really did. That's not going to be in the real interview, is it?"

"Of course not. I just wanted you to lighten up. No, this is all about your art."

Time drifted away as they spoke, and Jack forgot about his reservations, falling into the rhythm of a one-on-one conversation. He didn't think about the recording again until Stephanie asked her final question.

Stephanie cleared her throat. "Most listeners of our fine station know I keep a print of your most famous painting in my home."

"Do you really?"

"I do, right above my toilet."

Jack laughed. "I guess that's a good place for it."

"It is! It's a great conversation starter, you know? And I get asked by a lot of people, 'Where does your brother get his ideas?' I tell them it's not my place to answer, and I've long promised I'd get you on the air if given the opportunity. So, since you're back in your hometown, I thought I'd ask you directly about a pair of paintings, one of which graces my porcelain throne at home."

He leaned back and took a sip of water. *Here it comes,* he thought, bracing himself for the question he gets asked during every interview. He'd become a master of deflection with this topic, mainly because most folks wouldn't understand, but Stephanie had lured him into a comfortable space, and he felt drunk with honesty. The prospect of telling the truth about his art for once felt liberating.

"Okay," he said. "Shoot."

"Your painting *A Congregation of Jackals* deals with a rather touchy topic here in Stauford. For those of our listeners who've never seen the painting, it depicts a mob of figures in white sheets holding torches while a black child watches from a window. We both know Stauford's got a disgusting history when it comes to racism—what part of the country below the Bible Belt doesn't? But when I look at this painting…" She held up her phone, revealing an image of the painting in question. "…there's something personal to it. It isn't just about Stauford's racist roots, is it?"

Jack breathed slowly, measuring his words. After a full minute of silence, Stephanie reached across the desk and placed her hand on his. "We can skip this one if you want."

"No," he said, "it's okay. I don't think I've ever been asked before. Not about the personal nature of it."

"Are you sure? I don't mind skipping it, Jackie."

"It's cool, honest. So…" He took another breath, exhaled. "…the painting is *entirely* personal. When I drew the initial sketch, I wasn't trying to make a statement about Stauford's past reputation. Something most folks don't know about me is, I was raised by my grandmother. You might say she…saved me from a bad situation. And some folks in town, they thought she was a bad person for it." He paused, and Stephanie nodded for him to continue. "So, one of my earliest memories as a kid is of the Klan showing up at my grandma's door in the middle of the night. They'd come to burn a cross in her yard, taunt her, call her a witch. And…"

He trailed off, stopping short of the way Mamaw Genie commanded their flames, turning the fire against them. He remembered the heat, the smell of smoke, the screams and shouts as one of the Klansmen caught fire. And he remembered the blue light filling the house, surrounding Mamaw Genie in an azure aura, illuminating her so brightly her every feature was visible even in the night.

The blue light.

The idol.

Jack's mouth went dry. He felt so foolish for not making the connection before.

"Jack?"

He blinked. "Yeah, sorry. That's where the painting came from. Those men showing up to bully my grandmother."

"My grandma told me that story when I was a girl. I'm so sorry it happened to you and Genie."

"It's okay. She dealt with it the only way she knew how." His mind drifted back to the idol.

Trust your gut, he told himself. *She needs to know.*

"Last question, I promise. Answer however you wish, okay? I won't torture you anymore than is necessary." Stephanie held up her phone again, revealing the macabre image of *Midnight Baptism.* "What can you tell me about this?"

Jack frowned and closed his eyes. "Yeah, about that one. I do have something to tell you."

"I'm all ears."

"No," he said, meeting her gaze. "This is a story you probably don't want to hear. But I think you need to."

6

Riley slouched down on the plush sofa, half-listening to Stephanie and Jack talking through the speakers, half-focused on the screen of his phone. His mind was elsewhere, wondering how much trouble Rachel was in with her parents, wondering if he'd have a chance to talk to her at church tomorrow morning. Wondering if Ben and Toby were okay.

He took a breath, tried to push those thoughts away, but they kept squirming back to the forefront of his mind. Twenty-four hours ago, his friends were setting up their tents, chatting about what transpired at school, the look on Jimmy Cord's face when Riley socked him with a lunch tray, their homework for Mr. Pilman's English class.

Just a day ago, life was somewhat normal, or as normal as a teenager could expect in Stauford. How many days had they pined for something exciting to happen in their little Podunk town?

We got our wish, Ben. Now I wish it hadn't happened to you.

He thought of the figures in the woods and their glowing eyes. God, those eyes were impossibly bright, unnatural.

"—remember the blue eyes?"

Riley's breath caught in his throat. He looked up at the two adults talking in the other room. Jack spoke with a tremor in his voice, the words coming through the studio speakers loud and clear.

Stephanie shook her head. "I haven't thought about that in a long time."

"Yeah," Jack went on, "well, I've thought about it every night for as long as I can remember. Maybe it's a nightmare, but it feels real. It's got that dreamy quality, where everything is a blur, you can't remember how you got there or what came after, just that moment in the grotto."

Stephanie held up her hand. "Maybe we should stop here."

"No, let me get this out. I need you to hear it. Okay?"

"Okay." Stephane glanced through the window at Riley. He met her eyes, and for the first time he saw something he'd never seen in her before: fear. His badass aunt Steph faced the criticism and scorn of an entire town without batting an eye, but this? Her face was pale, her eyes glassy with tears, and her voice trembled. Riley wanted to tell her it would be okay, but she turned away before he could get her attention.

"I don't know about you, but one of my earliest memories is of the grotto beneath the church. The dark place, where the stars shone from within the earth. That's where he took the six of us, to baptize us."

"I don't..."

"Our father took us there, and our mothers watched. They gathered on the shore, beneath the stars, but I don't think they were stars at all. They were—"

"Eyes," Stephanie whispered. "My God, they were eyes."

"Yes," Jack said, "millions of eyes watching while Jacob marked us."

"Old lies above," she said, "new love below. Isn't that what he used to say?"

Jack nodded. "I've been haunted by that memory all my life, Steph. *Midnight Baptism* is the result of those nightmares, and it's kind of funny because most people think I made all this shit up. Except I was pulling those awful things from memory, not my dreams. I even had myself convinced it was all fiction, nothing more than a recurring night terror. Shit, I spent a fortune on therapy for myself just to arrive at the conclusion, but...it all changed last night."

"What do you mean?"

"I mean, I found this."

He leaned down and retrieved something, but Riley couldn't see over the mixing board. All he could see was Stephanie's confused reaction.

"I don't understand," she said. "Your grandmother kept a diary?"

"Not exactly. Look closer."

"She was researching the church? Wait, I've seen these symbols before."

Jack nodded. "Me too. We all have. They used to be inscribed over the pulpit in the church. And these symbols here, they're etched into Mamaw Genie's gravestone."

"What do they mean?"

"I'm not sure. But this isn't everything. Do you remember the idol?"

"How could I forget it?"

"My grandma paid someone to go get it for her. I found it with this notebook locked in her old writing desk. She left the key with Chuck. He gave it to me at the probate meeting."

Stephanie let out a low whistle and leaned back in her seat. "What do you think it means?"

"I don't know," he sighed. "It gives me a bad feeling, you know? It's like I've stepped into one of my nightmares. I've had the feeling ever since I arrived yesterday. I keep going back to memories of what happened. What I used to think was a dream. I keep thinking about what that sick bastard did to us, what our moms *let* him do to us. And our father's awful blue eyes…"

Riley's heart skipped a beat, and he exhaled a hot lungful of air. He was so caught up in their conversation he'd forgotten to breathe, filled with a growing fear his uncle's story might be related to his missing friends in the woods. Could the man with glowing eyes be their father? His grandfather? The boogeyman who burned to death in the church at Devil's Creek?

God, this is so stupid. No one comes back from the dead, you idiot. Except Jesus, and maybe that's even up for debate. His father's voice piped up in his head. *You're forgettin' about Lazarus, son. He came back, too.*

Riley waited at the door. Would they believe him? Would they pass this off as a troubled kid seeking attention? No, Stephanie wouldn't. And Jack? Maybe, maybe not, although Riley suspected Jack would believe him before anyone else. After telling a story like that, how could he not?

He opened the door to the studio and tiptoed inside. Stephanie turned to him.

"What is it, Riley?"

"I've seen him," the boy said. "The man with the blue eyes."

7

Jimmy braced himself as Amber stepped on the gas, urging her neon green Volkswagen around the curve at full speed, spewing chunks of gravel in their wake. They splashed down into a puddle of rainwater with a jolt, prompting a sudden yip from Amber followed by her shrill laugh. Jimmy hated her laugh, hated the piercing quality of it. Nothing was that goddamn funny, least of all her death-wish driving.

But when he looked over and saw her plump lips illuminated in the glow of the dashboard light, everything he despised about Amber Rogers drifted down below his waistline. He imagined kissing those lips; he imagined those lips kissing him, and not just on his face, either. *Soon,* he thought. The car bumped and caught air as they hit a pothole at full speed. Jimmy's stomach lurched, and his swollen nose throbbed when he clenched his jaw. *Maybe if we survive the trip.*

After another mile of fearing for his life, Amber pressed the brake and slowed the car as they rounded another bend. Their headlights lit up the back bumper of a rusty yellow pickup truck parked in the wet grass along the gravel path. Jimmy didn't recognize it.

"Looks like we ain't alone out here," Amber said. "You ever come out here before?"

"Sure," Jimmy said, the lie slipping from his mouth before he had time to think. "All the time."

"I love coming out here."

I bet you do, Jimmy thought, biting his cheeks to fend off a smile. He'd heard all the stories from the rest of Stauford's varsity players. Amber Rogers was the unofficial team mascot, having made her rounds not once, but twice with the rest of the team. Her conquests were legendary, even running a train with the entire team at Tommy Harmon's house party the weekend his parents went out of town last year. Jimmy knew those rumors were true, too—Tommy had photos on his phone to prove it.

When Amber first showed interest in Jimmy, he was somewhat disgusted by her advances. She was gorgeous, sure, and she had an amazing ass, but she'd also been held back twice, and would be eighteen in another month or so. He was practically jailbait to her, and the thought of being her sloppy fifths turned his stomach, but the rest of the team talked him into it. Fucking Amber Rogers was a rite of passage with the Stauford Bulldogs, and he'd intended to cement his place on the team.

Amber shut off the engine but left the radio on. This far out in the boonies, they couldn't pick up the Top 40 station in town, but the old rock station out of Knoxville came in loud and clear. She turned down the volume and unbuckled her seatbelt. Jimmy leaned back against the headrest and closed his eyes, trying to focus on anything but the pain.

"How's your nose?"

"Hurts like a bitch," he muttered. "That fucking guy is so dead."

She giggled. "Can I watch? When you kick his ass?"

"You'd wanna see that?"

"Damn right, I do. He broke your face." She smacked her fist into her palm. "And I love that baby face of yours."

Something stirred inside him, something he'd not felt since grade school when he gave Tiffany Bradford a flower at recess. A fluttering in his gut, an electric jolt in his heart. Such feelings were forbidden in his social stream and better left unsaid. If word got out Jimmy Cord felt something for this slut, his reputation as Stauford's rising football star would be over before it began. Emotions were out of bounds in this game. He knew he was the next name on the team's roster for Amber Rogers, as much a rite of passage for her as she was for him.

She reached out and traced her fingers along his jawline. The fluttering sensation climbed up his chest. He sucked in his breath, and for a moment, Jimmy let his mind wander into a forbidden territory of daydreams and fantasies. What if Amber Rogers really *liked* him? Hell, what if she *loved* him? And what if he felt the same way? His father would think less of him, and the guys on the team would ridicule him, but none of that would matter because he'd have her. In a flash, he saw them going to college together, maybe even getting married, maybe—

"So," Amber said, curling a lock her hair around her finger, "I made you a promise."

"Uh huh."

"Want me to keep my promise?"

Jimmy grinned, his face flushing with heat. He forgot all about the pain of his broken nose. His hormones were in overdrive, the rest of his body going numb as his blood redirected south. The world swam before him, filtered through a dirty lens, its edges hazy. In the center was Amber's flirty grin, her smooth skin, her big eyes reflecting the glow from the light of the radio dial. When she touched his arm, his skin erupted in gooseflesh, her fingertips like electric fire surging all the way down his body. He gasped.

"I'll take that as a yes. The seat reclines back, you know."

Jimmy swallowed hard, his heart racing, his numb hands fumbling for the release lever on the side of his seat. He pulled it too hard and the whole seat flew backward. They both laughed, their voices filled with an awkward nervousness—or was it an eagerness? A heated desire, something they'd both wanted for what felt like forever, but in reality, was only a couple of weeks. Two weeks felt like years to a couple of horny teenagers, each moment of wanting drawn out, second by agonizing second. God, Jimmy never felt this way before. The waiting, the anticipation of her lips around him, was almost euphoric.

Amber put her hand on his chest. "Lay back," she whispered, smiling. "Close your eyes."

"I want to watch," he said, almost in desperation, as if he needed her permission. And why wouldn't he? She was in control here. He was hers, now and forever.

She gave him a mischievous glance as her fingers found his zipper. Jimmy smiled, waiting for heaven at the tip of her tongue.

Something caught his eye above the back of her head, through the windshield. Movement.

"Hey," he mumbled. She giggled, her fingers fumbling with the fly of his jeans, but she did not stop. Something brushed past the windshield. Something pale blue glowing in the night. There were sounds, too. Muted chittering, shrill, almost sing-song in nature, a sound taking him back to elementary school when his class was set free to roam the playground across the street.

His mind was dragged away from the imminent euphoria happening below his waist. His heart raced—not from the feel of Amber's tongue, but from the sudden terror of something outside the car. Something unseen that sounded like children.

"Hey…" He pushed his fingers into her hair. "Stop for a minute."

"Uh-uh," she groaned, pushing him deeper into her mouth. Jimmy tried to sit up, hissing as her teeth scraped against his rigid flesh. Finally, she let go of him, frowning as he went limp in her hand.

"What's your deal? Ain't you enjoyin' it?"

He ignored her snide tone. "There's something outside."

"What?"

"It sounded like kids."

Amber leaned back in her seat, wiping spittle from her chin. She glanced down at his flaccid penis and smirked. "You ain't, like, a fag or anything, are you?"

"Goddammit," Jimmy spat. He tucked himself back into his briefs and zipped his fly. "It ain't you. I'm tellin' you, there's someone out there. Look." He pointed to his window, at the pair of dim lights beyond the tree line. "Don't you see that?"

She peered out the window and shrugged. "I don't see shit," and then, under her breath, "First time this has ever happened."

"What?"

"Huh? Oh, nothin'."

"No," Jimmy said, "what the fuck did you say?"

Amber laughed, driving shrill spikes into his ears. "I said, 'First time this has ever happened.'"

"What the fuck's that supposed to mean?"

"Means what I said. First time I ever had a boy go limp in this mouth."

"Yeah, I bet it's been a while since you had a first, ain't it?"

Her smile fell in shock. Jimmy smirked, returning his attention to the window. The shapes were gone, and after a minute of staring he wondered if anything had been there at all. Had he imagined the laughter? The movement?

"This is boring." Amber turned the radio dial. Tom Petty's drawl oozed through the car speakers, singing about one last dance with Mary Jane. Amber hummed along, and Jimmy followed the lyrics in his head as he searched the darkness for the phantom shapes.

They were both so caught up in the song they didn't hear the scratching along the outside of the car, the telltale drumming of small fingertips on the trunk, the back door, the driver door. Only when the latch released for Amber's door did she squeal, more from surprise than fear. She didn't have an opportunity to scream for real.

The door swung open, and in the time Amber cried out in shock, a pale hand reached inside and shoved its mud-caked fingers into her mouth. A boy with dirty hair and piercing blue eyes appeared in the opening. Jimmy scrambled backward, pressing himself against the car door.

"Jesus Christ!"

"False prophet," the boy hissed, shoving his hand further into Amber's mouth. She writhed in agony, gagging, gasping for air and swatting at her attacker. The boy's ruddy face looked familiar, but in the poor light, Jimmy couldn't be sure. He watched in horror as thick black worms protruded from the boy's naked arm. They seeped from his pores, crawled down the length of his arm toward his wrist, and slipped inside Amber's swollen maw.

Jimmy's gut lurched. He tasted bile at the back of his throat. Amber looked to him, blinking a silent plea for help as tears slid down her cheek. The black worms wriggled past her lips, some of them spilling down the front of her shirt, others working their way into her nostrils. One wriggled into the tender flesh below her eye.

Oh fuck, oh fuck, oh fuck. Jimmy's mind raced as he fumbled for the door latch. He tumbled backward into the night, landing with a dull plop on the damp grass. A cool breeze met his hot skin, kissing the back of his neck, attempting to soothe him in this time of panic. He scrambled to his feet, his head and face throbbing in force. *Need to get away. Run. Follow the road. Follow—*

"Come back, Jimmy. I want you to meet our god."

He *knew* that voice. Toby Gilpin. They had homeroom together. Toby was always goofing off in class, always getting on the teacher's nerves, cracking jokes, a little shit who wanted to be friends with all the cool kids but who never would. All the times Jimmy bullied him flashed before his eyes as he weighed his options. He could run, follow the road, or he could disappear into the woods, maybe follow the tree line for a while.

A pale face emerged from around the side of the car. Toby Gilpin's eyes glowed in the darkness, illuminating cheeks full of black, spidery veins. The sight forced all rational thought from Jimmy's head. He shot to his feet, gritting his teeth at the jolt of pain racing through his face, and darted into the woods.

Twigs and weeds snapped beneath his heavy footfalls as he raced into the dark, and errant branches slapped his face, scratching his cheeks as he pushed forward into the overgrowth. He lost track of time and distance. There was only his breathing, the heavy machine gun pattering of his heart, his aching nose, and the terrible clarity he was racing not toward safety, but deeper into unknown danger.

The world spun before him as his foot caught an exposed root. He pitched forward, crying out in pain as he met the hard earth.

"Hi, Jimmy."

He froze, looking up. His heart stopped, and a voice in his mind screamed. Not in fear, but in rage. Ben Taswell stood before him, his face covered in dirt and thin black cracks, his eyes awash in a deep blue light. Two men with glowing eyes stood behind him.

"Is this the one, Brother Ben?"

Ben smiled. "It is, Father Jacob. Can we keep him? Can he be saved?"

"All sinners will be saved, my child. All sinners will suffer."

One of the dark figures crossed the gap. Moments later, Jimmy Cord screamed. The forest listened, and somewhere deep in the earth, the god of Jacob Masters rejoiced.

CHAPTER FOURTEEN

1

Ozzie was fast asleep when Susan arrived home. She heard his buzzing snores from the front porch, felt the subtle vibration of air sucked through his massive frame. *Poor baby,* she thought, letting herself into the house. *It's too bad this has to happen.*

He lay on the sofa, his head slumped to one side, the room bathed in the glow of a late-night infomercial. A man with terrible hair demonstrated a cleaning device to a captive audience, men and women who looked bored but were probably paid to be there. "That's all it takes," the host said, followed by a canned clip of applause. "But the real question is, does *Susan* have what it takes?" She heard the voice from the TV but did not break her stride. If she'd waited, she would've seen the host turn toward the camera, would've witnessed the odd bluish glow around his eyes. Instead, she set down her purse and wandered upstairs into the bedroom to change out of her work clothes.

"I do have what it takes, Daddy." She stripped to her underwear and stood in front of the mirror, tracing her fingers along the scars at her thighs, the shiny pink ribbons at her ribs, the freshly cut wounds at her biceps, still wet with her offering, still alight with a sacrificial sting. The tattoo on her wrist had scabbed over since last night's weeping, but now fresh blood seeped from the wound, forming a glistening tapestry on her pale flesh. "I'll give you everything if I must."

The infomercial host's measured voice echoed from below, his tone deepening, distorting into the booming voice she'd heard all her life. The voice of her father's god from within the belly of the earth. "You would bleed for your father, but would you take a life?"

Warmth filled her ears like tide pools. She dabbed a fingertip at her earlobe and examined the dark tear of blood.

"Would you make his body your altar, his skin your robe, his blood your sacrament? Would you defile his remains in the white light of the moon?"

Susan pulled open the top drawer of her dresser, shifted an assortment of panties and black lingerie to the side, and retrieved her special blade. It was really nothing more than a carving knife, something she'd swiped from her grandfather's kitchen years ago in a moment of desperation before she understood the pressure building beneath her skin. Those were the days when she bled for nothing, when the sting of severing her flesh brought swift relief. In those days, she told herself she was freeing the demons from her body. Now she understood: her blood was sacred.

She held the blade to her forearm and opened a fresh wound, fascinated by how easily the flesh parted, how it was so resilient and yet so fragile in the face of something sharp, something foreign.

From downstairs: "I don't know, ladies and gentlemen. I don't know if our little girl has it in her to do this. What do you think?" Jeers and boos erupted from the TV. Susan walked barefoot to the staircase and then downstairs to the living room where her boyfriend slumbered. The infomercial host turned toward her and smiled.

"What's it going to be, Susan? Will you honor the Old Ways?"

Susan smiled, gripping the knife in her hand. Blood trickled down the length of her arm and dripped on the wooden floor.

"Old lies above," she whispered, "new love below."

2

Laura Tremly wasn't crazy. Oh, sure, *they* thought she was crazy, even if they wouldn't come right out and say it. They all thought she was crazy, like the Leifthauser woman in the room down the hall. *She* was the crazy one, catatonic except for occasional outbursts, drooling on herself like a child.

No, Laura was different. Who else could say they had stared into the eyes of a true god? Who else could say they had lain with god's apostle and birthed one of his many children? Once, she and her sisters in worship formed a covenant to serve their lord's apostle, attending to his every earthly desire, aiding him in building the foundation of a new paradise. Was she crazy to follow her faith? Was she insane to listen to the voices in her heart?

There were always more acceptable terms, like "troubled," "disturbed," or her favorite, "delusional." Clinically, Laura's diagnosis was a nice helping of schizophrenia with a generous side of paranoid personality disorder, equally sexy terms in this age of modern science, but her favorite would always remain "delusional" because it implied her beliefs contradicted reality.

Had they not seen her lord's wounds upon her body? Had they not witnessed her rebellion against gravity, held aloft by her lord's will alone? *Fools.*

Only cowards allowed themselves to be so blinded by their so-called science. Laura Tremly knew the truth, what the rest of the world was so afraid to see: her lord's apostle was coming home beneath the light of the moon, and He would bring an age of blood and fire. A new paradise would grow in His wake, watered by the blood of Stauford's sinful and weak. All the heretics, the liars, and the whores who walked the streets so brazenly would soon meet their day of reckoning.

And that day, brothers and sisters, was soon at hand. Her lord whispered the truth to her, speaking from the long shadows filling her sparse room when the sun hung low, the day drawing its last gasp into night. They may have strapped her to the bed to keep her from paying tribute to her lord, but her faith would not be contained by her restraints. Such fibers were made in the kingdom of man, and nothing of this world could stand in the gaze of her living god.

Soon, her lord whispered, as the door latch clicked. One of the nurses, a new girl by the name of Charlene Goodall, wheeled in her cart of pharmaceutical goodies.

"How are you this evening, Ms. Tremly?"

Laura said nothing, choosing instead to let her god speak for her. "All is well," she said, feeling her lips pulled upward to feign a smile. "You can call me Laura if you like."

She does not know, her lord said. *She is like a child in the wilderness, a lamb among wolves.*

"That's good to hear, Laura. It's time for your meds." Charlene reached for one of the small paper cups on the cart. Inside the cup were three pills, two blue and one yellow, that would send Laura into the throes of sleep, dim the light of her lord, and quiet his words. But not tonight. Not again. Not when their reckoning was so close at hand.

"Will they help me sleep?"

Nurse Charlene nodded, offering a faint smile of her own. There was fear behind her expression, the way a cat will purr even in distress. "Of course, Laura. We want to help you get your rest. So you can get better."

Such pretty lies, her lord said. *She thinks you are foolish, child. She thinks you are ignorant and is treating you as such. Do you remember what the Old Ways of your lord say about liars?*

Laura remembered. Those ancient words were inscribed in the halls of her mind, halls which she'd wandered for the last thirty years, often with nothing more than a candle to light her way. She promised her lord she would not forget, and tonight she would prove her devotion.

Nurse Charlene leaned down, offering the plastic cup of pills to her patient. Laura lifted her chin and opened her mouth but moved her lower lip just in time. The cup tipped, spilling the pills. Two of them rolled down the side of her cheek and came to rest beside her face.

"Oh, I'm so sorry," Laura said, meeting Charlene's gaze. "I'm so terribly sorry. Sometimes I'm too clumsy for my own good."

Charlene Goodall forced a smile, but her eyes flared with annoyance. "It's quite all right, Laura. I'll get them for you."

She leaned over the bed to retrieve the pills, exposing the pale flesh of her throat.

"Thank you," Laura whispered. "I'm so grateful for your kindness."

And unlike her nurse, Laura wasn't lying. She demonstrated her gratitude by sinking her teeth into Charlene's neck.

3

Stephanie looked in the rearview mirror as she pulled the car into Bobby's driveway. The house was dark but for the porch light.

"Your old man still goes to bed early, huh?"

"Every Saturday night," Riley said. He looked up at the house and sighed. "Can't I stay with you tonight?"

She wanted to frown but forced a smile anyway. "I've already pushed my luck by havin' you out so late. It's best you go on inside for now. Maybe you can stay over next weekend." She watched him climb out of the car. He was almost to the porch when she put down her window and called for him.

"Hey, Riley?" He spun around, his face lit up with excitement, hoping maybe she'd changed her mind. She hadn't, but the eager look on his face made her smile. "About what we talked about tonight, back at the station. Don't tell your dad. Not yet, okay? Your uncle Jack and I need to figure out some things, okay? You know how Bobby can be about…well, this sort of thing."

Riley nodded. She supposed he knew as well as anybody, maybe even more than she did.

"What if he gives me a hard time about bein' out so late?"

Stephanie smirked. "Blame it on your aunt, the Big Bad Influence."

They shared a laugh before saying goodnight. Stephanie waited until Riley closed the front door behind him and backed out of the driveway. She reached to turn up the radio but put her hand down in hesitation. Most days, music helped clear her head and focus on whatever tasks were at hand. Tonight, however, there was too much going on in her head, too many things to process. Music would only scramble the puzzle she was trying to piece together. She returned her hand to the steering wheel.

Should've known better than to bring up that shit. You knew the painting had something to do with what happened at the church. Even if you couldn't remember all that well, you still knew.

She *did* remember, better than she ever thought possible. The memories were always there, hiding beyond a curtain of ignorance. Sometimes those memories would surface as she slept, manifesting in the form of horrible nightmares no amount of sleeping pills or therapy could diminish, and when she awoke, they would sink back down in the murk of her subconscious like sharks, always swimming, always waiting.

Those awful things she thought she'd imagined—the grotto, the eyes, the chants and incantations, the places her father touched her, the abuse, the awful sermons, the glow of their eyes, and a hushed voice in her head telling her to be quiet, to close her eyes, to let it happen—were horrible memories of her childhood. All these years, she'd embraced the stigma of being one of the Stauford Six without really facing the terrible reality of what it meant to *be* one.

Stephanie drove on in silence, speeding through Bobby's neighborhood until she reached Main Street. From there, she followed the overpass toward the east end of town, passing the turnoff for her apartment, continuing toward the shopping center where teens in the 80s and 90s used to cruise in banal circles on Friday nights. She sat at a red light and peered down the hill toward the parking lot, its cracked pavement illuminated in the pale phosphorous glow of closed storefronts. Two police cruisers were parked side by side in front of the local Kroger, but otherwise, the lot was empty. No one cruised these days, not when social interaction could be performed from the comfort of one's home, at the touch of a button.

Everywhere I go is haunted, she thought. Every street, every storefront, every home she passed by was tainted with the memory of being one of the weird and strange. One of the outcasts, one of the tortured, and one of the misunderstood. One of the Stauford Six, a child whose childhood was stolen from her in the service of a nameless god. Stauford might've been her hometown, but it didn't love her, it didn't care who she was, and by all rights, it despised her. Maybe it despised them all, in its own way, and some more than others. Maybe, in some fucked-up sort of way, she'd stuck around Stauford in a half-assed attempt at earning back its love, like a scorned child trying to appease a parent—or in her case, a dead mother and father.

The light turned green, but she didn't move.

Looking down at the closed storefronts, Stephanie Green realized she'd been lying to herself all along: Stauford didn't give a shit, it would never change, and the tainted blood that built this apathetic place would perpetuate itself until the end of time. And despite the lies she'd told herself all these years to function and have a semi-normal life, those memories were true, they were real, and now with Jack's revelations tonight, they might not even be over.

Not if what Riley said was to be believed. And why would the kid lie about what he saw? She recalled the boy's trembling hands as he told them what he saw the night before in the woods. Jack's recounting of their time in the grotto, the impossible space deep below the foundation of their father's church, aided in connecting the dots. She remembered her father's hellish idol, with teeth too wide and crazed eyes filled with arcane knowledge. Why on earth would Genie Tremly want to have that terrible thing in her possession?

"Some sort of fucked-up memento, maybe." The sound of her voice startled her from her thoughts. She didn't care for the slight tremor of fear rippling through her words. Stephanie glanced up, saw the light turn green again, and stepped on the gas. The troubling thought of Genie's intentions followed her all the way to the next intersection. She flipped on the turn signal and merged on to the Cumberland Gap Parkway.

No, not a memento. Remember the other shit in the notebook? The news articles, the magazine clippings, and the notes on all those symbols? Something about moon phases? And didn't Jack say some of them were etched into Genie's tombstone?

For a moment, Stephanie considered driving out to the cemetery to investigate for herself, but the thought of walking through a graveyard this time of night was a bit much for her right now. Instead, she drove another mile before turning off the parkway, traveling past the old Layne Camp High School building, down the hill, and toward Standard Avenue.

Genie Tremly's house emerged above the tree line in the distance, towering over the surrounding subdivisions. There were lights on in the house. She imagined Jack was home by now, and when she drove by, his parked car confirmed it. Should she stop? And why? They were both tired, mentally and emotionally drained after the day they'd had, and at least one of them was doing the sensible thing by settling down for the night.

Stephanie's foot lingered on the brake, idling slowly in front of Ruth McCormick's home, staring up at the faint glow coming from the upstairs bedroom window of Genie's house.

You want to see it. You actually want to see the idol. Your brother's story wasn't enough. You want to see that infernal thing for yourself, in person, just to make sure you aren't insane. You want to hold it in your hands, maybe even destroy it...

In a way, she really did. The idol symbolized everything she hated about her childhood, the church, her bastard of a father. Maybe, in some way, the idol was the root of all their problems. And if not the root cause, then an extension of the source, like a dark antenna sending out a malignant signal, focusing, amplifying somehow.

Hadn't she seen her father levitate in its presence? Hadn't his eyes changed color? Hadn't darkness itself leaked from his pores?

"Enough," she spat. The empty car said nothing. "Go home, Steph. Get some rest. You're fuckin' arguing with yourself."

Stephanie glanced once more at the old Victorian before stepping on the gas. Jack's silhouette wandered by the living room windows, and a moment later, the lights went out. The dim glow upstairs pulsed. She kept an eye on it in the rearview until she crested the hilltop and the light faded from view.

Ten minutes later, Stephanie parked outside her apartment. She gathered her things and went inside. The feeling of exhaustion was immediate, announcing its presence in the form of a massive yawn reverberating through every muscle down to her toes. When she turned on the bathroom light to brush her teeth, her eyes fell upon the framed print of Jack's painting.

She took in its grim scene, the vivid detail with which he'd painted the congregation on the shoreline. Had this really happened? She couldn't remember every detail, but what was there in her memory was more than real—she felt errant fingertips upon her skin, caressing her flesh, touching her in places no child should be touched. She felt the hot breath on the back of her neck, expelled in desperate gusts while strange guttural words crawled from familiar lips. They were baptized there in the dark waters of a grotto, deep inside the earth and yet beneath a sky of impossible stars, the air still and pregnant with hushed voices of the Void.

A sharp chill raked down her body. Trembling, Stephanie Green took the frame off the wall and set it inside the hall closet. She didn't care to talk about it ever again.

4

"Hey. Honey. Wake up. Come to bed with me. I want to play."

Susan's words slithered through Ozzie's ears and writhed around his brain. He'd been in the grip of a nightmare, running from shadows with glowing eyes, and Zeke Billings was one of them. Everything else faded as her words infected his dream space, stirring the most primal parts of him from slumber. He had an erection even before his eyes were open.

Only she wasn't there when he awoke. The TV was turned off, as were the recessed ceiling lights, but there was a dim glow filling the room from somewhere else. He turned, wincing at a crick in his neck, his head still swimming in an alcoholic haze.

"Suze?"

A row of white candles flickered on the floor. They lined the hallway to the stairwell, an illuminated breadcrumb trail dotted with articles of clothing. Here was the black lace bra he'd bought her for Christmas. A few feet onward, her lace panties lay in a heap. He smiled and adjusted the iron bar in his pants.

"On my way, darlin'."

He rose to his feet and staggered to the side, nearly toppling back to the sofa. When the world stopped spinning, Ozzie wandered upstairs. *She must want to be romantic tonight,* he thought, feeling a little disappointed. He staggered into the door and pushed his way into the room.

"Hello, officer."

Susan lay on her side, covered in only a sheet. Her hair spilled over her pale shoulders, and shadows danced across her figure as his clumsy entrance disturbed the flames. Candles were arranged on the floor, on the dresser, and along the windowsill, filling the room with an inviting glow.

"Wha's all this?"

She rolled onto her back and stretched her arms, exposing the tops of her breasts. "I thought I'd set the mood. Don't you like it?"

"Uh, yeah, sure…" he slurred, nearly losing his balance as he took off his shoes. "Candles are fine, I guess."

"Oh, Ozzie," she purred. "Undress for me. I want to see how hard I make you."

He managed a smile. Imaginings of what he would do to her tonight bobbed along a sea of whiskey in his head. Susan gasped when he finally stripped off his pants, and he beamed with pride. *Yeah, look at that thing,* he thought, *you know you want it.*

"I've been waiting for this," she cooed, reaching out to trace her fingers along his shaft. "Why don't you join me here, Chief? I need to place you under arrest."

"That so, huh? Wha's the charge?" He pulled back the sheet, revealing her beautifully naked body, pale as creamy moonlight. His mouth watered, and when he swallowed back the saliva, he tasted something gritty, something metallic. Something like dirt.

"Failure to appear in court." Susan grinned, wrapping her hand around him and pulling him down to the bed. She kissed him, placed her hands on his chest, and slowly pushed him back against the headboard. "You're in contempt." She leaned over to the nightstand and retrieved two pairs of handcuffs. "How do you plead?"

He grinned, feeling stupidly drunk, his vision suddenly clouded with dark shadows. The gritty dirt taste in his mouth grew stronger, enough when he tried to swallow it back, the flavor almost made him gag.

"G-guilty, your Honor." He forced a smile and lost himself in the pendulous swing of her breasts as she leaned over him, cuffing his wrists to the bedposts. "Take me to jail."

"Mmm," she purred as she climbed off him, lightly tracing her finger along his cock, delighting as he rose to attention on her command.

"The old boy's got a mind of 'is own."

"Yes he does, Chief." She met his glass stare. "I want to do something different tonight, Oz. I want all of you tonight. I want to do *everything* to you." She slipped two fingers between her legs. "I'm so wet just thinking about it."

Oh Christ, he thought. *Never seen her this horny before.* And yet he'd never heard her talk like this before, either. Sure, they got wild in the bedroom, but usually he was the one leading the charge, guiding her, instructing her where to bite, to kiss, to suck. This new Susan excited him and unnerved him. *Maybe it's the booze,* he thought.

Susan took her wet fingers and slid them up the length of his shaft. All rational thought left Ozzie's brain in a single gasp of air.

"I-I'm yours," he stammered. "Do whatever you want. I just want you."

"Anything I want?"

"Yes," he groaned, smiling as she took his permission to retreat to the dresser in front of the bed. He watched with drunken curiosity, admiring the view of her shapely ass in the warm glow of candlelight. A moment later, Susan returned with two more sets of handcuffs. He wasn't surprised by their appearance—although he'd been the one to introduce bondage to their bedroom, Susan took to it almost immediately. She once said she loved the thought of dominating him, of having him all to herself to do with as she pleased. And Ozzie couldn't complain, either. She rode him like a madwoman atop a bucking bronco, sometimes moaning, sometimes near the point of screaming in ecstasy as they climaxed together.

She closed the handcuffs around his ankles and then fastened them to the posts at the foot of the bed. He winced from the pressure, the metal cuffs cutting into his flesh and pinching his circulation.

Ozzie met her gaze and grinned. "When you gon' come here and take me for a ride?"

"Not yet," Susan whispered, "but soon, Daddy. Soon."

Daddy? That was a new one. He laughed it off, taking joy in watching her naked figure haunt the bedroom before him. She tiptoed toward her side of the bed, reached under the pillow, and retrieved something he couldn't see.

When she turned to face him, the first thing he noticed wasn't the blade but the distant look in her eyes. The world fell away from him, his heart frozen, his blood displaced with the burning chill of ice water, and the thick churning taste of bile climbing up the back of his throat. His instinct was to jump out of bed and charge her, disable her ability to use the weapon, cuff her, and interrogate her—except he could do no such thing. He was helpless, hopelessly cuffed to the bed by wrist and ankle, about to become a case study in idiocy and another sex crime statistic.

I want to do everything to you.

"S-Susan, whatcha got there, babe? You're makin' me nervous."

"I hate that it's come to this, Oz. I really do. We had some good times."

The sultry tone of her voice was gone, displaced by a different sort of Susan, one he'd only caught fleeting glimpses of here and there. A phantom of her personality, there and gone again in a blink, a quality that only came out during arguments or intense conversation about her siblings. He'd shrugged off such sightings, figuring she'd overcome anger management issues in her youth. Now, as he lay bound naked to the bed, Ozzie realized he was terribly wrong.

"Suze, listen to me. Whatever you're plannin' to do, you don't have to. Whatever I've done—"

"It ain't what you've done, Oz, it's what you're gonna do. You know what Zeke means to me, and I can't let you blame him for doing what he was told."

Ozzie blinked, the haze of intoxication clearing for a few precious seconds, and some of the pieces came together. His heart sank. *Oh fuck.*

"Our father asks so little of us, so when He does speak, we must listen. I can't let you arrest my brother. Not when you were the one who sent him out there in the first place."

His mind raced. *How? How the hell could she possibly know?*

Susan turned toward the window and tilted her head, listening. All Ozzie heard was the racing of his heart, the settling of the house's foundation, and the stir of tree limbs in the breeze outside. *She's fucking crazy, she's lost her goddamn mind, everyone told me she was nuts, oh fuck, I should've listened, one of the Stauford Six is gonna kill me—*

"Yes, father. I will prepare this vessel." She smiled. "I'll be waiting for you tomorrow morning."

Susan turned back to him, and her smile faltered. "For the longest time, I thought I was crazy. I thought the voices I was hearin' in my head were because of trauma, because of what happened out at my daddy's church. But I know that's not true. My father speaks to me, Oz, and He's told me something wonderful. Something so beautiful I can't wait for tomorrow to come."

"What's happenin' tomorrow, Suze?"

"A reckoning, my love. The god of my father will free the sins of Stauford, like He wanted to all those years ago. This false Babylon will fall, and it all starts here."

Ozzie tested his restraints. The cold metal dug into his wrists and ankles. Pain shot through his arms and legs.

"Please, my love. The heretics of this city have blinded you. Let me peel back your veil, help you see the truth."

"Yeah, what truth's that?"

"There ain't no salvation without suffering, Oz."

And before Ozzie Bell could scream, Susan Prewitt gave a demonstration of her father's Old Ways.

5

Fifteen miles away, Tyler Booth stirred in his sleep, troubled by lithe shapes emerging from the dark. He was back in the pit beneath the church, a dream so vivid he could smell the musty earth surrounding him, his nose itching from the dust and ash afloat in the air. The impossible passageway yawned before him, illuminated by flickering torchlight, and beyond its mouth was a sky full of eyes. They blinked erratically, separately, each focusing on him in their own time, examining his frail dream-shape beyond the passage.

In the impossible logic and perception of dreams, Tyler knew he wasn't alone, the eyes beyond notwithstanding. There was someone in the temple with him, buried beneath his feet—and she was climbing her way out.

"Tyler," Imogene said, her voice nothing more than a rasp of dry air. A plume of ash shot up from the floor. *"I did it. The ritual worked. I'm coming back."*

And in the dream, Tyler knew she was speaking the truth—except something went wrong somehow, despite his memories speaking otherwise. He was there that day, watching her conduct the final rites beneath the light of the full moon, and at the passage of that brilliant celestial body, so had her life passed from her lips. As above, so below.

But here in the dark dreamscape sculpted from his worst fears, Imogene's rites cheated her, twisting their meaning to suit the dead pastor's evil desires. Her rotting fingers breached the ashen earth, scraping the surface, seeking, pulling. Dead fingers became dead hands became the pallid bones of Imogene's arms, and Tyler tried to scream, but an impossible cacophony of voices screamed for him from behind the passage.

"I'm coming back," she rasped. *"I'm coming back for you, darlin'."*

The cracked dome of Imogene Tremly's skull protruded from the earth, flaps of wet skin and matted hair falling in clumps around her. The orbits of her eye sockets rose, filled with a sickening blue light, and when those awful eyes turned toward him, Tyler screamed.

He screamed so long and loud he woke himself with a start, kicking off the thin sheet and scrambling to his feet in a fit of panic. He searched the dark, crying out, still haunted by the fading visions of a woman he'd once loved crawling from the earth. And with each panicked breath, each tremulous beat of his frail heart, the old professor's dream seeped back into the shadows of reality. The contours of his bedroom fell into focus, illuminated by moonlight filtering through the open window.

Tyler wiped sweat from his face, wandered down the hall to the bathroom, and ran water in the sink. He gasped at the feel of cold water on his cheeks and reeled as a tremor of tears overcame him. *Oh God,* he thought, fighting and failing to hold back the sobs. *God, Genie, what did you do? What did we do?*

Tyler sank to the floor and leaned back against the cool tile, waiting for the tears to pass. He felt his age, felt every bit the frail and lonely old man he'd become. And he hated himself for what he'd let her do to herself. Maybe if he'd stopped her, she'd still be here with him and not six feet in the ground.

"You're a coward, old man. You couldn't stop her then, you couldn't tell her grandson the truth, and you're too chickenshit to see if her plan worked." He wiped his nose, snorted back the phlegm collecting at the edge of his throat, and sat for nearly an hour before he made up his mind. Tomorrow, he'd pay his fallen friend a visit that was long overdue, whether he liked it or not. He'd give himself some closure and try to move on with what little life he had left.

Rising to his feet, groaning at the aches in his knees, Tyler looked at his reflection in the mirror.

"And what if her plan worked?"

His reflection didn't say anything, and it didn't have to. He already knew the answer. The possibility kept him awake for the rest of the night.

CHAPTER FIFTEEN

1

A slow fog rose from the banks of Laurel Lake and crept into town like a quiet intruder. Streetlights acquired ringed halos in the haze, and the stoplights on Main Street flashed cautionary yellow like blinking eyes, quietly signaling a warning to all who would travel at that ungodly hour. For the god of Stauford's people wasn't there, having slipped away into the long shadows drawn by the full moon above. There would be a new lord waiting for them on the morning of their Sabbath, and many suffered from troubled sleep, their heads filled with dark dreams of primal urges and pagan sacrifice.

Strange symbols were etched into their skulls and lit with the orange glow of dancing flames. These glyphs possessed meaning and pronunciation in their dream space, impossibly linked with one another by a primal magic which lacked a name in any language, or a human tongue capable of describing it. The link simply *was,* the meaning universal, and through those carvings they understood the grim fate of their quiet little town. Men and women would don the ceremonial robes of their ancestors, wear the masks forgotten by time, and utter rites not performed in a millennium.

Even as the sun rose and the fog subsided, the people of Stauford awoke to an uneasiness wrought by their dreams. The air was swollen with a sort of anxiety many of them had never experienced before, a powerful gravity pulling them down, anchoring them to the earth with invisible chains. Parents and their children regarded one another with lingering doubt, side-eye curiosity, and a tacit understanding between them that something would happen today, although no one could say what. So, too, were they hesitant to discuss the obscene bacchanalia inhabiting their dreams.

Instead, the men and women, boys and girls of Stauford stumbled to their kitchen tables, ate their breakfast in silence, perused their Sunday edition of the *Stauford Tribune*—"Search Continues for Missing Boys," the headline read—and prepared for the early morning services at First Baptist downtown. The old church from the days of the Stauford Six still stood on Kentucky Street, but had been the subject of many renovations. In the last thirty years, the old church was swallowed by modern excess, sporting several new conference rooms for such activities as the Wednesday night business meeting of the church's many officers, the weekly Thursday night youth group meeting, or the bi-weekly Fellowship of Christian Athletes meeting every other Friday.

As Jack Tremly discovered earlier, for all the changes in the years of his absence, the old ways remained. The gears of Stauford's ancient machine were still turning, and its people were locked in the same routine as they'd always been. Sunday School began at ten, with morning services beginning at eleven on the dot. Afternoon fellowship would follow in the cafeteria (with light refreshments), and evening services would begin at 7 p.m. For each session of worship, First Baptist's bell would chime, announcing the lord's house was now in session. Come all ye sinners, the doors are open for business.

2

Jack Tremly lay fast asleep, shirtless and sprawled across the sofa in his grandmother's living room. The nightmares ripped him from sleep the night before, and he'd done what he'd always done when the terrors denied him rest: he created art, sketching out the demons haunting him. One hand dangled over the edge of the sofa, hovering above a scattering of charcoal pencils and a sketchpad filled with erratic shapes culled from the darkness of his memories. There were shapes of men and women emerging from a formless gloom, dragging behind them the bodies of the damned. He'd fallen asleep as the sun rose and wouldn't awaken for several hours.

His sister, Stephanie Green, also slept on a sofa, aglow in the erratic flash of her TV screen. Early morning infomercials not unlike those cheering on Susan the night before played on the screen, but Stephanie didn't see them. She was still fast asleep even as sunlight poured through the open blinds of her apartment living room. In her dreams, she ran from unseen phantoms down the endless corridors of a labyrinth, sprinting toward something terrible and fantastic at the center, something that would reconcile her childhood memories once and for all. She snored lightly, her fingers twitching in the throes of her dream, and when the rays of light inched toward her, she stirred briefly, burying her face in the cushions.

Chuck Tiptree, however, was wide awake, although he didn't understand why. Sundays were his days to sleep in, had been for years, but something pulled him from his precious slumber. An ominous feeling, like he'd forgotten something long ago and glimpsed the tip of memory off in the distance but could no longer grasp what it was. Annoyed and puzzled, he sat on his front porch, sipping coffee to ward off the early morning chill and watching the fog sink into the earth. Across the street, Mr. Samson's German Shepherd, Ox, squatted and shat in front of Mrs. Jourgensen's prize-winning hydrangeas. Chuck watched with mild amusement, while the far-off part of his brain chased down what he'd forgotten. Was it something he'd dreamed about? Something from long ago, perhaps, when he was still a chubby little kid and terrified of his own shadow? When he was afraid the shadows would return to claim him? When he still had to sleep with his bedroom light on? Ox the German Shepherd finished his business, and Chuck sipped idly at his coffee, digging for an artifact he could no longer remember.

Nor did Susan Prewitt sleep. She sat at the foot of her bed, marveling at the pretty designs she'd carved into Ozzie's pale body. He'd fainted from the blood loss long ago, but his chest still rose and fell in labored breaths. The proof of her labors soaked through the sheets and into the mattress, crimson pools so deep and dark they looked like black paint. She'd started with his feet, carving a story one glyph at a time, inching up his legs, across his groin, along the canvas of his chest, and down his arms. The tale was older than man, one of a god living within the earth, fluid like water and blacker than sin, a god of eyes and mouths drinking from the pool of sanity and tears of pain. A god speaking to men from below, teaching them its ways from beyond the cosmos, where time is a dream and space a vanishing memory. At first, Susan only carved what she could remember from the teachings of her father the apostle, but as Ozzie's pleas diminished, the hands of her lord guided her. Ozzie's body was a new testament, writ in blood and agony. As the swollen wounds glistened in the early morning sunlight, so too did the tears on Susan's cheeks. Her father would return, and soon. *My cup runneth over,* she thought.

Bobby Tate was already awake, rehearsing the morning's sermon in his head while he tied his necktie. As with most of his Sunday sermons, he tried to relate current events to the teachings of his lord; for this morning's lesson, he chose the wanderings of Moses in the desert to relate to the boys lost in the wilderness. There would be salvation following great hardship, and even in times of crisis, the people of Stauford needed to remember to put their faith in their god. *And they will, my son, but not in you, and not in your god. They're going to put it in the faith of your daddy. He's disappointed with you, boy, lettin' the god of the heretics steer you wrong, but He will show you the error of your ways and bring you back into His flock.* The voices from his nightmare seeped into his thoughts, and he was so startled by their appearance he missed the loop and had to start over with the tie.

Down the hall, Riley Tate sat on the edge of his bed, rubbing sleep from his eyes and wondering if he could possibly get out of going to church today. Then he remembered Rachel would be there, and there might be a chance for them to talk between Sunday school and morning service. Riley reached under his pillow for his phone and sighed. The battery indicator flashed red, dropping from 15% to 14% as if to mock him. Annoyed with himself, Riley checked his messages. He'd sent her a text before going to bed the night before: "Can we talk tmrw?"

He frowned. She'd read the message half an hour ago but hadn't responded. *Great,* he thought. *Just fuckin' great.*

In the master bedroom, his old man hummed a church hymn out of tune, and Riley tensed. He'd expected twenty questions when he got home last night, but his father was already fast asleep. The last thing he wanted was an interrogation first thing in the morning, and Riley wasn't sure how to even begin to answer the inevitable questions. *Uh, yeah, Dad, I was out with Aunt Steph and Uncle Jack, and we figured out that maybe one of the guys who took Ben and Toby is your dead father. Oh, and I know all about what happened to you guys when you were kids, too. What's for breakfast?*

Instead, Bobby Tate stuck his head in the doorway of Riley's room, gave his son a once-over. "You need to get ready for church, son."

"Yes, sir."

The questions Riley expected never came, and later, he'd regret they never would.

But what of Zeke Billings? The youngest of the Stauford Six sat behind the wheel of his dead friend's truck. The grimy engine growled as he stamped the gas pedal, spitting back gravel as they tore down the length of Devil's Creek Road. Father Jacob sat in the passenger seat, and Amber Rogers's Volkswagen trailed behind them, carrying the other corrupted youth.

Together, their caravan traveled toward Stauford's city limits, unremarkable and unnoticed, just in time for Sunday School.

There, Father Jacob would deliver a sermon thirty years in the making and call his children home.

3

On the opposite side of town, Ruth McCormick stepped outside into the morning fog. She carried a stack of paperwork, comprised of notebooks and loose sheets of printing paper, volumes one and two of her lord's gospel.

The old radio still hissed static from within, which to the uninitiated sounded like nothing more than errant white noise. To Ruth it was the clipped guttural voice of their lord, commanding she prepare for the revival at First Baptist downtown. Somewhere far away in the back of her mind, Ruth heard herself screaming, and for a moment she was confused by the suggestion of a revival. First Baptist's fall revival wasn't for another three weeks, and she would know because she was on the planning committee.

But the screaming voice faded, dimmed, and died away in a breathless whisper. In its place was the voice of the one true god, a powerful being from below the earth, eager to reward the believers and punish the heretics.

Spread the gospel, her lord said, and like a good servant of the faith, Ruth obeyed.

4

"I'm coming, my lord."

Laura Tremly crouched in the overgrowth, hidden among the brambles and kudzu as a squadron of police cruisers sped by. She waited until the sirens faded into the distance before lifting her head above the weeds. She'd made her way down the hillside behind the hospital in the dark and waited in the brush before continuing. For those few unsettling hours, Laura curled herself into a ball beside the trunk of a dead tree and rocked in place, muttering the prayers her lover taught her in the starlit grotto beneath the old church.

Your love is below, Your ways are the truth. I give this flesh to feed You, my lord. My blood for You to drink. My soul to be one with Your essence in the earth. Your love is below, Your ways are the truth...

Sleep found her before dawn, and Laura Tremly dreamed she was back in the grotto, wading into those warm waters with Jacob. He was shirtless, his sallow flesh lit with a pale glow in the undying light of the eyes above. Jacob took her in his arms, kissed her forehead, and marked the symbol of the moon upon her flesh. *You will be mine forever,* he whispered, *if you would do but one thing for me, my lamb.*

Anything, she told him. *I'd give my life for you, my love. Anything. Just say it.*

Our son has something that belongs to our lord god below. Your mother stole it long ago, while I was still asleep in the earth. I want you to go get it back. Can you do that for me, my lamb? Will you do it for us? For your lord?

"Yes," Laura whispered, waking herself from the dream. The sun was up, the fog dissipating. She wandered through a copse of trees until she reached the nearby highway. A gas station stood on the other side. Traffic was light this time of morning, and she had no trouble crossing.

A powder blue pickup truck was parked at the pumps. An older man dressed in a green John Deere cap and overalls leaned against the truck bed, whistling while he pumped gas. He was blissfully unaware of his impending death, even as Laura's fingers gripped the side of his chin. The old man's neck snapped with a quick twist. Minutes later, Laura sat behind the wheel of the truck, speeding along the Cumberland Falls Highway toward Stauford.

5

9:18 a.m.

Bobby Tate parked in the lot behind the building. Riley followed him inside, into the small office his father occupied most days during the week. The room was sparse, decorated with a few framed landscape photographs sporting Biblical passages, a painting of Jesus suffering on the cross, and a coat rack in one corner. A desk sat in the center, adorned with a small desktop computer, a daily planner, and a pair of framed photographs of Riley and the late Janet Tate. Bobby took a seat and asked his son to do the same.

"Join me in prayer, son."

Riley slumped in his chair. "I really don't want to, Dad."

Bobby stared, fighting the urge to frown and voice his displeasure. Instead, he nodded and said, "Understood. I'll pray for both of us, then."

He didn't wait for his son to reply. Bobby bowed his head, closed his eyes, and thanked his god for a beautiful morning. He thanked God for blessing him with a son, even if his son had yet to accept their faith; he thanked God for blessing him with a beautiful wife, even if her time on this earth wasn't as long as he'd liked; he prayed for a safe return of the boys who were taken in the forest on Friday night; and he prayed Ronny Cord and his son would learn to forgive Riley's transgressions.

And please, oh Father in heaven, spare me from the awful dreams of my youth. Spare me from the horrors that tainted me as a child. I have dedicated my life to serving You and Your will, to atone for the sins of my father as You gave your only son to atone for the world. Please take this cup from my lips. Please—

A voice spoke up within his mind, echoing from dark chambers long thought buried: *Drink deep, my son. Your suffering is just beginning.*

Bobby opened his eyes, startled by the intrusion, expecting to see his son smiling or even laughing in mockery. But Riley was still slumped in his seat, his eyes half-open and trained on the screen of his phone.

Once again, Bobby Tate turned to the visage of his dying lord for answers. The white-washed depiction of Jesus, with his eyes upturned in cosmic agony, said nothing—but there was the slightest hint of a smirk on his bloodied lips. Bobby did a double take, his heart aflutter with panic, but the painting was as it had always been: Jesus in indescribable pain, suffering for all eternity in silence.

10:00 a.m.

The first bell clanged from First Baptist's steeple. Out of all the renovations and improvements at the church during Reverend Tate's tenure, the one constant was the old bell, which still had to be operated via rope in the church's foyer. A vote occurred during last Wednesday's business meeting, appropriating funds to replace the bell with a more modern digital speaker system in the first quarter of the following year. Everything was sacred at First Baptist, except the things that weren't.

Downstairs, the classrooms filled with their eager students, young and old. Even Reverend Tate was in attendance, but not as a teacher. No, that honor belonged to David Sparks, one of the new deacons. Across the hall, Riley sat in the back row of the youth class, watching helplessly as Daniel Taswell struggled to keep his composure and give the morning's lesson. Dark circles accented his eyes, his face too pale, and his voice cracked when he spoke. Riley wished Daniel had stayed home. *Seeing me here probably doesn't help,* Riley thought, his cheeks flushing with shame. When their eyes met briefly, Daniel looked away.

10:05 a.m.

Further down the hall, the older ladies of the senior group awaited their teacher, Mrs. McCormick, whom no one heard from all weekend. Agnes Belview believed the poor woman was sick but wouldn't elaborate further, and the rumors flew quietly among them as the morning church bell ceased its chimes. The senior ladies' group eschewed its usual lessons for the better part of six months in favor of meeting to discuss how to combat the evils of that demonic radio station, but without Ruth there to guide and channel their disdain, all their misplaced contempt found other cracks through which to seep.

Ruth waited for classes to begin before making her appearance. She pushed open the door, interrupting a lively gossip session among the group. Agnes gasped at the sight of her dear friend, unaware her hands were shaking.

Ruth smiled, clutching the volumes of the new gospel to her chest.

"Ladies," she began, turning toward the door. "I've prepared a new lesson for this morning's class. *Hallelujah.*"

A metallic click punctuated her words when she flipped the lock.

11:02 a.m.

A yellow Ford pickup truck and a neon green Volkswagen pulled along the curb out front of First Baptist. Zeke Billings turned to his father in the passenger seat and asked, "Will you need me?"

"No, my son. Your sister is waiting for you."

Zeke smiled. "Thank you, father." He looked up at the church. "Are you going to show the heretics the error of their ways?"

"Oh yes. The flock must be called home, and I am their shepherd."

Jacob exited the truck and walked back to the Volkswagen. The two children in the backseat climbed out to meet him.

"Are we going home, father?"

Jacob looked down at Ben Taswell, admiring the glow in his innocent eyes, the blackened marks of the lord on his cheeks. "Yes, my little lamb. Today we all go home."

Jacob turned back to the young sinners in the front. The blonde whore in the driver's seat lowered the window. Jacob reached in, took her chin in his hand, and traced his thumb along her lips, smearing black sludge across her flesh.

"Go spread the gospel as you once spread your legs, child." He looked up at the young man in the passenger seat. "And you, boy, spread the gospel as you once yearned to spread your seed."

Amber and Jimmy smiled, speaking in unison: "Yes, father."

Jacob Masters stepped away from the car. He looked up at the front of the old church, which had changed during his years in the earth. The symbol of Stauford's decadence had transformed, twisting further into an icon of sin.

Go, my apostle. Show them the error of their ways. Spread my gospel.

Jacob traced a blackened tongue across his teeth. "By Your will, my lord, my love, my light."

6

The morning service at First Baptist began as always: with a moving rendition of "The Old Rugged Cross," albeit without the church's choir director, June Crabtree. There were other notable absences in the early minutes of the morning service—Ruth McCormick, Agnes Belview, Janet Thirston, and Mona Cartwright, to name a few—but the routine of morning worship would not be halted.

Reverend Tate led the congregation in song, something he hated doing because he thought his singing voice was cringe-worthy at best. No one else seemed to mind, though, and when "Rugged Cross" concluded, several congregants shouted *"Amen!"* and *"Hallelujah!"* Bobby smiled at their show of spirit. This sort of fellowship is why he wanted to spread the gospel in the first place. Not just to bury the horrors of his past and atone for the sins of his father, but to lift the hearts and spirits of those around him. Together, they would walk hand in hand into the light of Jesus, hallelujah.

Bobby cleared his throat as everyone took their seats. He adjusted the microphone at the pulpit, frowning as a whine of feedback squealed from the speakers. Before he opened his mouth to speak, Bobby surveyed the room, noting the empty seats. He didn't see Ronny Cord or his son, but then again, he never saw them on Sunday morning; nor was the Matthews family in attendance, a fact which saddened him as he'd hoped to have a word with Don Matthews after the services were over. What did surprise him, however, was the sight of the Taswells and Gilpins, parked on opposite sides of the room halfway down the aisle. They glared at him, and while he didn't back down from their gaze, he didn't linger on them for too long, either.

Satisfied his flock was settled, Bobby leaned into the microphone. "Amen, brothers and sisters. It's another beautiful day in the kingdom of the lord." He waited a moment and then bowed his head. "Let us pray."

Prayers came easily to Bobby Tate. They were little whispers in the dark, hopes for better things sent up to the sky, love letters to God in Heaven, and he was never lacking in hope for better things. He was so caught up in dancing around the subject of praying for those poor boys in the woods without naming their names that he did not hear the front doors of the church swing open.

What finally tore his attention away from the prayer was the growing uneasiness in the room, a sort of heated anxiety clinging to his face and throat, suffocating him. He paused long enough to reach for the plastic cup of water on the lectern. That's when he saw the boys walking down the center aisle.

He knew who they were, even if he had a tough time believing his eyes. *Oh, thank you, Jesus,* he thought. "Thank you, God," he whispered aloud, his voice magnified through the church's sound system. Murmurs arose in the congregation as the two youths walked toward the pulpit.

They were pale, their clothes covered in dirt and grime and stained nearly black by what could only be engine grease of some kind. Leaves and soil clung to their hair, matted in thick clumps. Although no one said it—no one said much of anything, the air seemingly sucked from the room, the tension palpable—a thought crossed the minds of everyone in the church, including those of Ben's and Toby's parents: Were their eyes always blue?

Bobby Tate was so thrilled by the appearance of the boys, he stepped down from the pulpit and walked to meet them in the aisle. Grant and Linda Taswell rose from their seats, followed by John and Phyllis Gilpin, but Bobby reached the boys first. He knelt and took the boys into his arms, fighting back tears, not just in relief of their safety, but in relief that for once his son couldn't be blamed for something horrible.

"We're so glad you're safe," Bobby whispered, clutching the boys close to him. "Thank you, Jesus."

But there was something wrong. Their clothing was damp, their skin nearly pruning as if they'd been submerged in water for hours, and the sensation of their touch made his mind scream. *This is what touching a dead body must feel like,* he thought, a suggestion so startling he immediately felt shame for it.

Bobby pulled away, noticing the two boys didn't hug him back, didn't show any sort of emotion whatsoever. Their eyes pulsed with a glow reaching all the way back into Bobby's memory, yanking back something he'd long thought buried, something that terrified him every night of his childhood.

Ben Taswell smiled. "His will and the Old Ways are one."

Toby Gilpin placed his hand on Bobby's shoulder. "All heretics must suffer for their sins."

Bobby Tate's mind froze, his inner voice uttering a silent scream, and his muscles refused to react.

Ben and Toby opened their mouths, freeing a viscous sludge darker than midnight that dribbled down their chins. They clutched Bobby's shoulders, holding him in place with a firmness he couldn't resist.

A dark figure emerged at the end of the hallway. A figure he'd not seen since he was a child but had dreamed about in some form for the last thirty years. Their eyes met, Bobby's fear manifesting in the piercing glow surrounding Jacob's gaze, and he heard his father in his head: *Bobby-boy, my little lamb. I've come home. Give your father a kiss.*

And Bobby wanted to pull back, wanted so badly to scramble away in retreat, but the mind-freezing fear rooted him in place. Ben and Toby leaned in as if to kiss him, and when he turned in startled terror, a single word crossed his lips.

"*Please—*"

A stream of the black vomit erupted from Ben's maw, interrupting Bobby's words and invading his open mouth. The taste of dirt and oil filled his throat, the gut-wrenching stench of rot and offal invading his nostrils. Bobby collapsed backward, retching and coughing, trying to spit the awful black bile from his mouth, but the thick gunk refused to leave. It slid down the back of his throat like snot. Bobby spat, gagging on the black phlegm as it worked its way inside him.

"Dad!" Riley knelt beside him, and Bobby was struck with the impulse to kiss the boy, to share the black essence between them. *No,* he thought, struggling to get a grip on himself, resisting the foreign urges infecting his mind. *No, this is what he wants.*

He pushed Riley away. "Go…get my keys…"

His son didn't linger, ran to the door at the far end from the pulpit and disappeared. *Good boy,* Bobby thought. *Your mama would be proud.*

Cries among the congregation tore his mind away from the horror he'd swallowed. As Bobby climbed to his feet, Ben Taswell and Toby Gilpin infected their fathers with the blackened corruption nesting inside them. More cries erupted near the entrance, and when Bobby turned to look, he saw the missing women of the senior ladies' group. Ruth McCormick led the way with her gospel in hand, babbling a hymn in another language. She and the other ladies fell to their knees and raised their hands in devotion to their lord's apostle.

Jacob Masters hovered above the floor, his arms held out in mockery of the crucifixion, laughing as Bobby's congregation writhed and screamed in pain around them.

"Dad, come on!"

Riley stood at in the doorway at the back of the room. Bobby turned back only once to look at the horrible bedlam unfolding beneath the holy rafters of First Baptist, before retreating out the backdoor to the parking lot.

7

Inside, as the essence of his lord worked its mysterious ways upon the heretics of First Baptist, Jacob Masters walked in midair toward the pulpit. A small table sat before the lectern with words etched in its surface: IN REMEMBRANCE OF ME. He vomited a pile of dirt and worms upon the table. When he was finished, Jacob turned back to his new flock, the converted.

Many of them found peace with their new lord, their eyes aglow with His divine light. The rest writhed in agony, coughing in vain to dispel the essence from their bodies.

"My little lambs," Jacob said. "The Old Ways of our lord demand sacrifice, torment of flesh and suffering through the blood. There is no salvation without pain, but as your lord's apostle, I will guide you to a most righteous path. Together we will build a new kingdom on earth, and from the seeds of this falling Babylon, so too shall it grow."

"Old lies above," Ruth McCormick cried, "new love below!"

"Old lies above," Agnes Belview chanted, "new love below!"

One by one, the corrupted members of First Baptist joined, chanting the gospel of the infernal god sleeping below Stauford, following the scripture of the Old Ways. Jacob Masters watched in ecstasy.

Soon, my lord, you will have the blood of the damned, and fire for your great purge. The world will drown in your essence, and a new paradise shall grow. As above, so below.

Near the front of the room, Ben Taswell pulled on the rope, chiming the bell above. No one outside the church took much notice, even if it was chiming far too early. Inside, the morning services were just beginning.

8

Miles away, while Bobby and Riley made their escape from the hell unfolding inside First Baptist, Dr. Tyler Booth turned left off the Cumberland Gap Parkway and drove up the hill toward Layne Camp Cemetery. After he parked, Tyler made his way along the small path over the hill, walking carefully between the hundreds of gravestones.

After all his years digging up the old gravesites of indigenous cultures, stepping into a modern cemetery still made him uncomfortable. Maybe it was the notion of stepping on hallowed ground that bothered him so much. He'd never been one for the church, in any of its many forms, but the esoteric teachings to which Imogene exposed him piqued his curiosity. Maybe more than he'd cared to admit. When her grandson told him yesterday about the Hermetic maxim on her gravestone, Tyler wasn't surprised.

As above, so below. Microcosm and macrocosm. Life above, life below, life within, life without.

As he walked among the rows of markers, looking for Imogene's grave, he recalled what she'd told him about Jacob's ways. He'd perverted the maxim in his teachings, spouting "old lies above and new love below," another way of brainwashing people to believe in his malignant majesty underground.

But what else had she said? Something about the binding ritual he'd performed the night they burned down his church.

So below, as above. The inversion of the maxim. He bound his death to our lives, Tyler. Don't you understand? When we're all gone, he will return. To finish what he started. I can't let him. I have to protect Jackie. I have to protect the rest of the kids.

Tyler smiled. She was the perfect grandma all the way to the end. Why had he let her go through with the ritual? That was an easy one. He didn't think she'd actually do it. Not when she had him. Not when they could spend the rest of their time together in quiet retirement.

Panting from the brisk pace and riddled with heartache, Tyler stopped near a white marble mausoleum to catch his breath. He wiped tears from his eyes.

Go on, old man. Get it over with. You know what you're going to find. It's all a pipe dream. Genie was crazy, all messed up from what she witnessed in that cult, and you're too stubborn to admit it to yourself. You fell in love with a mad woman, old man. Accept it.

Tyler started walking and nearly fell into an earthen hole ten feet away. He lost his balance, fell backward, and landed hard on his ass. He groaned in pain from the impact, and after the bright sparkling lights cleared from his vision, he realized what he'd almost stepped into.

"No," he whispered. "Genie, God, no, no, *no!*"

The wound in the earth sat at the foot of Imogene Tremly's gravestone. The mound of dirt surrounding the opening was piled outward, with thin lines traced there hours before by fingers he'd once held on long evening walks. Bits of splintered wood and concrete littered the area, and a fresh set of footprints led away from the gravesite.

Tears flooded Tyler's eyes, not from relief but from pure terror. Imogene's ritual worked. Staring at her gravestone, incredulous despite the reality set before him, Tyler read and re-read the Latin inscription etched in marble: *Et quod est superius est sicut quod est inferius. As above, so below.*

CHAPTER SIXTEEN

1

Amber Rogers did as Father Jacob bade her, spreading the gospel as gleefully as she spread her legs. After leaving the church, she drove Jimmy to his neighborhood at the south side of town. Stauford's Ghetto, some called it, although Jimmy would always have words with anyone who said as much to his face. Truth was, the only thing elevating Jimmy Cord to the height of social magnate in Stauford High School was his place on the football team. People in Stauford always seemed to ignore who lived down the street from a trailer park when football was involved.

Jimmy looked up at his home when they parked along the curb. He followed the trail of sagging gutters, all the places where the old nails were loose in the rotting wood, where all the shitty patch jobs his father did himself to save money had failed anyway. He'd never noticed them all before, or how the house, with its limp roofing, peeling paint on crooked siding, and cracked windows, looked more like a bloated wasp nest than a home. God knew he'd suffered his share of stings inside its crumbling walls.

His god knew a lot of things Jimmy wanted to forget, but that was part of his suffering, remembering all the horrible beatings his father gave him, even the ones before he was born. The beatings he heard from within the womb, when his mother carried him and tried her best to mask the tears while she hid her bruises. She'd been dead for five years now, rotting in the earth in the sweet embrace of the buried lord.

Jimmy turned to Amber and took her hand. Black tears leaked from her eyes, striping her cheeks with dark lines bleeding into the veins pulsing beneath her skin. He leaned over and kissed her, their swollen tongues tasting each other with primal urgency. Her hand was already down his pants when Jimmy's father called out to him from across the street.

"Boy, what the hell you doin'? Have you been out all gaw'damn night?"

Ronny Cord stood on the front porch, hands on his hips like he always did when he was pissed and itching for a fight. He'd just come home, having worked more than his share of a third shift down at the railroad. He was buzzed from the whiskey flask he kept in his work vest and the fire in his eyes was paramount.

"Your daddy's mad," Amber cooed, sliding her hand up and down. "Why don't you tell him about the lord?"

Jimmy turned from her and stared dreamily across the street at his fuming father. He pulled her hand out of his pants, zipped himself up.

"The old man ain't gonna believe I've been to church."

"Make him believe, baby."

"For sure," Jimmy said, opening the door. "His will and the Old Ways are one."

Amber waited, watching from the safety of her driver's seat while Jimmy wandered toward his father. She didn't flinch when Ronny smacked his son across the face, nor did she look away when he punched Jimmy in the gut. Instead, she giggled at the shock on Ronny Cord's face when Jimmy caught the old drunk's fist, twisted it back, and snapped his forearm in two. There was a moment of silent understanding between the two of them before the pain reached Ronny's booze-addled brain and the screaming began.

She climbed out of the car as Jimmy silenced his father's screams with the essence of their lord. Thick black tendrils dripped from Jimmy's throat, curling into the agonizing maw of his father, seeping into his guts, his eyes, his lungs.

Amber rubbed herself through her jeans while she watched the old man writhe in agony, his body crippled and convulsing as the dark mass worked its way inside him.

Jimmy knelt beside his father. "I met God, old man. He's real, He's here right now, and soon you'll meet Him too. But first you need to suffer. That's what the Old Ways say you have to do." He looked up at Amber. "Do you think he's sufferin' enough, babe?"

A mischievous grin flashed across her face, her eyes darkening. She licked her lips.

"No," she gasped. "Hurt him more."

"Okay," Jimmy said, grinning.

Ronny Cord wasn't a religious man, but now he was praying to Jesus and all the angels in Heaven. They couldn't hear him over the sound of all that screaming.

2

While Jimmy dragged his groaning father inside the house, Amber drove up Gordon Hill. From there, she followed Barton Mill Road to her neighborhood, where she found her younger sister, Candy, playing on the sidewalk in front of their home. Before her awakening in the glory of the lord, Amber Rogers used to hate her little sister.

If asked, Amber would probably tell you her parents conceived Candy just to fuck up Amber's life. She was annoying, always messing in Amber's business, always wanting to tag along, and tattling on her every chance she could. And with Amber's recent acquisition of a driver's license, her parents were asking her to take Candy here, take Candy there, pick up Candy from school, drop her off at this friend's house, or worse, to take Candy with her wherever she was going.

Candy Rogers, who never shut up and went snooping in Amber's room. Who, a few months ago, told her parents about the pack of condoms Amber kept hidden in her nightstand. There was the incident over her stash of Plan B pills, too. Her father never shut up about that one.

Now, Amber didn't hate her sister. She pitied her. This pitiful child, so blind in her supposed innocence, living outside the light of the one true lord, was agonizing in the heretical ways of their parents. This little beast would go without salvation if left to her own devices, a divine gift squandered in the name of a false god.

No longer. Her lord granted her permission to spread the gospel, and like Jimmy's father, suffering would occur. Suffering was *necessary*. Like the sacrifices of old, the beasts of the heretics would feel this suffering. Through them, the adults would soon see the light.

"No seeds will sprout without the sustenance of nature," Amber whispered, watching her sister draw on the sidewalk with a stick of pink chalk. "This earth must be fed. It is Your will in the Old Ways, my lord."

Amber shut off the engine and exited the car.

Candy scrunched up her face. "You're in so much trouble. Mommy and Daddy know you snuck out last night. I told 'em you were probably with a boy. What's wrong with your face?"

"Are Mommy and Daddy home now?"

"Uh huh. Want me to go get 'em?"

"No," Amber said, kneeling next to her sister. She took a piece of chalk and drew a pink sigil on the concrete, tracing the symbol of her lord. "I'll go see them when I'm done."

Candy watched her sister, visibly uneasy now Amber was so close. "What's wrong with your face? Did somethin' happen, sis? You look sick."

Amber finished her drawing and met her little sister's stare. Thick black tears slipped down her cheeks, and she licked them away from her lips, relishing the taste of the earth, the dark, the gritty essence of her god.

"I've never felt better, Candy." She leaned forward to Candy's ear and whispered. "Can I tell you a secret?"

Candy blushed. She wasn't used to this sort of attention from Amber. It excited and scared her, and she couldn't decide whether to lean in or run away in terror. *Mommy* lingered on her tongue, ready to be cried out at a moment's notice, but the word would never be uttered.

What Amber told her was too confusing and left her head reeling with a funny feeling. She felt like a top wobbling on its axis, and something stirred deep in her belly. A new voice occupied her mind, and the darkly curious things it said to her made her cry. *Your parents have lied to you, child. They don't deserve a little lamb like yourself. Let me show you the true way to salvation.*

"I met God last night," Amber said, "and I want you to meet Him, too."

"H-How…" Candy whimpered, sniffling back tears.

Amber gripped a fistful of her little sister's hair and leaned forward as black worms inched their way from her mouth, her nose, her eyes, seeking the flesh of another innocent beast.

3

While Candy lay gagging and seizing on the sidewalk, Amber went inside her home to share the gospel of her lord with Joseph and Grace Rogers. When she was finished, she stepped outside and marked the front door with the half-moon sigil of her lord.

From there, she went next door to the home of Jeremy and Christina Hanes, who used to yell at her for leaving her hula hoop in their front yard all the time; the home of Ms. Viruett at the end of the cul-de-sac, with her obnoxious poodle, Dandy, whose blood-drenched limbs were used to form the sigil on the front stoop; the residence of Tom and Priscilla Maxwell, where their two ginger sons Ricky and Beau were playing a game of catch in the front yard until Amber introduced them to the Old Ways; the newly remodeled home of Randy and Carolyn Eberle, whose newborn, Charlie, nearly suffocated before the black essence could be absorbed into his frail body; and finally, on the opposite side of the cul-de-sac, the three-story trophy home of Steve and Cassie Robinson, one of Stauford's socialite couples who were proud members of First Baptist but who rarely went, and who were the only two in the neighborhood with enough sense to try and call the police before Amber silenced them.

The call went through to Stauford PD's switchboard, which was already lit up with a dozen other pending callers, as Jimmy Cord did his share of spreading the gospel at the trailer park next door. Officer Gray wasn't present at the station when the first frantic calls erupted with reports of children attacking their parents, vomiting black sewage and babbling about the ways of a new god. Marcus was on the other side of town, having gone from one murder scene to the next, first at Baptist Regional and then at the small gas station down the road. All his attempts to reach Chief Bell were met with the same monotone voicemail message, and within a couple of hours, a computerized recording would tell him Bell's inbox was full.

The few officers who were dispatched to the homes of those first terrified callers would arrive to scenes of struggle and bloodshed. First there was Officer Timothy Martin, who drove out to Harmony Heights, the trailer park down the street from the Cord residence. He knew the neighborhood well enough, having broken up several drug deals there over the summer, and when he received a call from dispatch about a domestic dispute, he expected more of the same.

What he found were two pale-faced boys standing outside their doublewide trailer, circling the squirming bodies of their parents while dropping stones. The children arranged the pebbles around the bodies in a bizarre design, giggling to themselves while they worked. Black bile streamed from their eyes and noses. Officer Martin exited his cruiser and called to the kids when he was assaulted from the side by a young girl with dirty brown hair in pigtails. She looped her fingers around Martin's service belt, hoisted herself up on her toes, and projectile vomited a stream of black filth into his face.

Three blocks away from Harmony Heights, Officer Shawna Scott arrived at the private residence of Darrel and April Brown where she found their daughter, Michelle, standing over them with a carving knife. Michelle Brown had cut into her father's rotund gut and was slicing bits of his intestines into pieces to complete the ceremonial sigil of her lord. She stared intently at the blood-drenched curl of meat in her hands, her tongue stuck between her teeth, oblivious to Officer Scott's presence or the groaning agony erupting from her twitching parents.

"Little girl," Shawna said, swallowing back the dry lump in her throat as she unbuckled her holster. "Baby girl, I need you to put the knife down."

Michelle Brown said, "I have to get this right for my lord." She sliced through another chunk of her father's intestine and arranged it carefully in the grand design, nearly dropping the blood-slick flesh.

Officer Scott's stomach lurched as she readied her weapon. *Am I really doing this? Am I really going to* do *this? Oh God, am I—*

A crowbar silenced her troubled thoughts. She was so caught up in her moral quandary she'd failed to notice the two Rapino boys from next door creep up behind her. While one child vomited the black essence into Officer Scott's face, the other circled her body with stones from the gravel driveway.

In the distance, church bells were ringing.

FROM THE JOURNAL OF IMOGENE TREMLY
(3)

1

Notebook entry dated April 5th, 2012

Cosmic alignment serves as catalyst for focus of power. Follow cycles of the moon. If you ever go through with this, it must be before the full moon. The dead roots below Stauford always stir by moonlight.

2

Notebook entry dated June 14th, 2017

Tyler convinced me to go to a doctor. Wish I hadn't, but there's not much else I can do about it now. I won't poison myself to extend my life when the outcome will be the same. Jacob will have his day, but so will I. Calling Chuck in the morning to break the news and arrange for the next steps. Jackie, I'm so sorry.

3

Notebook entry dated August 17th, 2017

Important to follow instructions to the letter. Three circles—mind, body, spirit—to represent the afflicted temples. Salt to bind them, sage and incense to purge the air, candles to scare off the shadows. Something to mark the sigils of purging around the temple of mind. I'll need a bit of earth worms for the temple of body, as that's where Jacob resides, and that is where he is consumed. The idol of the nameless resides there as well.

Chuck's helped me make the arrangements for afterward. My darling professor isn't happy about it, but he knew what he was getting into. My heart aches for him, regardless, but this is something I have to do. It's what I've always known. I just pray this works.

I pray I'm able to stop him when he returns.

I pray Jackie forgives me.

4

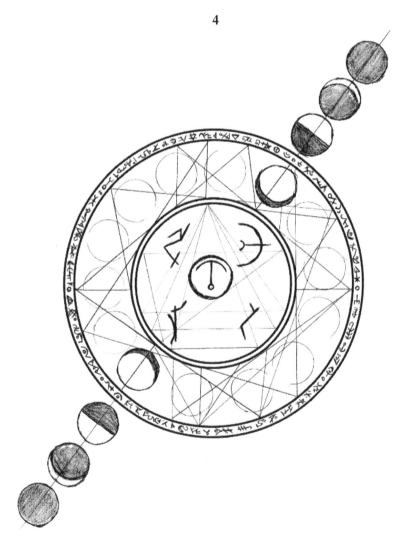

PART FOUR

BLOOD AND FIRE

Stauford, Kentucky
Present Day

CHAPTER SEVENTEEN

1

Across town, Jack Tremly stirred in his sleep. He was no stranger to dark dreams, but since his return to his hometown, the nightly phantoms were restless, defying even the strongest of his prescriptions. Jack found himself back in the temple beneath the church, knee-deep in a pit of ash and bone while the cries of children surrounded him. His mother stood at the far end of the temple, near the gateway to the twilit grotto.

Come to me, Jackie. She held out her arms to him, beckoning with a proud smile. *You can do it. Take your first step, baby boy. Come to Mama.*

And he wanted to. God, he wanted to, only his toddler limbs wouldn't work. They were trapped in the ash, his tiny feet slowly sucked down by something from below. When he glanced down, he saw the brittle bones of baby hands and feet, tiny skeletal remains reaching from the earth.

Come to Mama, honey.

But in this dream, Jack resisted his mother's call. There was something standing behind her, an impossibly horrible thing stretching along the walls, dripping into every crack and etching, embodying the very words carved in stone. Something with arms and eyes and teeth. There were so many teeth, a devourer of worlds and stars, buried here in this tumor of the earth.

You can do it, Jackie. Come to me.

He resisted, staggering in place over the crushed bones of the babies who'd gone before him. Their hands were still down there, beneath the surface of ashen earth, waiting to pull him down.

His mother stamped her foot, angered by his hesitation, her gaunt cheeks flushing red. Above her, the living shadow trembled like heat in the distance, a visible echo in the air reflecting her anger.

Jack Tremly, you will do as I say right now, little boy. You will come to me, or so help me, I'll tell your father.

Those awful words were enough to spark terror in any child, a universal edict carrying the promise of punishment even inside this hellish dreamscape. Jack froze, his tears watering the soil beneath him, and from their dampened clumps sprouted bony fingers, seeking his feet to pull him down. The children who'd gone before him, be they of his mother's womb or from some other faceless woman, cried out his name in victory. He was one of them, one of the damned, and soon he would join them. The ash of charred remains and bones would fill his lungs, his beating heart slowing in the earth, suffocating in the bosom of a buried god.

Buried, but not sleeping.

Waiting.

Pulling him down one inch at a time. Deeper into the dark, into the pit of bones with all the other children.

Jack awoke from the nightmare and opened his eyes.

Laura Tremly stared down at him, her lips and chin coated in dried blood. Black trails streaked from her eyes and mingled with the coagulated mess on her face.

"Baby boy." Her hands were on his throat before he could scream.

2

Riley kicked open the front door, wincing as the doorknob slammed into the wall. Bobby Tate leaned against his son's shoulder, hacking up a lungful of black gunk. Thick clots of the dark gore fell in clumps to the floor, writhing with unseen things beneath the surface, and filling the house with an overpowering stench of rotting earth. Riley propped his dad against the wall as he closed the door.

"I'm calling 911."

"No," Bobby rasped. He coughed so hard he lost his balance and fell to the floor in a shuddering heap. Whatever it was Ben and Toby vomited into his father's face was working its way into the man's system. Dark veins burst around his eye sockets, pulsing their way down the sides of his face while black tears dribbled down the ridge of his nose. They'd barely made it home before the toxic mess took an effect. Bobby's Acura was still in the ditch next to the driveway, its blinker still on, the engine still idling.

Riley watched his father wince in agony, frozen by the prospect of losing another parent, and for the first time since his mother died, he found himself crying out to God. *No, not him too. Please, don't take him away from me. He's all I've got left. It's not fair, damn you. You can't have him. You can't.*

He unclenched his fists and set his shaking hands on his father's shoulders. "Come on, Dad. Get up. We're going to get you to the bathroom, and then I'm going to call an ambulance."

"No," Bobby said again, but he was too weak to protest his son. Riley heaved his father's arm over his shoulder and cursed under his breath as he tried to lift dead weight.

"You gotta work with me, Dad. Please."

Another hoarse cough tore through Bobby Tate's convulsing frame. A runny clump of black phlegm shot from his mouth and splattered at the foot of the stairs.

"Oh, Jesus fucking Christ, that's gross."

Riley's father found his footing and reached for the banister. Whether it was the expulsion of the toxic matter or his blasphemy that got Bobby moving, Riley would never know. In either case, Bobby Tate managed to pull himself up the stairs without the help of his teenage son, collapsing in front of the bathroom door.

"Dad—"

"Call…Stephanie…"

"I will, but you really need a doctor—"

Bobby crawled into the bathroom and vomited on the tile floor. He turned back, hooked his foot against the door, and met his son's gaze.

"Riley, I love you more than anything…please don't ever forget that."

"Dad, enough. I'm calling 911."

"Goddammit, Riley, listen to me for once." Riley stared at his old man, dumbstruck. "Go to your room and lock—" Another heaving cough tore through the good reverend's shuddering body. He turned and hacked up another mess of black phlegm. "—lock the door. Don't let anyone in. Not even me."

"Dad—"

"I SAID GO!" Bobby Tate kicked the door closed with such force the walls shook. Riley stared at the blank door in shock, listening to his old man retch on the other side. *Is he dying? Oh God, is he dying? Is he dying?*

He was so caught up in the racing fear that for a moment he forgot about calling for help. Instead, Riley faced the prospect that he was going to lose another parent. His *only* parent. The prospect of being without a father scared him, but the imminent possibility of being truly alone in this world downright terrified him.

Beyond the bathroom door, Bobby vomited into the toilet, muttering a prayer to God for release from this awful poison coursing through his body. Only Riley heard him, and the sound of his father's agony was enough to spur him to movement. He ran down the hall to his room, locked the door behind him, and fumbled for his phone through a cloudy haze of tears.

"Oh God," he cried, wiping his eyes. "No, no, no, not now. *Not now!*"

His heart sank. The battery indicator flashed on the screen, and he glanced toward the far wall where the charging cable hung limp from the outlet. Riley's phone was dead.

3

The world spun for Jack Tremly, the rooms of his grandmother's home tinged in shadow while an expanse of colorful stars burst before his eyes. His gut lurched, and he was halfway out of consciousness when he realized he was flying. No, not flying. *Floating,* held aloft by an unseen force while his mother cackled madly from somewhere beyond the creeping dark.

I'm still dreaming, he thought. *Still back in the temple beneath the church, still a child, still terrified.*

And he *was* terrified, but the effect of adrenaline slowed time, slowed his responses to everything. The world didn't move to catch up until he heard the creak of the basement door, and from that moment, everything happened in the impeccable high definition of stone-cold reality.

Jack hovered at the precipice of a darkened maw leading down into the basement. Laura hovered with him, her dirty toes scraping the wooden floor of the kitchen. She held him by his throat with an impossible strength, the cords of her neck standing out, the muscles in her blood-soaked arm bulging with blackened veins. Thick rivulets of black oil seeped from her glowing eyes and streamed from her nostrils. A black puddle riddled with thick clumps formed at her feet.

"I never got to say goodbye to you, Jackie. My, how you've grown. You look just like your daddy."

Words failed him. After years of imagining what he'd say to his mother if he ever saw her again, all the anger and sorrow drained from

264

him. Now, more than ever, Jack wanted to breathe again. He wanted to feel the comfort of gravity. And he didn't want to go down into the darkness of the basement.

Laura Tremly had other plans.

"The old bitch can't protect ya now, Jackie dear. And you and me, baby boy, we got some catchin' up to do."

His mother puckered her lips and blew a kiss. Her rancid breath sent the world spinning, and Jack realized he was falling backward, the light of the doorway rolling upward as he tumbled. Jolts of pain shot through his back as he met the sturdy wooden stairs. The burning agony traveled down his waist and gut as he rolled the rest of the way, collapsing hard on the concrete slab below. A familiar warmth spurted from his nose as a white heat surged between his eyes, and stars sparkled before him while he sought to make out shapes in the dark.

A groan escaped him when he tried picking himself up from the floor. More than the pain in his head and throat, more than the terror of waking to face his mother, there was the unsettling realization and agony of finding himself in the dark of his grandmother's basement. Even when Mamaw Genie was still alive, he avoided this terrible place. His therapist told him it was a trick of his mind, a way of projecting early trauma on present surroundings, a flight response triggered by what happened to him when he was a child. Here in the deep dark of the earth, all the old demons were waiting for him, folded up in the shadows like old decorations, covered in dust and cobwebs. *Jackie,* they said, *you've finally come to play.*

Jack groaned again as he forced himself to his knees, his mind racing to get to his feet, to gather his wits and defend himself against his attacker. Blood gushed from his wounded nose, pooling on the concrete between his shaking hands. He knocked over a pair of cobweb-laden brooms and his old wooden baseball bat from a million years before. They clattered to the concrete, the harsh noise chiming in his head like cathedral bells.

"Yes, my lord," Laura Tremly croaked, descending the staircase like a fallen angel. "I'll find your prize, and I'll make sure my boy gets what he deserves. Your will and the Old Ways are one." She fell upon him before he could find his footing. "I thought I raised you better, baby boy. But look at you. You've gone and fallen in with the heretics."

Laura hooked her hand around Jack's neck and heaved him across the room like a twig. He collided with a stack of packed boxes, and Christmas decorations clattered on the floor, strings of lights and decorative balls shattering from the force of impact.

The world swam before Jack's eyes once more, and he fought to maintain consciousness while his whole body shrieked with pain. His mother's words flirted with the dull ringing in his ears, swirling with the dark colors accumulating in his palette of vision.

"More useless trinkets for a false god," Laura mumbled, picking through the strewn Christmas paraphernalia on her way toward him. "Did the old bitch ever tell you she used to shun such things? She ever tell ya she used to be one of us?" Laura found him bleeding amid the crushed boxes. He opened his eyes, glared up at her, but lacked the strength to speak. "Even her false god punished traitors. Only she didn't need thirty pieces of silver. No, all it took for her was a little baby boy. Just you. You, and the rest of your kin."

"What do you want?" he grunted, wincing as he eased himself up on his side. "Why the fuck are you here?"

Laura clicked her tongue. "Always so disrespectful to your mama."

"You might be my mother, but you're not my mama." He spat blood at her feet. "Genie raised me while you were rotting in the hospital. I always hoped you'd die there."

"My lord saw to it I got out, baby boy." She kneeled before him and took his chin in her bloodstained hand. "He gave me a job to do, and I aim to do it. The old bitch took something from my lord many years ago and you're going to give it back to me."

"I don't know what you're talking about."

She squeezed his cheeks. "I can pull that lyin' tongue from yer head, Jackie baby. My lord ain't kind to liars, and I follow His ways to the letter."

"But I know who might," Jack said, bracing for impact. "Someone like *him*, maybe."

The baseball bat struck the back of Laura's skull before she could react. Jack turned away as a thick clump of black sludge splattered the wall above him. His mother's unconscious body slumped to the side, revealing a sweating old man in dirt-covered khakis and a tweed jacket.

Professor Booth let the baseball bat clatter to the floor. Panting, he pulled a handkerchief from his breast pocket and wiped his forehead. "You okay, son?"

"Never better," Jack said, gritting his teeth as he rose to his feet. The swirling shadows before his eyes finally got the better of him, and before he knew what was happening, the world was swimming once again. The last thing he saw before the darkness overtook him was a surprised look on the old man's face.

Tyler Booth still had a hell of a swing from his boyhood days of playing on the field, but he was long past the age of carrying a full-grown man up a flight of stairs. Instead, he dragged Jack's unconscious body away from the bloody wretch to the opposite side of the room. He knelt and put a finger on the young man's neck. *Come on,* Tyler thought, *don't die on me, boy. I need you.*

The pulse was there, and strong, too. Nothing some bandages and aspirin wouldn't fix. Tyler wiped sweat from his brow and thanked a higher power he'd come along when he did. After his discovery at Genie's grave, he'd debated on packing up his things and leaving town but knew he couldn't live with himself if he abandoned his love's kin.

Instead, Tyler drove the quick couple of miles to Genie's house, hoping he'd find Jack there. He'd knocked twice when the front door creaked open, and that's when he'd heard the struggle within. Less than a minute later, he'd found himself standing at the foot of the basement steps, staring at the back of a haggard creature defying all logic and gravity. Finding the stray baseball bat at his feet seemed like more than luck to him—it seemed like divine intervention, or at the very least, a small gift from Genie.

Satisfied Genie's grandson wouldn't die on his watch, Tyler turned his attention to the bleeding bitch on the other side of the basement. A dark mixture of blood and something like oil seeped from the wound in the back of her head, pooling in a misshapen halo around the top of her skull. Tyler wondered if he'd killed her.

He knelt again, grimacing as his aching knee popped under pressure, and spotted the plastic ID bracelet on her wrist.

"And who might you be?" he muttered, lifting her limp wrist and turning it over in his hand. He read the tag: LAURA JEAN TREMLY. The color drained from his face as realization sank in. He stared at the woman's features, trying to see through the blood and black murk staining her skin, wondering how Genie could've ever given birth to this horrible woman.

A conversation from years ago replayed in his mind, the night he and Genie sat in her backyard, watching for shooting stars. They'd each had their share to drink that evening after dinner, imbibing a full bottle of wine he'd brought for the occasion.

"I used to sit out here with my daughter, you know. Me 'n Laura would do what we're doin' now, watchin' the stars."

"That so?"

"Yes, sir. She wasn't always bad. Wasn't always locked up in a hospital. No, she used to be a good little girl, before she fell in with Jacob. I tried to do right by her, but…well, some things can't be saved, I guess. Maybe some of us are born rotten. I failed her, and then she failed Jackie. I won't make the same mistake twice."

It was the only time she'd ever brought up her daughter around him. Even toward the end, when she went all-in with her plan to combat Jacob's binding ritual, she never brought up Laura Jean Tremly. For the longest time, he suspected Genie was trying to protect her grandson, but now he realized she was trying to spare herself the heartache. *Maybe you were right,* he thought. *Maybe some of us* are *born rotten, Genie.*

Laura stirred in her sleep, her eyes moving behind their lids. A thick bead of black goo slowly rolled down her cheek, carrying with it a musty stench of rotting leaves and grass. The smell took him back to a place he swore he'd never go again, and from within the dark shadows of his mind rose a chorus of voices he wished he could forget: *We see you, child.*

"You were right," he whispered. "All along, Genie, you were right."

Tyler walked toward a dusty workbench in the corner, its strewn contents of misplaced hammers, nails, and other hardware covered in a thin sheet of cobwebs. He found a bundle of twine in one of the drawers.

"This'll have to do." Tyler looked up and pulled the dangling chain from the bare bulb above. Pale light flooded the room, illuminating a design of circular glyphs on the floor and wall in all their esoteric glory.

How many years had Genie devoted to deciphering the nature of the ritual? He couldn't say but knew she was researching the glyphs for as long as they'd known each other, and probably even longer than that. Tyler reached out, tracing his index finger along the dusty chalk lines drawn on the wall and recoiled with a jolt. He rubbed the tip of his finger against his thumb, watching his flesh turn red and blister.

I wish I'd stopped you.

Instead, he'd obeyed her like the lovesick fool he was. Now she was gone, and he was alone to deal with the fallout. He looked down at Laura and then back at Jack. *No,* he thought, *not alone. But first things first.*

A few minutes later, after he'd bound Laura to one of the beams in the middle of the room, Tyler tried to rouse Genie's grandson. Blood caked Jack's nose and lips, his throat was bruised and swollen, and whenever Tyler said his name, Jack groaned errantly but did not wake.

Nervous, Tyler pulled his phone from his pocket and dialed 911. A recording announced all circuits were busy. He tried the number again and met the same result.

"Shit."

He paged through his phone's contact list, searching for the name of the only other person he could call. The one person he'd sworn never to speak to again, for helping Genie carry through her final wishes.

Tyler stared at the name CHUCK TIPTREE, frowning. "The hell with it."

He dialed the attorney's number and closed his eyes.

5

Bobby knew what was happening to him. He hadn't recognized it at first, not when he sank to his knees to greet the two missing boys, and not when their corrupted filth spread among his congregation. No, he didn't realize what was happening until he felt the awful darkness spreading inside himself, when the dark sludge worked its way into his guts, his blood, his soul.

He'd seen this once before, seen the effects on an otherwise normal human being, and for the longest time he thought they were nightmares culled from less sinister memories of his time beneath his father's church. He'd prayed to God to quiet the darkness of his childhood, to keep those vile things from bubbling up within, and for a while his prayers were answered.

Now, as he crawled his way out of the bathroom and across the hall toward his bedroom, Bobby Tate understood his prayers would no longer be answered. He was being punished for his instinct to cry out to God, each muttered prayer ending in a crescendo of agony as his guts ripped themselves apart, the viscous sludge seeping further into his core. Soon it would reach his heart, and what then?

Then you're gone. Then you're His. Like you used to be. Like He always wanted.

Bobby winced, crawling along the floor of his bedroom toward the bed. Thick ropes of the dark sludge streamed from his nose and the corners of his mouth. *Fight this.* He pulled himself up onto the bed and collapsed into his pillow, wincing at the deep ache inside his skull, the awful taste of bile and dirt in the back of his throat. *Fight this for Riley.*

A voice spoke up from across the room. *Oh, son, why fight this? Why fight your true lord? Why fight your father? When we both know this is the way things are supposed to be?*

Bobby lifted his chin and stared straight ahead, expecting to see his dead father, but there was only the stillness of the room. The chest-of-drawers stood silent, cluttered with some of his late wife's things he couldn't bring himself to remove, the dark screen of a small television, and a cross hanging on the wall.

Your father knew the true meaning of sacrifice, my child. He, too, was once a man of a false faith, a follower of a heretical god. But he saw the true light, not from above, but from within. He read the scripture of the Old Ways, etched those ancient words in his heart, and followed a narrow path of the one true faith. He spilled his seed for me. He suffered for me. He gave his life for me. And I have raised him up from the clutches of death, free from the bounds of the earth, for the earth is my domain. No cage of the earth will hold you if you would suffer for me, Bobby. Your father is my apostle. Will you not be one too?

A tiny metallic *ting* filled the room, and the cross fell to the floor. Bobby sucked in his breath and looked away, blinking dark tears from his eyes. Something plastic scraped along the wooden flooring. The voice grew louder.

Your wife is one of my children now. I can free her from the prison of the earth, child, and give her back the life stolen from her. Would your false god do such a thing for her? I alone heard your prayers all those nights, while your darling Janet rotted in the earth. I alone heard your anguish, your quiet cries for her return. And by the mandate of the Old Ways, my son, I will give her life once more if you would open your heart and suffer for me. Would you shred your soul to be one with me? Would you suffer to let your wife be with you once more?

Bobby turned his head and clamped his eyes shut, struggling to contain the rank sewage spilling up his throat, slowly drowning him from within.

"Honey," Janet Tate whispered, her warm breath tickling his ear. *"Don't you want me back? We can start over. We can be one again and make another baby for our lord. We can give Riley to the Nameless and begin anew."*

The scraping intensified, growing heavier, transforming into footfalls across the room toward the bed. Bobby wanted to cover himself like a child, to hide from the monster in his bedroom, praying that if he couldn't see it, then it couldn't see him. The thing speaking to him was not his wife, dead or otherwise. This thing speaking with his wife's voice was a liar, a puppet of the dark god his father conjured from the earth. The real Janet would never trade Riley for anything.

"So foolish," Janet cooed in his ear. He felt something like a hand trace its way across his cheek, down the back of his neck like she used to do, and then down along the side of his thigh. *"Honey, my darling reverend, you can't hide from the one true god. He is eternal. His roots run deep beneath this home, beneath all of Stauford, and if you would suffer to come unto Him, He would reap the fields of the earth."* The hand moved up, cupping his groin, massaging him through his slacks. *"If you would suffer for Him, then you could fuck me again. I would do things to you in death I never would in life. Because you were too timid to ask. Our new lord doesn't judge our desires, honey. Your lust is not a sin."*

Her voice deepened, tainted with the rot of a thousand years. She was no longer at his ear, but inside it, inside the chamber of his mind. *"I want you to do terrible things to me, Bobby. On an altar of blood, beneath the unblinking gaze of our lord, I want you to ravish me. I want you to spread me open, taste the honey of wasted years, and consummate our union."*

"No," Bobby groaned, rolling away, hiding his face in the pillow. His cheeks burned with a heat he'd only known in the quiet moments of the night, after his wife's untimely death. The rigid discomfort in his pants betrayed his refusal, and the thing infecting his body and mind knew as much. A deep laughter filled the chambers of his head, shaking the world around him.

If not your wife, then perhaps your false god. I know what lies in your heart, Bobby Tate, even if you choose to ignore your very nature. The only other thing you loved more than your wife is a dead idol. You loved your faith more than your own son, just like your false god. So be it, child. Open your eyes and gaze upon the pained face of your savior.

Bobby worked up the energy to cry out in one final act of defiance. He would not let this evil thing possess him. He was a man of God, a servant of the light, and he would not stand for these blasphemous atrocities. Finally, with the last ounce of his strength, Bobby Tate opened his eyes and gave voice to his rebellion: *"ENOUGH!"*

The room was empty, the air sucked from its open spaces as quickly as the air from his lungs. There were no dark shapes standing before him, no decomposed figure of his deceased wife. He was alone except for the gripping, tearing sensation in his guts.

It's all in your head, he told himself, leaning back on the bed. *It's all in y—*

A bloody hand reached up from below the foot of the bed, followed by another. Together they pulled up a bruised shape soaked in darkened gore, its torn and tortured flesh hanging in thick folds from scrawny arms. A head emerged beyond the edge of the bed, adorned with a crown of bleeding thorns. Thick spikes jutted from the figure's wrists, their wounds seeping black oil on the duvet. Black tributaries ran down the forehead of Bobby Tate's savior, pooling in the wells of glowing blue eyes.

"Suffering is the way to salvation, my little lamb. Will you suffer for me?" The bleeding Christ crawled toward him, its face twisted in agony, twin streams of black phlegm pouring over its cracked, sunburned lips. *"I am the way, Bobby boy."*

But Bobby Tate was no longer listening, his mind held firm in the grip of his father's buried god, the darkness inside him seeping into his heart. He closed his eyes and laughed.

❧

6

"My little baby, my sweet angel. I know you're still alive, little lamb. I can hear you breathin' all the way over here."

Jack stirred, the sound of his mother's raspy voice like something from a bad dream, syllables dragged over stones and across jagged glass. Her voice was smoky darkness, sour with the heated rot of something roiling beneath the surface, and when she spoke, his heart slowed in fear.

He opened his eyes to the stark contrast of light cutting through the dark. Sunlight poured down the dusty basement steps, illuminating errant particles in the air. A man's muffled voice bled through the walls, his footsteps creaking the floorboards overhead.

The man's name rose from the fog in his mind, and the rest followed slowly, filling his conscience with fragments of what came before. The throbbing ache of trauma returned, and his whole body sang a chorus of agony when he moved.

Laughter echoed through the room. Jack peered into the shadows, trying to make out the shape huddled against the support column.

"Oh, my darlin' boy, I can see you. Do you feel that hurt? That sweet pain ain't nothin' like what's waitin' for you in the dark where the lord's eyes never look away."

Jack ignored her, gritting his teeth as he pulled himself upright and leaned against the wall. He reached up and touched wet warmth on his face. *Booth's upstairs calling for help,* he thought. *Maybe an EMT. Maybe I'm concussed. Lucky she didn't break my goddamn neck.*

"I never forgot about you, Jackie. Not in all the years I was locked away in the hospital. Your daddy would tell me things about you, how you'd grown up, how you still dreamed of us and the night of your baptism."

"Please shut up."

"Is that any way to talk to your mama, Jackie?"

Laura Tremly's eyes glowed a sickening blue, illuminating the dark veins splintering from her eyes. *Just like my dreams,* he thought. *Just like the idol—*

What she'd said earlier echoed in his skull. *The old bitch took something from my lord many years ago.*

"Your grandma was always too soft on you, baby boy. I s'pose grandmas always are when it comes to their grandbabies. She didn't teach you nothin' about respect."

"She taught me plenty," Jack spat. His mother chittered in the dark. Even in the dim glow, he could see she was grinning at him, her mouth a wide chasm splitting her face. "You mock her memory all you want, but she taught me more than you ever did. At least she loved me."

"I loved you plenty, baby boy, in my way. I just loved my god more."

Jack opened his mouth but found he had no response to match her chilling honesty. What could he say? He believed her. She *did* love her god more. What he remembered of his mother was rigid devotion and unshakable faith, a follower to her lord with the discipline of a general in his infernal army. The innocent Christian girl who grew up in this house was long dead, strangled and buried by the woman she'd become.

"Once your daddy gets hold of you, Jackie, he's gonna set you straight."

Jack's breath hitched in his throat. He met her glowing stare and tried not to look away. "So it's true? He's alive?"

"Oh yes, my darlin' boy. He lives again. Even now, He's out doing our lord's work, spreading the gospel of the Old Ways." Laura cracked a smile and laughed. "But you knew that already, didn't ya? Felt it in your bones, deep down in your belly. In the dark while you sleep."

Jack looked away. She was right. He didn't have to say so. She already knew.

"Like it or not, Jackie, you're family. All you kids are. And your daddy's comin' to finish what he started all those years ago."

A chill crept over him, and the upstairs light dimmed at the sound of her words. A moment later, the basement door creaked open, revealing the silhouette of the professor. Jack didn't wait. He clenched his teeth and climbed the stairs one step at a time.

Behind him, his mother Laura giggled madly with a grating voice of broken glass.

7

Officer Gray sat in his mud-splattered cruiser, listening to frantic chatter over the CB radio. Across the gas station's parking lot, Officers Deal and Curtis taped off the crime scene where the old man's body still lay surrounded by a pool of his own blood. The forensics team was supposed to be there thirty minutes ago.

When he was a kid, Marcus Gray thought being a police officer meant day-to-day adventure, hunting down bad guys and saving old ladies. The reality of being a cop in a no-horse town like Stauford was far removed from his boyhood fantasies. He'd thought about quitting and getting himself a real job, maybe as security down at the railroad.

That all changed when shit hit the fan. Those were Ozzie Bell's words, of course—Marcus was a good church-goin' boy, never one to blaspheme or curse out of turn—but they were so fitting for the last several days. No matter how often he played back the last couple of days in his mind, no combination of words fit so well as "shit hit the fan." First with those missing boys, the Tremly woman escaping from the psych ward, and then the murder here at Ricky Rader's gas station early this morning. Now, from the sound of the chatter coming across the police band, the whole damn town was falling apart.

Shots fired in multiple districts, reports of children attacking their parents, neighbors attacking neighbors, a report of smoke billowing from the steeple of First Baptist downtown, a mob outside the church chanting prayers—not to mention the endless 911 calls overloading the switchboard. Marcus tried calling the chief again. He closed his eyes and listened to his panicking heart. *Count back from ten,* he told himself. *Ten. Nine. Eight.*

"Voice mailbox is full."

Officer Gray canceled the call and then dialed Chief Bell's phone number once more. Chief Bell would know what to do. He'd know how to manage this chaos, in his own brash sort of way. He'd chide Marcus for not keeping his cool, for falling apart at the worst possible moment, when seconds counted most.

Five rings. Six. Seven.

He opened his eyes and looked at the phone. He'd dialed the chief eleven times since arriving at the crime scene forty-five minutes ago. *Are you really this helpless? Shit hits the fan while you're on duty and you fall apart. No wonder the guys at the station make fun of you.*

But he'd never been caught in a situation like this. There was supposed to be a chain of command. Sure, maybe he wanted to be chief someday, but not *this* soon, not *today,* and not while feeling hopelessly out of his element.

He thought back to the Saturday after he graduated from the academy, when his parents held a surprise celebration party in his honor. Ozzie Bell took him aside, back to the far corner of Harlan Gray's yard. There, hidden in the shadows of the storage shed, Ozzie told him between mouthfuls of chocolate cake, *"I'm only doin' this as a favor to your old man. If you fuck this up, if you make me look bad, if you get anyone killed, so help me, boy, I'll put you down myself. You got me? This cake is fucking dry."*

Marcus frowned. He still remembered the shock, the cold look in Ozzie's eyes even as he spoke with a smile, and the awful metallic taste bubbling in the back of his throat as the chief of Stauford's police department spat a mouthful of cake and frosting onto Marcus's loafer.

"I read you," Marcus whispered, as a recording announced a full inbox once again. "I read you loud and clear."

He wasn't going to fuck this up, no sir, but he still needed to know if he was on his own. There was only one place Ozzie Bell could be right now. The whole town knew, had been whispering about it for a while now, and even Marcus heard the talk.

In some ways, Marcus thought it made perfect sense. Ozzie didn't seem like the sort to fall in with a safe, homey type. From what he knew of Ozzie's conquests back in the day, the chief was every bit the Stauford hellion the tales made him out to be. A good ol' boy down to the bone, football star, infamous bully and troublemaker.

But Susan Prewitt had a reputation of her own, one the guys at the station only spoke about in whispers. They said she was crazy from the trauma she'd suffered as a child, marked by the devil, and all sorts of other spooky shit. They said she had a fling with her brother, bathed in her own menstrual blood, and danced naked during the full moon.

All rumors, of course, but in a town like Stauford sometimes rumors were all there were to go on. One might even say the town thrived on them, suckling rumors from the populace like marrow from bone, and Chief Bell's interest in the Prewitt girl fueled the rumor mill for months. Tomorrow, he was sure, new rumors would surface.

Rumors the chief ditched his official duties in favor of spending the day in bed with his latest conquest. Rumors he'd left Officer Dipshit in charge to oversee the town's downfall. Rumors that would surprise no one, because the whole damn town knew he got the job because of a favor and not merit. *What did you expect? Leave a stupid kid in charge and the whole town tears itself apart under his watch. Typical.*

Not if I can help it, Marcus thought. *They might speak rumors, but they won't be about me. No, sir. This time I'm in charge. This time I'm the one tellin' the story. I won't take the blame for this town fallin' apart.*

Marcus started the car and called over Officer Deal. "Wait for the forensics team. Shit's hitting the fan in town, and I can't reach the chief."

Officer Owen Deal, three years Marcus's senior, blinked and waited for the punchline. Marcus stared, lifted his chin, and spoke again. "I'm going to find Ozzie. Stay here."

Officer Deal smirked, nodded, and tapped the roof of the cruiser. "You got it, sir."

Officer Gray didn't say anything else. He put up his window, dropped the cruiser into gear, and turned onto the Cumberland Falls Highway.

8

Riley sat on the edge of his bed, chewing his thumbnail while the battery indicator flashed on his phone. He scolded himself while he plugged in the charger. *So stupid. You shouldn't have run it down at church. You should've charged it last night.* Only he didn't. He'd fallen asleep with the phone by his side, hoping for a text from Rachel, or maybe even from Ben.

Ben.

God, what happened to him? Ben's pale face flashed before him. He remembered the strings of black phlegm oozing from the boy's eyes and nose. The attack on his father played in Riley's mind on a loop. His dad turned away, but not in time. Some of the dark gunk went into his mouth, his nose, his eyes.

Riley's gaze fell upon a stack of books on his desk. Some texts for school, a couple of horror anthologies centered around Lovecraft and Bloch, and a thick graphic novel called *Gothical.* He'd picked it up at the bookstore downtown because of the cover, which he'd later discovered was drawn and painted by his uncle Jack.

On the cover, a lone figure in crimson armor rose above a throng of zombie-like men and women, brandishing a weird weapon: an amalgamation of sword and axe that would only make sense in a comic book. The zombie army was drenched in an oil-like substance, thick and shiny, covered in a pale sheen from the eerie light streaming from their eyes.

An infection, Riley thought, running his finger along the cover, tracing along the border of the nearest zombie. *Whatever's inside them is infectious. They infected Dad. Contagious. Whatever the blue-eyed man did to them, his corrupted army did to Dad and everyone else.*

A low erratic laughter erupted from down the hall. Riley froze, looking up at his door. The lock was turned, but he didn't have much faith in the door itself.

If Dad's infected, he can pass it on to me. A thick wad of cotton lodged itself in his throat. *Dad knew.*

Riley forced back tears. Now wasn't the time for crying. He returned to his bed and checked the phone. The device lit up, its battery still in the red but showing ten percent. Enough to call his aunt.

The laughter grew louder, and the whole house shook beneath heavy footfalls. "Riley! Did I send you to your room? I didn't ground you, son. I ain't mad. Come to your father. I want to tell you about the lord."

Riley swallowed back air, fumbling for the phone to dial Stephanie. He lifted the device to his ear and listened to the thrumming of his heartbeat, erratic, pulsing faster with each approaching step.

"Son," Bobby Tate said, his muffled voice an octave deeper, raw, like he'd chain-smoked a pack of Camels in the last hour. "An angel of the lord visited me in my time of need. And do you know what he said? 'Take your son on high and deliver unto me a sacrifice worthy of your devotion.' And I said, 'Lord, I will do what thou wilt, for Your will and the Old Ways are one.'"

The footsteps stopped at the bedroom door. An instant later, the doorknob rattled.

"Riley boy," Bobby said. "I need to purify your soul, son. My lord commands it. Riley? *Riley!*" The room shook as his father slammed the wall.

No, Dad, no, not you. Please, no. The phone rang in his ear. Once, twice, three times—

A click. His aunt's voice on the other line.

"Hi, you've reached Stephanie. Leave a message."

Riley's lungs deflated. His father slammed the door once again, harder, so hard a thumbtack holding one of his posters dropped to the floor.

He dialed Stephanie's number again while he scanned the room in panic. How long would the door withstand his father? Could he hide under the bed? No, that wouldn't work, it was too obvious, too silly.

His aunt's voicemail picked up once again. *Goddammit, Steph, don't you ever answer the phone?*

He canceled the call and checked the screen. The battery charge was at twelve percent. His father began to sing.

"Oh, give me that old-time religion. It's good enough for me." Bobby slammed the door and the walls shook like Jericho. "And it'll be good enough for you, Riley. The lord said so, son. You'll see soon enough. All you need to do is suffer." He beat on the door again. *"Oh, give me that old-time sufferin', give me that old-time sufferin', give me that old-time sufferin', it's good enough for me!"*

Riley shoved the phone into his pocket and looked to his bedroom window. Some nights, he plotted escape routes in his mind. In those daydreams, he tore off into the night on the back of his bike, sometimes visiting Ben or Rachel. Sometimes, when he was particularly pissed at his old man, he'd ride out of Stauford for good.

But those were daydreams. He'd never attempted a climb from his second-floor window. The fifteen-foot drop was enough to deter him from trying such a stupid feat.

"RILEY!"

A section of the door exploded in a cloud of splinters as Bobby Tate thrust his fist through it. Riley screamed, shot to his feet, and moved for the window.

"Oh God," he whispered, thrusting the window open. A rancid stench of compost and earth permeated the air. From somewhere else in the neighborhood, a car alarm sounded endlessly, and there was a dog barking. Gunshots. A panicked voice was cut off mid-scream.

Behind him, Riley's father shoved his arm further through the hole, seeking the doorknob. Riley lifted his leg and straddled the windowsill.

He stared at the shrubbery below.

I can't do this. I can't, I don't want to get hurt, I'll break my legs, I'll—

"I see you," Bobby crooned. Riley looked back and saw his father's glowing eye peering through the hole in the door. "Where d'you think you're goin', Riley boy? Open the door for your old man, huh? You know I can tear this down any time I want."

Riley swallowed hard. His father stepped back and shoved his arm through the hole again. The wooden panel creaked under Bobby's weight, cracking wider as the good reverend reached further inward and gripped the doorknob—

His phone buzzed. He pulled it from his pocket, hoping to see a text from his aunt, but instead there was a message from Rachel: "Neighbor attacked my mom and dad. Something is wrong w/ them. Riley I'm scared!"

"No," Riley whispered, shoving the phone back into his pocket. "Not you too."

The doorknob clicked. Bobby Tate pulled his arm back through the hole, and the door slowly opened.

"It's time, son." Bobby stepped into the bedroom. "It's time your old man teaches you about the Old Ways."

Riley took one look at the thing that used to be his father. Dim light filled Bobby Tate's dull eyes while blackened gore streamed from his nostrils and lips, staining his Sunday best. A quiet voice spoke up within Riley's head, a voice belonging to his late mother. *You can do this, kiddo.*

Bobby Tate took another step toward his son.

Riley didn't wait. He pushed himself out the window and fell toward the chaotic world below.

CHAPTER EIGHTEEN

1

She was naked when her brother arrived. Sitting at the edge of her bloodstained bed, watching the life seep out of Ozzie Bell, Susan Prewitt remembered the night she snuck into her half-brother's room and teased him to orgasm. Even then, she heard the voice of her father in her head, willing her to satisfy her fleshly desires. *Go on,* her father told her, *do as you wish.* She would've, too, if the sound of her grandfather's footsteps hadn't startled them from their bedroom trance.

Susan leaned back and sighed as she slid her fingers between her legs.

Memories of Zeke's shocked face filled her mind, playing back like a private film reel, preserved with the clarity of formative memory. How could she forget? The trepidation in his voice when he asked what she was doing, the innocent reluctance, his yearning eyes alight with desire, the way he chewed his bottom lip when she ran her fingers over him, the subtle gasp of breath, the desire to stop her despite visibly being unable, *unwilling,* to do so—all these images flashed before her as she touched herself, willing her brother to be there now, to join her, to finish what she'd started all those years ago.

Blood seeped from the tattooed glyph on her wrist, dotting her thigh, forming a lover's trail to the promised land between her legs. She held his image in her mind, the horny boy she knew, the messed-up addict he'd become, praying to her father's god to bring Zeke to her.

But will you follow through this time?

The voice echoed in her ears, a raspy thing that was at once her father and yet something else altogether. Something older, its very presence filling her with the slightest hint of trepidation, its voice numbing her skin and vibrating in her bones. The voice of her lord, turning a mirror upon the trespasses of her youth.

She'd gone to Zeke's room, driven by hormonal lust and a deeper desire to rebel. Rebellion against morality, rebellion against the faith of the heretics, rebellion against the tenets of a false god—Susan had many causes to choose from, and when paired with her hormones, little else mattered. But while she sat at Zeke's bedside, touching his erection through a thin white sheet and driven mad by the deep groan escaping his terrified breath, a smaller voice spoke from within. *This is wrong. Stop before this goes any further. Before you do something you'll regret later.*

In the years since, Susan supposed the voice belonged to the false god of the heretics, trying to lead her astray from her desire. Even now, she was ashamed of not doing as her lord bade her, and she would atone for her sin.

I was a foolish child. Let me prove my faith to You, my lord. Your will be done.

The air in the room grew stale, heated, filled with the breath of something beyond her scope of understanding. She felt the gaze of her lord upon her and found she couldn't open her eyes to behold its glory. The fear of what she might find staring at her was too great. Her skin erupted in gooseflesh, her nipples hardening to stone.

Will you prove yourself, child? Will you give yourself to him as you've promised yourself to me? If I give you this gift, will you go all the way for me?

"Yes," she whispered. Ozzie stirred beside her, moaning incoherently. She ignored him, lifting her chin and her free hand in praise. "Let your spirit move through me. I will become Your vessel. Your will and the Old Ways are one, my lord."

So be it, child.

A rush of heat swept through her in orgasmic waves, stealing her breath and freeing a shrill cry of surprise from her lips. Susan arched her back in the throes of ecstasy, fingering herself on the edge of the bed while her boyfriend bled out.

Susan sighed. "Is that you, Ezekiel?"

The stench of sweat, blood, and rancid earth wafted into the room, followed by the creak of footsteps behind her. Coarse fingertips caked in dirt traced along her naked back, along the nubs of her spine, following the contours of her shoulder blades before moving up to her hair. Her whole body tingled at his cool touch.

"It's me, Susie. Our father sent me to you."

"I've been waiting. Do you see the sacrifice I made to honor our lord?"

"I do. You did well. You've taken a filthy spirit like Ozzie Bell and turned him into living scripture."

"He was going to have you arrested. He was going to keep us apart. I couldn't let that happen. You were doing the lord's work. It wasn't fair to punish you."

"I know." Zeke's hand slid down to her shoulder, his fingers caressing the nape of her neck. Susan cooed in response. "I've wanted you for so long, Susie. Ever since that night."

"I was a stupid little girl. Let me make it right. This body is yours."

"Yes" he whispered, "but first I've gotta ask you something."

"Anything," Susan said, her voice rising an octave as his hand slipped between her legs. "I'll do anything to make it right for you."

His hand left the moist heat between her thighs, trailing upward between her breasts, and stiffened around her throat. Susan Prewitt opened her eyes and swallowed back a scream.

The gaunt face of Zeke Billings looked down on her, the blue light of his eyes illuminating the blackened worms protruding from his cheeks. Dark phlegm streamed slowly from his nose and the corners of his mouth in thick strands shivering with life. Tendrils of black ichor sought the air, flexing outward in search of a host.

"Would you suffer for me, Susan?"

Zeke didn't give her time to answer.

2

Dark colors burst before Riley's eyes, clouding his vision with splotches of color as a stabbing pain shot from his hip to his knee. He'd landed hard in the bushes below his window and was lucky enough not to break anything, but the pain was ever-present in those moments when he limped across the lawn.

Somewhere behind him, his father bellowed in anger, crashing through his childhood home. *Keep moving,* he told himself. *Don't look back.*

The pain muddied his thoughts, however, and he fought the urge to vomit. *Maybe I did break something,* he wondered, plodding across the grass in slow motion. But his limbs cooperated with his wishes despite the pain, and in moments he was around the side of the house and standing before the garage door.

"Fuck."

In his panic, he'd not thought ahead. The garage door stood closed. His bike was inside. He couldn't run for long, not with every step shooting needles into his muscles. Swarms of dark spots swirled about his vision, threatening to steal consciousness from him. His father's heavy footsteps pounded across the house, down the stairs.

Panicking, Riley's gaze fell upon his father's car in the ditch. Bobby Tate had left it running in his haste to get inside the house.

I can't drive, Riley thought, his feet shuffling across the driveway. *I've never driven before in my life.*

Except that's not true, his mother said. *Your father took you out last year and let you drive in the shopping center's parking lot after hours. You had fun doing it, even if you wouldn't admit it to him.*

Riley sucked air through his teeth and stumbled ahead, focusing on what he remembered from that evening in the parking lot. He couldn't remember why his father took him out that night. All he remembered was his old man wanting to go for a drive, and then, to Riley's surprise, Bobby had relinquished the wheel.

It's a rite of passage, Bobby had said, dropping the car in park before exchanging seats with his son.

"RILEY!"

Bobby Tate pulled open the front door with such force it slammed into the foyer wall.

Cold white panic flooded Riley's mind as adrenaline took control. The boy ignored the pain, pushing himself through the carrion colorations eager to pick away at his consciousness, and closed the gap between himself and the car. He scrambled inside, slammed the passenger door, and engaged the locks.

Bobby Tate slammed his fist against the glass.

"Open the door, son."

Riley shook his head, grunting as he pulled himself over the center console and into the driver's seat.

"Riley, I mean it. This is your father talking to you. You're supposed to honor your father, boy." Bobby leaned his head against the window, leaving a dark snail-trail of black gore on the glass. "I want to tell you about the lord, son. Our lord and savior doesn't have a name. He's glorious and comes from within. Old lies above, son. Old lies above and new love below. So it says in the Old Ways. And I can show those to you, Riley. I can show you everything you'd ever want to know about the Old Ways, but you need to suffer first."

Riley placed his hands on the steering wheel and his foot on the brake. He looked over at his dad and realized he was crying.

"I'm sorry," Riley whispered. "I love you, old man."

Bobby Tate grinned, revealing a mouth of blackened teeth. Something slender and slimy like a leech protruded from his left nostril and slid along the glass. He didn't speak again. Instead, Reverend Bobby Tate raised his fist and thrust it through the window, shattering the glass in one pulverizing blow.

Riley reacted without thinking, pressing the brake like his father taught him and shifting the car into drive. He slammed on the gas.

The car shot forward along the rut of the ditch before reconnecting with asphalt in a shuddering bump. The tires squealed in complaint as they met the road, and as Riley sped away in his father's car, he thought he heard his old man shout, "Don't look back."

Riley did, but he'd spend the rest of his life wishing he hadn't.

3

Stephanie's phone vibrated across her coffee table and clattered to the floor. She awoke with a start, sitting up with a soft cry. Figments of the nightmare from which she'd sprung still danced before her—immeasurable dark things with a universe of eyes and teeth like stalactites—and she struggled to discern reality from dream while the phone vibrated along the floor.

Just a dream, she told herself, wiping sleep from her eyes. But her heart was still racing, her breath like a freight train, and when she looked about the room at the late morning sun streaming through the windows, dark phantoms skirted the edges of her vision. The vibration stopped, and she finally reached for the phone.

She thumbed through a list of missed calls. Several from Riley, one from Jack. Stephanie frowned. Seeing their names brought the previous evening's revelations racing back to her, culminating with a shiver crawling down her back. She clutched the afghan on the back of the sofa and pulled it down around her shoulders.

All the messages from Riley were hang-ups. Stephanie smirked. *Such an impatient little shit.* The one call from Jack, however, yielded a voicemail: "Hey Steph, it's Jack. Need you to drop by ASAP. It's about our chat last night." He paused. There were muffled voices in the background. "…Chuck's on his way. Good. Yeah, Steph, please get here as soon as you can."

"So ominous, Jackie." She thought about the painting she'd hidden in the closet the night before, of her father's bright blue eyes, and what Riley told them last night about the man he saw carrying his friends into the night.

Stephanie dialed Riley's number. The call went straight to voicemail.

"Hey Riley, it's Steph. Saw you tried to reach me. I'm going over to Jackie's place soon, but if you need me, just call. I promise I'll answer this time."

She canceled the call and rose from her nest on the sofa. Her body protested with a symphony of cracks and pops, and she took a minute to stretch out her aching muscles.

This was supposed to be my weekend off, she thought. *Whatever. No rest for the wicked.*

When she was finished, Stephanie went to her bedroom to change clothes. Outside, police sirens rose and fell in the distance.

4

Riley was two blocks away from his home when he finally switched his father's radio station. Bobby Tate was a devout country fan, which only amplified his disapproval of Stephanie's potential influence over the boy. Now, as the surge of adrenaline slowly left his system, Riley found himself hesitant to change the station. An artist named Sturgill Simpson sang about flowers and thorns and dancing with demons, topics which Riley hadn't expected to hear discussed in a country song. As he reached the end of the street, Riley realized he was humming along and felt foolish for doing so.

He switched the radio over to The Goat. Danzig filled the car, setting his mind at ease, the aural equivalent of a warm security blanket. His heart slowed, his breathing steady, but the cavernous pit in his gut was still there, a sort of emptiness he'd not felt since his mother died.

You can't save Ben, he told himself, *but maybe you can save Rachel.* He remembered the warrior on the cover of his comic book, rising above a throng of blue-eyed monsters. Could he be that strong right now? Or that brave?

"I have to be," he whispered. The street was empty of traffic, an oddity for an early Sunday afternoon in Stauford, when most churches were freeing their congregants to the world. Sirens cried out from somewhere in the distance, firing off in different cadences, and he couldn't tell if they were police, ambulance, or fire related. He thought of the horrible scene at the church before they'd fled and wondered if any of those people made it out alive.

His mind wandered back to the text from Rachel. What happened at the church was happening elsewhere, and right now, she needed him. If she was still alive. If she was still normal.

"Riley!"

His father's roar gave him a start. He looked in the rearview and saw a lone figure walking in the center of the street. Bobby Tate was less than a block away.

Riley didn't wait. He stepped on the gas, and the car shot forward so fast he panicked and lost his grip on the wheel. The car turned wide, over the opposite lane, and jumped the curb. Riley cried out in surprise as he twisted the steering wheel and let off the gas, guiding the sedan off the sidewalk and back into its proper lane. The tires gave a shrill cry when they met the pavement once more.

"Holy shit," Riley gasped, checking the mirror once more. Bobby Tate grew smaller in the reflection. "Holy shit. *Holy shit.*"

A cool breeze swept his hair back as he traveled along 7th Street, and when he rounded a curve, his father finally disappeared. Riley's heart slowed as the panic subsided, and he turned his attention toward the road ahead.

The way along 7th Street trailed up an incline, lined by several split-level homes. He went to school with a few kids who lived in this part of the neighborhood, but he'd never gone out of his way to socialize with them. They were just faces he recognized outside of school, names on the morning roll call.

Are they okay? Did they end up like Dad?

A burst of static hissed from the speakers, drowning out the rock music and filling the car with unbearable white noise. Riley cringed, reaching for the dial to change the station, but as he did so, a thick gurgling voice formed from the static.

"We are one, Riley. Your father is one of Us now. Your lovely Rachel is, too. Soon, you will be one of Us. Soon, you will know the Old Ways."

All along the street, the front doors of homes on both sides slowly opened, revealing their occupants clothed in weird dresses. Riley did a double take to his left. *Not dresses,* he thought. *Robes.*

Mothers and fathers stepped outside, wrapped in bedsheets and curtains and whatever else they could find to serve their dark purpose, all covered in those familiar black stains. Their infernal children followed, taking their parents by the hand and leading them toward their front yards. Some of them smiled, revealing blackened mouths full of dark writhing creatures; others raised their hands and beckoned to him as he drove on. "Sinner," they chanted. "Heretic. Interloper. Outsider."

Other families joined in the chorus, chanting their condemnations of him as he stepped on the gas. *Sinner. Heretic. Interloper. Outsider.*

"You can be one of Us, Riley. Your sweet suffering will set your soul free."

He slammed his palm against the radio, silencing the awful voice spewing from its transmission, and placed both hands on the wheel.

The crowds standing on their lawns pointed at him as he drove past. He reached the summit of the hill, took a left onto Phillips Drive, and then a right onto Tanglewood. With each turn, he met more of the same: families corrupted by the filth of his late grandfather. The phone buzzed in his pocket, but he was too afraid to take his eyes off the road, too afraid one of the possessed fanatics would dart in front of the car. He drove on, guiding the sedan over the hill along Tanglewood Road toward South Stauford and the home of Rachel Matthews.

Sinner. Heretic. Interloper. Outsider.

"Whatever," he muttered. "Story of my fuckin' life." The words sounded good aloud, and he wanted to feel brave, but deep inside he was screaming.

5

Officer Gray stepped on the gas as he sped past the pandemonium of First Baptist Church. He only glimpsed the chaos, but what he saw was enough. Men, women, and children congregated outside the building, babbling and raising their hands into the air, their eyes aglow with blue light, their clothes covered in oil. Black smoke billowed from the upper windows of the church, obscuring a hint of flames licking the air, while smaller fires burned on the sidewalk outside. Children danced around these fires in jubilation as the adults tore pages from their Bibles and cast them into the flames.

Chatter on the police band filled the car with reports of attacks all over town—North and South Stauford, Gordon Hill, Barton Mill, from the Cumberland Falls Highway to the Cumberland Gap Parkway, the whole town was erupting into chaos. All EMS services from Baptist Regional were already dispatched, and some police units were not responding to inquiry. Although Stauford's fire department was called, the fires at the church and elsewhere downtown burned unchecked. There was no word if the fire departments of Landon or Breyersburg were called to assist.

His hometown was tearing itself to pieces, a sudden reality which fueled the anger simmering in Marcus Gray's heart. Where was Ozzie Bell, Stauford's elected official who'd sworn to serve and protect its people? Where was Chief Bell, who'd abandoned a search for two missing boys? Where was Chief Osmond Lucas Bell, who'd failed to report for duty this morning when all hell broke loose?

He's at Susan Prewitt's house, Officer Gray thought, white-knuckling the steering wheel. *Fucking or sleeping or stoned, it doesn't matter. The town needs him whether he likes it or not.*

And Officer Gray would make him do his job. Even if persuading Ozzie meant pulling a gun on him. Oh yes, Officer Gray had found his balls, and he intended to let them swing. He'd show Ozzie and the rest of the squad Marcus Gray wasn't the timid dipshit they all believed he was. There would be a reckoning, on this day of all days, thank you, Jesus.

And yet, as he drove on down 4th Street, Marcus couldn't shake the suspicion that even if he managed to kick Ozzie's ass into gear, there might not be much of Stauford left by the end of the day. The scene at the church stirred within him a foreboding sense of déjà vu.

I dreamed this, he thought, recalling the awful visions that plagued his sleep over the last couple nights. Marcus didn't understand how he knew these things, and he wasn't sure where the dreams came from, but their stark certainty chilled him. *It has eyes. It could see inside me. It still does.* And then its words rose from his throat, spilling over his tongue like the mantras they taught him in Sunday School.

"His will and the Old Ways are one." Marcus blinked, easing off the gas as he rounded a curve. "What does that even mean?"

A surge of static spat from the radio, filling the cabin with a guttural churr like an animal clearing its throat. Words bled into one another, babbling forward and backward, overlapping, transforming into a language all its own—a language which inexplicably made sense to him.

"Salvation through suffering, My child. Bear witness to My apostle and weep."

Laughter burst from the CB radio in a thick chortle of static before dissipating into the frenzied chatter of the police band. Marcus slowed the car and switched to a different frequency. He held his breath, dreading the sound of babbling voices, and was relieved when static filled the cruiser. He closed his eyes and wiped sweat from his brow.

What the hell is happening to me?

He blinked and swallowed back a bitter taste in his mouth. The incident left him spooked but unshaken, and he continued his way toward the intersection of 4th and Stamper Streets. Susan Prewitt's house sat on a corner, nestled against the slope and partially hidden in the shade of several oak trees.

Chief Bell's cruiser was parked in the driveway. A yellow pickup truck camouflaged with patches of rust was parked along the curb. Marcus parked his cruiser behind the pickup and gave it a once-over, certain the vehicle looked familiar. If he'd had more time, he would've run the plates to be sure, but for now he'd have to rely on his instinct. He marched up the driveway toward the small stoop in front of the house.

The door stood open in invitation. He was struck with the absurd notion they knew he was coming to pay them a visit. Any other time, Marcus would've laughed off such a ridiculous idea, but after what he'd experienced in the car, the world seemed less tethered, reality somewhat more malleable than it used to be. He pulled his weapon from its holster and held his finger against the trigger guard.

"Chief?"

His voice echoed in the void of the house. The foyer was dark except for the slanted rectangle of light piercing from the doorway. He hated the way his voice shook, betraying any sense of authority he might've commanded, and in that moment, he felt the world stop. There was no wind, no birdsong overhead, not even the hum of locusts in the trees. There was only Officer Marcus Gray, standing here at the threshold of some unknown chasm decorated to look like an ordinary 1970s split-level home, his pounding heart the only sound in all the universe.

An acrid smell permeated the air, filling his nostrils with the stench of something sour, rotting. There was heat to the smell, like the makeshift compost heap his dad made in their backyard a decade ago, so thick it coated his lungs with its stink. There was something else, too, something metallic.

He raised his weapon and stepped across the threshold into the dark living room. He swallowed air, grimacing at the sour taste in his throat.

"Chief Bell?" His voice fell flat, echoing off the foyer walls. He felt every bit a stranger in this woman's house, and his skin crawled with the urge to turn and run. Melted candles and discarded clothing marked a path from the living room up the stairs. Dusty photos of Susan's grandfather, Henry Prewitt, decorated the stairwell of the dim foyer. There were other photos of Susan as a little girl, sitting on what must have been her mother's lap. He was about to move on to the living room when a soft groan traveled down the stairs, startling him so badly he nearly dropped his weapon.

Marcus took a breath and tried to calm his racing heart. *Keep it cool.* He listened. Another moan filled the hallway upstairs. Not a moan of pain, but of pleasure. He sighed and shook his head. No wonder the chief wasn't answering his phone. He holstered his weapon.

The moans grew louder and more erratic as he climbed the stairs, rising to a crescendo that was almost comical given the circumstances. The air inside the house had an almost surreal quality, and he questioned if he was truly awake and not back at home in his mother's basement, still asleep, still dreaming up horrible happenings in his hometown.

You could take your turn with her.

Marcus hesitated, mere feet from a half-closed door. The voice in his head buzzed with static, the same voice he'd heard through the cruiser's radio, and the hallway swam before him in dark splotches. He heard the noise of a church congregation in his head, a million babbling voices speaking in tongues.

When my child is finished, you may have her if you want, Marcus. You can fuck the whole town if you wish. Man, woman, child, my lord won't judge you. Sins to the false god are virtues in our faith.

He steadied himself against the wall, trying to hold back the waves crashing inside his head. His guts twisted and churned.

I have but one thing to ask, Marcus. Will you suffer for me? Will you honor the Old Ways and heed my will?

Marcus stumbled forward, fighting off the wave of sickness spreading through him to no avail. A thick clump of his undigested breakfast shot from his throat and filled his mouth as he crossed the threshold of the bedroom.

Ozzie Bell lay naked and cuffed to the bed, his lifeless body carved up into bloody symbols like a scroll of flesh. Susan Prewitt stood naked at the edge of the bed, bent forward while her brother Zeke Billings fucked her from behind. She moaned with each thrust. Dollops of the black sludge spilled over her lips.

"You could take your turn with her," Zeke grinned, slapping Susan's bare ass so hard the snake tattoo on her thigh danced from the impact. "She's all yours if you'll suffer for us."

Susan looked up and flashed a smile of dirt and grime.

"I can't…" was all Marcus could say before words failed him completely. Zeke unmounted his sister and approached the doorway. Marcus reached for his holster, fumbled for the butt of his weapon, and cried out in terror as Zeke Billings laid his hand over Marcus's face.

"You will," Zeke said.

6

Chuck Tiptree knocked on the front door of Imogene's old house and waited, listening to the muffled footfalls and voices inside. He craned his neck and assessed the damage from the vandalism Jack reported two days earlier. Flecks of red paint still clung to the surface of the front porch, and although the shards of glass were gone, the plastic Jack hung over the shattered window was torn. Curtains fluttered inside from the low afternoon breeze.

He shifted his weight, checking his watch while clicking his tongue. The old house had always given him the creeps, even before everything went down with Imogene's passing. When he and Jack were kids, he'd always ask to play in the yard and never in the house. The place felt wrong to him, the way walking into a church always gave him a chill, like he wasn't meant to be there.

Swore you'd never come back here, he told himself.

"Swore I'd never see him again, either."

But here he was, at Dr. Booth's request yet again, and he scolded himself for answering the phone. Last time, he hadn't known any better, but now he had no excuse. He was as stubborn as the rest of his kin, whether he wanted to admit it or not. He'd made a career out of being exceptionally stubborn, even when the odds were against him.

The door opened, revealing Jack's bruised face.

Chuck gasped. "What the hell happened to you?"

"My mother happened. Hi, by the way." Jack managed a wry smile. Chuck gaped at the wounds on his brother's face, the darkened marks around his throat. "Look, I'll explain later. Just come inside already. There's coffee brewing. When Steph gets here, we'll get down to it."

"All right," Chuck said, reluctantly stepping over the threshold. The musty smell of the old place still lingered, accented with mothballs and dust, but there was something else in the air. Something off, like fruit on the verge of turning, or gone bad. He followed Jack into the kitchen where a familiar face stood at the counter, pouring himself a cup of coffee.

Chuck stopped abruptly, unsure of what to say. What *could* he say? Their last meeting was anything but pleasant, and if it hadn't been for Imogene, he was sure it would've turned violent. But that was months ago. Maybe things had changed. Maybe not. Either way, Chuck was stunned to find the old professor's name on his phone's screen. Perhaps that was why he answered after all—incredulity, or even shock.

Dr. Booth turned, offered Chuck a cursory nod, and reached into his pocket for a silver flask. He tipped its contents into the coffee. "Want some, Mr. Tiptree?"

"No, thanks."

"Jack?"

Jack shook his head at first but thought better of it and nodded. "Might take the edge off."

"Good man." Dr. Booth poured a finger of bourbon into Jack's coffee and capped the flask. "Thanks for coming, Chuck."

The three men sipped their coffee in silence, standing awkwardly in a kitchen far too small, its walls too close together.

"So…" Jack began, "do you guys mind telling me how you know one another?"

Chuck smirked. "Yeah, Doc. I'll let you take this one."

Professor Booth scowled at him, taking another long sip of his spiked coffee. Chuck waited, almost eager to hear the words tripping off the old man's tongue. How much did Jack know? Had Dr. Booth told him about the ritual Imogene spent the last years of her life preparing? Or the relationship they'd had over the last decade?

Probably not, Chuck decided. Observing Jack and the professor, he sensed that much was true. Jack wore his heart on his sleeve, always had, and if he'd known what the professor helped Imogene do, odds were Dr. Booth wouldn't be standing in this kitchen right now.

The dual honk of a locking car stole their attention from the silence between them.

Jack set down his mug of coffee. "I think Steph's here." He gave them both a concerned glance before walking toward the front door. "Maybe you two can sort this shit out, huh?"

Chuck nodded, watching his brother exit the room before meeting the old man's eyes. "Does he know about you and Genie?"

Dr. Booth closed his eyes and sighed. Chuck's face fell.

"You fucking lied to him?"

"I did. I was trying to protect him. Like Genie would've done."

"Genie was crazy, Doc. I know you loved her, but goddammit, she was nuts and it cost her her life."

"No," Professor Booth muttered. He downed the last of his coffee in a single gulp and winced. "That's where you're wrong, Chuck. It's why I called you here. It's why you should reconsider having a drink from my flask."

Chuck shook his head. *Unbelievable,* he thought. He ran his hand through his hair and shifted nervously. "It's that sort of belief that got us here in the first place, entertaining this hocus pocus bullshit. You're supposed to be a man of fucking science, for God's sake." Chuck looked toward the hall, where he heard Stephanie approaching. "Besides, I thought you had a change of heart?"

Dr. Booth opened his mouth to speak but stopped short when Stephanie Green walked into the room. Jack followed her.

She gave Chuck a playful punch to his shoulder. "Long time, no see."

"Yeah," Chuck said, forcing a smile. "Glad you're here."

"So am I," Jack said. He opened a cupboard and pulled a mug down from the shelf. "Professor Booth and Chuck here were about to explain to me how they know each other, among other things."

Chuck and Dr. Booth exchanged glances. This time the professor did not hesitate, and for once, Chuck was grateful to hear the old man speak.

"I will. I'll get to that. But first, I think we should all take a seat. I've got a lot of ground to cover, and we don't have much time."

7

Since his mother died, Riley turned to his daydreams to cope with the horrors of reality. His growing distaste for Stauford in general, its favoritism toward athletes, the hypocrisy of its people on Sunday mornings, the widening gap between himself and his father—these fantasies saved him from real life so many times, comforting him in the twilit hours when the tears came so easily.

In his daydreams, Riley Tate fancied himself an antihero, the bad boy with a heart of gold from countless miles of Hollywood celluloid. He was the director of his own private film, and he was also its star.

In this fantasy, Riley was the kid who used his art to shine a light on Stauford's hypocrisy. He fought back against the bullies who threatened him—kids like Jimmy Cord, adults like his father or Assistant Principal Meyers, the whole regime governing Stauford's social classes—and played by his own rules. He never did his homework, failed the daily quizzes, and still aced the exams. He always got the upper hand of whatever stood in his way, overcoming insurmountable odds, and despite his underdog status, still won the day. He was lauded for his efforts and rejected the establishment's praise.

Riley was a savior and a sinner, a troubled youth and prodigy. And at the end of this private movie, Riley saved the girl. The girl's identity changed over the years, but ever since he'd started high school, Rachel Matthews played the part. She was the heroine in his fantasy film, the plucky foil to his antihero, the girl from the other side of the tracks whose love thawed his frozen heart.

The beauty of his daydreams was, when the film ended and the credits rolled, he could always start it over, changing whatever he saw fit. Before launching himself out his bedroom window merely an hour ago, the film often featured Riley's midnight ride to Rachel's house by bicycle. But the narrative changed, the film edited to reflect Riley's circumstance.

Now the film took place during the day, the bicycle traded for his father's car. Even as Riley drove into Rachel's neighborhood, a ritzy development known locally as Forest Hills, he was daydreaming about the way this new film would end. He would still show Stauford the error of its ways. And, more importantly, he would still save the girl.

But today, Riley discovered no matter how much he changed the narrative in his mind, he would still have to face a harsh truth: reality is far less appealing, far less friendly, and far, far less forgiving.

When he slowed the car in front of Rachel's home, Riley Tate realized he was holding his breath and slowly exhaled. A small mound of twigs and leaves burned on the Matthews's front lawn. A plume of gray smoke snaked lazily into the air. Laura Matthews stood naked in the front yard, convulsing with laughter and spewing black bile over her breasts, which jiggled frantically with her erratic movement. She held a Bible in her hands and was tearing out the pages one at a time.

"He loves me, he loves me not, he loves me, he loves me not…"

Beside her, Don Matthews was in the process of undressing. He stripped off his khakis and tossed them on the fire. His wife handed him one of the torn pages, which he wrapped around his exposed erection. Masturbating, Don Matthews lifted his chin to the air and shouted, "His will and the Old Ways are one, hallelujah!"

"Hallelujah!" Laura shouted, stripping a handful of pages from her oversized Bible and throwing them on the fire. The flames engulfed them in a singular whoosh.

God's not here, Riley thought, recalling all the Sundays he'd spent in his father's church, listening to fairy tales written by men long dead. *Even if He was, He isn't here now. Maybe He never was.*

A sudden smack startled him from the hideous ritual happening outside the car. Riley's eyes shot front. His heart sank.

Rachel Matthews stood outside the car, her hands on the hood. She smiled, revealing blackened teeth. Something gray wriggled along her upper gum line, seeking the air, and fell from her mouth. It landed with a thick plop on the hood.

"You came to save me," she said. "But I've already been saved, Riley. I suffered for salvation, and you can, too."

"No. Goddammit, *no.*"

Rachel walked around the car toward the driver's window. She pressed her face against the glass. Black ooze squelched from her nostril and slithered along the surface. Her eyes glowed with blue light.

"It's okay, Riley. I can show you the Old Ways. And then we can be together. I'll let you kiss me if you want. You can have this body, too. Do you want to fuck me? I can be yours if you'll be His."

Any other time, under any other circumstances, Riley would've let his hormones take control—but not today. Not now. The Rachel Matthews he'd adored, crushed on, fantasized about was no longer here. She'd been stolen from him by whatever dark corruption now roiled inside her.

"Is that your boyfriend, honey?" Don Matthews walked to the edge of the lawn, absently jerking himself off with the torn page while black tears dripped from his glowing eyes. He peered through the shattered passenger window. "Does he want to stay for dinner?"

"No, Dad, it's not like that." Rachel shot Riley a wink. "Unless you want it to be. Why not join us? I want to show you the Old Ways, Riley. Like your father, and his father before him. It's your birthright."

Rachel's voice changed. Guttural, choked with the black filth inside her, and reminiscent of the awful voice speaking from the radio. He put his hand on the glass, his eyes burning with tears.

"I'm sorry, Rach." His voice rattled like empty tree branches, their leaves dried and fallen and dead. "Maybe I shouldn't have kissed you the other night. Maybe it was too soon, and I made things awkward. I'm sorry I didn't take things slow." He swallowed back a dry ball of cotton in his throat. "But I'm just—I've lost my friend. I'll miss you."

He didn't wait for her to reply. He stepped on the gas and drove until he was out of the neighborhood, back onto the Cumberland Falls Highway, and found a vacant lot near the old Stauford Drive-In.

The tears came fast, his chest heaving so hard his abs ached, his lungs filled with fire. First his mother, then his father, and now Rachel. He sucked in his breath, held it, waited for the sobs to pass, and let it all out in a quick rush of air.

Alone, he thought. *I'm all alone now except for—*

The phone. How could he have been so stupid? He was so caught up in getting away from his dad and finding Rachel that he'd forgotten about Stephanie. He pulled the phone from his pocket. The battery symbol flashed red. Less than five percent left. He'd had a missed call, and he remembered the vibration in his pocket while driving through his neighborhood.

"So stupid."

He listened to Stephanie's message and nodded. Jack's house—old lady Tremly's place. The Stauford Witch. His great aunt. Everyone knew where she lived, and if he drove down the Stauford Bypass circling the city, he could be there soon.

Minutes later Riley was back on the road, determined to find a new ending for the movie playing in his head.

CHAPTER NINETEEN

1

What does he know about Genie's passing? I assume you didn't tell him."

Jack met Chuck's eyes across the dining room table as the old man's words sank in. Stephanie's face fell in shock. She placed her hand on Jack's almost instinctively, a comforting gesture he would've appreciated under other circumstances.

"Chuck?" Jack stared at his brother, measuring the words he wanted to spit out, and then turned toward the professor. "What do you mean?"

Chuck put his elbows on the table. "Goddammit, Tyler, she didn't want him to know."

"We're past that point, young man."

"I never should've gotten involved with you two. Fuck this, I'm out." Chuck began to rise from his seat. Jack slammed his fist on the table, startling a sharp cry from Stephanie.

"Sit down. You're not going anywhere until you explain what the fuck is going on, Chuck. You too, Tyler." He shot a glance at Stephanie. "Do you have any idea what they're talking about?"

She shook her head. "I'm as clueless as you are."

"Great. Would someone please enlighten me?"

"Fine," Chuck sighed. "But understand this, Jack. Genie didn't want you to know."

"Want me to know what?"

"That she was dying."

A cold silence slipped between them as Jack processed Chuck's statement. The tick of the hallway clock filled the house, punctuating the dread seeping into the room. In some absurd way, Jack wasn't at all surprised by the revelation. He'd often suspected she hadn't been truthful about her health. She was always so quick to change the subject on the phone or to sugarcoat her answers to his emailed questions.

No, what hurt most was his brother's willingness to keep the information from him. Even if it was Imogene's wish her poor health be kept from Jack, he still deserved to know.

"Wow. Okay."

"Look," Chuck began, "I had a duty to my client—"

Stephanie snorted. "Save it, Chuck. Stop."

"—to uphold her wishes as she dictated—"

"Steph's right," Jack said. "Just stop, Chuck. I need a minute."

Jack sipped the coffee, relishing the warmth of the bourbon in its mixture, and downed the rest of his mug. The fire in his gut eased the screaming in his head, his joints, his back. But it didn't ease the pain in his heart. Booze couldn't touch that.

"Dying, how? They told me she had a heart attack." Jack frowned, his gaze burning a hole through Chuck's face. "*He* told me she had a heart attack."

"And she did," Dr. Booth sighed. He plucked his glasses from his face and absently wiped their lenses with the hem of his shirt. "That part's true. He didn't lie, but—look, son, it's complicated."

Stephanie shook her head. "It's time you spit it out. Both of you."

Jack nodded. "Listen to the lady."

Chuck opened his mouth, shut it again, and gestured to the old man. Professor Booth had the floor.

2

"There was more to what I told you yesterday, son. I'm guilty of lyin' by omission. Me and your grandma, we were pretty close." Dr. Booth wiped his eyes with a shaking hand. *"God, she always talked about you, people you'd met, places where you'd shown your work, she was always singing your praises. She loved you more than anything. And I loved her. Asked her to marry me a couple of times, but she turned me down."*

Jack smiled, caught off guard by the man's show of emotion. There was a tenderness in the old man's face that hadn't been there before. Tenderness, and a streak of melancholy. Jack knew that kind of heartbreak, the regret of not saying what you wanted, a thousand nights spent replaying some pivotal moment, wondering what could've happened differently, wondering what could've been said to change course. He loved her, *Jack realized, and he restrained himself from reaching out to take the professor's hand in comfort.*

Instead, Jack cleared his throat and asked, "Why's that?"

"Because she was married to her quest. All the bad shit that happened at the church when y'all were babies, well, she had this notion your daddy put a curse on her before all was said and done. She died trying to reverse it. All these years later, son, she was still tryin' to protect all of you."

Tyler watched her gather the supplies he'd collected for her, still telling himself this was insane, this was dangerous. Still believing he could talk her out of it. *But you know better. Once Genie sets her mind to somethin', there's no changin' it.*

And she wouldn't. Not this time. Not when he'd pleaded with her to rethink her decision, or on all those late evening walks through the neighborhood when she recounted her plans, the preparation she would undergo, the agony she would subject herself to.

An assortment of items were spread out on the dining room table: two containers of salt, boxes of candles, a box of matches, white chalk, a quart of red paint, multiple bags of incense, a bottle of cheap tequila, a small coffee can full of earth, and writhing somewhere inside the can, a handful of nightcrawlers. The idol she'd sent him to acquire more than a decade before sat in the middle of the table like an infernal centerpiece, its eyes shimmering even in the afternoon light. He tried not to stare too long at the awful thing.

"Did you remember the sage? I don't see it here."

"I did," Tyler muttered, pushing aside a box of candles. A bundle of sage was underneath, wrapped in a plastic bag. "Right here."

Imogene looked at him with her good eye. She wasn't wearing the eye patch this morning, and he reminded himself it was because she was comfortable around him. He didn't have the heart to tell her that seeing her bad eye set him on edge, gave him the creeps.

"I guess that's it, then. Thanks, love."

She smiled, and he forgot about the dead orb staring back at him. Her smile fixed everything. He put his hand on her shoulder and pulled her to him. When she embraced him, the world sank away, and for a moment, he forgot about her grim plan. There was just the two of them, alone in the universe, alone but for each other. It was all he'd ever wanted. All he'd ever need.

Tyler kissed her forehead. "Genie, please."

"Honey. We've been over this. I'm the last one left, and Dr. Parks gave me less than three months. The cancer's eating me alive. If I don't do this now…" Imogene stepped back from him, squeezing his hands in hers. "I'm doin' this for Jackie. For the babies. He's going to come back to finish what he started, Tyler. If not me, then who—?"

He sank to his knees, gripping Imogene's hands so tightly in his own that she gasped. Tears flooded his eyes, something that would've embarrassed him in his younger years, but now was different. Now was a time of desperation. He needed her to hear him, and if his humility could break through the wall of resolve she'd built for herself, if he could delay this awful plan for one more day, he might find a way to save her life.

"Genie, darlin', please listen to me. *Please.* There's treatment for what you've got—"

"Chemo ain't about quality of life—"

"—and I can't watch you throw your life away."

Imogene yanked her hands from his, the emotion bled from her pale face. She clenched her teeth and wiped a tear from her good eye.

"Foolish. Is that what you think I am? After all this time, Tyler Booth, you think I'm crazy like the rest of that godawful town?"

Tyler sank back, taking the weight off his aching knees. "No, darlin', that's not what I mean. You know that's not what I mean. I just…I can't abide you throwing your life away like this. How do you know this will even work?"

"I don't." She gathered the containers of salt and turned toward the basement door. "But I have to believe it will. For Jackie."

"And what if it doesn't?"

"Then my pancreas will rot, and I'll rot with it."

Jack frowned. "Pancreatic cancer?"

Dr. Booth nodded. "Advanced. She'd been losing weight and I finally got her to go to the doctor. After some tests, her doctor gave her less than three months to live."

The professor's words sank in, and Jack replayed the last time they'd spoken on the phone. He'd offered to fly her to New York. She'd never been, and he wanted to show her the sights—Rockefeller Center, the Statue of Liberty, the gallery where some of his work was featured—but she'd passed on the opportunity, something which seemed odd at the time, but now made perfect sense. A hole opened in his gut, threatening to swallow him up from the inside.

"Did she kill herself?"

The words seemed so odd on his tongue, but aloud, they were nasty things that offended his ears. Mamaw Genie wouldn't. Never. Life was precious to her. She'd spent years trying to teach him that. You only get one, she'd told him on so many occasions, so you make the most of it. He'd taken that edict to heart and tried to live by it as best he could. The thought of his grandmother giving up on her life so easily left him unsettled.

"Well," Chuck said, "the coroner report was accurate: she did die of a heart attack, despite the advanced stage of her cancer and…the predicament in which she was found."

"That doesn't answer my question, Chuck." He looked at the professor. "What was she doing in the basement, Tyler?" He turned back to Chuck. "What did she do? What 'curse' was she trying to break?"

Chuck crossed his arms and locked eyes with the professor. "This is your area, not mine."

"It's more appropriate," Tyler said, "if we consider the intent. We already know the outcome."

Tyler wished he'd not relented to his curiosity that day she appeared in his classroom. Until then, Tyler Milford Booth was blissfully happy with his ignorant place in the world.

He had a decent job, was well-respected in his field, had contributed to the greater understanding of the cultures that came before our day. Tyler had everything he wanted, or so he thought—until the day this beautiful silver-haired queen walked into his life. She'd opened a door to something greater and far more mysterious than any ancient culture he'd studied in his career, and he'd followed her with wide-eyed curiosity into the dark places beyond.

He grew up believing the occult was a farce, a word ascribed to fortune tellers and so-called psychics, another way to part a fool from his money. In the brief years they'd known one another, Imogene Tremly showed him the occult was more than a shell-game of faith, but another method of understanding this reality and the next, whatever it may be.

After what he'd witnessed down in the temple below Calvary Hill, his curiosity finally overcame the fear inherent in his bones, blood, and soul. Witnessing the darkness wasn't enough; Tyler needed to understand, or at the very least, grasp the concepts with which he might correlate all he'd seen.

So began his partnership with the one-eyed witch of Stauford, a connection that blossomed from friendship to love, forever teetering on the brink of obsession for both: he in his yearning for her devotion, and she in her damned quest to protect her grandson from his father.

All she'd told him about Jacob Masters played back in his mind as he followed her downstairs to the basement, trailing at her heels like a scolded puppy.

He cursed me that day, Tyler. I betrayed him. We all did, and he bound his death to our lives. Don't you see? Death for life, and life for death. When we're gone, he will return, and no one in this awful town will be able to stop him. Now I'm the last one left. I have to find a way to beat him at his own game.

Imogene flipped a switch and lit up the room. Old boxes and storage totes were pulled away from the far wall, the floor swept free of dust. She set down her bags and turned to him.

"Tyler...if you're going to stand there and judge me, I'd rather you not be here at all. I've spent most of my life bein' judged by this awful place. I won't suffer it from you."

"You're runnin' from a dead man. He's gone. Thirty years, he's gone, and you're still lettin' yourself be haunted by his ghost. Now you're going to..." He motioned to the bags with a trembling hand. He'd left his flask at home, and his nerves cried for it now more than ever. "...look, Genie, he's already taken so many lives. Why are you going to let him have one more?"

She knelt, wincing at the sudden pop in her knees, and rummaged through the plastic bags until she found the chalk. "All those smarts and you still haven't listened to a damn thing I've said." She pulled a stick of chalk from the box and drew a circle on the floor. When she was finished, Imogene met his eyes. "Even after what you saw down there, you still won't believe me."

"Oh, for God's sake..." He trailed off, watching as she traced the next circle along the floor. *It's not that I don't believe you,* he wanted to say. *It's that I'm fucking terrified of facing it.* His sojourn into the pit below Calvary Hill opened his eyes to things no one, least of all himself, was ever meant to see. Like lifting a stone to discover all the squirming insects underneath, he could not displace the knowledge of their existence; they were there, always were, and would be long after his approaching expiration date. Acknowledging what he'd seen that day meant acknowledging everything Imogene confided in him was not only a possibility, but a reality.

Imogene finished the second circle, climbed to her feet, and traced the third on the wall.

"I wish I'd met you sooner," he mumbled.

"Me too, old man. Me too."

He smiled, feeling at once flush and weak, his heart full but flawed with cracks. There was no talking her out of this. He'd always known it, but rebelled against the notion, clinging to the hope his love would be enough to change her mind.

Selfish old bastard, he thought. If she was right about everything, then Stauford would need its witch. And somewhere else in the world, a fortunate young man would need his grandma. For all the chaos in the universe, nothing remained more constant than the resolve of a grandmother to protect her young'uns. He couldn't argue with her, knew it wasn't even worth trying.

"Your circles are off." He crossed the room, rummaged through the bags, and produced a spool of string. "I thought you might need this. Tie it to one end of the chalk. Here, I'll show you…"

"We spent an hour drawing the configuration. Circles for body and mind on the floor, one circle for soul on the wall. Tenets of what she called a 'right hand' path, to counteract the 'left hand' nature of Masters's curse."

Jack nodded, the pieces finally coming together. "So those symbols on her gravestone, the ones marked 'cleansing runes' in her notebook…"

"Right," the professor went on, "those were used in the ritual to cleanse herself of the binding Masters placed on her."

"In theory," Chuck said, and was about to say more when Stephanie shot him a scowl that told him to shut the fuck up.

"She'd studied the different disciplines of magic, researching Crowley and the Golden Dawn, the tenets of Hermeticism and the nature of balance in a chaotic universe. I did my best to keep up with her, but she was always a step ahead of me. She was always talking about scans of old grimoires she'd found online, some barely legible, some dating back to the early days of the printing press, but I trusted she knew what she was doing." Tyler took a sip from his flask, craned back his neck, and drained the final drops of the bourbon. "That was a mistake, of course. To be honest, I don't know if she knew what would happen. Not really."

Stephanie put her hand on Tyler's. "Tell us what happened."

His nostrils tingled from the scent of burning incense. Imogene wandered around the basement, waving the smoking bundle of dried sage in each of the corners. Tyler finished lighting the candles, careful not to disturb their placement, as Imogene consulted her notes to ensure the correct configuration. When they were finished, they stepped back and surveyed their work.

A series of runes filled in the three circles they'd drawn on the floor and wall, surrounded by the candles he'd lit. A ring of salt surrounded the circle of body, in the center of which sat a mound of earth and nightcrawlers. Sticks of incense burned around the open can to ward off the acrid stench. She'd placed the idol in the center of the mound to serve as a crude representation of the dark thing dwelling in the earth below Calvary Hill. Its eyes cast a pale blue glow about the room.

On the wall, a dripping border of dark red paint surrounded the chalk circle representing the soul. Tyler thought about asking what the paint was supposed to represent, but decided he'd rather not know.

The final circle was of mind, positioned on the floor closest to the wall, between the circles of body and soul. The four cleansing runes marked the four corners of the circle.

"Where's the tequila?"

He reached in the bag and retrieved the bottle of amber liquid, purchased from the bottom shelf of the local liquor store. Imogene took it, examined the label, and unscrewed the cap. She drank.

Tyler snorted in confusion. "It's not for the ritual?"

"Not exactly," she said, grimacing at the awful taste burning its way down her throat. "It's for my nerves. I don't know how this is going to go. Want some?"

He was repulsed by the notion—tequila never treated him well—but after a cursory glance of the odd symbols on the floor, he thought better of it and took the bottle. The cheap liquor tasted every bit of its price, numbing his tongue and lighting a fire in his gut, and he regretted the drink immediately. Imogene laughed at his expression, taking the bottle from him and imbibing once more.

"What's a classy lady like you drinkin' swill like that?"

"I have my moments, Professor Booth." She flashed him a smile, capped the bottle, and turned toward the configuration. "I guess I should get to work, huh?"

A dry lump found its way into his throat. He wanted to tell her no, to repeat the many reasons why he didn't want her to go through with this, but seeing the conviction in her eye reaffirmed the answer he already knew she'd give. Whether he argued or pleaded, the outcome would be the same; instead, he chose to spend their last moments in an embrace, wrapping his arms around her and pulling her close. He kissed the top of her head, breathing in the sweet smell of her hair one last time.

"I love you, Genie. I hope you know that."

"I do," she whispered. "I'm sorry I couldn't give you what you wanted."

It's okay, he wanted to tell her, but the words didn't feel right. It wasn't okay. He would never be okay with it—but he wouldn't ruin this for her and make it harder than it already was.

She took a step back from him, gave him a once-over, and put her hand on his cheek. "I've enjoyed these years with you, old man."

"Me too." Tears slipped from his eyes. No sense in trying to hide them. Imogene wiped his cheek with her thumb and smiled.

"Chuck's taken care of my affairs. You remember what I asked you to do?"

He did, and even if he didn't agree with leaving her research for Jackie to find, he would honor her wishes. "When it's over," Tyler said, "I'll return the idol and lock it up in your desk. Then I'll call Chuck."

Imogene nodded. "He'll take care of the rest." She stepped toward the circle of mind and began to undress, revealing a series of dark tattoos along her shoulders and down the ridge of her spine. They were the same cleansing runes decorating the floor, marking the corners of her circle, and would soon decorate her gravestone.

Tyler tried not to stare but found he couldn't look away. Even with her imperfections, the wrinkles, sagging flesh, and darkened spots of age, she was beautiful in his eyes. She tied her long silver hair back in a bun and offered him a coy smile. Twenty years ago, the look would've set him on fire. Even now, it set his heart ablaze, but this old machine was nearly out of gas.

"When I step into this circle," she said, "I won't be able to leave. The boundary will be sealed. No matter what happens, do not try to pull me out of this circle."

He nodded, but with some hesitation. She'd told him everything that would be done to prepare, but she'd not divulged what would happen during the ritual itself. He had no idea what to expect, and as much as he wanted to flee in terror, he found he was curious about what he would witness.

"Tyler," she snapped. "I'm serious. Don't break the seal."

"I won't."

Imogene nodded, took a breath, and stepped into the center of the circle.

Stephanie smiled. "Genie Tremly had tattoos?"

"She did," Professor Booth said. "Several, all along her back. She waited until he moved out."

Jack shook his head, smirking. "She used to go on and on about one's body being their temple."

Stephanie held up her hand, showcasing the tribal design tattooed around her wrist. "Ain't nothing wrong with glorifying your temple, Jackie."

"Indeed," said the professor. "In her case, it was more about taking extra precautions. She believed the cleansing ritual would work but needed to demonstrate her conviction. The tattoos were just the start of it. She'd fasted for three days. A total cleanse of her body, including her medications. She was a trooper. I can't imagine the sort of pain she was in. The cancer was already eating her up inside. She thought she could hide it from me, but I knew. I saw how she clenched her jaw whenever she moved,

*heard whenever she sucked air through her teeth to hold back the ache." The old man
reached for the flask again, stopping short when he remembered it was empty. Instead,
he threaded his fingers to keep from fidgeting. "I can't imagine the sort of pain she
went through when things started happening for real."*

Tyler sat at the bottom of the basement steps and watched her
meditate. He assumed that's what she was doing, sitting cross-legged in
the center circle, her back arched forward while she rocked in place. The
candle flames trembled with her movement, and for a while, he adopted
her breathing pattern, mimicking the rise and fall of her fragile frame.

Outside, the sun arced across the sky, the song of birds slowly
displaced by the chirp of crickets in the fading light. Twice he retreated
upstairs to relieve his bladder, and she was still in her sitting position
each time he returned. Still rocking, still breathing deeply. Each time he
returned, the shadows were longer, held at bay by the flickering candles
and glow of the idol.

She didn't speak until sunset, in a different language with a different
pair of lungs.

Here the professor failed in his retelling, unable to reproduce the
words she made, successful only in his description of the sounds
ululating from her throat: a guttural hum in time with her breathing,
punctuated by the uncomfortable noise of air strained through
congestion. A deep phlegmy sound carrying in waves, rising in intensity
as she rocked in place. The candle flames surged, pulsing in time to her
raspy voice, flaring in a crescendo as she spat a wad of black earth from
her lungs. The dark expectorant oozed down the wall and collected in a
wet puddle.

Tyler rose to his feet, eager to yank her from the circle but too
terrified to move. The candles dimmed, their flames slowly extinguished
by a rustling of air, and he could not see where the breeze was coming
from. As their light faded, the azure glow of the idol filled the room,
coating them in its haze. A pungent stench of rancid soil and dung filled
the room, overpowering the incense and assaulting his nostrils with such
force he struggled to keep his nausea at bay.

Imogene gasped, her voice choked from her by a sudden pain writ
upon her body. She trembled, holding herself while violent spasms tore
through her. Her naked back rippled and seized, the skin pulled taut over
bone, and the tattoos along her shoulders and spine bled. Black
tributaries snaked their way down her back and collected in a pool on the
floor, seeping toward the outer rim of the circle.

A red glow emanated from the painted circle on the wall, intermingling with the blue haze pulsing from the idol, filling the room with an eerie light. Tyler put his back to the wall, bracing against the assault of sensation, and watched in helpless horror as his dear friend, his love, his darling, was subjected to a cosmic force by her own calling.

She cried out in pain as her body left the floor, lifted into the air like a doll, her arms limp at her sides. Dark streams of blood pooled in the circle beneath her, seeping into the cracks in the foundation.

Tyler wanted to run to her, free her from her unseen captor, but the horror of what emerged from the wall rooted him in place. The painted circle began to spin, turning on an axis like a locking mechanism; as it moved, the red glow grew brighter, overpowering the idol's haze. The circle turned, sinking backward into the wall with each revolution, drilling its way into an impossible space from which came a collective sigh and brisk, stagnant air.

"My God," Tyler whispered, lifting a trembling hand to his mouth to stifle a scream. The universe peered back through the opening, a cosmos full of eyes focused on the naked queen levitating before their maw. Murmurs erupted from the portal, more of the same language spoken by Imogene during her meditation.

Each enunciation was a guttural sound of consonants and cosmic bodies colliding, planets forming and dying, stars swelling into nova and shrinking into black holes of immeasurable mass. The sounds spilling from the tear was the universe, unfiltered, undefinable, and agonizingly chaotic. There was no order, no air with which to breathe, no time in which to think. There was only the essence of their existence, suddenly miniscule in the grand scale of everything but granted an audience with the eyes of something older, wiser.

Something impartial.

Something crawling along the strings of a universal lattice, plucking at fate when it pleased.

In her dying moments, Imogene lifted her head to stare into the infinite. *"Cleanse this soul of the nameless within and grant me life beyond life!"* A harsh vibration ripped through the air itself, shaking the house on its foundations, the beams above their heads groaning in protest. The red light dimmed, and with a relieved gasp, Imogene uttered her final words: *"As I am above, so shall I be below."*

3

Jack sat with his arms crossed, listening as the professor's words degenerated into sobs. He wanted to be angry, felt like he had every right to be, but he also felt such a profound sadness that hearing the old man cry brought tears to his eyes. *He loved her,* he thought. *Mamaw Genie always had a way of getting into your heart.*

But her lover's story was something he'd not expected. Even after a lifetime of nightmares, even after the conclusions he'd reached with Stephanie and Riley the night before, he didn't expect to hear this other side of his grandmother. He wasn't even angry with her secrecy—far from it, in fact. He was more impressed she'd managed to keep it from him all that time, but even then, he wasn't surprised.

While Stephanie comforted the old man, Jack retreated upstairs and gathered his things. Chuck arched an eyebrow when Jack placed Imogene's notebook on the table.

"What's that?"

"Remember the key she left for me? It unlocked her old roll-top desk upstairs. This was in it." Jack slid the notebook across the table. Chuck flipped it open, read the inscription on the first page.

"So…she was keeping a scrapbook? About us and what happened? I don't—"

"This was with it." Jack placed the grinning idol in the center of the table. Chuck's expression fell, his face draining of color. He pushed back his seat and stood.

"That's not fucking real, man. That—I *dreamed* that. I made it up. It's—no, man. No way." Chuck stepped back until he'd pressed himself against the wall, knocking a framed photograph of Jack's late grandfather askew. The idol sat in silence, its empty black eyes slowly leaking blue light, forever grinning like a child with a horrible secret.

"It's real," Jack said quietly. "It's important we come to terms with it right now."

"He's right," Stephanie said. "What happened under the church that day—shit, even in the years before that, it all really happened. We've talked about the nightmares, Chuck. They're more than that. You know it. I know you do."

Chuck sank to the floor, shaking his head, unable to take his eyes off the awful thing on the table. "I can't accept this. Okay, so, there's a stone carving, and our crazy father worshiped it, but it doesn't mean the rest of this shit is real. Genie was crazy, she—" His face fell when he met Jack's stare. "Sorry, Jack. I took her money, okay? She paid me to put her affairs in order, make the arrangements, pull some strings where they needed pulled. I didn't ask questions and, really, who else would? She's the Stauford Witch. Nobody cared when she passed, except us, maybe."

"Maybe that's true," Jack said, "but it doesn't change the truth. It doesn't change what happened, or what's happening. Even if the professor hadn't called you, I would've. Because there's something you need to know."

Stephanie returned to her seat and faced Chuck. "We think the man who took those boys Friday night is our father."

Chuck laughed and shook his head again. "This is insane. Listen to yourself, Steph. You, of all people—fuck, I never expected you to go all-in with this voodoo bullshit."

Jack reached for the notebook and threw it at his brother's feet. "It's all there, Chuck. What was it my grandma said? Death for life? There's shit in there about moon rituals, something that bound our father to our grandparents. When they're gone, he rises under the light of the first full moon." He knelt before Chuck and flipped open the pages about the ritual. "Everything Tyler told us is in here. Binding rituals, life and death, joined with the cycle of the moon. Friday night was the first full moon since Mamaw Genie died. Friday night, those boys went missing—" He gestured toward Stephanie. "They were, what, five miles from Devil's Creek? Three? Holly Bay's not far."

She nodded. "Riley told us—"

"Oh, great. Riley told you." Chuck threw up his hands in mockery. "The preacher's goth-wannabe rebel son, who idolizes you and would do anything to win your approval, told you he thinks our dead father came back to life to ruin a church group's camping trip? *Please*, Steph. The kid is starved for attention and will do anything to get it. You're too blind to see it because you're his part-time mother."

"You're such an asshole, Chuck."

"Enough." The professor's voice startled them all from their argument, and they turned to him like scolded children. "We don't have time for this." He pointed to the idol. "Chuck, whether you want to believe it or not, this thing is real. What happened back at the church wasn't a dream, but what's happening now is very much a nightmare. And I can tell you, as terrified as I am to admit it, I believe Genie was right."

Chuck scoffed. "Of course you do."

Tyler ignored him. "The whole reason I came here this morning was to tell Jack about what I found." He turned to Imogene's grandson and sighed. "My conscience got the better of me, son. After you left yesterday, I couldn't help but wonder, was she right? Did her ritual work? So, I went to visit her grave this morning. She isn't there anymore."

Jack's face went white. "What do you mean she's not there?"

"I mean there's a hole where her grave should be, and a hole in her coffin. She dug herself out."

Silence squirmed between them, the air pregnant with a kind of skepticism better known in the pews of a church. Jack studied the professor's face for a hint of a smile, but Dr. Booth's sunken eyes and thousand-yard stare suggested no punchline.

Chuck broke the silence with a loud snort. "Well. That's enough for me." He shot to his feet and pulled his keys from his pocket. "Jack, Steph, nice to see you. Dr. Booth, I wish I could say the same. Me, I'm going back home to pretend this fucking meeting never happened."

He'd advanced no more than five steps from the dining room when dry, croaking laughter echoed from beyond the basement door. He froze, pivoting on his foot. "What the hell was that?"

"It's my mother," Jack whispered. Both Stephanie and Chuck turned to him, stunned. "She came looking for the idol. She would've gotten it, too, if Tyler hadn't shown up."

"Christ," Stephanie whispered. "I thought she was locked up in the psych ward at Baptist Regional."

"She is," Chuck said. He gestured to the bruises on Jack's throat, the blood caked around his nostrils. "What do you call this in your line of work, Jack? Performance art? Some shit like that."

"Steph's right," Jack said. "You're an asshole, Chuck."

Chuck sighed, holding up his hands in apology. "Okay, that was a cheap shot. I'm sorry. But consider what you're all saying. Just because the idol is real doesn't mean our father is alive and walking around. We all saw him take a bullet. God, how I could ever forget?" He paced back and forth in front of the table, working up his defense with one brick of logic at a time. He reminded Jack of a frightened animal. "So, your mom broke out of the hospital. I can believe that more than this bullshit about rituals, curses, and the dead returning to life. This is reality, okay? Stauford's boogeyman is no more alive than its witch"

Jack bit his tongue. *You overbearing asshole,* he thought, and was about to retort when Stephanie did so on his behalf. She slapped Chuck so hard his cheek glowed red with the imprint of her hand.

"You unbelievable prick. Your grandpa raised you better. Jack's your brother, for fuck's sake."

A jubilant cackle erupted from below, so loud its force shook the foundation of the house. It was a laugh with which the children of Devil's Creek were well familiar, culled from their recurring nightmares. The mere sound raised the hairs on their arms and necks, the sensation of chilled air on a brisk winter night, cold enough to steal one's breath.

The voice did not belong to Laura Tremly.

"No bickering, children. Come, let me look at you."

4

Less than a mile away, Riley Tate slowed his father's car to a timid five miles an hour. His trip around the outskirts of town via the Stauford Bypass went without incident, allowing him time to grow comfortable behind the wheel, a brief respite from the living nightmares miles back.

As he left the bypass and turned west along Breyersburg Road, signs of the corruption grew more apparent, and his heart sank when he realized how far it spread. Mile after mile, house after house, he saw more of the same blue-eyed horror from which he'd escaped on the other side of town. Figures clad in makeshift robes walked hand in hand down both sides of the road, heading west toward the heart of town. Adults and children alike made their unholy pilgrimage, called forth by the same corrupting force.

I wonder if Dad's doing the same thing. He'd always thought of his father as an automaton of sorts, living his life by a book that didn't make sense to the boy, spending more time in servitude of an invisible all-seeing entity than with his own family.

Before she got sick, Janet Tate spent every evening with Riley, discussing his homework, talking about his day, chatting about what books he was reading or the music he listened to. Janet didn't share his interests, but she didn't shy away from them, either. Not like his father, who spent more time trying to find ways to convert people to his way of thinking, his way of believing.

Riley was so caught up in the past, he almost missed the turn for Standard Avenue. Old Lady Tremly's estate wasn't far now, just around the bend and at the top of the hill, but the mass of bodies congregating in the street forced him to slow. There were men and women, boys and girls of varying ages, clad in their shoddy robes and walking hand in hand down the center of the street. Together, they sang the chorus of an old church hymn, one he'd heard at his father's church once or twice before.

"Give me that old-time religion, give me that old-time religion…"

He slowly pressed down on the gas, but the mob in front of him had thickened. He held his breath and tried to hold back a rising panic in his chest, hoping none of them noticed his presence.

"Hello, Mr. Tate."

Riley cried out in surprise and slammed on the brake. Assistant Principal Meyers stuck his head through the shattered window and grinned. Thick rivulets of black gunk squelched from between his lips and dribbled on the passenger seat like hot tar. A vein bulged from his forehead.

"I'm willin' to let bygones be bygones if you'll suffer for me, son. Will you do that? Will you suffer for the lord?" The vein in his forehead burst with a sickening plop. A tear of black fluid leaked from the opening, followed by a worm working its way toward the open air. A pair of them emerged from beneath the man's eyes, coated in the same viscous sludge. "Come on, Mr. Tate. Let me teach you about the Old Ways."

Riley didn't wait for the scream rising in his throat. He stamped the gas pedal and shot forward, plowing through the corrupted mob. A young woman in stained drapery flew onto the hood of the car and shot into the air. The young boy she was carrying smashed into the windshield, bouncing off with a dull thud as the glass cracked from the impact. The child's infected blood coated the right side of the car like thick blackberry jam. Riley finally freed the scream building within, a rattling cry of fear and disgust and anger filling his mouth with the bitter taste of bile, the heat of hatred.

His gut lurched as the sedan cleared the fallen bodies and returned to asphalt. Panicked, his tears clouding his vision, Riley slowed only once to look in the rearview mirror. The mob was still coming, stepping over the bodies of those he'd crushed, their singing more pronounced than before. Some of them were laughing in the cloud of fumes.

Riley watched them in the rearview for a moment longer until he saw the figure of Stauford High's assistant principal emerge from the crowd. David Myers's face had split open, flaps of skin held aloft by the worms protruding from his skull. Before Riley turned away, he thought he saw dark fingers poking out from the man's gaping mouth.

"Hallelujah," he chanted. "Give me that old-time religion."

Riley swallowed the taste of bile and stepped on the gas.

5

"Ah, my little lambs. Don't be shy. Come, let me see you."

Jack led the way down the basement steps, half-expecting to see his father waiting for him at the bottom. What he remembered of Jacob Masters was forever ingrained in his mind, a dark blue-eyed specter haunting his dreams for the better part of thirty years. The notion that Jacob would be down there waiting in the dark with Laura didn't seem implausible.

But when he reached the landing and switched on the light, there was only his mother, still bound to the support beam. Dark tears streamed from her cheeks, and something black squirmed from one of her nostrils. A blue aura surrounded the orbits of her eyes. She smiled when she saw them. A thick clump of black mud dripped from her mouth.

"I've missed my lambs. Time's been good to y'all."

Stephanie gasped, raised her hand to her mouth. "What's wrong with her voice?"

"That isn't her," Jack whispered. He turned to Chuck, who stood dumbstruck at the bottom of the stairs. "Does that look like performance art to you?"

"Jack, I—"

"Ever the Doubting Thomas, little Chuck. I remember the first time I fondled your tiny cock, you tried stopping me. I told you, 'Don't worry, little lamb. It's the lord's will.' And you know what you said to me?"

Chuck blinked back tears. "I don't believe you."

Laura Tremly leaned her head back against the beam and laughed. *"Do you remember everything else I did to you down there in the dark where the lord was watching? You couldn't sit down for days."*

"You fucking bitch," Chuck growled. He raced forward and struck Laura with the back of his hand. "You're not him. *You're not him!*"

Dark sludge streamed from Laura's nose. A long dark worm slipped from her nostril and writhed along the floor toward the shadows. She looked up and laughed. *"Still doubting the power of your father, child. I wish I'd slit you open for our lord to eat your guts."* Her eyes rolled up in her head. *"I still may, if my other children don't get you first."*

Chuck balled his hand into a fist, was about to take a swing when the professor caught his arm. Tyler shook his head.

"Is it really him?" Stephanie asked, holding back tears. She stepped forward, hesitant to get any closer but unable to stop herself. Here was the beast they'd escaped all those years ago, speaking through his most faithful servant, in captivity for all to see. Stephanie stopped short of Laura's feet and crouched before her. "Father?"

"Little Stephanie. Not my favorite lady, but close. You always put up a fight when I took you down to the temple. Not like your sister Susan. She was a good little lamb."

Stephanie struggled to keep her composure. "How is this possible?"

"As the lord speaks through me, I speak through His followers, for I am His apostle. You could be one of my flock, child. Just like your sister Susan, or your brother Zeke. Even your brother Bobby saw the light. So shall you all."

Jack knelt beside his sister, put his arm around her in comfort. "What do you want, Jacob?"

"Callin' your daddy by his name don't make you a big man, Jackie. I want what I've always wanted. A pure world, a heaven on earth. I want to spread the seeds of Eden and free my lord from His earthly prison. I want what I promised your heretic grandma the day she killed me. I want blood and fire." Laura's eyes rolled toward the old man. *"And I want what you stole from me."*

Professor Booth met Laura's glowing gaze, his resolve withering, a visible tremor rippling through his elderly frame. He stepped away from Chuck and back toward the wall. Jacob's laughter swelled, exploding from Laura's mouth in a burst of chortles and chunks of earth.

"I heard you step into my house that day, teacher. Heard you fumble your way through the dark. You glimpsed the nature of god and didn't even know it. Whole lot of good all that education did for ya." Laura closed her eyes and inhaled, relishing the rancid scent wafting through the room. *"I know my lord's idol is here. I sent my love to retrieve it, and she will. A little carving of a hungry baby, and what is God if not hungry? I am His apostle, His caretaker. I will give my lord what He wants. I will give Him the blood He desires, and in return, He will give me the world I want."* Laura craned her neck toward the basement window and sighed. The black veins spreading from her eyes deepened, cracking her flesh. *"My children have been busy. While you've been bickerin', I've been preparing Stauford for the reckoning it deserves. Soon, very soon, I'll finish what I started, and then my perfect kingdom of suffering will be chartered, hallelujah—"*

A car horn startled them, blaring in three quick beeps as tires squealed to a halt outside. Jack shot to his feet. Stephanie followed, approaching the basement window. She stood on her toes and looked outside.

"That's Bobby's car."

They all went upstairs together, eager to leave the maddening sermons of their father behind. Outside, Bobby Tate's Acura sat at a crooked angle, its engine ticking as it cooled. Riley Tate sat on the edge of the driver's seat, hunched over and vomiting on the ground. Stephanie was the first to reach him, shocked to find her nephew instead of her brother behind the wheel. She put her hand on the back of the boy's neck to comfort him, whispering that it's okay, he'll be okay.

Chuck walked around the side of the car, exchanging confused glances with Stephanie when he saw the boy.

"Riley," Stephanie said. "Honey, where's your dad."

"Gone," Riley croaked. He wiped his mouth and blinked away tears. "Dad's one of them now."

"One of who?" Chuck asked.

The boy climbed to his feet and pointed down the hill. The mob of corrupted neighbors marched along Standard Avenue toward the home of Stauford's one-eyed witch. Jack Tremly walked to the edge of the driveway, shielding the sun from his eyes as he peered down the hill. A cold snake slithered through his gut.

"One of them," Riley said.

CHAPTER TWENTY

1

O*ne of them.* Stauford was no stranger to the phrase. The upstanding members of Stauford's elite, families that lived within the city for generations, and even Riley's father to a degree, did everything they could to bury that part of the town's history. But if they were to go digging along the foundations of Main Street where Jacob Masters and his children now marched, they might find in the earth a festering boil, covered in a thin layer of dirt and stone, ready to be lanced.

They might discover the very foundations of Stauford were built upon a fragile attitude of "them" and "other," making a mockery of the Christian ideals they claimed to uphold. They might discover cracks in the mortar, years upon years of layered sediment, scar tissue in stone, poured with each generation's refusal to confront the blemish of truth at the core of Stauford's necrosis.

Before today, if you were to ask anyone in town, they might say Stauford's only controversy was the burning church in the woods back in '83. And why would they say anything different? Generations of white-washing and silent indifference saw to that. History always tends to fall prey to revisionists, especially in an echo chamber like Stauford, Kentucky.

The truth was this: Stauford's tainted history didn't begin at Devil's Creek. It didn't begin with the burning of a church, a ceremonial suicide pact, or six surviving children.

It began with a poker game, a town awakened in the middle of the night by mob justice, and a passionate preacher's fiery condemnation of those involved.

2

Jacob Masters thought of these truths as he left the mind of Laura Tremly and rejoined his children on the streets of a town that shunned his family. The whispers from the grave ignited his hatred for the decadence of this town, its hypocrisy, its lies. For over thirty years, he'd lain dormant in a shallow grave while the world moved on above him, and in that time, cocooned in the husk of his decaying body, the lord whispered to him.

They have forgotten you and *your hate. You must remind them, Jacob.*

And he would. Only Jacob remembered his father's sermon of revelation and retribution to a bleary-eyed congregation of hypocrites one Sunday morning. Only Jacob remembered the cause of the old man's fury.

His children frolicked down Main Street, singing the hymns of old while they smashed windows and set fire to Babylon. He stopped at the corner of Main and 3rd, staring up at the building formerly known as the Hinkley Hotel. It was a brewery and taproom now, a place for the sinful to imbibe and poison their temples. He watched with proud glee as a boy with black tears streaming from his eyes smashed the glass door and climbed through the jagged opening.

The foundations were rotten here, a black river of sin flowing below the masonry. He heard the babble of whispers lost to time, echoes from the phantoms who'd lost their lives one night in 1919. He heard the raucous, drunken laughter of men over a poker game one warm Saturday night. He heard their footsteps as two of them stumbled their way out of the Hinkley Hotel, around the corner, and toward the railroad tracks across from Depot Street.

Jacob followed in their footsteps, breaking away from the violent singing mob of his own making. There, across the street, near the slope leading up to the tracks, those two men were held at gunpoint by a pair of black men. Only they weren't black at all—Jacob knew now, another secret given to him by the grave, made clear across the cosmic expanse of death and the universe. No, they were two white men who'd arrived in town the week before by way of the railroad, looking for work but finding most laboring jobs filled by a small community of black men across town. They'd heard of a poker game at the hotel happening

Saturday night, and wouldn't it be something if they could get their hands on some of those winnings?

They'd covered their faces in engine grease, dirtied their clothes to look like two good-for-nothin' niggers, and waited for a drunk poker player or two to wander their way.

Jacob tasted the air with his leathery tongue, breathing in the smell of smoke. He supposed his father's crusade was foolhardy given the time and place, but without it, Jacob's communion with the lord would have never come to pass. The lord, He did work in mysterious ways.

The drunks who were robbed at gunpoint that night staggered back to the hotel and told their friends what happened. What followed was a shameful act of cowardice and fear, of supposed racial superiority and white ignorance. Hours later, the screams of men and women and children filled the night as they were marched down the street, driven from their homes by a mob of angry white men.

He heard the phantoms of their conspiracy, indignant remarks about too many blacks in Stauford, and what good did they do, anyway? They were there to help while the men were away at war, and the Great War was over, had been for almost a year. The men were home and they needed work. Stauford was a white town, and the last thing they needed were a bunch of blacks muddying the waters, marryin' their women, taking their jobs, and getting rowdy in town on the weekends. They needed to know their place—and that place wasn't here, friend. No, sir.

As Jacob walked back to Main Street, he heard the bubbling river of sin below, for here the black abyss ran deepest, thickest. These streets were paved over the blood of the innocent, where men were whipped and beaten as they were marched toward the railyards. There, they were loaded onto a series of cattle cars and sent south to Chattanooga. The few who tried to run were either shot or lynched from the bridge over Layne Camp Creek.

A plume of flame engulfed the steeple of First Baptist in a cloud of orange and black. Cheers erupted from the crowd, raising their hands to the sky as they shouted *Hallelujah,* and Jacob joined them. *Let their temple burn. Their bed of sin was made there. So shall they lie in it.*

The morning after their purge, the same men who'd spilled innocent blood wandered through the doors of First Baptist, took their seats, and feigned their faith before Jacob's father. Thurmond Masters heard what they'd done, heard they'd even set fire to the small one-room church outside of Stauford the black folks used for worship, and his fury was unmatched. Following the passion in his heart, Reverend Thurmond Masters preached a different sort of sermon, one of fire and brimstone and revelation visited upon those who'd knowingly turned away from the teachings of Christ.

Amen, they'd said, nodding their heads in agreement. Thurmond Masters, hands shaking, his brow coated in sweat, slammed his fist on the lectern and screamed, *"You are all murderers in the house of the lord!"*

These men, these white men who'd exiled entire families from town on account of their skin color, were more than just murderers—they were landowners, business owners, elected officials in town. They were on the side of public opinion, held a higher office than the local reverend, and they saw to it Thurmond Masters preached his final sermon at First Baptist that humid Sunday morning in 1919.

He was cast out like Adam and Eve from Eden, a bad seed who would soon take root in the wilderness outside of town. There, he claimed the voice of God called to him among the trees, leading him with whispered direction toward a knob of earth standing solely in a clearing. God told him to build a temple for His children, and good Thurmond Masters, ever the man of faith, did as his lord bid him.

And so, the Lord's Church of Holy Voices was established, its walls blessed in the name of the father, the son, and the holy spirit, amen. For decades they prayed and sang to a false god above, decrying the decadence of the Babylon beyond the trees. Soon, Pastor Thurmond preached, a reckoning would come to Stauford, a reckoning of blood and fire raining down from the heavens. God's retribution for the people exiling their only voice of purity and reason.

Jacob remembered his father's sermons, and he remembered Stauford's scorn. *He's one of those crazy holy rollers. They ran his father out of town. He's one of* them.

In the eyes of Stauford's families, he'd always *been* one of them. And after years of following his father's footsteps, he finally heard the voice he'd yearned for. The voice didn't come from the clouds, the stars, or the heavens beyond; no, the voice came from below, soothing the wounds in his fractured soul.

The burning steeple of First Baptist caved in upon itself, and in a rush of flames, vanished from view. The mob's joyous cries filled the air.

Jacob Masters smiled. Their temple was burning. *So shall they all.*

3

Breaking glass and laughter woke Skippy from his slumber. He opened his eyes, confused to find he wasn't in his room at Stauford Assisted Living, but in an alleyway downtown. A group of pale-faced children surrounded him, staring down with curious glee.

Skippy sat up and grimaced. His body ached from sleeping against a mound of trash bags. Memories of the night trickled into frame. He'd gone for one of his late-night walks in town and fallen asleep. He'd walked too far for too long, and he'd grown tired.

One of the kids whispered into the ear of another. They both looked at him and snickered.

He didn't recognize them; the children he'd befriended years ago were all grown up, and he'd since been asked politely by the principal of the elementary school not to visit the playground anymore. Besides, there was something wrong with them. Their eyes were all funny and blue, and they were crying tears like black oil.

"Hi," he said, hoping not to scare them away. He was going to ask if they wanted to play Kick the Can when a little girl with blonde pigtails and blood smeared on her face chucked a pebble at his face. Skippy cried out, cradling his head. "That hurt!"

The children giggled. "He's different from the others."

Skippy touched his forehead. Blood smeared his fingertips, the wound throbbing with a pronounced ache. He blinked tears and looked at the children, confused.

"What'd you do that for? I didn't do nothin' to you."

A young boy in stained bib overalls picked up a chunk of asphalt. He threw it and struck Skippy on the cheek.

"He still bleeds," the little boy said. "He can still suffer for God."

There's somethin' wrong with 'em, Skippy thought, wincing. He scrambled to his feet, crying out as his knees popped and sang with arthritis, and pressed himself against the brick wall, hoping his fear would make them leave him alone.

A tall girl in torn jeans and a stained Slayer T-shirt reached out and touched his cheek, sliding her fingers through the curly gray streaks of his beard. She pursed her lips, squelching worms between her teeth.

"God says I can fuck an older man if I want." She ran her hand down the front of his shirt, picking the buttons free. "Do you want me? You can have me if you'll suffer for it. You could take me right here."

Skippy Dawson closed his eyes. He didn't want to be here, wished he was still back at the nursing home, wished he hadn't listened to that voice calling him into the night. A voice calling from the earth, beneath the streets, chanting *He Lives, He's Risen, He's Returned.*

Black veins beneath the girl's eyes deepened into cracks, her skin shifting and separating like tectonic plates, revealing the dark folds of sinew beneath. When she opened her mouth again, he saw fingers in there. Dark fingers coated in the same oily substance, writhing and twitching, reaching forward into open air to take hold of the world. To take hold of *him*.

Skippy screamed, shoved himself off the wall and past the gang of children. As he neared the corner, the sound of a parade filled his ears. There was singing and cheering, the smell of smoke in the air, sirens and alarms and breaking glass. Confused, he looked over his shoulder expecting to see the children giving chase, but they were where he'd left them. They smiled at him, eyes aglow in the alley shadows.

When Skippy turned the corner, he saw men and women dressed in bed sheets and drapes, their children clad in tattered clothing, all drenched in the same black goo. They walked with purpose, singing an old church hymn while they deposited their Bibles in a massive pile at the corner of 1st and Main. Smoke slithered from the shattered windows of Whitacre Bank, its alarms blaring while police officers danced in circles on the sidewalk.

"Gary Dawson. I dreamed of you in the grave, child. Let me have a look at you."

Skippy turned, startled by the sound of his real name, startled by the voice he'd heard so often in his dreams. The dead reverend had haunted him for years after the church burned, after Skippy's motorcycle accident nearly killed him.

"The grave never loses touch with its own," Jacob Masters said. "We might as well be brothers, you and I. And in the eyes of my lord, we are."

"I dreamed you," Skippy whispered. "You ain't real. You're dead."

"I am. Ain't I, brothers and sisters?"

"Hallelujah, Reverend!" A woman in a Tiffany blue bathrobe flicked a lighter and set the mound of Bibles on fire. They went up in a rush of orange flames. Skippy shielded his face from the sudden heat and blinked away tears.

"What's wrong with everybody? What'd you do to 'em?"

"I showed them the ways of my lord," Jacob said. "I showed them the Old Ways. It's my will. They are one." He held out his hand. "Would you join us, Gary? My lord answers prayers. My lord will heal your mind, heal the pains of your failing body."

Hesitant, Skippy considered the reverend's gesture. "What do I have to do?" Reverend Masters smiled and stepped back, allowing a young man to approach from the crowd. Skippy lit up with a smile. "Mr. Gravy! Why ain't you at the Gas 'n Go?"

David Garvey returned the smile, revealing blackened teeth and a squirming shape wriggling out of sight beneath his lower lip. "I quit my job, Skip. I have a new one now."

"What's that?"

David pulled a dark tendril from his nose, curled it around his finger and shoved it into Skippy's mouth before the old man could protest. "I make others suffer for the lord."

Reverend Jacob smiled with approval and strolled on down the street toward the bonfire. He joined his children as they linked hands and swayed in a circle around the blossoming flames, singing the hymns of their lord. Even on that humid September afternoon, the warmth was exquisite.

4

The mob was already there when Cindy Farris parked in front of the radio station. Her lungs deflated at the sight of them. There were at least twenty by her count, men and women and a few kids, all draped in weird shrouds. They'd formed a half-circle in front of the building, holding hands while they sang a church hymn.

So this is how it goes down, she thought, fishing through her purse for her phone. *They've finally snapped. I warned Steph this would happen. Ryan warned her, too.*

She'd imagined militant rednecks would show up at the front door of the station someday, shotguns and Bibles in hand, demanding they stop playing the devil's music—except, these people weren't rednecks, they didn't appear to be carrying firearms or religious materials.

One of the men in the chain of religious nuts looked over his shoulder and smiled. Cindy's heart sank.

"Ryan?" She rolled down her window and leaned out. "Ryan, what are you doing? What is this?"

Ryan broke away from the mob, holding out his hands to welcome her as he approached her car. "It's the greatest thing, Cindy. A true revelation. A god that doesn't judge me for my sexuality. All I had to do was suffer."

A stench of rotting compost permeated the air, sweeping a wave of nausea over her. She wrinkled her nose and fought her gag reflex.

"Victor didn't believe me, so I helped him understand."

A dark stain painted the front of Ryan's shirt, wet and shining in the afternoon sun. Thick globules of viscous sludge bubbled from his nostrils, and when he smiled, Cindy glimpsed something moving beyond his tongue.

Oh God, I'm going to be sick. She found her phone beneath a can of pepper spray. The screen lit up, showing a full charge but no signal. "Fuck." She held up the phone to the car's ceiling. "Come on, goddammit."

Ryan remained in front of her car, sizing her up like an animal. "There's a purge of blood and fire comin' to Stauford, Cindy. It's already begun. Can't you hear the music in the wind?"

She could. The whole damn town seemed to be screaming with alarms, gunshots, and a weird chanting in the breeze. Something about old-time religion. Something about a god from within and old lies above. A song about heretics and the many ways they burn.

Cindy rolled up the window, muffling the outside world. The phone signal was nonexistent, dead since this morning. If she could make her way inside the station, maybe somehow lock herself in, she could broadcast for help.

The mob of fanatics turned toward her, staring with strange eyes. Ryan tapped his knuckles on the hood of her car.

"The lord has a plan for you, Cindy. Has a plan for us all. And you can be a part of that plan. All you need to do is suffer, girl."

"No thanks," Cindy whispered. She put her foot on the brake and started the car. Judas Priest sprang from the speakers, a concussive beat spurring Cindy on as she dropped the car into reverse. "I should've left this dump months ago."

A hand shot through her window, shards of shattered glass spraying her face and the car's interior. Its fingers gripped a handful of her hair and yanked her toward the opening. Cindy shrieked, scratching at the fingers holding her, trying to pry away their grip. She felt her hair ripping free of her scalp, and in a moment of blind desperation, reached into her purse for the can of pepper spray. A jet of orange liquid shot from the can.

Her attacker recoiled, his glowing eyes burned and swollen from the spray. Grinning, he snatched the can from Cindy's hands and returned the favor, blanketing her eyes.

Cindy screamed, slamming on the gas pedal. The car shot backward across the parking lot, squealing tires as it jumped the curb and careened over the embankment.

Shrieking in agony and blind terror, Cindy jerked the wheel to correct her course, but momentum held her in its grip. The car turned, tipped onto its side, and rolled down the kudzu-covered hillside where it collided with a copse of walnut trees. Cindy lay crushed beneath her seat, struggling to breathe through the burning in her swollen throat. Consciousness left her with the slow seeping of blood from a wound on the side of her head.

Minutes later, the corrupted wandered down the hill, led by Ryan. Her suffering was just beginning.

While the residents of Stauford followed the whims of their new god, one silent figure made her way through the chaos unnoticed.

To the corrupted, she looked no different, indiscernible from the other lambs frolicking through the streets. Her good eye possessed the same sickly glow. Her clothes—stolen from a wash line on the north side of town, less than a mile from Layne Camp Cemetery—were a size too big and bore the telltale stains of fluid leaking from her nose, her eyes, her ears. A thin sheet of dirt and dust hid her pale complexion, and if it weren't for the silver hair tied back behind her head, anyone paying her notice might've mistaken her for a young lady no older than fifty.

She clutched a folded sheet of paper in her hand. A piece of thread was looped through a small tear at one end of the page; the other side was tied to her left index finger, a reminder of what she had left to finish and a promise to do so. She was pleased her final wishes were followed to the letter.

Little had changed in the weeks since her death, except for the smell in the air. The living would only recognize it as the stench of sour earth and compost, of rot and slow decay. To her, it was the scent of the grave. Stauford reeked of it, even if its people didn't know it yet. But they would. By the look of things, oh yes, they would know it soon enough.

She watched from the summit of Gordon Hill while the fires in lower Stauford spread north. She saw the steeple of First Baptist collapse upon itself, heard the horrible clang of the bell as it fell from its tower. Somewhere down there in the chaos, her adversary was rejoicing, believing he'd won.

You lack the conviction, he'd once told her. After being a member of the Lord's Church for more than a decade, leaving her family behind was the hardest thing she'd ever done. She'd lost her daughter because of it, almost lost her grandson because of it, and in the quiet spaces of the nights since, she'd wondered what she might've done differently if only she'd gathered the courage sooner.

None of that mattered now. She had a job to do. Jacob was down there somewhere, and while he counted the spoils of his temporary victory, she would slip past quietly. She would make her way back to where this nightmare began and seal the rift for good.

Before turning away from the town and resuming her pilgrimage, Imogene Tremly looked toward the horizon in the direction of her home. *Be safe, Jackie.*

CHAPTER TWENTY-ONE

1

Jackie wasn't safe. The mob was nearly at his doorstep, marching hand-in-hand up the long driveway toward his childhood home. They sang about their religion, about the glory of their god; they sang about the purity of suffering and honoring the Old Ways. Their voices filled him with an overwhelming sense of dread he'd not felt in the waking world since he was a child living at Devil's Creek.

"Get inside," Jack told his siblings. Stephanie and Riley stood beside Bobby's Acura, staring in horror at the approaching crowd. Chuck remained at Jack's side, watching down the hill. Jack turned to him. "You too, Chuck."

"This is ridiculous," Chuck whispered, staring at the mob, noting their choice of clothing, the song they sang. "This can't be happening."

Jack clutched Chuck's shoulders, gave him a good shake. "Wake up, man. I need you, okay? If we're going to get out of this together—"

"Jackie Tremly," a voice cried out. He turned toward the crowd. There were at least thirty, maybe even forty people standing before them draped in improvised robes, their faces caked in black sludge. An elderly man emerged from their center, his eyes aglow, his back bent like a snapped candy cane. Half his face was masked in scar tissue, a wax dummy held too close to a flame, the result of ancient skin grafts from an unsophisticated time.

Jack didn't recognize him. Not at first. Not until he spoke again, clearly, amid the silence of the day.

"Last I saw you, boy, you were about yea high." The elderly fellow raised his hand to his hip. "Course, you were hidin' behind your grandma, then."

Can't be, Jack thought, recalling the night the Klan showed up at their door. They were all wearing white robes and those idiotic white hoods, but he remembered their voices. He remembered the man who caught fire, remembered his voice shrieking into the night, *This ain't over, witch.* More than thirty years had passed, but as soon as the disfigured old man opened his mouth, Jack knew him.

"Get off my property. All of you." He caught Stephanie's eye, cocked his head toward the house. She pulled Riley back, marching the boy across the yard toward the porch. "I don't know you, mister, but take your people and go."

"You *do* know me, boy. You know this face." The old Klansman traced his fingers over the waxen patch of skin covering his cheek. "You know what your old bitch of a grandma did to me." He took a step forward, and then another. Jack sucked in his breath and stood his ground. "You got any pagan magic to protect you this time, boy? Can you throw fire like your grandma?" The Klansman held out his hand, and the crowd presented a brown bottle. A dirty rag hung limp from the neck. "Because I can."

Jack held up his hands, eyes wide, unsure what to do. Should he make a move for the bottle? Stop this idiot from setting his house on fire? Or should he retreat? His mind circled back to that night the Klan arrived on their doorstep, back to the blue light filling the house, the porch. Back to the image of Mamaw Genie wielding fire like a comic book hero.

The idol, he thought. Until this weekend, he thought what he saw was the workings of an overactive imagination, the wind had stirred the fire— but not now. The idol had something to do with it. She'd channeled it somehow, used its power to control the elements. The idol was an effigy of the dark thing beneath Devil's Creek. She'd channeled it to protect them, channeled it to complete her ritual—

"Jack, get back!"

A gunshot ripped through the air and struck the Klansman in the shoulder. Stunned, his ears ringing from the report, Jack turned around, wildly seeking the source of the bullet. He found it in Chuck's shaking hands. His brother stood beside the BMW's open passenger door, his arms braced on the car's roof, a handgun pointed at the crowd. The Klansman staggered backward, grunted, and regained his composure. Blue light leaked from the old man's eyes, and his whole face glowed as he struck the lighter in his hand.

"Chuck, don't—"

"Get in the fucking house, Jack!" Chuck fired off another round, more a warning shot than anything else, but the mob wasn't fazed.

Jack backed away just in time. Chuck's next round struck true, shattering the bottle in the Klansman's hand, lighting up the old bastard like a match. Jack shielded his face from the rush of heat, retreating up the porch steps.

The Klansman collapsed, his flesh sizzling as it cooked, but he wasn't screaming. Something sprouted from his face, something long and tendril-like, licking the air along with the flames. A living shadow in the shape of a slender arm with fingers at its ends.

"My God." Chuck slammed the passenger door and climbed over the railing onto the porch. The mob watched their brother's transformation and rejoiced when he rose to his feet, flames be damned. Chuck stood beside his brother. "What the hell's happening to him?"

Jack ignored the question. "Where the hell did you get a gun?"

Chuck grinned. "Any self-respectin' southern boy carries a piece. Me, I keep mine in my glovebox. Those lessons at the range didn't hurt, either."

Jack shook his head. "Get inside with the others. We need to figure this out, and right fucking now."

2

Stephanie was on her phone when the gunshots erupted outside, and she nearly dropped the device as she sank to the floor. Riley stood at the window next to Professor Booth, gaping at the mob, and Stephanie was torn between scolding and applauding him for his sense of self-preservation. *Definitely not like your old man,* she thought, readjusting the phone against her ear. Chuck shouted something to Jack, but she couldn't make it out. In her ear, a recording told her all circuits were busy.

She tried 911 again, received the same recording. She looked up at the old man and shook her head. "Can't get through to the cops."

"You won't," Professor Booth said. "Tried that earlier."

"The whole town's borked." Riley sank to his knees beside her. "It started at church this morning. It's an infection."

She squinted, shook her head. "I don't understand. An infection? You mean what's wrong with them is like a cold?"

"No, it's like—whatever that black shit is, it gets in their heads. It's controlling them somehow. Just like in my comics." Jack burst into the house, followed by Chuck. They engaged the lock and braced their backs against the door, panting. Riley cocked his head in their direction. "It's like the cover he painted for the *Gothical* comic." The boy's expression fell, dragged down with a sullen realization. "It got Dad."

Stephanie forced herself to smile, but inside, her heart was breaking. *You poor kid. First your mom, now your old man.* She wanted to reach out, pull him to her, and hold him tight, but now wasn't the time for comfort.

She dialed 911 again and put the phone on speaker. A friendly woman told them all circuits were busy, please try again later.

"This is insane. Did you *see* what was coming out of that guy's mouth?" Chuck brandished the handgun, pointing it toward the torn plastic covering the broken picture window. "And this is going to do us a whole lot of good, Jack. Great fucking job. Did you even call that guy about fixing this?"

Stephanie climbed to her feet and pulled back a curtain. The mob remained in the driveway, staring at the house. *An infection. It gets in their heads.*

And then she remembered. They'd all spent their time in the grotto, a place that hadn't made sense to her even then, because a place that far underground couldn't possibly have an open sky above. But there were stars. She remembered them—and she remembered the dark things erupting from the mouths of the congregation.

All of them, including her own mother, stood at the edge of waters in the twilit grotto with their chins lifted to the stars above. There was something extracting itself from their mouths. Long, worm-like, squirming with eager ferocity as it licked the air, the essence of a living shadow somehow given flesh with the power of their blasphemous faith. Dark hands reaching for the god in their sky, the stars its eyes, unblinking from their home in the tangent cosmos as its children baptized sacrifices in its name.

"They're getting closer." Professor Booth watched the mob advance across the driveway toward the porch. Stephanie put her hand on Riley's shoulder and pulled him from the window.

"You stay with me."

The boy shrugged. "They can get in here if they want to. There's nothing any of us can do to stop them."

"A little optimism might go a long way right now, kid." She checked her phone again, saw there were three bars of service. On a whim, she dialed the radio station to see if any lines were open. Silence followed by a hiss of static and the trill of a ring on the other end. She held up her hand and shushed everyone. "It's ringing."

Stephanie put the phone on speaker once more and set it on the table. They huddled around it like a tribe, waiting for their deity to answer their call. On the third ring, someone picked up.

"Yes, hello?" Stephanie cleared her throat. "Cindy? Ryan? Can you guys hear me?"

A low rumbling laugh tested the boundaries of the phone's tinny speaker. Ryan Corliss spoke: "Howdy, *Stevie G.* You callin' to make a request?"

"Ryan, listen, this is kind of an emergency—"

"I know, darlin'. My lord told me all about it. He told me you'd be calling." The air left her lungs in a slow breath of defeat. She closed her eyes, pounded her fist on the table. *I need you to radio the state police barracks in Landon,* she'd wanted to say. The words still hung there on her tongue, eager to be voiced, eager to ignore the stark reality breathing through the other side of the phone line.

"You still with me, Steph?"

Tears coated the rim of her eyelids. "I'm still here."

"Glad to hear it. My god's got a message for y'all."

The feeling in her legs left her, their consistency like rubber. She listened to the hum of static on the line, the ratcheting beat swelling in her chest. "What's your message?"

"Stauford belongs to us now. Give us the idol and let Laura go." Ryan's voice changed, cracked, distorting with the sound of layered voices speaking over one another. "Your lord commands it. Our will and the Old Ways are one."

The signal strength dropped to nothing, and the line fell silent.

Outside, the mob began their chanting, led by the burning Klansman. The old man's face split horizontally, his charred skin cracked and blistering from the flames, while a thick tendril protruded from the wound of his mouth. Fingers sprouted from the tip of the dark shape, bent at their knuckles like the old man's spine, a dark puppeteer positioned above its marionette. The impossible thing was impervious to the flames engulfing its host, towering nearly two feet above the man's cracked face. He walked with an almost comical gait, his neck craned backward to accommodate the shapely appendage, arms limp at his sides, legs full of jelly and marbles. Like a human marionette, controlled by the malignant god infecting his mind.

The Klansman walked toward the porch, reached out, and placed his hand on the support beam. Flames spread up the column, along the banister and railing.

Somewhere below, a woman laughed.

3

"I knew you'd come for me, my lord. My love. My light."

Laura Tremly craned her neck toward the basement window and watched her lord's followers march closer to the house. Her head hummed from Jacob's voice inside her mind, a slow vibration filling every inch of her body with a kind of ecstasy she'd not felt since he ravaged her in the grotto all those years ago. Down in the dark, amid the eyes of God, they conceived a vessel of flesh which would serve as a sacrifice to signal their utter devotion. A tremor rippled upward from between her thighs and took her breath away. If she concentrated, she could almost feel him there, his fingertips inside her, his breath against her neck, in her hair, in her ears.

You are mine, one body and mind, one soul. And we will be together again soon. We will start again.

"Yes," she gasped, straining against her bonds. "I will give you this body, this womb. I will be your kingdom on Earth, my lord. *Hallelujah.*"

Hallelujah, my lamb. Will you take back what is ours? Will you bring it to me?

"Anything for you." She pulled at her restraints, twisting her wrists, sucking in her breath as the coarse twine dug into her skin. "My suffering for you."

I will wait for you in the city. Our flock will bring you to me, and then we will consummate our union where our kingdom began. We will rebuild on the ashes of Babylon, at the shores of this lake of sin.

And like a whisper, he was gone from her, the aches in her bones returning, her muscles crying out once more. Black tears rolled down her face and she clenched her jaw, biting back the pain digging deeper into her wrists. Such suffering was miniscule, a tribute to their buried god, but the sting was still there. A reminder of her earthly nature, the ache of mortality writ in skin and bone and blood, etched forever in the temple of her body.

Laura pulled against the beam, pulled until her fingertips tingled from a loss of circulation, until the sharp sting of twine cutting into her flesh dulled to numbness. Until her bindings finally broke free, loosing her upon the world once more. For years she'd lain dormant and drugged in the town's psych ward, waiting for the return of her god and lover, waiting for the time when she would do her part to fulfill Jacob's prophesy.

Tonight, she would join him, and the world would quake at their union. But first, there was a matter of the idol, of the heretics upstairs, and her rebellious son.

Laura walked to the bottom of the stairs and peered up. Rivulets of blackened corruption dripped down her wrists and pooled on the floor. The basement door stood open, light from the kitchen falling down the stairwell in a rectangle of dust motes and frantic shadow play. She heard them speaking frantically up there, panicked by the mob outside, bickering about which way to scatter.

Because rats always scatter, she thought. *Cowards.*

"You all need to calm down. This isn't solving anything."

The old man's voice brought a smile to her face. The back of her head still ached, an exquisite throb to the tune of her corrupted heart, and she decided she wouldn't let his transgressions go unchecked.

Thief. Interloper. My lord's will would be done by now if not for you.

Laura waited and listened. Their voices rose and fell, dancing between muffled syllables and profane clarity. She heard her son say the house is on fire, and she nearly cried out with joy.

She cursed her mother in her mind, but Imogene Tremly didn't respond. There was only the chorus of chanting rising from outside the house, the shuffle of footsteps and panicked chatter above, and the slowed beating of her black heart.

Laura Tremly gripped the banister and climbed the stairs.

4

"—the fucking house is on fire, Chuck. What would you have us do?" Jack held out his hands, waiting for his brother to respond. Chuck gestured to the phone.

"Try 911 again? Shit, I don't know, Jack."

"You all need to calm down. This isn't solving anything." Professor Booth stepped between them. Sweat dotted his forehead and his hands were shaking, but a career of wrangling students never truly left him. "Get whatever you need from here and go out the back door. They're standing out there, waiting for us to go out the front."

"Out there," Chuck said. He shook his head, incredulous. "Are you out of your goddamn mind, old man? Did you *see* what's wrong with them?"

Stephanie didn't wait. She took Riley's hand and pulled him away from the window, crossing the dining room toward the den. Jack scrambled to gather his things, stuffing his grandmother's notebook into his messenger bag. He reached for the idol but hesitated. The stone carving pulsed with light, its hollow eyes staring forever, its grim smile mocking them all.

"That's coming with us," the professor said. He put his hand over it, moved it into the open compartment in Jack's bag. "Genie made me get it for a reason, son. It can't go back to Devil's Creek, no matter what."

Stephanie called from the living room, "We need to go, gentlemen. Right now."

"What about your mom?" Chuck looked at Jack, surprised by his own words. He knew better, or thought he did. Jack's stare said everything it needed to. Chuck frowned and left the room to meet Stephanie and Riley on the back porch.

A haze of smoke filled the room, tickling Jack's nose and burning his throat. He slung the bag's strap over his shoulder. As he crossed the threshold from the dining room, Jack heard the professor utter a startled cry. Jack turned, and his heart sank into his gut, his veins flushed with ice water.

Laura Tremly clutched the back of Tyler's neck, her fingers digging into his sagging flesh.

"Give me what he stole, baby boy."

"Don't," Tyler rasped. The professor's face screwed up in agony as she dug her fingers into his neck. Jack slid his hand under the flap of his messenger bag, traced the contours of the idol's grinning face.

"Laura," he said. He swallowed the lump in his throat. *"Mom."* The word left his tongue coated in a bitter taste. "Let him go. I'll give you what you want. Just let him go."

His throat burned from the smoke, his eyes watering as he suppressed an urge to cough. The smoke grew thicker, the heat palpable, and he heard the crackle of flames as they spread to the second floor. The windows of the dining room were aglow, the front door engulfed, and through it all he heard the cheers from the mob outside.

"Don't, Jack—"

Something collapsed upstairs, followed by a rush of flames, the sizzle and pop of cinder.

"Shut up, Tyler." Jack removed the idol. The malignant light brightened the room, illuminating the swirls of smoke dancing between them. Sweat dripped down his forehead into his stinging eyes. He strained to meet his mother's gaze through the smoke. "You let him go and I'll give you the idol."

"Jack…" the professor growled. His eyes widened, glaring across the room through the curtain of smoke. "…it opens the rift—*ulk!*"

Professor Booth's neck snapped with the effortless twist of Laura's wrist. She flung his body to the side. He crumpled into himself like a wet paper bag, his face frozen in the pained expression of determination. Jack fought the urge to puke, fought against his limbs going limp. In that moment, watching the old man's lifeless body collapse, he wanted nothing more than to curl into a ball and cry. None of them deserved this nightmare.

And there, in the center of his despair, Jack found an anger he'd not felt since he was a teenager. An anger he'd submerged in a well of uncertainty and confusion, a well he'd covered over and hidden away as an adult.

Laura grinned and leaped at him with her teeth bared. Time slowed, Jack's heart stopped, and in a frozen moment, he reopened the well.

Jack raised the idol and roared at his mother, channeling all his frustration and resentment and hate. The light dimmed, focused itself around the stone figure's hollow eyes, and erupted in a pulse of force.

Both mother and son were propelled away from each other in a violent shockwave. Laura's limp body shot through one of the dining room windows, through a wall of flame and shattered glass. Jack flew backward, sprawling through the air into the living room where he collapsed with a pained grunt. The world swam and his whole body ached from the impact, his heart racing as he struggled to regain his breath.

The idol.

Jack sat up, searching the floor around him, but the idol wasn't there. He looked toward the dining room for its dull glow but only saw flames spreading into the room.

"Jack, come on, we've gotta go. Riley, give me a hand." Stephanie and Riley clutched him under his armpits and dragged him to the back door. He tried to stop them, tried to tell them the idol was missing, but his throat was scorched from the smoke. All he could do was clutch the strap of his messenger bag, saving what mattered most.

A cool breeze swept across his face as they pulled him free of the burning house. He watched the inferno eat away at his childhood home. *So ends the Tremly legacy,* he thought, before a painful cough erupted from his lungs. He gasped for air, tried to spit out the taste of smoke. Stephanie knelt beside him on the grass, her hand on his back.

"Breathe. It'll be okay." She looked up at Riley. "Is he coming?"

The boy stood near the edge of the house, peeking around the corner. He glanced back and nodded. A moment later, Chuck's black BMW appeared, chewing up the lawn as he steered toward them. The car slid to a halt in front of the back porch.

"Get in."

They piled into the car, and within minutes were headed toward the parkway. Behind them, the silhouette of the Victorian house slowly collapsed into itself. The eyes of Jacob Masters's followers lit up the hillside like blue fireflies, their hymns of victory lifting the ceiling of Heaven for all the angels to hear.

5

Laura Tremly's fingers twitched, curled into fists as a roar ripped through her chest and out her charred maw.

The mob cheered as they watched her step through the broken window into the inferno. She returned a minute later, a smoldering figure born from nightmares.

Laura held up the grinning idol. Its glow pierced through the haze of smoke. The Klansman knelt before her, followed by Riley's assistant principal and the other men and women from the neighborhood. They bowed in reverence, praying to the visage of their new god, the faith of their apostle, the love of the sacred mother.

She gripped the idol, lifted it to her blistered, blackened lips, and kissed the face of her god.

"Take me to the lord," she said. "He requires his prize."

6

Stephanie kicked the underside of the glovebox. "No fucking signal. No cops. Nothing." She tossed the phone onto the dashboard. "We might as well be on the goddamn moon."

Riley snorted, screwing up his face to contain his laughter. "Well, it *is* Stauford."

She looked back from the passenger seat, shook her head, and laughed. Jack joined her but was stopped by another round of coughs tearing through his lungs.

"This isn't funny," Chuck muttered, shaking his head. They were headed west along the Cumberland Gap Parkway, through North Stauford and toward the I-75 ramp. Dozens of smoke trails snaked their way into the sky from the south, tumbling upward from the fires downtown. "This is wrong. People are dead. The old man's dead." Chuck took a breath, stepped on the gas. "We need to get the fuck out of here."

Jack cleared his throat. "We can't leave."

The car fell silent. He didn't wait for Chuck to protest; instead, he spoke through short breaths about what the professor told him. Stephanie turned in her seat and stared him down.

"You mean the grotto. The one from your painting. From when we were kids."

Jack nodded. "If what Tyler said is true and my grandma's walking around, then she's on her way there now." He waited a beat, thinking. His fingers were still numb from the jolt. "I left the idol back there. I have to assume they have it now, and that's not what she'd planned—"

"So what?" Chuck looked up at his brother's reflection in the rearview. "Look, I don't disagree some weird shit just happened, but let's think about this, guys. Even if Genie Tremly is back from the dead— even if our fucking father is back from the dead—what's to stop us from getting on the highway and leaving town right now? Huh?" He geared up, speeding through a red light. "This isn't our fight. Let Genie and Jacob duke it out, man." Tears slipped down his cheeks, and Jack realized Chuck wasn't trying to convince them. He was trying to convince himself and failing horribly. "I never liked this fucking town, anyway."

"Because if we don't, it'll spread. It spread to my dad. He tried to spread it to me. It's an infection, guys. Can't you see that?" Riley turned to the window, blinking away tears. "I hate this town, too, but it's my home." His jaw quivered, his words reduced to a blubbering jumble of syllables. "It's all I've got left."

Jack put his arm around the boy, pulled him close. "It's okay," he whispered. "Let it out."

"Riley's right," Stephanie said, fighting back tears of her own. "We need to help Genie. We need to go back to Devil's Creek."

Another blanket of silence fell over them, the hum of the car's engine and the buffeting of tires on asphalt the only sounds. The sun hung low on the horizon, thick fingers of smoke occulting its gaze. They drove for another mile along the empty highway until they reached the intersection of the parkway and US 25. Chuck grunted in disapproval as he turned left, speeding back toward town, toward the fires eating away at the cancer of Stauford.

Half a mile later, Stephanie pressed her face to the window and gasped. Flames lit up the summit of Gordon Hill, just beyond the girders of Stauford's water tower. Riley leaned forward to comfort her but was stunned to silence as they caught a glimpse of downtown beyond the hill. Chuck slowed the car to a crawl and gaped from the open window.

Fires raged unchecked for as far as they could see. A massive crowd rejoiced in the streets, their faces lit up by thousands of unblinking eyes, an army of insects swarming over a rotting corpse. Whitacre Bank stood in ruins, its remains a charred, hollow shell. In the center of Main Street, a bonfire burned as tall as the Stauford Tribune, one of the city's oldest structures now reduced to a squat rectangular jack-o-lantern with flames shooting from its windows. A block away, Devlin's On Main was engulfed in the inferno.

Chuck parked the car and ran to the edge of the overpass. He slammed his fist on the railing. "Goddammit," he whispered. "Goddamn you all."

Stephanie, Jack, and Riley joined him at the rail. Chuck wiped his eyes, shook his head, and laughed. "You remember when we were kids? We used to daydream about burning this shithole to the ground."

"Yeah," Jack said. "Yeah, I guess we did, didn't we?"

Stephanie snorted. "Can't say our old man never gave us nothin'."

"He's probably down there right now," Riley said. They turned to him, his words hanging ominously in the air. "Don't you think?"

Jack closed his eyes, nodded. "Probably. Which means we need to get going. Beat him to the punch."

Chuck rapped his knuckles on the railing and returned to the car. Stephanie and Riley followed, but Jack remained a moment longer, watching the smoke roll over Stauford like a dark wave. *I hope you're out there, Mamaw. I hope we're doing the right thing.* He smiled grimly, his eyes alight with the glowing embers of a dying city.

FROM THE JOURNAL OF IMOGENE TREMLY
(4)

1

Notebook entries dated February 14th, 1997

Had dinner with Tyler again. Conversation was light, mostly small-talk. I wanted to talk business, but he wanted to talk about family, and I humored him as much as I could. Mostly talked about Jackie, how he was doing in school, about his art. We didn't talk about the past, even though he wanted to.

I let him see me to the door, and I kissed him on the cheek, thanked him for a nice evening.

I know he knows who I am, but he's been respectful so far. Maybe I'll talk to him about it when I'm ready. Maybe I never will be. Maybe I had too much wine tonight. Maybe I just need some sleep.

Nightmares tonight. Dreamed I took Jackie back to the church for one of Jacob's evening sermons and sacrificed the boy at the altar of the nameless. I can still feel the warm blood on my hands. For as long as I live, I'll never forgive myself for becoming involved in that man's madness.

Maybe we were all just so eager to get out of Stauford, eager to believe in something that was pure. Something that wasn't bogged down by the town's hypocrisy. It's hard to sit in church on Sunday, watching everyone around you pray for forgiveness, put their dollars in the collection plate, and listen to the man at the pulpit scream about damnation when you know they'll be back to their gossip, their drinking and drugging, their whoring and adultery, their bigoted rage.

That's the way it's always been, for as long as I can remember. Even when I was a little girl, I knew how the wind blew in Stauford. That's what drew me to the Lord's Church outside town. I think that's what drew most of us, if I'm being honest. We just wanted something different, something that wasn't the same hypocritical rhetoric. All that stigma around the "scary church in the woods" was just more gossip from the Stauford rumor mill. One always has to consider the source, and when it's the Stauford Elite, always swallow it with a grain or two of salt.

Personally, I never doubted the intent behind the formation of the Lord's Church. Thurmond Masters was a good man, a principled man. We'd all heard the story about the church's founding, how he and his family were cast out from town because of the things he'd said during his final sermon at First Baptist, and we didn't blame him for it. Anyone who's lived in Stauford for a while understands a man like that has no place in a town like this. There was a saying some years back, the sort of thing you'd hear passed around in friendly circles whenever news of corruption or scandal would surface, that Stauford had killed the last good man in town.

Thurmond was that man, in so many ways. They hadn't killed him, but they'd killed his reputation, driving a spear right through its side. Most men would've despaired, picked up their roots and moved elsewhere, but not Thurmond. He chose to stay, chose to rebuild his congregation, and rededicate his faith while the people of Stauford slandered his name. They mocked him for shining a light on their wrongs, cast him out for holding up a mirror so they could see how awful and rotten they were inside. No, a man like that didn't belong in Stauford at all.

Maybe you could argue it was pride that drove him to build the Lord's Church and preach about the evils in town. I wouldn't disagree about that, no sir, but at the heart of his message was a condemnation of Stauford's ways. Of loving thy neighbor on Sundays when everyone's watching, after herding them out of town on cattle cars the night before.

His son, on the other hand, was cut from a different cloth. Jacob was every bit as devoted as his father, but he had a charisma about him that his father lacked. When Jacob would stand in for Thurmond during some mid-week sermons, he always got the congregation worked up, "feeling the spirit," as we used to say many years ago. He was in favor of the old hymns from simpler times, preached about living a simpler life, and was utterly devoted to his faith. It's no wonder we all fell under his spell.

Jacob Masters was, at one time, a good man. His heart was in the church for all the right reasons, and if he carried any sin at all, it was that he scorned Stauford just like his father. Maybe even more than Thurmond. Every hardship Jacob had ever known came from being born an outcast.

I guess maybe that's why he was so easily corrupted by the evil in the earth. Maybe that's why we all were.

Just looked at the clock. 3:32 in the morning. Let's give this sleep thing another try.

2

Notebook entry dated February 15th, 1997

Tyler called. He heard from his friend in New England, Dr. Walter Crawford, a fellow professor in "occult studies," if you can believe it. I didn't know there was such a thing. He was intrigued by Tyler's description of the idol and asked to see photos. Guess I'll need to get film for the Polaroid…

3

Notebook entry dated February 23rd, 1997

Spoke with Dr. Crawford on the phone this morning. He's intrigued by the photos I sent him. Seemed curious about my knowledge of the greater implications of the idol's existence. I played dumb, of course. Told him I hadn't the slightest idea what it meant, that it sure seemed really old, and did he think it might be worth something?

"Priceless" was his word of choice. I told him I was interested in learning more about it, asked if he could point me in the right direction. He said he might be able to pull some strings and get me copies of the old texts they keep at his university's library. Then he told me to tell Tyler he owed him one. I laughed, thanked him, and told him I'd pass on the message. This might bear fruit after all.

4

Letter dated March 3rd, 1997 from Dr. Walter H. Crawford, Professor of Occult Studies, Miskatonic University.

Dear Ms. Tremly,

I hope this letter finds you well. Enclosed are the Polaroid photos you provided, for which I must extend my gratitude once more. The photographs proved to be somewhat anomalous among my peers. Although we are not strangers to the various idols, carvings, and runes in our chosen studies, your artifact has drawn much speculation from Miskatonic faculty, leading us to consult with the grimoires kept in the university's private collection.

Our mutual friend, Dr. Booth, mentioned his theory of sacrificial rites used by the local native culture, one which perhaps predates the accepted known record within global archaeological and anthropological circles, but there are still enough holes in that theory through which any number of anomalies can slide—your grinning idol notwithstanding. That said, we did find a few short passages which fit the idol's description within a number of tomes.

The artifact—and more specifically, the entity carved in effigy—appears to have no formal name on record, but several corollary Latin translations refer to it as *sine nomine inanis*—or simply, "void without a name." What passages we found spoke of corruption and cleansing rites centered around the cycles of the moon, the mandate of blood offerings, and a distinct lack of form. Illustrations depicted its presence as a shadow with blue eyes.

As I promised, you will find enclosed photocopies of select pages from these grimoires for authentication purposes. Of note are the pages excerpted from the *Necronomicon* and *De Vermis Mysteriis,* and it's worth mentioning that the sigils found within closely resemble those found in the seals of the *Arcanum Arcanorum.*

Speaking personally, what I find more intriguing than the notable absence of information, is how something like this ended up in southeastern Kentucky. I suppose our friend Dr. Booth will have to fill in that part of the puzzle. Please give him my warmest regards.

If you do decide to part with the artifact, please contact me before considering other venues. Miskatonic's Department of Occult Studies is willing to make an offer that may be worth your while.

Kind regards,

Dr. Walter H. Crawford, Ph.D.
Department of Occult Studies
Miskatonic University, Arkham, MA

PART FIVE

MIDNIGHT BAPTISM

Outside Stauford, Kentucky
Present Day

CHAPTER TWENTY-TWO

1

Dust and gravel filled the air in a dark cloud as the stolen pickup truck barreled down Devil's Creek Road. A cool breeze swept back Imogene's silver mane, and she drove with her elbow perched over the open window.

Even in the years after the incident, she'd never traveled back to these roads, this wilderness, or the ramshackle village they'd built. The same rundown houses were still here, dotting the landscape like open sores, and kudzu had claimed most of the surrounding area as its own. Even the barn bearing the name "Devil's Creek" in janky lettering was still there, its roof sagging from old age and the burden of gravity on rotten wood. She slowed as she drove by the barn, watching it with quiet regard, as though it were a sleeping beast that might awaken and alert its master at any moment.

Imogene had no illusions about the nameless thing living under the earth. It knew she was coming. She'd communed with it in the grave, felt its fingers trying to touch her soul, trying to pry her free of the void holding her in stasis. *Be with me,* it whispered to her. *Be one with me, child. I will give you life again. I will raise you above my children, make you a general in my army, if you would but kneel in devotion to me.*

And for an instant, cradled in the shell of her corpse, the essence of Martha Imogene Tremly considered the offer. What sort of world could she help shape with that sort of power? One free of anger and hate, free of the bigotry and racism and hypocrisy which fed the great beast of Stauford.

But the universe shielding her essence upheld its part of the bargain she'd sealed in her basement, a pact which would not be reversed. *It lies,* the void said, and spoke no more.

Even now, as she stepped on the gas and sent the pickup sputtering past the collapsed barn, Imogene felt the tickle of its many fingers trailing down her spine. The nameless thing would always be there, trying to win her back.

The pavement gave way to gravel, the truck's suspension groaning from shock as the carriage bounced over the divider. In another couple miles, the road would dead end at a roundabout in the forest. From there, she would continue her journey on foot.

You can't win, the nameless thing said. *My son won't let you.*

Imogene Tremly gripped the piece of paper tied to her hand and ignored the voice lapping at her ears, behind her head, hidden in the shadow of her soul.

2

The people of Stauford swarmed toward Main Street from all corners of town, leaving fires in their wake, ensuring there would be nothing left of this unholy Babylon when the sun rose again. They joined their lord's apostle at the bonfire in front of Whitacre Bank, throwing the vestiges of their former faith into the purging flames. Bibles, heretical symbols cast in gold and silver, their filthy clothing of excess, their laptops and phones and other totems from the false gods of technology. They stripped themselves of their former lives down to bare skin, frolicking amidst the cleansing inferno, their flesh stinging from the cloying heat.

Be one for me, their lord said, and they were.

The citizens of Stauford shed their inhibitions, entwining themselves with each other, engaging in the pleasures forbidden by the god of heretics. Main Street slowly transformed into an orgy of flesh and flame, burning maggots writhing over a corpse, and conducting them all in this orchestra of pleasure was their lord's apostle, Jacob Masters.

He hovered above the bonfire, the flames blackening the soles of his feet, watching with grim satisfaction while the people of Stauford fucked themselves into a mindless stupor, their cries of pain and pleasure filling the evening air like the call of cicadas. Their intermingled chorus rose and fell in waves, punctuated with the occasional orgasm, the gasp of agony, the sob of fear, regret.

The children of Stauford congregated on the side streets, dancing freely among the flames and rejoicing with each structure's collapse. Their lord set them aside, the seeds of Babylon from whom a new paradise would grow. Jacob heard their heartbeats, the pitter-patter of their bare feet slapping upon the pavement as they danced in celebration. He heard their cherubic laughter, smelled their innocence, and felt himself harden. His time in the grave had not dulled his base nature, but for as much as he wanted to claim their innocent flesh, he knew they served another purpose.

By your will, my lord. All must suffer, even your most devoted apostle.

A procession of cars exited the overpass and approached the bonfire. The mass of men and women ceased their copulation and allowed the cars through. Jacob watched Laura Tremly step out of the first car. Her face was badly burned, half her hair scorched down to her scalp, but the horrible disfigurement did nothing to steal the smile from her face. She met her lover's gaze and raised their lord's idol.

"You've done well, darlin'."

Jacob descended, his tattered slacks and suit coat like the fractured wings of an avenging angel. He slipped his arm around Laura's waist, pulled her close, and pressed his coarse lips to hers. The grim idol's hollow eyes glowed, bathing them in a shimmering light. When Jacob pulled away, Laura raised her charred hand to his face, ran her fingers along the sigil burned into his forehead.

"Your will and the Old Ways are one," she whispered. Black tears slithered down her cheeks. She shivered in anticipation. "It's been so long, my lord. Will you take this body once more? I've saved it for you."

"Oh yes," Jacob growled. He licked his lips, tasting the lust in the air, and spun his lover around, bent her over the hood of the car. "Our lord demands it."

3

The city of Stauford disappeared behind them as Chuck sped down the Cumberland Falls Highway, its burning buildings obscured by rolling hills and the tops of trees. Smoke rose above the tree line in thick tendrils. Straight ahead, the sun drifted toward the horizon, painting the path before them in shades of orange flames and long, drawn shadows.

Stephanie leaned against the window and listened to her brothers conspire in the front of the car, grateful she'd let Jack ride shotgun. Riley sat with his head on her shoulder. His fingers twitched, his breath a slow whistle through his nostrils, and she shifted her arm to cradle him against her in comfort. *Hell of a day you've had,* she thought.

She tried to remember what she was thinking that morning when she awoke, if she had any idea what sort of nightmare awaited her today. Her apartment was probably nothing but ashes at this moment, all her clothes, her art, her vinyl. Gone up in smoke and cinders like her dream job.

Her heart dropped into the pit of her belly. All the photos of her grandmother. The ones hanging on her walls, countless others in shoeboxes in her closet and under her bed. The loss of her radio station was a huge blow, but nothing compared to the loss of those few good things she wanted to keep from her childhood. Stephanie took a breath and buried the desire to cry, but the tears remained, lingering at the edge of her vision.

God, she wanted a cigarette. She hadn't smoked in nearly five years, but the urge to take in the smoke and calm her nerves was palpable. Instead, she tried to find her spiritual center, a place to soothe her worry and reassure her everything would be okay. But it wouldn't be. There was no way it *could* be. Even if they made it out of this alive, what would be left for them?

She'd locked up every cent she had in the radio station and the restaurant, and while they were paying for themselves, she wasn't exactly rolling in the dividends. And then there was Riley. The poor kid had no one left except for her. Janet Tate's parents were back in town, their minds probably crawling with black worms.

Riley's breath hitched, and he uttered a low moan in his sleep. Stephanie leaned over and kissed the top of his head.

You're all he's got, her grandma Maggie reminded her. Stephanie smiled. She remembered the old lady's constant nagging after Stephanie finished college. *Steph, when are you gonna find a nice man and have a couple of kids? You should be thinkin' about settlin' down.* And she'd always put her career first, always told Mamaw Maggie she was too busy to have a kid, when the truth was she was terrified of raising a kid in Stauford. A small town like this ate children alive, and she'd promised herself years ago she'd never raise a kid here.

Now Stauford was a burning trash heap. She supposed there was some poetic justice in that.

And yet there was something about the place she found alluring despite all the scars she'd endured—and not all of them were formed exclusively in the depths of Calvary Hill.

The halls of Stauford's schools, in the classrooms where she'd heard the gossip, the laughter and snide looks, the antagonizing notes found in her locker, and cruelty of false friends all did their part to carve lines into her soul. Those false friends wounded her most, and she'd done more than her share of cutting lines into her arms out of hesitation, trying to psych herself up and end it already, because that's what a crazy cult kid would do.

She looked at the tattoo on her wrist. A trio of roses with bleeding thorns hid the ribbon scars in her flesh. Mamaw Maggie treated her to the tattoo when Stephanie was seventeen, proudly signing the consent form at the parlor in Landon. *You can always start over,* Maggie Green told her later, when her skin was on fire and glistening with fresh ink. *Now, later, it don't matter, honey. You can always start over. Here or a thousand miles from here, it don't matter. You make your future. It's yours. Take it.*

Stephanie looked down at Riley, her heart swelling for the first time since they'd left the burning city behind. *You can always start over,* she thought, brushing the boy's dark hair back from his face. *We just have to make sure we have a future first.*

Jack pointed at a road sign up ahead. "There."

They turned off the highway, and Stephanie caught a glimpse of the road sign. Her blood ran cold. The sign read "DEVIL'S CREEK RD."

4

The sun had vanished behind a curtain of smoke by the time Jacob was finished with her. Even in her ecstasy, the pain was so intense Laura was sobbing uncontrollably by the end, and she recoiled from him like a wounded animal. Their coupling severed the final link in her sanity, dropping her mind into an abyss. She curled up against the car, staring vacantly at bloodstains on her hospital gown. Jacob stepped away from her, tucked himself back into his trousers, and wiped his chin. The taste of Laura's blood lingered on his tongue.

His children were with him now, standing among the crowd at the bonfire on Main Street. Dearest Susan, a true keeper of the faith even after all these years, stood naked with her brothers. Zeke held his arm around his sister's bloodstained shoulder, and behind them both stood Bobby, former practitioner of the heretical faith. Jacob stopped before them, looked them over as a general would his troops. He took Susan's chin in his hand. She sighed, smiling.

"Father."

"My little lamb," he said, tracing his finger along her cheek. "Why didn't you tell me you'd arrived?"

"We didn't want to interrupt, father."

"Nonsense." He pressed his rotten lips to hers. "You should've joined us."

A black tear rolled down his daughter's cheek. "I've missed you so much. I never lost the faith. I prayed to our lord, and I heard you calling to me. I did everything you asked."

"I know, my lamb. I know. You did good, darlin'. You made your daddy proud." He turned to Zeke. "I'm proud of you both."

"Thanks, Papa."

Jacob looked to Bobby Tate and frowned. "I can't say I'm proud of you, child. You took up the mantle of a false god while the grave held me."

"I was wrong, father. I've renounced the faith of the heretics. There is only your will and the Old Ways. They are one. Forever."

Jacob lifted his chin, peering at Bobby with a hint of pride. "I knew you'd see the light, boy."

Susan leaned her head against Zeke's shoulder. A sliver of earth dripped from her right nostril, followed by a plump worm. The invertebrate fell on the asphalt with a sick plop. "What do we do now, Daddy?"

"We rebuild the church, darlin'." He looked back to the cars where Laura sat crying to herself, cradling the idol of their lord in her lap. "We finish what was begun when you were all just babes. We finish the sacrament…starting with the blood of the damned."

Jacob went to Laura and took the idol from her trembling hands. The stone effigy burst into flames in his palm. He willed himself free of the earth, pulled into the air by the power of his god, and hovered above the bonfire once more. For as far as he could see, naked bodies writhed and squirmed over one another down the concourse of Main Street, tirelessly copulating in a parted sea of flames.

"No more," he said, and they obeyed their savior. From the next street over, the sing-song worship of Stauford's youth overpowered the stark silence on Main Street. Jacob lorded over them like the avenging angel his father only dreamed of being.

"The path of the Chosen is gilded in fire, forged in blood, and patterned across the bones of the damned." He lifted his free hand to the air as he'd done every Sunday morning, marching back and forth along the length of the pulpit. "Do you love your lord?"

The people of Stauford raised their hands. *"Yes!"*

"You've all suffered for your salvation, but I ask you, brothers and sisters, would you *die* for your lord?"

They fell to their knees, supplicants to a darker will, their minds crawling with an infection of the earth, their hearts writhing nests of blackened worms. *"Yes!"*

"Would you walk into the fires of Hell to make amends for your sins? Would you rend your flesh and carve penitence into your bones?" He raised the burning idol and willed his lord another sacrifice. "Would you feed your soul to God to sate His hunger? *Would you?*"

"*Hallelujah,*" they chanted, rising to their feet once more.

Jacob smiled. "Then I beseech you, brothers and sisters, would you *prove* your devotion?"

"*Amen,*" they said, thousands of voices echoing down the fiery chamber of Stauford's last living artery. "*Your will and the Old Ways are one, Father Jacob.*"

One by one, the people of Stauford willingly strolled into the flames of their burning city. They did not cry out in agony, but instead sang the old hymns of the church. "*Give me that old-time religion,*" they cheered amidst the crackling hellfire, their flesh bubbling, blackening, slowly peeling from bone. "*It's good enough for me!*"

Behind the bonfire, Laura Tremly climbed to her feet, steadying herself against the open car door. Blood trickled down her legs, causing her hospital gown to stick to her thighs. She shuffled slowly to the edge of the bonfire, raised her hands to the flames, and slowly walked into the heat. She caught Jacob's eye as she threw herself upon the pile of cinders.

Jacob watched her burn until her body was ash. *I love my god more.*

5

Imogene approached the clearing, now little more than an overgrown hill sprouting from the wilderness. The flagstones they'd used to mark the path up the hill were still there, shrouded in tall weeds, and several of their torch holders remained, jutting from the earth like broken bones.

When she was a little girl, her father told her stories about the woods outside of town, how they were haunted by living shadows. As an adult, she thought her father's stories were just that: stories told to scare a little girl from wandering too far away from their home. Now she knew the truth, having witnessed the shapes haunting between the trees, a void given form and presence.

She stood alone in the clearing, listening to the absence of sound. Here there were no crickets, no chirping birds, no call of cicadas or locusts. The void was here, all around her, and with the insight gifted to her by the grave, she finally understood the stories of her childhood. Shadows dripped from the limbs of the tallest trees, folding in upon themselves as they skirted away from the failing light, watching her from beyond the safety of the forest. Their eyes shimmered, their voices like waves crashing upon a shore, and from deep within the earth came a vibrating hum.

Welcome home. Your lord has waited so long for your return, child.

Imogene steeled herself, took air into her dead lungs out of impulse, and marched forward through the overgrowth. The earth moved before her, alive with skittering insects and other vermin, driven to the surface by the hum from within. Black worms reached up from the ground like earthen cilia, slipping along her ankles. Ants crawled over one another, joined by centipedes and beetles, forming a writhing river of carapaces and limbs all the way up the hill. They crunched underfoot as she made her way to the summit.

What do you hope to accomplish, child?

"Your end."

The earth grumbled and shook with a low chortle of dissonant voices, the sound of many screaming as one, mocking her purpose, her drive.

There is nothing for you here, child. My son has won. Your journey is for nothing.

The insects were drowned by a viscous sludge seeping up from the soil, forming a black river oozing down the hillside like a lava flow. Imogene walked among them, feeling the tickle of insects squirming along her skin as the sludge anointed her feet. She'd felt this once before, long ago before Jackie and the others were born.

You remember the Old Ways. Once you have seen, you cannot unsee, you cannot unknow. Your lord is with you, always.

A slow-motion movie reel of heated regret, embarrassment, and hate flashed before her. Pastor Jacob had called a special sermon. They'd all arrived to discover the church aglow in lamplight, their faithful pastor sitting at the pulpit, his clothes caked in dirt and sweat. A massive hole was torn open in the center of the church floor, the pews pushed away, with tools and piles of earth scattered about.

"There's a temple below us, my lambs. A true temple of our faith, and on its walls is a testament far older than the one I've preached to you every Sunday. I want to show it to you, if you'll let me."

She mouthed his words silently as she walked the black carpet of sin leading her up the hill, recounting the moment she made her greatest mistake. She chose silence in the face of Jacob's madness like everyone else, and the decision cost her Laura, almost cost her Jackie, and in the end, it cost her life.

Oh, child, you came so willingly into my temple.

She lowered her chin, staring intently at the top of the hill. Yes, she'd followed her friends down into the temple below. Yes, she'd listened to

Jacob spout the teachings of a new scripture. And in her heart, she wanted to speak up, to shout down his madness and wake her friends from this horrible spell he'd cast on them all, but—

Your fear was so delicious, child.

Imogene closed her eyes. She was terrified as Jacob's devotion transformed into obsession, and later, into pure madness. By then, she'd given nearly everything to his cause—her life, her daughter, her reputation—all in the name of a god she was too frightened not to believe in. Not for fear of divine retribution, but for what might happen to her here on this plane of existence. When Jacob made his intentions known among the community—

"The Old Ways demand innocent blood be spilled upon our lord's altar."

—she'd finally found her voice, rallied the few sane friends she had left, and stood against him.

She opened her eyes and carried on.

When she reached the summit, Imogene surveyed the church's foundation. Here, the liquid of the abyss dissipated, seeping back into the ashen pit, leaving behind the trampled weeds, rotted timbers, and cracked foundation stones. Someone had left a sign to warn others about the opening in the ground, but it lay on its side now, its bright neon pink letters obscured in the tall grass. A series of ruts in the earth led away from the opening, revealing where her adversary emerged. On the far end of the old foundation, she spotted a blood-soaked hand protruding from the weeds.

Imogene recognized him, had seen his face in the newspaper more than a handful of times for various arrests. Possession, mostly, or the occasional DUI. Waylon Parks's reputation was widely known across Stauford, one of the bad apples from the other side of Moore Hill. Last she'd heard, little Ezekiel had fallen in with this low-life. She examined his bloody face, forever frozen in a twisted agony of terror, and the cavern of his chest cavity.

Jacob was hungry, she thought, thankful to have been spared from such desires. She did wonder, though, if more time in the grave would've given her an unearthly appetite. Her two weeks were nothing compared to Jacob's thirty-plus years.

The earth shivered beneath her feet.

You have come all this way, child. Would you come further and pay tribute to your lord? Let us commune.

She turned from Waylon's corpse and approached the tear in the earth. A soft halo of light pierced the darkness below, illuminating the rungs of their old extension ladder. Down there were the bones of countless innocent children, sacrificed at a stone altar to appease a nameless god, joining a sculpture of worship as part of a dark tradition that went back for centuries. Others tried to contain this place, sealing it one brick at a time, covering it with earth as they covered their dead.

They sealed it, she realized, *because they couldn't destroy it.*

The thought troubled her, and doubt needled its way into her mind. Her resolve was stronger, her faith unshaken, and she threw off the shackles of fear attempting to root her to the earth.

Imogene descended the ladder, taking one rung at a time. This time, she hoped, would be the last.

CHAPTER TWENTY-THREE

1

Riley snapped awake when Chuck cut the BMW's engine. He sat up, bleary-eyed and panicked, his heart gearing up for a marathon. Fading fragments of a dream still hung before him, slowly transitioning into the car's leather seats, the two men sitting in them, the dense row of trees beyond the safety of the windshield, and the concerned, curly haired lady sitting next to him.

"You okay, Riley?"

"Yeah," he told her, wiping a slick film of drool from his cheek. He looked at her shirt sleeve, saw a dark spot in the fabric, and blushed. "Sorry about that."

"Not the first time I've been spit on. You were sleeping so well, I didn't want to make you move."

"Thanks." He rubbed his eyes and peered out the window. The sun set behind the trees, filtering between them like jagged slits of fire, and fireflies rose from the tall weeds at the road's edge. He tried to remember the dream he was having, but all he could recall was something about shadows and eyes. Especially the eyes. Blue orbs hovered in the dark, peering at him from some great cavern, and whatever they belonged to was calling his name.

"Looks like we aren't alone." Chuck pointed straight ahead. There was a pickup truck parked near the end of the gravel turnabout. Its windows were open and its driver was missing. "Do you think it's your grandma?"

"No way of knowing until we get there." Jack turned in his seat. "I'm guessing neither of you ever came back out here?"

"No way," Chuck said. "Those years when we were kids was enough for me, man. You couldn't pay me to come back. I mean…" He looked out the window, shook his head. "This place hasn't changed at all. Christ, not one bit."

Stephanie sighed. "I did. Once. I was home from college for a weekend. My roommate, Lizzy Warner, talked me into taking her to see where it all went down, so I brought her out here to shut her up. We got as far as the shacks. I wouldn't go farther than that." She looked out the window to her right, where the overgrown trailhead disappeared into the forest. "I'm still not sure if I can."

Jack turned to Riley, offered a thin smile. "What about you? I can't imagine your old man ever brought you out here to go hiking."

"No way. Dad told me if he ever found out I was out here, he'd ground me for the rest of my life." Riley paused, thinking about their conversation. "I asked him what was out here. He told me it's nothing, just a void."

Silence fell over them, the air inside the car too hot, suffocating. Stephanie opened her door, prompting her brothers to do the same. For a moment, Riley wondered what it was he'd said, but he understood as soon as he opened his door. The air was different here, possessed with an unnatural stillness as though time itself were standing in place. There was no breeze, no sound of animals or insects. Now he understood his father's ominous statement.

He stared at the gravel turnabout where the truck was parked. *It's a fucking dead end,* he thought, smirking. He was struck with an urge to text Ben, but his heart sank when he realized his error.

"Riley?"

Stephanie watched him from the other side of the car. He forced a smile. "What's up?"

"You okay?"

"Yeah. I'm…taking it all in. You know?"

She nodded. "Got it."

He watched her tie back her curly hair, noticed the way her hands were shaking, and felt a little better knowing she was as terrified as he was. Jack and Chuck walked around to the back of the car and opened the trunk.

An Army surplus duffel bag filled out the BMW's trunk space.

"I invested in one of these bug-out bags a few years ago," Chuck said. He unzipped the duffel, revealing a first-aid kit, a carrying case for a second handgun, four heavy-duty flashlights, a jumbo pack of batteries, road flares, and several loaded magazines. At a glance, Riley thought there was enough ammunition to start a small war, but even with all their hardware, he didn't think they were any better off. They were as ill-prepared now as they were back at Jack's house—except now they were exhausted, hungry, and capable of shooting each other by mistake.

"So…this is it." Chuck reached in, opened the carrying case, and retrieved his second handgun. He offered it to the group. "Any takers?"

None of them volunteered, exchanging uneasy glances among one another. Riley hesitated, considered holding out his hand, but Stephanie's gaze stopped him. She stared at him intently, forcing the smile of a terrified mother.

Chuck sighed. "Someone needs to take this."

Stephanie reached out and took the weapon from her brother.

"You know how to use this?"

She pulled the slide, chambered a round. "No, I was too busy cooking and birthing babies to learn how to shoot, Mr. Patriarchy."

They shared a nervous laugh together, but his aunt's levity did little to quell the dread growing in Riley's gut. Minutes later, Jack slung the duffel strap over his shoulder and walked to the edge of the road, tramping down the weeds at the foot of the trailhead.

Riley watched him move, watched the careful hesitation in his mannerisms, the uncertainty in his steps. *He's terrified,* the boy realized, looking from Jack to Chuck to Stephanie. *God, they all are.*

When Jack looked back at them all, he did so with pale resignation, his eyes pleading silently for this to be over. His uncle didn't say anything, only looked at each of them for a moment before clicking on his flashlight and forging ahead into the forest. Chuck did the same, crunching across a carpet of dead leaves and weeds without a word.

Stephanie followed but hesitated at the tree line and turned back to her nephew. She held out her hand. "I don't have any breadcrumbs to show you the way."

Smiling, Riley took her hand and followed her into the dark.

2

Stauford's children returned to Main Street to watch the adults slowly roast in the flames. They were drawn to the spectacle with the same fascination as children at a carnival, wide-eyed and agape with awe. Their lord set them free, and they danced barefoot in the streets to celebrate the dawn of a new age. An age of their lord to mark the decline of the heretic god and the beginning of a paradise on earth. *Their* paradise.

And it would all take root here in Stauford before spreading across the world like the most tenacious of vines.

They frolicked from one end of Main Street to the other, dancing between the walls of flame and the skeletal remains of the town's structures, the desecrated temples of Stauford's false gods. From South Stauford, where the remains of the high school collapsed in upon itself, to the central part of town where First Baptist was now long gone, and to the north where the bank, the radio station, the newspapers, and other businesses were still burning, the seeds of Babylon rejoiced and sang the praises of the lord in the earth. The nameless void. The smiling god of their dreams, calling them home to an ocean underground, beneath a darkened sky of eyes and teeth.

Their lord's apostle beckoned them to his pulpit of fire. They answered his call, young and older children alike, skipping along in sing-song fashion while the flesh of their elders blistered, cracked, and slipped from bone in charred sheets.

Ben Taswell and Toby Gilpin were among the crowd. Their faces were split open, chunks of bloody flesh held suspended in the air by the dark worms protruding through the viscera. Thick fingers of blackened corruption jutted from their open maws at odd angles, swirling in the air, feeling their way.

Amber Rogers's younger sister, Candy, walked with her eyes suspended inches from her face, held aloft by thick stalks of writhing filth, while her tongue was a nest of crawling worms. Amber herself crawled along the asphalt of Main Street, held upright by a swirling mass of dark tendrils sprouting from between her legs. One of those tendrils wrapped around her waist, snaking up her torso, into her gaping mouth, and down her throat.

Jimmy Cord walked toward the apostle's pulpit with a grin on his face and the blood of his father on his clothes. He'd watched his old man stroll into the burning storefront of Rick's Hardware a mile back. Ronny Cord screamed in glee as the flames ate the flesh from his bones. Jimmy walked on, humming his new father's sacred hymn, and pushed his way to the front of the crowd encircling the bonfire at the end of Main Street.

There, he watched Jacob Masters lead a prayer consecrating the dawning of their new age. When he finished, the children shouted "Amen!" as loud as they could, and Jimmy joined them. The Old Ways stirred something in Jimmy's soul, something he always felt but could never voice. A need to free the primal creature living below his skin. To be free of society's restrictions. To rend and tear, to bleed, to taste, to fuck and devour. Jimmy raised his hands in the air, "feeling the spirit" as his daddy used to say, and pledged his devotion to their lord's apostle.

A great surge of heat filled his face, following the blackened veins around his eyes and cheeks, spreading along the ridge of his jaw and into the chasm of his throat. A cluster of black worms erupted from his Adam's apple, splitting his gullet in half. Clumps of soil and writhing insects spewed from the wound, crawling over his body, cocooning his face in a helmet of skittering limbs. He fell to his knees and praised his god, hallelujah.

"And now, my little lambs," Jacob went on, "I must return to our lord's temple and complete the rites as dictated in the Old Ways. Rejoice, for tomorrow we begin anew."

Their lord's apostle turned to the trio at his side. Susan, Zeke, and Bobby led their father back to one of the cars and piled inside. Minutes later, they were on their way home to Devil's Creek.

3

They reached the footbridge as the sunlight finally failed them, draping the forest in thick shadows. Jack led the way, his flashlight beam bobbing along the ground in tandem with his steps, but Chuck discovered he still remembered the way. The trail took a hard turn up ahead at a pair of elm trees, ran down a small slope, and into a gully where the creek babbled away in the dark.

Shouldn't have lied, Chuck thought as they neared the bridge, but supposed it didn't matter. Like Stephanie, he'd come home one weekend from school, had a few drinks, decided he was bold and brave enough to confront his demons, and drove stupidly all the way out here to do so.

The legend of the place was in full swing back then, the turnabout lined with cars and trucks belonging to stupid kids who all wanted to experience something creepy. Music filled the forest, some forgettable hip hop song, and the trail was teeming with flashlights and laughing teenagers, discarded plastic cups reeking of beer, the crisp forest air suffocated with an acrid haze of pot smoke.

He'd gone as far as the footbridge when something called to him from beyond the trees. The music was still going on, punctuated with the laughter of a party that wouldn't end for hours, and yet he still heard his name amidst all the noise. *Charles,* the voice said, which was enough to give him pause. Curious, Chuck stepped off the trail and followed the creek toward the sound of his name.

The passage of time erased any sense of distance from his memory. Chuck couldn't remember how far or for how long he'd walked into the dark, but what he did remember were two beady blue eyes in the distance, peeking from behind a gnarled tree on the edge of the water. Its roots were exposed, and half the trunk hollowed out, frozen forever in an expression of anger.

Charles, welcome home.

He couldn't remember what drew his attention to the limbs above. Maybe it was the appearance of blue light, or maybe it was the movement of shadows, the dark separating from itself and taking on formations in the void. When he looked up, dozens of sapphire eyes peered down at him. He stumbled backward and fell into the creek bed. The shadows laughed, mocking his terror while he splashed his way out of the water.

Never again, he'd vowed, and yet here he was, standing on the footbridge once more. He pointed the flashlight toward the water and spotted the hollowed-out tree. The trunk now lay collapsed to the side of the creek bed, its dead roots jutting out over the water.

"Chuck?"

He looked up, straining to see Stephanie's face in the failing light.

"Yeah?"

"You all right?"

He nodded. "Just thinking. Come on, let's get going."

Stephanie frowned, made to say something but decided against it, and turned to join Jack and Riley beyond the bridge.

Chuck turned back toward the creek, pointing his flashlight into the shadows, expecting to see eyes. There were none, but in the back of his mind, he heard the hushed voice repeating itself. *Charles, welcome home.*

4

A quarter mile from the footbridge, they encountered their former compound. Two wooden posts marked the entrance, one on either side of the overgrown trail, and both were almost consumed by crawling ivy. The metal hooks which once held lanterns were long gone, the wood too rotten to hold them. Stephanie smiled when she saw them. She and Zeke used to race each other through the village every night, eager to be the first to light the way for any lost souls stumbling in the dark.

Father Jacob told them they served a higher purpose, their births signaled the spark of a new light for all, and to young Stephanie Green, she took that meaning literally. Carrying the lantern to the edge of the village every evening was the best part of her day.

She'd told this story to her roommate, Lizzy, the day they'd hiked beyond the footbridge. Standing now at the edge of her former home, while her brothers and her nephew forged on ahead, Stephanie remembered the look on Lizzy's face when she'd drunkenly admitted to being part of a cult. Of course, there was alcohol involved, so much Stephanie couldn't recall parts of the conversation as their night went on, but she did remember two things: telling Lizzy about her childhood and fumbling her way into a kiss. The retelling of her childhood was the awkward part.

Riley pointed his flashlight at her feet. "Steph? You coming?"

"Yeah. I'll catch up in a sec."

The forest had grown over the trail even more, leaves and weeds blanketing the earth before them, but the other lamp markers were where they'd left them all those years ago. Lizzy's voice spoke in her head, in a shrill bubblegum pitch of innocence Stephanie once found so endearing. *"So you lived out here with, like, no electricity? No running water?"*

No, Stephanie told her, *the adults had forsaken those things.* She didn't experience modern amenities like warm showers or microwaved food until she was older, after the church burned to the ground. She didn't dare tell her roommate about the circumstances, though.

Up ahead, Stephanie saw the first of the metal shacks, its flimsy surface marred with rust and graffiti. Someone had painted a crude Confederate flag on one side. A stark white swastika glowed beneath the beam of her flashlight, and she turned away when she realized what it was. Riley, Chuck, and Jack were farther along, chatting amongst themselves, peeking into a few of the sagging structures.

Poor Lizzy, she thought. This was where their hike stopped, where their budding relationship ended before it even began.

The details were fuzzy—what they'd talked about on the drive down to Stauford, what they'd eaten for lunch—and the event nearly twenty years gone by that point, but other things jumped out of her memory with pure clarity. When the living shadow emerged from one of the shacks, Stephanie hadn't seemed all that surprised, as if its appearance was expected.

Lizzy wasn't prepared for it, though. She laughed off Stephanie's warnings, and because Stephanie had a thing for her, because they might've fooled around that night for the first and only time, she'd acquiesced when Lizzy suggested they visit the old compound.

Stephanie pointed her light at the next shack on the trail, its roof caved in, the rusty metal walls covered in vines. The shadow had emerged from there, extracting itself from the dark the way oil separates from water, slipping into their reality without a sound. The impossible thing towered over the two women, standing nearly eight feet tall when it was done forming itself into being, and looked down at them with bright blue eyes.

We knew you'd return, little Stephanie. Your father sleeps with Us in the earth. Will you join him?

She remembered Lizzy's shriek, the way the poor girl backed away from the dark creature like a terrified child, toddling backward until she lost her balance and fell. The living shadow turned away from Stephanie, looking down at the hapless creature crawling through a mound of dead leaves. Lizzy screamed, crying out for Stephanie to help her to her feet, only Stephanie was running by that point.

"Hey, Steph?"

She took her eyes off the collapsed shack and looked down the path at her brothers. Jack shook his flashlight to get her attention.

"Yeah, sorry. I'm coming."

"You'd better look at this," he said.

Stephanie nodded, trudging through years of dead leaves past the old shack. She couldn't remember who'd lived there—one of the deacons, maybe—but supposed it didn't matter now because they were long dead. As she walked toward them, Stephanie's mind wandered back to her roommate. Lizzy wandered out of the woods half an hour after their encounter, shivering, her running mascara painting her face like a harlequin. Stephanie sat in the front seat of the car, crying. Her roommate never said what happened after Stephanie left her there, and Stephanie never asked. A week later, Lizzy broke their lease and moved out. They hadn't spoken since, and Stephanie thought it was for the best.

Walking toward the boys, she felt the familiar urge to turn and run. The impulse to tear off into the forest, take their car, and speed away from Stauford as fast as possible was paramount—but she was older now, maybe even stronger. And while Jack and Chuck could handle themselves, there was still Riley to think about. She wouldn't leave him for the world. Whatever was waiting for them down in the bowels of Calvary Hill, she would find the courage to face it—if not for herself, then for her nephew.

"What did you find?"

Chuck turned to her, was almost smiling. "You won't believe this."

She peered into the open shack. Jack's flashlight lit up the small room. At least a dozen propane tanks sat on the floor, along with several containers of chemicals, tubing, matches, and a camping stove.

"A meth lab," she said. "Or what was going to be one."

Jack stepped inside and lifted one of the tanks. "It's full," he grunted, returning the tank to the floor. "Shit, I bet they all are."

When Jack looked up at them, Stephanie found she couldn't help but smile. She stepped inside. "You're still a troublemaker, Jackie. Thank the gods for that."

5

Unlike his siblings, Jack never felt the need to return to his birthplace. Growing up here was enough. Stauford always felt haunted to him, but Devil's Creek was a living nightmare always one step behind him no matter how far he ran. They were marked by this place, a fact which uncovered a deeply rooted anger in his youth. Thousands in therapy bills helped him tame the anger. He'd learned to channel it into his art, building a career and a small fortune on the back of his pain, but the anger was still there, the fire still burning. Revisiting this place stoked the fire inside. Everything that happened to him here—to them all—poisoned his life, his soul.

Walking down this backwoods rendition of Main Street USA, Jack came to understand everything he was began here. The last several decades of trial and ridicule, anxiety and depression, his whole life a road atlas of misery that inevitably led back to this godforsaken place. His obsession with the macabre. His distrust of authority. His disdain for religion. All of it began here in this ground zero of sadness and agony, a mecca of madness and a monument to one man's hubris. The compound of Devil's Creek, the Lord's Church of Holy Voices, and Calvary Hill were all part of a greater cancerous mass on the earth that had to be excised.

Finding the meth lab might have been merely fortuitous but Jack chose to believe otherwise. If he and his siblings were here for any purpose at all, if there was any sense of justice in this chaotic universe, this had to be it. The circumstances were too perfect for him to believe otherwise. He'd never felt such conviction for anything else in his whole life.

Jack lifted one of the propane tanks again and carried it outside.

Stephanie followed him out. "Jack, you've got that look on your face. What are you plannin' to do?"

He set down the tank with a heavy thump and shook off the sting from his fingers.

"Come on," Chuck said. "Out with it. What's on your mind?"

Jack nodded, grinning. "Let's blow it up." He didn't wait for them to protest. "I don't know about you guys, but this place has haunted me for as long as I can remember. Every bad thing I can remember started in the temple below that hill over there." He pointed toward the clearing up ahead. "Whatever god our father prays to is down inside that place. I say we cut off the head of the snake now, while we have a chance to do it."

"This is insane. All of you are insane," Chuck said, sighing. "But we don't have much else to lose, do we?"

Stephanie smiled. She turned back and pointed her flashlight inside the shack at the other propane tanks. "Do you think this will be enough?"

"I have no idea," Jack said. "But it's worth trying with the flares in Chuck's duffel bag. At the very least, it'll make me feel better." He looked down at his nephew, nudged the boy's shoulder and grinned. "Come on. Let's go blow up this motherfucker."

6

Jack grimaced as he lugged the propane tank up the hill, following the remains of a footpath reclaimed by nature. The hill itself was steeper than he remembered, but he was also much older, much heavier than he'd been the last time he climbed to the summit. The tank in his hands didn't help matters.

When he reached the pinnacle, Jack dropped the tank and looked back at the three white beams bobbing up the hillside. Satisfied, he trained his flashlight along the ground, searching for the tear in the earth. He hadn't thought much further ahead than blowing up the temple; after climbing the hill, he wondered if a dozen propane tanks would be enough to destroy the masonry entombed within. Doubt crept in, voiced by his late mother.

You dumb little shit, always thinking with your heart and never thinking things through. What possessed you to think you could blow up something as ancient as this place? Your daddy's god is eternal, child.

Jack shook his head. "Nothing is eternal. Everything burns." He thought back to his grandmother's home, felt a pang of regret in his gut. Maybe the tanks wouldn't be enough, but they had to try. Whoever built the temple managed to keep the nameless thing contained for centuries. There had to be a way, and he wouldn't give up until he found it—or until he was dead.

He followed the perimeter of the church's crumbled foundation, searching for the entrance to the temple below. The last thing he wanted was to fall in and break his neck. He followed the cracked stones, stepping over patches of weeds and charred timbers. A sound caught his attention as he neared the far end, a churning hum feeding into itself, rising and falling in pitch.

"Jack, did you find it yet?"

Chuck dropped the propane tank at his feet with a huff. Jack turned, shone his flashlight on his brother's reddened face. "Not yet."

Something lit up in the corner of his eye. A faint light seeping from the earth, rising and falling in time with the cyclical hum rumbling within. He pointed his flashlight toward the rift. Thick clumps of earth surrounded the opening, sprouting weeds that crisscrossed one another in a pale green weave.

"Hey," Jack called out. "It's over here but be careful." He knelt near the hole and planted his flashlight into the silt of ashen earth, its beam splitting the night. "Don't go past that light."

"That's fine." Chuck was doubled over, heaving for breath. "I'm gonna wait here a minute." Stephanie and Riley joined him a moment later, adding to the cluster of tanks at the opposite end of the foundation.

The humming ceased, and a voice echoed from the dark below. The sound woke every hair on his neck and covered his arms in gooseflesh.

Singing. Someone was singing down there about the walls of Jericho. A dozen memories flashed before him, each one of his grandmother on her riding lawnmower, singing at the top of her lungs while grass clippings flew in all directions, *"And the walls came tumbling down."*

Mamaw?

Even with all the impossible horror he'd witnessed in the last 24 hours, the mere thought his dead grandmother was down there tested his sanity.

"Jack, are you coming?"

He turned back, saw the trio of shadows at the far end of the hill. Stephanie placed her hands on her hips, waiting impatiently.

"Yeah," he said, "I'll be there in a minute." He hesitated. *I'm going to climb down and check something out,* he wanted to say, but thought better of it. He heard mutterings between them, certain Chuck was voicing his complaints. They would try to stop him, and none of them had time for another debate. Somewhere out there beyond the forest, he was certain his father was on his way back here to finish what he'd started. If the bastard's communion with the god below their feet granted him any kind of omniscience, then he was most certainly on his way to stop them now.

He reached out, fingertips poised for the ladder, when the supports shuddered and creaked—and a pale face appeared in the opening. Jack fell back into the weeds with a shrill cry, his breath stuck in his throat behind the beating of his racing heart.

"Jack?" Stephanie now, her soft footfalls racing across the hillside toward him. Chuck and Riley joined her, and they watched in terror as a figure emerged from the pit below. Jack scuttled backward, desperately trying to crawl away from whatever was climbing out of the temple.

Together, the quartet watched the lone figure emerge, dust itself off, and turn toward them. Shaking, Riley trained the flashlight beam on the figure's face. One of her eyes was milky white, the other a bright piercing blue, and her silver hair shimmered in the light. She looked at them all and smiled.

"My babies," Imogene said.

CHAPTER TWENTY-FOUR

1

Oh, Genie, you couldn't leave well enough alone, could you?

Jacob felt her presence as they neared the turnoff for Devil's Creek Road, felt it like a needle driven into the back of his skull. They'd both given themselves over to the grave following the rites drafted by the nameless gods of the void, and through their pact they were bound on opposite ends of the same cosmic string. He hadn't thought much of her in the beginning, when they were still tainted by the words of a false god, but as the years progressed, Jacob found himself continually surprised by Martha Imogene Tremly. She'd proven herself resourceful if nothing else, and in a grim sort of way, he admired her.

Reversing the binding ritual was a clever gambit on her part. He'd gone to the grave with the satisfaction of knowing his time there was temporary. That Imogene would be the last of the six did not surprise him; that she'd divined her own way of cheating death by bargaining with the void, however, not only surprised him, but impressed the hell out of him.

I didn't think you had it in you, darlin'.

Imogene was the consummate Christian lady. She always sat on the front pew, never missed a Sunday sermon, was the first to lead the choir in song. After his revelation, she'd followed Jacob's teachings to the letter, never batting an eye when he asked for her daughter to conceive a child, and later, always looking away when he had his way with her grandson in the bowels of the temple. No, Imogene was nothing more than another mindless sheep in his flock, a follower through and through.

Up ahead, the car's headlights lit up the front of the old barn. Jacob smiled, tracing his gnarled fingers along the contours of the idol on his lap. He turned to Zeke, who sat behind the wheel, and then to Bobby and Susan in the backseat. They met him with smiles of their own, eyes alight. Soon, they would return home, and he would lead his family back into the belly of their living god.

2

Jack climbed to his feet, unable to look away. He thought he was ready to face the possibility she'd returned to life, but now that she was standing before him, he found he could barely keep his composure. Tears crept in from the corners of his eyes, the hot sting forcing him to wipe them away with an errant hand.

"Jackie," Imogene said. She shuffled around the rift, the cuffs of her baggy jeans dragging the dirt, and her loose shirt slipped down one shoulder. She held out her hands, and Jack took them without hesitation.

"Mamaw," he croaked. His jaw quivered as he fought back the surge of tears. She put her hand on his cheek.

"No tears, Jackie. We ain't got time. But, my goodness, I missed you somethin' awful. Let me give you a squish."

She pulled him close, wrapped her arms around him, and he was assaulted by the stench of the grave, but he did not care. He didn't get to say goodbye when it mattered. Now, even by the cruelest of fates, he had the chance once more and would not let it go. Jack put his arms around her, held on tight, and finally freed the tears from his eyes. The world around them disappeared, his brother and sister and nephew gone for only a moment, and he was ten years old again, holding on desperately to the only mother he'd ever loved.

"I told you not to cry," she said softly. "I can't cry with you. This body ain't what it used to be."

Imogene stepped back, wiped the tears from his face, and smiled. "You've done good for yourself, Jackie. I knew you'd make your mamaw proud." She turned to Stephanie and Chuck, and then down to Riley. "You've all done good."

The three of them stood there in cautious awe, afraid to accept what they were seeing, afraid not to. Chuck reached out and pressed his finger against the old woman's shoulder, recoiling when he felt the cold tightness of dead flesh.

Imogene grinned. "Ever the Doubting Thomas. Yes, it's really me, Chuckie. I never did thank you for helpin' me with my affairs. I trust you followed my instructions to the letter."

He nodded, hesitant to speak. Jack took the burden from him. "He did, and your friend Tyler helped, too."

"So he did. How is the old man?"

"Mamaw, he…he didn't make it."

A cool breeze swept past them, stirring the weeds into a hushed whisper, the whole hillside alive with conspiracy. Imogene studied his face. "How?"

Jack told her what happened, about Laura, the fire, the idol. When he told her about how Tyler died, a sharp cracking sound erupted from her mouth, her molars shattering as she clenched her jaw in anger. Imogene turned away from them, contemplating the encroaching darkness.

"That old fool," she whispered, and turned back to them all. "You shouldn't have come back here. None of you. If Jacob has the idol—"

Her head cocked to one side, listening to a slow murmuring coming from within the earth. At first, Jack heard nothing but the whisper of the wind through the weeds and leaves, the groan of old limbs rattled loose in the trees. But as he trained his ears, he *did* hear something else—a chorus of voices singing a language he didn't know but found so familiar. They were children's voices, cherubic and innocent, speaking in tongues with sing-song cadence. *Angels within the earth,* he thought, wondering if the phrase was culled from a childhood memory. When he turned to the others, he saw they heard it, too.

The ground trembled beneath them. A pale light erupted from the opening, piercing the night like a beacon, the old temple calling its people home. Imogene met their stares, frowning.

"Your father is near. We don't have much time."

3

Imogene's dead heart ached, knowing no amount of time with her grandson would ever be enough. She was here by the grace of a contract with the universe, and her time was fleeting. There was so much she wanted to tell them, so much knowledge of the cosmos to share from her brief time in the grave, but her adversary's presence interrupted the little time they had together.

When panic fell across their weary faces, Imogene saw them not as adults, but as the doe-eyed children she remembered fondly. She found herself torn between the bargain she'd made during the cleansing ritual and the maternal desire to shield her babies from the onslaught of their dreadful father.

Jacob was near. So near the idol's presence opened the rift down below. She'd thought her communion with the dark being entombed within would be enough to open it on her own, but the hours of meditation and incantation left her feeling drained, and she'd needed to collect her thoughts, think of another way. Finding her grandson and his siblings at the surface was a shock, albeit a welcome one.

But her true purpose called to her from below. Her time outside the grave was limited and not without cause, a deal struck for the sake of shared interest.

The enemy of my enemy, she thought, casting a side-eyed glance toward the stars above. Jack was talking to her now, his words spilling over one another. Something about a plan to blow up the hill, something involving the tanks of gas they'd found in the old village in the woods, but Imogene wasn't really listening. Her ear was tuned to the subtle murmurings echoing from within the temple, the hypnotic inhalations of the thing sleeping in the safety of its own reality.

She'd hoped to keep the idol as far away from here as possible, but now this setback could prove to be a boon after all. In the moments between her warning and Jack's explanation of his plan, Imogene made up her mind on what to do. She waited, and when Jack finished telling her about his intentions, she nodded in agreement. "While y'all are getting those tanks, I'll head back down to get things ready."

Jack looked at her for a moment, puzzled by her reply, but she didn't give him a chance to question her. Instead, she wrapped her arms around him, pulled him close, and pressed her dry lips to his cheek.

"I'm proud of you," she whispered, "and I love you more 'n anything, kiddo. Don't you ever forget that."

He returned her embrace, and while he was reciprocating his love, she slipped the folded piece of paper into his pocket. A moment later, they were on their way back down the hill to gather the rest of their arsenal. Imogene waited until they were gone before returning to the ladder. A vacuous hum erupted from within. One way or another, she'd end this for good. A greater purpose was at stake here, and she prayed Jackie would forgive her when it was all said and done.

4

Chuck's second trip carrying a propane tank up the hill was far worse than the first, and by the time he was on his third go-round, a stitch opened in his gut. Years of sitting behind a desk every day and having dinner every night at Devlin's—washed down with a beer or three—took their toll on the burgeoning attorney. He held an image of his treadmill in his mind with every aching step, its usage falling behind on the trail of good intentions.

Compounding the aches and pains was an anxiety building in his head and chest. A list of questions rattled off in his mind as he trudged across the clearing toward the forest once again, following Riley's flashlight trail into the dark.

Were they sure all these gas tanks would be enough to level the temple inside the hill? No.

Had Jack ever done this before? No.

Had any of them, for that matter? No.

Could they trust the reanimated corpse of Martha Imogene Tremly? To be determined.

Chuck stood at the bank of weeds near a poplar tree. He looked back, watching Jack and Stephanie's silhouettes hobbling up the hillside, their propane tanks in tow. Their flashlight beams bobbed like errant spirits, darting across the landscape, and for a moment Chuck wondered if he'd lost his mind.

You let them talk you into this, he thought. *You should've left when you had the chance.* If he'd had his way, they would be well on their way to Landon by now—hell, maybe even Richmond or Lexington, checking off the miles along I-75. They could've made an anonymous call to the state police barracks in Landon. They could've, maybe they should've, but none of that mattered now. Here he was in the middle of nowhere, wandering around in the dark. Charles Tiptree had clearly lost his mind.

You have, a voice said, *but it's not too late, Charles. You can turn back. You can slip away into the dark when they aren't looking. Leave them to their fool's errand.*

"Yeah," he muttered to himself, clutching his side as he walked slowly beneath the forest canopy and into absolute darkness. His flashlight cut a slim wedge from the void before him.

What makes you think you can trust the old crone on the hill? Didn't she confide in you? Didn't she help the other grandparents steal the church's money? How could you trust a thief like that? And besides, didn't those rumors of her being a witch turn out to be true, Charles?

"Well, yeah," he mumbled, straining as he lifted his leg and stepped sideways over a rotten log. "But it's Genie, though. She'd never—"

She defied your god, Charles. She's led you astray. Let your father guide you home and fulfill your purpose.

He stopped, suddenly aware of a cold spike driven deep into his gut. No one called him Charles, only his grandfather, and Gage Tiptree had been dead for a decade.

Charles.

He twisted in place, shakily moving the flashlight beam around the forest. Countless trees lit up before him, their trunks buried in the overgrowth, ferns and twigs and poison ivy, clusters of bushes and weeds, a handful of deadfalls, and the trail leading to the village. Chuck was alone except for his nephew, and Riley was much farther along, his light a bulbous white eye hanging in the dark.

"Hey, Riley?"

The boy didn't answer, but the forest spoke for him, the breeze through the leaves filling the night with a low hiss of judgment. A bead of sweat rolled down Chuck's forehead and across the bridge of his nose. He turned back toward the clearing, questioning if he should wait for Stephanie and Jack before venturing off into the dark, but a nagging voice—his own this time—chipped away at his resolve.

What if something's wrong with the kid? What if he needs your help? What if—

Somewhere ahead, twigs snapped in the brush.

"Riley?"

The dark swallowed his voice. He waited, counting to five before calling the boy's name again. Something crackled in the breeze.

You dumb shit. You should've been paying attention. Ah, fuck it. This is ridiculous. We don't have time for hide and seek, kid.

He gathered his wits and trudged forward, following his flashlight toward the shack, trying not to think of the blue-eyed shadows that mocked him years ago. Imogene's ominous warning rang inside his thoughts like a fire alarm: *Your father is near.*

The hollowed corpses of his former home fell into view, spotted with rust and choked with weeds, ivy. Chuck tried to force Imogene's words out of his head, but as he drew closer to the boy's flashlight, he found he could no longer silence them. Riley's light sat perched on the roof of the makeshift meth lab, pointing in the direction of the clearing.

He called the boy's name again, frowning at the trepidation in his voice. The forest said nothing in return. Chuck reached out, took hold of his nephew's flashlight, and was about to turn back when plodding footsteps caught his ear. A figure raced out of the dark, struck him in the shoulder so hard he nearly spun like a top.

Disoriented, Chuck fumbled with the flashlight, the beam darting among the tree trunks and empty shacks until he found the silhouette backing away down the path. Riley's face was pale in the white light, his eyes wide with terror. Sweat glistened on his forehead, and he was trying to say something between gasps of breath.

"Riley, what the hell?"

"Chuck…" the boy stammered. "My dad…coming."

His blood ran cold as Riley's words sank in, and when he turned to look back down the path, he saw the source of his nephew's terror. Four pairs of glowing eyes approached from the shadows, so close Chuck smelled the stench of rancid earth, sweat, and death.

Time slowed, the air thickening to molasses, and a single thought raced through his mind before they were upon him: *Slow 'em down.*

He reached for the handgun tucked into his waistband, pointed it into the air, and fired a single shot. Riley cried out in surprise somewhere behind him, but Chuck could not hear him over the ringing in his ears. The first pair of eyes stepped into the beam of light, revealing his brother Zeke's distorted face. Thick black worms protruded from Zeke's nostrils, a dark fluid streaming from his eyes.

Chuck didn't think. He fired again, blinking at the force of recoil. The shot went wide, ricocheting off a nearby tree with a dull crack. Zeke Billings closed in, gripping the gun barrel, his flesh searing from the heated metal.

As his corrupted brother's hand fell over his face, Chuck Tiptree shrieked his final words into the darkness, hoping his nephew could hear him. *"Riley, run like hell!"*

5

Riley ran as fast as his aching legs would carry him. His heart raced, his head light and fuzzy from a day without meals, but still he pushed on while his muscles screamed for him. *So stupid,* he told himself, the words echoing a mantra in his head to the pace of his frantic heart. *So damn stupid.* And he was, falling victim to the most cliched action this side of a slasher film: he'd heard a noise, and without thinking, gone off to investigate.

Someone whispered from the forest. Hushed voices overlapped one another, like radio chatter played asynchronously, filling out the still spaces all around him. And then a familiar bluish glow caught his eye in the dark, but this was different, hovering higher among the trees.

Afraid of calling attention to himself, he'd placed his flashlight on the roof of the meth lab, waited for his eyes to adjust to the gloom, and crept on ahead into the shadows. By the time he'd reached the center of the village, there were more than two eyes hovering in the air. Dozens, maybe, although he'd had no time to count.

A naked woman emerged from beyond one of the shacks, her pale face illuminated in the glow of her eyes. Three men followed her. One of them looked like his father. Riley turned, caught his foot on an exposed tree root, and stumbled with a shrill yip. He didn't know if they'd heard him, didn't wait to find out, but when he'd regained his footing and raced back toward the beam of light, he heard the soft shuffle of legs rustling through the overgrowth behind him.

And then he'd collided with Chuck, and—

Two gunshots thundered from the dark.

"Riley, run like hell!"

His uncle's words chilled him to his core, flooding his veins with adrenaline and regret. He wanted to turn back and try to save Chuck, but his mother's voice spoke from within. *Keep running, go as fast as you can, you can't help him.* Chuck's gagging cries filled the night.

Tears clouded his vision as he raced from the forest and up the hillside. His muscles burned while a sharp pain stabbed between his ribs, every breath like fire in his lungs, every movement another spike driven deeper into his joints. Stephanie nearly trampled him when he collapsed at her feet. He reached for her, panting for breath, the tears flowing freely down his burning cheeks.

"Riley? I heard gunshots, what's—oh God."

The darkness surrounding the edge of the forest converged, flowing like water between the trees, lit up with the occasional blue eye like fireflies dancing through the air. Four figures emerged from the trail.

Stephanie knelt beside him. "You okay?"

Riley shook his head. "I'm fine, but…" He forced himself to look her in the eye. Her face was glassy through the tears and the sweat, and he all but choked on the word clinging to the inside of his throat. "Chuck."

The boy didn't have to say any more. Stephanie frowned, averting her gaze to the figures standing at the foot of the hill. The world ceased its spin, the air still and heavy, while above the moon and stars judged them silently. At the bottom of the hill, the forest was alive with the sentinels of their father's buried god, the very shadows stretching into gaunt figures towering over creation. They stood among the trees, regarding the trespassers with silence, their eyes shrouding the hillside in sickly light.

Jacob Masters broke away from the group, walking a few steps up the hillside path. He held the idol before him, a talisman burning bright with an impossible flame.

"My darlin' lambs, you ain't got nowhere to run. Why fight the eternal? We only want to share the rewards of salvation with you. All that must be done is sweet suffering in the belly of God." Jacob turned back toward the path. A pair of shadow sentinels parted, and Chuck Tiptree wandered into the clearing. His eyes glowed.

"Amen," Chuck cried.

"Amen," Susan Prewitt said. Zeke joined her, as did Riley's father. When he heard his father shout hallelujah, Riley's gut twisted into a knot.

"Come on," she whispered, helping him to his feet.

"Where are we gonna go? Where *can* we go?" His voice cracked as he tried to swallow back a sob.

"Inside the temple," she said.

"Inside?" He stopped, but she pushed him along, looking back over her shoulder. "I thought we were gonna blow it up?"

But Stephanie didn't say anything, and when he looked back, he saw the dark silhouettes advancing. Riley sucked in his breath and raced after his aunt, wondering what the hell they were going to do, and too afraid to ask.

6

This is all wrong, Jack thought, stepping off the final rung of the ladder. His grandmother wasn't anywhere to be found. She'd climbed down here twenty minutes ago, promising to "get things ready" as they pushed the propane tanks down the shaft. Now she wasn't answering him, and he was alone in the gloom.

He looked down from the earthen pillar where the ladder was extended, marveling at the eerie blue flames flickering along the sconces built into the stone walls of the temple. Shadows danced across the surface, filling in the etched carvings of his father's so-called "Old Ways," lending them the almost animated quality of crude cartoon strips. A cluster of propane tanks were scattered across the ashen floor. Up above, he thought he heard the distant crack of gunfire, but the sound was muffled, fleeting.

"Steph?"

She didn't answer. His heart raced, and the worst memories of his childhood rushed back in a flood of dripping shadows. He remembered his father dragging him down here, landing in the pit of dust and bones, and fracturing his arm in the process. His arm ached now when he thought about it, along the length of his radius, an old wound that never truly healed.

But long before that fateful day, he'd been down here plenty of other times. Times he'd locked away in the back of his mind to protect himself, to protect his sanity. Staring down the chiseled stone steps from the earthen pillar, he remembered his mother dragging him by the hair while he kicked and screamed in protest, remembered the icy fear coursing through his young veins when he first laid eyes on the bones of other children who'd gone before him. Those bones were still here, half-covered in ashen earth. The jawbone and fractured orbit of a child's skull peeked from their home in the dirt. *Hello,* that broken grin said, *won't you join me?*

The echoes of children's screams haunted this forgotten place. He felt their presence with every breath, their unseen eyes watching from beyond this mortal veil, the gravity of souls pressing down upon him, constricting his chest, pushing on his heart.

Jack realized he was holding his breath and exhaled a loud rush of air. All around, the flames shuddered and danced, welcoming him home. The shifting shadows afforded him glimpses of the Old Ways etched into the stone walls, crude glyphs and runes arranged in patterns that made his eyes hurt. A dull throb emerged in the center of his forehead, and he forced himself to look away.

He was struck with an odd thought, watching the shadows dance across the floor. *This is where I was born.* Maybe not in a physical sense, but the soul of everything he'd become was birthed from the womb of this cavern, and he found he wanted nothing more than to burn it to the ground.

When he reached the bottom of the steps, Jack saw prints in the dirt, scattered between the shallow graves of those who'd gone before him. Toward the center of the room was the stone altar on which the idol once sat, its surface still stained with the blood from his father's exit wounds. A mound of dirt sat off to the side of the altar, surrounding the hole where Jacob was buried.

A curtain of shadows parted before him, driven away by a pair of flickering sconces, illuminating an opening in the wall. The breach expunged a gust of sour air, sweeping back his hair, and twisting his guts with its awful stench.

Bare footprints led toward the mouth of the tunnel. *This is where Mamaw must've gone, but…this is impossible.* The air inside wavered as though with heat, yet he felt nothing but a chill emanating from the rift. There was a grim light at the far end. *Like the moon. But that can't be. I'm underground. I'm…*

Home, a voice spoke from beyond the opening. *You are home, child.*

Memories assaulted his mind, biting and scratching their way free from the mental graves in which he'd buried them, harsh ghouls eager to devour his sanity. He remembered his mother carrying him down this passage, the hem of her robe dragging the earth with a soft slipping sound. There was the rancid smell of compost and decay, the breath of a living god that was ageless, nameless, forever. And beyond the corridor, there was a sound of water churning against stones. Tides, maybe, driven to shore by a moon—or was there more than one? Surely there were more. He remembered ill light everywhere, bright enough to illuminate their actions, but it was always shifting, changing, moving to follow them like the gaze of eyes.

Countless eyes. Eyes forever, watching us, guiding our parents to do those awful things. A million eyes in the sky like stars in the cosmos.

Jack remembered the congregation standing at the shore, their faces wrapped in shrouds while his father walked with him into the shallow waters. He remembered the warmth of the liquid, but it wasn't water at all. It was thick like old motor oil, reeking of dirt and something else, something he couldn't place. Something ancient, older than time itself. Something alive.

I will baptize thee in the name of our lord, Jacob said, and Jack remembered looking up at his father with wide-eyed wonder, proud to be a part of something greater than himself. Proud because he knew no different. *And when you are ready, your blood will sate our lord's hunger, and from that great feast a new day will dawn when the scripture of the Old Ways will be known once more.*

Jack stared slack-jawed down the corridor before him, his eyes wrapped in tears, his heart racing so hard his chest ached. All his worst memories, the endless nightmares, were now beckoning to him in the flesh. The place of his baptism was beyond this impossible passage, an anomaly of space that could not exist, leading toward some other place where the moon was alive, the stars were eyes, and the only light was gifted by the god that birthed it.

He wanted to turn and run, to leave everyone behind, race back through the forest to the car, and drive as far away as he could. All his courage drained from him while he faced down the path to his fate. *I can't do this,* he told himself. *I can't. I can't—*

"Jack!"

The ladder rattled from above, and he saw Riley and Stephanie descend from the surface. The boy let go, skipping the last few rungs and landing hard on his feet; his aunt followed a moment after, and together they raced down the stone steps to meet Jack in the center of the room.

"What's wrong? Where's Chuck?"

Riley stammered, blinking tears away while Stephanie shook her head. "They're here, Jack. And Chuck's…"

His sister's tears finally came, and Jack closed his eyes. The strength left his body, his muscles suddenly jelly. "What about the gun?"

Stephanie's face fell as she reached to her waistband. She raised a trembling hand and covered her mouth, shaking her head in disappointment. "I must've dropped it. I can't—fuck, I can't believe I did that."

It's okay, he wanted to say, but there was no time for consolation. He looked back to the opening, praying to whatever was listening that his grandmother was somewhere in there, praying she could save them.

A voice spoke from above, filling the chamber with a roaring echo that flooded his heart with ice water. Jacob Masters peered down from the opening, his cool blue eyes shimmering in the dark.

"My little lambs. I'm so glad you've all come home."

Jack didn't wait. He took Riley and Stephanie by the hand and led them toward their only exit. The corridor shimmered before them with hungry anticipation, and from the other side, a guttural chirr erupted as if in laughter.

CHAPTER TWENTY-FIVE

1

Their flashlights lit the way before them, revealing a floor alive with vermin of the earth. Worms and other insects writhed over every surface, slithering and crawling along a slow tide of the black liquid seeping from the other end of the corridor. The stone walls were covered in a shimmering membranous film like windows in the rain. A smell of salt punctuated the stench in the air.

"How can this place be?" Stephanie's dry voice echoed across the narrow chamber.

"We're underground," Riley said, squeezing her hand. "Why is there light? Do you guys see that?"

"I do," Jack said, catching Stephanie's stare. "We've been here before."

An uneasy silence fell over them as they walked cautiously along the squirming floor. The air was alive with a low hum, filling Stephanie with a mounting dread she could not escape.

I've been here, she thought. *This is where it happened. That son of a bitch tainted us here. Raped us here. Wanted to kill us here.* A chill spread across her neck and down her back.

Chuck's voice echoed from behind, filling up the cavern with the bellowing resonance of her name. "Steph, you can't run from us. Trust me, it ain't so bad. I promise. All you have to do is suffer."

Jack put his hand on her shoulder, urging her forward. "Don't look back. Trust me, okay?"

She did trust him, but the impulse was too great, an almost instinctual reaction to do the very thing he'd told her not to. When she looked back over her shoulder, she saw their father standing in the mouth of the tunnel, his bare feet dragging across the dirt as he hovered above the floor. Susan stood at his side, her naked body caked in blood and black filth. Above, Zeke crawled along the ceiling, insectile in his movement, and her stomach lurched when she realized his eyes were suspended from his skull. Bobby joined him, walking along the ceiling on all fours, his stained tie hanging down like a limp antenna. *Oh my God, what happened to them? What—*

"Steph." Chuck appeared from behind their father, knelt at the old man's feet, and proceeded to crawl along the river of worms. He slipped his hand into the squirming current, lifted a handful of dirt to his mouth, and swallowed. When he was finished, Chuck looked at her and grinned. "We can be one with the Old Ways, Steph. A little suffering and it's done." He slurped a plump earthworm between his dirt-caked lips like a strand of spaghetti. "Will you suffer for your lord?"

Stephanie turned away, her broken heart aching as she pushed Riley forward. All around them, the tunnel shimmered and writhed, its stone masonry giving way to a bulbous, fleshy growth seeping dark ichor from its pores.

This isn't a tunnel. It's a throat, and we're being swallowed.

2

I've seen this before. In Jack's painting.

Riley froze when they stepped out of the tunnel onto a rocky shore. A cold dark tide seeped forward, rolling over the toes of his sneakers, stealing his breath. Riley stared across the desolate landscape, feeling a bizarre sense of déjà vu as his gaze fell over the stones, the flat monument rising from the dark waters before them, and the veil of darkness cloaking the horizon. Millions of stars twinkled down upon them, filling the grotto with a sickly light, forcing shadows to crawl and dance before their eyes. In the distance, the half-lidded eye of a pale moon hung among the starry expanse, its surface featureless and smooth, a cosmic bulb suspended from a formless abyss.

Riley turned, craning his neck up at the sheer cliff from which they'd emerged—except it wasn't stone at all. It was a fleshy appendage, a hunk of gelatinous meat crawling with carrion beetles and worms. Dark slime rolled down the surface, coating every inch with a thick film shining in the moonlight. The wall of flesh stretched on forever, consumed beyond the veil of shadows above. An acrid odor of offal and earthen rot met his nostrils, and he turned away to fend off a wave of nausea.

"The grotto," Jack said, and Stephanie nodded in agreement. Riley, however, didn't understand. An underground ocean in this part of the world was too much to process. They were far below Calvary Hill, deep enough to hit ground water, but here was a whole sea. For as implausible as it was, the landscape before them was more like a shoreline than a grotto, and when he trained his ears, he heard the distant lapping of waves.

The world dimmed, and when Riley looked up, he saw the moon vanish along with some of the stars. Others blinked into existence along the horizon. As he watched the sky, he discovered all the stars were blinking, twinkling in and out of the shadows, and a cold serpent coiled around his guts when he realized they weren't stars at all, but eyes. His throat was dry, and his balls shriveled between his legs.

In the last 48 hours, Riley Tate thought he'd learned true fear, but losing his friends and his father paled in comparison to losing his place in the grand scheme. He'd often wondered if the god his father prayed to was real, if there could possibly be goodness in any sort of divinity, and when Riley saw the pallid eye of the moon open in the sky and look down at them, *through* them, with a chilling indifference, he realized he had an answer: there was a god far below and it did not care. The concept of empathy was something foreign to its nature, and he considered the plight of ants in a magnifying glass.

The entity cast its gaze upon them, and every nerve in Riley's body grew numb. *We shouldn't be here,* he told himself. *We've seen too much.*

He was so entrenched in the implausibility of the creature above them, Riley didn't hear his aunt and uncle urge him forward, didn't hear the cries and mockery emerging from the opening behind them. Stephanie pulled him into the water, and the icy liquid stole his breath, snapping him from his fearful trance.

"Come on." She gripped his wrist, pulling him across the shallows. "They're behind us."

Riley looked over his shoulder almost dreamily, his mind lost among the stars above, and saw the visage of his father barreling down the passageway toward them. Bobby Tate crawled along the tunnel's ceiling, his tainted eyes shimmering in the dark, his mouth a silvery black grin of dirt and worms.

"You can join us, son. The lord can put all that suffering to use. I never wanted you, but the lord does. The lord wants us all, and it will have us in time."

Riley turned away, blinking tears from his eyes. He forced the last good memory of his father to the forefront of his mind as he splashed across the water.

Riley, I love you more than anything. Please don't forget that.

He wouldn't, but with the corrupted vessel of his father's body chasing him down, Riley struggled to disconnect the two. The thing behind them wasn't his father anymore.

The water grew deeper, thicker. Something brushed against his legs, coiling around his ankles, rooting him to the rocky floor. He pulled, gasping at the stark sensation of cold, of something slimy.

"Steph—" he began, pausing when he realized Stephanie was struggling as well. Jack plunged his hand into the icy darkness, grit his teeth, and pulled out a black root-like tendril from the depths below. The dark thing writhed around his wrist, tried to snake its way up his arm, and he flung it aside. It landed with a thick splash a few yards away.

Oh God.

Something tightened around Riley's foot. He resisted, pulling against the unseen tentacle, and his sneaker slipped away into the murk. A moment later, something weighted down his other foot, holding him in place.

Jack turned back to them, the look of pure white terror in his wide eyes. *We're going to die here,* Riley thought, struggling against the gelatinous waves lapping around him. He looked skyward, staring with resentment at the million eyes watching their plight from afar.

From behind, Jacob Masters called out to the void above. "My lord below, we have come to complete your sacred rites. *Amen.*"

3

Jack broke free of the tendrils spiraling around his legs. He twisted himself around with one final bout of strength, but his muscles were already on fire. *I've killed us,* he thought, his heart sinking deep into the pit of his gut. *Walking into this murky shit was exactly what he wanted me to do. We're his now. Goddammit, we're his.*

Defeat crashed over him in a cold wave. Stephanie met his eyes, the fear etched prominently upon her face, and they shared a moment of tacit understanding. He reached out and linked his hand with hers. Her warmth was a comfort in this dark place, and he was grateful for it. Stephanie did the same, reaching out with her free hand to take Riley's in hers. If they were going to die, then they would do it together, knowing they'd done all they could to escape the fate waiting for them here for more than thirty years.

Jack scanned the rocky shore, looking for a trace of his grandmother. Had she been pulled down to the depths of this black bog? Had they stepped over her drowning body in their escape from his father? Jack kept searching, trying to keep the panic from overtaking him completely.

Jacob hovered across the surface of the water, a wingless angel of the dark. He came to rest at the foot of the stone slab rising from the water and placed the glowing idol. To one side of the altar sat a slender blade with a hilt carved from bone, its surface notched and pitted from usage over the centuries.

On the opposite shore, Jack's siblings waded into the murky waters.

The dead reverend's voice carried across the water like a siren's call, and Jack's mind began to itch. "We began this rite so long ago, child. Do you remember?" Jacob beckoned to Stephanie, who withered in her father's gaze. "Or you, little Stephanie? No, I thought not. That is what the sinners of Stauford have done to your minds. They've tainted your purpose, made you forget the Old Ways, made you cast aside your true callin'. But no longer, my lambs. No longer."

Susan Prewitt was the first to reach the altar. She stepped out of the murk, her naked body coated in a film of the dark fluid, the serpent tattoo weeping blood down the curve of her ass. Jacob embraced her as he would a lover, his hands slipping down her sides, smearing blood and filth across her cheeks. When she lifted her chin and pressed her lips against Jacob's, Jack turned away in disgust.

"One of my darling daughters kept the true faith. She will be the first to enter into the embrace of the nameless, as she was the first to be baptized in its waters." Jacob beckoned to them. "You were all bred for this purpose, whether you would claim this burden or not. The rites of the Old Ways demand suffering, yes, and they demand blood, but they also demand flesh, my lambs. My lord is a hungry god, and you will all be devoured in its belly. There is no greater honor, no greater sacrament."

Susan knelt before her father, smiling as he lifted the ceremonial blade from its place on the stone altar. He slid the curved blade around Susan's neck. The arterial spray coated the altar in a thick crimson geyser. Even from across the grotto, Jack heard the almost orgasmic sigh passing her lips as she slumped to their father's feet. Dark tendrils rose from the water, slipped around her bleeding body, and pulled her down into the abyss.

Zeke followed, kneeling before his father. Jacob regarded the pitiful man with a bittersweet smile.

"I raised you as cattle, and you were cast out among the wolves. You had a terrible go of it, my son, but for your loyalty I will grant you peace. Go, then."

The blade sliced through Zeke's artery, his neck a fountain of blood and blackened earth. As with Susan, so too was his body pulled down into the depths of the water by thick tendrils of shadow.

Chuck followed, and Stephanie struggled against the dark roots holding her in place. Tears streamed down her cheeks as she tried to break free. Jack squeezed her hand, but she resisted.

"No," she cried, "Chuck, don't do this. This isn't you. This isn't any of you. Please, just stop. *Don't.*"

The man who was once Charles Tiptree turned and stared at his sister across the expanse of dark water. A grim smile cut across his face, freeing blackened gore from his lips. "Oh, Stephanie," he said, "this is everything I've ever wanted. You'll understand soon enough. It's why we're here. What greater purpose is there than to serve our lord?"

He knelt before their father, accepted the razor-thin blade of the sacrificial knife, and was dragged below the surface. Jacob wiped the blade clean against his tattered sleeve. A slow sigh of ecstasy erupted around them, the grotto filling with a rush of sour air from points unknown. Overhead, the eyes blinked and shimmered, some rolling upward to reveal white orbs wrought with blackened veins. When Jack looked up, he saw a black pupil develop in the center of the moon. The squirming orb split in two like a great cell. Those two pupils divided again into four.

Gaze upon your work, you sadistic fucker.

Last upon the altar was Riley's father, Bobby. He was the only one Jack hadn't seen during his time in town. Out of the six of them, Bobby was the only one who'd bothered to find some form of faith. The Bobby Tate he remembered was a scared child afraid of his own shadow; the one he saw now, even under the guise of their father's corruption, was a tall man who looked like he'd found peace despite all his hardship. He looked ready for what was about to transpire.

When Jack looked across the water at Riley, he wished he could break free and stop Jacob from claiming the boy's father. He wished and he hoped and he pulled, but the roots tethering them to the earth would not relent. All Jack could do was watch the tears slide down Riley's face as Bobby fell under their father's blade.

Riley croaked as his father slipped beneath the dark waves. "Dad," he said, his voice barely more than a whisper. The sound filled Jack with a devastating rage, but no matter how hard he pulled and thrust against his restraints, he could not break free. Across the water, their father leaned against the altar and crossed his arms, clicking his tongue.

"My son, Jackie Tremly. I admire your passion, boy."

"Fuck you."

"You were the one who always put up a fight. Even when the other children accepted their fate, you resisted. I guess you got that from your grandmother." He turned toward the sky, beckoning to the multi-pupiled eyes watching the ritual unfold. "My lord, would you grant my son passage? Would you let his wayward soul come home to be one with you?"

The air grew still, and a voiceless hum reverberated through the expanse above. The tendrils holding their legs finally slithered away, allowing them to move.

"Please tell me you've got a plan." Stephanie's voice was little more than a whimper, her face frozen in a rictus of fear. Jack looked at them both, his heart breaking, a sullen emptiness in his chest.

"Be ready to run." He didn't wait for her to reply. Jack waded through the water toward the place of his baptism, the place of his final sacrifice.

4

He remembered his father being much taller, a slender giant of a man whose smile was as disarming as it was chilling. Jack stood at the foot of the stone altar, looking up at the desiccated remains of Jacob. Blue light seeped from the old man's sunken eyes, illuminating the dark veins spreading from his dry cheeks. Little else had changed with his father since that day in 1983, save for the scar traced into his forehead.

Jack remembered the glyph from his grandmother's notebook, a half-circle split down the middle with a straight line. The old bullet wound puckered around the contours of the glyph itself.

When he looked over his shoulder, Jack saw Stephanie and Riley making their way to shore, and felt content they'd at least have a chance of escape. That was all he could hope for now. His grandmother had vanished, and he wanted so desperately to believe she had a plan, that she'd not abandoned them to their fate, but as the minutes ticked on, he found his belief was faltering.

"My darlin' Jackie," his father said, beaming down at him. The altar sat atop a jagged rock, its surface carved from the stone itself, and surrounded by chiseled steps with edges smoothed over time by the churning waters. Jacob set down the blade on the stone slab and traced his fingers along Jack's cheek. "You were always my favorite. It's the passion burning inside you. You've got it going like a pilot light, son." A gray tongue slithered across his father's teeth. "I want to snuff it out like the light of the world. Such a light can only be good for sin, and my god can't allow that."

"Did you ever love me? Love any of us?"

The question took Jacob by surprise. Jack often wondered what he might say to his father if given the chance to relive their last moments together, and the question of love was at the top of the list. Now he questioned the point of such inquiry. What he remembered of his father was limited to their time in the church—he couldn't recall there ever being moments of joy or play outside its walls. There were only fractured memories of what happened in the shadows, the feel of fingers where they didn't belong, the sharp pain, the blood, the sour stench of sweat.

Jacob blinked, met his son's gaze, and smiled. "No."

Decades of anger tempered Jack's heart against the pain of his childhood, but he still felt the ache of sadness with his father's admission. They truly were sacrificial lambs to him, nothing more. Anger flashed through Jack like a crash of lightning, and he did something he'd only dreamed about for years. Jack snatched the blade from the altar and jammed it into the old man's gut. The light in Jacob's eyes dimmed, and Jack twisted the hilt, slicing the serrated edge in an upward motion toward his father's sternum.

"You like that?" Jack growled. He drew close, put his nose to his father's cheek, baring his teeth like a rabid dog. "Is that enough suffering for you? You sick fuck."

Air escaped Jacob's deadened lungs in a single exasperated gasp, driven from him by the six-inch blade buried deep in his torso. Jack felt triumph, a wedge of hope driven deep into the block of despair weighing so heavily on his heart, but it was not meant to last. The light was in Jacob's eyes again, and when his breath returned, it did so with the raucous fury of a victor's laughter.

"I would save you for last," Jacob hissed, "but I want your sacrifice to set an example for your sister and Bobby's little heretic bastard."

Jacob took hold of Jack's wrist, and with a singular motion, twisted the young man's arm away from the blade's hilt. Jack fell backward, collapsing against the altar, sending the idol clattering from its resting place. The stone effigy rolled down the steps into the murk. An instant later, Jacob fell upon him, bearing the blade down on Jack's throat.

"The nameless will feast on your bones. You will be devoured forever in the void of its belly, and you will feel every moment even beyond death. The grave does not relent, boy, and neither does your father. And when I'm done, Jackie, I will spread the lord's gospel across this world. My paradise will be built atop earth fertilized with your blood."

The tip of the blade neared Jack's neck, and he pushed with all his strength against his father's dead weight. He clenched his jaw, squeezing air through his teeth in a desperate gasp of fear, his heart racing frantically as it gave way to panic. The blade drew closer, poised for his gullet, and part of him wanted to let it happen. A warm resignation washed over him as he accepted his fate.

Run, Steph. Take Riley and go. I can't hold him back. I can't—

Stagnant water erupted in a geyser beside them, startling his attacker long enough for Jack to push the blade away. A dark figure emerged from the abyss, clutching the burning idol in one hand, one blue eye piercing the dark and lighting the way. Jacob cried out as the figure wrapped its free arm around his neck and pulled him from the altar, dragging him into the thick sludge churning at its steps. Jack rolled off the slab, gasping for breath as two figures struggled against one another in the murk.

"Jack!"

Stephanie's voice echoed across the grotto. He looked up, saw his sister and nephew standing on the shore near the entrance. *Go,* he wanted to shout, but the words wouldn't come.

Jack turned back to the figures wrestling in the water. Imogene pinned Jacob below the surface, clutching his throat with one hand. With the other, she gripped the burning idol, reared back, and smashed it against the bastard's skull. Thick tendrils reached upward from the churning waters, driven to the surface by the agitated god above them. Joining their ranks were hundreds of tiny hands, the bloated fingers of children taken in the centuries before, drawn to the surface like worms to the rain.

Jack looked up, felt his insides shrivel into themselves. The sky was alive with eyes, watching the struggle unfold between these two figures, every star peeled wide and bulbous, illuminating the grotto like grim stage lights. Imogene smashed the idol against his father's skull once again. She paused long enough to catch Jack's eye.

"Go, Jackie. Leave us."

He wanted to remain and help her, to emerge from this place victorious with the woman who'd raised him, but the reality of their situation was apparent: she was dead, and never had any intention of walking away from this place. Jack saw the reality in her good eye, and rather than utter a word, he merely nodded and blew her a kiss before darting across the grotto.

5

The world groaned around him, the blackened waves shivering with disappointment, and Jack resisted the urge to look back. Stephanie and Riley had already gone on ahead, retreating through the opening of the writhing passageway. A guttural roar filled his ears as he reached the shoreline, the sound of a mountain uprooting itself from the earth to give chase, shifting his heart into overdrive, pumping adrenaline to his muscles. He ran across the tunnel's threshold, his heart racing to beat the devil, the very air in his lungs combusting into flames.

Muscles screaming, Jack ran as fast and as hard as he could, through the tunnel of flesh and stone, and into the temple chamber. Stephanie and Riley were already climbing up the ladder. When he looked back, he saw a darkened mass assembling at the far end of the tunnel. The shape was amorphous, a blob of blackened corruption folding and tumbling in on itself, spotted with blue eyes and shining white teeth.

We will be fed.

Terror clutched at his resolve, but the adrenaline kept him one step ahead. Jack cupped his hands and cried out to his sister. "Push the tanks into the hole!"

The shapeless thing advanced, squeezing its way through the tunnel toward them. A stream of black water surged from the grotto into the chamber, mixing with the ashen earth, washing over the bones of past meals. Jack slowly backed away, past the small stone altar in the center of the room, and toward the coarse steps of the earthen pillar.

"Bombs away!"

Riley's voice echoed down into the chamber, and a moment later, several propane tanks fell to the floor with a dull thud. There were ten in total, falling one after the other like crabapples from a tree—*thump, thump, thump*—and when they were done, Jack went to work opening the valves on the tanks, watching with growing panic as more and more of the viscous sludge streamed into the room, flooding the pit below. With the valves open and the stink of propane filling the room, Jack kicked the tanks into the black ooze slowly filling the room.

Heart racing, his mind struggling to fend off panic, Jack took to the ladder. His muscles screamed for him to slow and rest, but his mind said otherwise, and when he reached the surface, the shapeless mass of flesh and eyes and teeth reached the end of the passage. Blue orbs rolled up and stared at him as he climbed out of the temple. Myriad voices echoed in his mind, shrieking for retribution and sustenance.

Stephanie waited at the edge with the flares. When Jack was free of the ladder, she struck the cap and winced as a jet of flames spewed from the flare.

"Run," Stephanie screamed, tossing the flare into the pit. Jack yanked Riley to his feet, and together they raced down the hill.

Behind them in the bowels of Calvary Hill, the seething gas caught fire, engulfing the mass of Jacob Masters's nameless god in an explosion of cleansing flames.

All around them, the earth shivered and groaned as the fabric of reality shriveled, contracted. The ground beneath them shook violently, throwing them off their feet and sending them rolling down the hillside. An agonizing voice echoed into the night, crying out with the rage of defeat, the fear of final oblivion, but then it, too, was snuffed out in the fires below. A bright orange-blue fireball shot out of the opening at the summit, tumbling over itself in a coil of smoke rising toward the heavens.

A series of smaller explosions popped and cracked from within, the shockwave rippling through the earth, and all through the forest, the living shadows shrieked as they lost substance. Half the hillside imploded upon itself as the temple collapsed in a gust of smoke and dust.

The rumblings from below continued for the better part of fifteen minutes, and the trio of survivors took refuge beneath a tree at the edge of the clearing. Jack leaned against the trunk, waiting for his racing heart to calm itself while the fires burned within the earth. Riley sat with his head against Stephanie's shoulder, half-crying, half-laughing at what had happened, and when another burst of flames shot out of the hill, Jack pointed toward it.

He looked to them, a smile of relief painted upon his face. "See? I told you I'd blow up that motherfucker."

They shared a nervous laugh between them, afraid to question, afraid to voice the obvious. Was it dead? Was the nightmare finally over? They had no answer. Together, they waited beneath the tree, while the moon completed its slow arc overhead. It held no answers, either.

CHAPTER TWENTY-SIX

1

Dawn drove away the forest's shadows, revealing the extent of their work the night before. Calvary Hill had collapsed into itself on the far side. Smoke billowed upward into a hazy golden sky. A network of veins was burned into the clearing, erratic patterns reminiscent of a lightning strike, reaching as far as the surrounding forest before vanishing in the overgrowth. Bits of stone protruded from the disturbed earth like fragments of bone, and when Jack surveyed the damage, he thought the hillside now looked like a collapsed skull. Looking at it reminded him of his grandmother's final moments, using the idol as a weapon against their father, and he turned his back to the smoking husk of earth for the last time. He would look at it no more.

Stephanie and the boy were asleep under the tree, and he considered letting them sleep a little longer, but the thought of remaining here filled his belly with a sour warmth. This place had always felt haunted to him; now it felt like a cemetery, inert, silent, cloaked in a palpable sadness that would never abate.

"Hey guys." He tapped Stephanie's knee. She sat up with a jolt, ready to run. Jack put his hand on her shoulder, smiling. "Easy now. It's okay. We just need to go, that's all."

Relief washed over her, and she roused Riley from sleep. The boy sat up and yawned. He looked at them both in a daze, and after another sudden yawn, he asked, "Can we get breakfast?"

Jack smirked. "Yeah. I'm buying. Come on, let's get out of here."

2

They drove as far south as Williamstown, sticking to the backroads, wondering how far Jacob's corruption spread. Some fires were still burning, some roads teeming with the fallen bodies of men and women and children covered in dark mounds of sludge and corruption, but they drove on, hoping they weren't the only people left alive. EMS and fire engines barreling down the two-lane highway quelled their fears, and although none of them acknowledged it, they all breathed a heavy sigh of relief.

On the other side of town, Jack pulled the car into a Waffle House parking lot and asked for Riley to hand him the messenger bag on the backseat. After the boy did so, Jack fished out his wallet, and as an afterthought, his cell phone. The screen lit up to show more than a dozen missed calls and texts. The battery had less than ten percent left. More importantly, there was service.

"You guys go on inside and get a table. I'll be there in a minute."

After they were gone, Jack finally called his agent. Carly Dawes answered on the third ring, her voice dry and groggy, and when she realized it was him on the line, he heard the relief in her voice through the angry cursing.

"You don't answer my fucking calls for days, Jack! I was so worried! What happened? Are you okay?"

"Yeah, I'm fine, just a little beat up."

"Beat up? You got into a fight? Christ, do I need to get your publicist on the phone? Do I—"

Need to fly down there, she was going to say, but he cut her off. "No, no fight. It's kind of a long story, Carly. Listen, I wanted to let you know I'm all right, and I might miss that gallery show. There's…well, something came up. I have a little family issue I need to take care of. Can we postpone the show?"

A low electric hum buzzed on the line as she fell silent. A moment later, Carly said, "This is important, isn't it?"

"It is."

"Okay," she sighed. "I'll see what I can do. Take care of whatever you need to. I'll handle everything from here." Before they hung up, Carly said, "Jack?"

"Yeah, Ms. Dawes?"

"You okay? I mean, really?"

He looked outside. His sister and nephew sat in a booth near the entrance, watching him from the window. Riley raised a hand and waved.

"Yeah." Jack waved back. "I'm okay. I promise. My battery is about to die, so I'll call you later. I promise."

"That's twice you've promised me something, Jack Tremly."

"I know, I know." His phone beeped a low battery signal. "I've gotta run, lady. I'll call you. Promise."

"That's three."

"Yeah, yeah," he said, and hung up.

3

Their bellies full of carbs and grease, the trio of survivors took the entrance ramp to I-75 North and drove alongside unassuming travelers for the next fifteen miles. A state police barricade waited for them at Exit 25, diverting potential visitors off to the next exit. Several cars stopped along the highway to question the state police officers redirecting traffic, but Jack stepped on the gas and kept driving.

Pillars of smoke rose from the eastern horizon, towering above the tops of trees along the ridge. A few miles away, the remains of downtown Stauford were a smoldering ruin. Stephanie leaned her head against the glass, watching as the dark trails vanished into a yellowing haze hanging above the town like smog. Jack looked over at her, wanted to ask what she was thinking, but thought better of it. He already knew.

When they were kids, they used to sit on the banks of Layne Camp Creek, talking about how they hated Stauford, how everyone treated them like freaks. In some sick sort of way, Stauford molded them all, shaping them from the salt of the earth into the band of successful misfits they were today.

Now the town was gone, burned to the ground by the very sinners who'd built it, collapsing beneath the weight of its own hypocrisy, and the misfit outcasts lived to see another day. Some of them, at least. And in the great purging fires, they'd lost everything for the second time in their lives, their livelihoods stripped away in a different cleansing ritual.

He thought of Imogene, wondering if this is what she'd intended. She'd hated Stauford as much as the next person, maybe even more. Had she enjoyed watching it burn? Even Jack had to admit seeing the smoke on the ridge filled him with a sense of retribution, glee. The place that robbed them of so much finally suffered its own trauma, and in the process—perhaps by Mamaw Genie's doing, no less—set them free once and for all.

Maybe, he thought. *Just maybe.*

Exit 29 loomed ahead, but unlike the South Stauford ramp, this exit wasn't closed. Jack flipped the turn signal and eased off the highway.

4

The devastation was greater than they'd first realized, with the full extent of Jacob Masters's curse reaching beyond the city limits and across the outlying suburbs. They witnessed emergency fire crews fighting flames while EMS workers struggled to make sense of the casualties strewn about the parkway.

"Something happened when we…killed it, I guess?" Riley's voice startled them both. The boy had been silent since they'd left Williamstown, and Jack thought him asleep this whole time. "If it can be killed, I mean."

Stephanie turned in her seat. "Not sure I follow you, Riley."

He pointed to the bodies loaded on stretchers alongside the road. They'd reached a stoplight at the shopping center a mile from downtown, and the road leading into Stauford proper was closed by a police barricade. Beyond the state police cruisers was a pile of bodies, their heads torn open and bleeding, stewing in a black puddle.

"They were connected somehow. When it…died, I guess, it took them with it. It looks like they all went *pop*."

Riley made a popping sound with his mouth. Stephanie and Jack groaned. A moment later, the light turned green, and they sped on.

5

Jack cursed under his breath when they rounded the curve of Standard Avenue and the Tremly estate fell into view. The once proud Victorian was nothing more than a charred, hollow shell. Plumes of smoke snaked lazily toward the sky.

"Oh, Jack." Stephanie put her hand on his. "God, I'm so sorry."

He remained silent as they parked in his grandmother's driveway. Jack climbed out of the BMW and surveyed the landscape. Most of the homes in his grandmother's neighborhood survived the burning, adding insult to his injury. Jacob targeted this place, knew what the estate meant to Imogene's family, and now it was a smoking corpse of the Tremly legacy. Now there was only Jack, and the burden of possibly building something even half as grand weighed heavily upon him.

While Riley and Stephanie walked aimlessly around the perimeter, Jack leaned back against the car and closed his eyes. He stuffed his hands into his pockets—and felt something there.

"What the hell?"

He pulled a folded slip of paper from his pocket. A loose bit of twine hung limp and knotted from one corner. Confused, he replayed the previous day's events in his mind, retracing every step until—

Mamaw. Her final embrace.

Jack opened the door to the BMW's backseat, unzipped his messenger bag, and retrieved his grandmother's journal. He flipped it open to the back, where the jagged remnants of a torn page stood out from the binding, and unfolded the sheet of paper. Tears welled up in his eyes as he scanned his grandmother's final scribbled words.

6

FROM THE JOURNAL OF IMOGENE TREMLY (5)

Entry not dated

Jackie—

Well, my darling boy, if you're reading this, then everything I've planned has come to pass. I've died and returned from the grave, and so has your father, and if there is any justice in this chaotic universe, then you are reading this in a moment of peace. I'd like to think you are. It's how I imagine you'll be. I have to.

What's happened between my death and now, I cannot say. Contrary to what most of those awful people in town think, I can't tell the future. I can hardly keep track of time. Tyler is supposed to be here within the hour, and then…well, I'll be doing what I've spent the last thirty years preparing for. You probably already know by now.

If there's any cause for these words, it's for me to tell you I love you. I love you more than anything. You might not have been my son, but I raised you like one, and the only thing to match my love is my pride in you, boy. You've given me a second chance in the latter half of my life. I feel like I did a whole lot of wrong when I was younger, but you made me believe I could fix it all. You gave me a chance to do it all over the right way.

A second chance is what this journey of mine has been all about, Jackie. I hope when you read this, you're able to put this all behind you. I hope the nightmares no longer haunt you. I hope you can leave this town behind you once and for all. I hope all your brothers and sisters can do it, too. Hope is about there always being a second chance, son. A chance to amend, to right wrongs, to move forward, and start over.

That's my hope for you.

I love you, little Jackie, and I'll be watching from the stars. Make me proud. I know you will. You already have, more times than I can count.

—*Mamaw Genie*

7

He closed the notebook and wiped his eyes. A warmth washed over him, the soft embrace of love from a lady long dead but still alive in his heart. Jack closed the car door and joined his sister at the remains of the front porch. A pile of charred rubble stood there now, smoking lazily in the morning light.

Stephanie looked at him, saw the tears drying on his cheeks. She nudged him. "You okay?"

"Yeah, I'll be fine. What about you?"

"I think so. I mean…" she trailed off, watching Riley wander around the side of the hollow house. "I think I have to be now. For him."

"If you need any help, I can—I mean, I'm offering. Just say the word."

She smiled. "I appreciate that, bro."

Jack rolled his eyes, grinning. "Ugh, God, don't say that ever again. 'Bro' sounds wrong coming from the great Stevie G."

"There's a first time for everything. For a second time, maybe." Her words trailed off on the breeze. A haze of smoke turned with the wind, forcing them to walk around the side of the house. In the distance, fire sirens cried out in emergency, as their responders traveled from one ruin to the next.

"Do you think they'll rebuild it?"

He knew she was talking about the city of Stauford, but when Jack turned back toward the skeletal remains of his family home, a thin smile crept along his face. "Maybe," he said, "but not here."

The breeze picked up again, changing the direction of the smoke. Jack Tremly put his arm around his sister's shoulders, and together they walked through the billowing white curtain toward their nephew.

Their shadows drew long in the morning sun, and the day was just beginning.

September 27th, 2007—March 7th, 2019

ACKNOWLEDGMENTS

I t's been a long journey down Devil's Creek Road, and there are many praises I must chant before I'm to make the hike to Calvary Hill.

Many thanks to my agent, Italia Gandolfo, for championing this book to others and trusting my vision. The same goes to my editors, Amelia Bennett, Kenneth & Heather Cain, and Renee Fountain, for imparting their wisdom, keen eyes, and blessings upon this manuscript.

I owe a debt of gratitude to Ken McKinley at Silver Shamrock for taking a chance on this monster and allowing me to be involved in the particulars of its creation. You wouldn't be holding this book in your hands if not for him.

Words can't properly express the appreciation I have for the friends and family who cheered me on throughout the writing of this book. First drafts may be written alone, but a book isn't born without the support of others. You all know who you are, and I love you dearly.

My wife, Erica, has been patient with me over the years while I fumbled through the dark with this story's many stops and starts. She was my light at the end of tunnel. I don't know how many nights we sat up late talking about the plot and characters, but I cherished them all. Thanks, love.

And then there's you, Reader. Thanks for visiting Stauford and coming along this journey with me. Calvary Hill is just a mile or so up the trail. Did you bring your robe? Good. Now, take my hand. Repeat after me: *Solve et coagula.*

Todd Keisling
Womelsdorf, Pennsylvania
October 27th, 2019

TODD KEISLING is the author of *Devil's Creek*, *The Final Reconciliation*, and *Ugly Little Things: Collected Horrors*, among other shorter works. He lives somewhere in the wilds of Pennsylvania with his family where he is at work on his next novel.

Share his dread:
Twitter: @todd_keisling
Instagram: @toddkeisling
www.toddkeisling.com

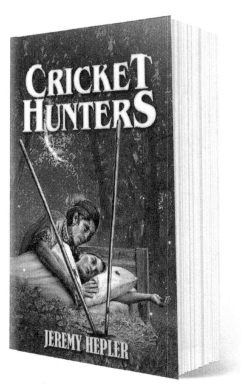

"An unpredictable, page-turning roller coaster."

—Chad Lutzke, author of *The Pale White*

Celia (Garcia) Lundy was fifteen in the fall of 1998 when Abby Powell, one of her five friends who called themselves the Cricket Hunters, disappeared without a trace. Cops scoured the central Texas town of Oak Mott searching for Abby. Interviewed everyone. Brought in the Texas Rangers to assist. Three key suspects emerged and were focused on, but no evidence was found. Eventually, the case went cold, and the passage of time buried the truth of Abby Powell's fate.

Fifteen years later, as the anniversary of Abby's disappearance approaches, Cel's life is upended when her husband Parker, also once a Cricket Hunter, goes missing. When bizarre clues surface that point to a link between Parker's and Abby's disappearances, Cel is forced to delve back into the past in order to navigate the present. With the help of her abuela, a self-proclaimed bruja, she embarks on a tumultuous journey fraught with confrontation and trickery, spells and spirits, theft and murder, in order to find out what happened to her husband, and why.

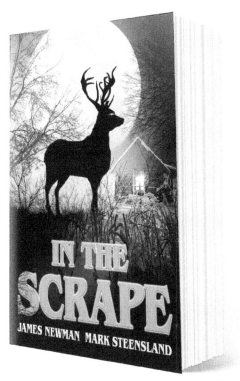

"A stand-out book for 2019."
—Sadie Hartmann, *Nightworms*

Most kids dream about a new bike, a pair of top-dollar sneakers endorsed by their favorite athlete, or that totally awesome videogame everyone's raving about. But thirteen-year-old Jake and his little brother Matthew want nothing more than to escape from their abusive father. As soon as possible, they plan to run away to California, where they will reunite with their mother and live happily ever after.

It won't be easy, though. After a scuffle with a local bully puts Jake's arch-nemesis in the hospital, Sheriff Theresa McLelland starts poking her nose into their feud. During a trip to the family cabin for the opening weekend of deer-hunting season, Jake and Matthew kick their plan into action, leaving Dad tied to a chair as they flee into the night. Meanwhile, the bully and his father have their own plans for revenge, and the events to follow will forever change the lives of everyone involved...

Made in the USA
Monee, IL
07 July 2021